SECRET SANTA

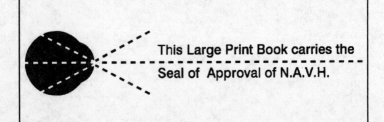

This Large Print Book carries the
Seal of Approval of N.A.V.H.

SECRET SANTA

FERN MICHAELS
MARIE BOSTWICK
LAURA LEVINE
CINDY MYERS

WHEELER PUBLISHING
A part of Gale, Cengage Learning

GALE
CENGAGE Learning·

Detroit • New York • San Francisco • New Haven, Conn • Waterville, Maine • London

Compilation copyright © 2013 by Kensington Publishing Corporation.
"Mister Christmas" copyright © 2013 by MRK Productions.
"The Yellow Rose of Christmas" copyright © 2013 by Marie Bostwick.
"Nightmare on Elf Street" copyright © 2013 by Laura Levine.
"Room at the Inn" copyright © 2013 by Cynthia Myers.
Fern Michaels is a registered trademark of First Draft, Inc.
Wheeler Publishing, a part of Gale, Cengage Learning.

LIBRARY OF CONGRESS CATALOGING-IN-PUBLICATION DATA

Michaels, Fern.
    Secret Santa / By Fern Michaels, Marie Bostwick, Laura Levine, Cindy Myers. — Large Print edition.
        pages cm. — (Wheeler Publishing Large Print Hardcover)
    ISBN 978-1-4104-6401-9 (hardcover) — ISBN 1-4104-6401-6 (hardcover) 1. Christmas stories. 2. Large type books. I. Bostwick, Marie. II. Levine, Laura, 1943- III. Myers, Cindy. IV. Title.
PS3563.I27S44 2013
813'.54—dc23   2013036256

Published in 2013 by arrangement with Zebra Books, an imprint of Kensington Publishing Corp.

Printed in the United States of America
1 2 3 4 5 6 7 17 16 15 14 13

CONTENTS

■ ■ ■ ■

MISTER CHRISTMAS

FERN MICHAELS

■ ■ ■ ■

PROLOGUE

December 18, 2013

"You can't be serious?" Claire said, though deep down inside she knew he was as serious as the disease with which he claimed to have been recently diagnosed. "Christmas is one week away. I promised my brother I'd spend the holidays in Colorado with the family this year." Claire O'Brien paused as she listened to Donald Flynn's litany of reasons why it was imperative she come to Ireland, first thing in the morning. Lastly, he explained to her that it was a matter of life and death, that his disease was fast-moving, and there wasn't much time left, though she didn't believe him. She'd just spoken to him last week and he hadn't even hinted he was ill, let alone about to meet his Maker. "I'm ill, Claire. Can I count on you?"

She'd said of course.

No, he had something up his sleeve. She

was far from naive. Living in the land of glitz and glamour had wizened her real quick-like to the ways of the rich and famous. Claire O'Brien was used to all sorts of people. Demanding. Spoiled. Rude. Whiny. But this? She wasn't sure what to call it. A plea maybe? She'd met Donald Flynn four years ago, when she was introduced to him at a party given for the firm's newest partner, Lucas Palmer. According to managing partner Brock Ettinger, Donald had been completely taken with her and had requested that all of his financial dealings be turned over exclusively to her.

And now he was dying, or so he says. "Bull. He's up to something."

Requesting her presence immediately, and she detested flying. Donald certainly didn't sound ill, or fearful. Just his usual commanding self. Though Claire had to admit, she truly liked the old guy even if he was a bit demanding at times.

As she calculated the necessary changes to her schedule, she realized that she would be lucky to catch a flight by midnight. Hopefully, some airline would have an international flight available on such short notice. Though she hated the thought, as much as she wanted to spend the holidays with her family, a part of her was almost relieved knowing she had a good reason to bow out, albeit with her usual excuse. Of course, the flying part wasn't good, but it is what it is.

Work, her usual excuse. And always valid.

Her family was used to it by now. Ever since her niece Shannon died from a rare blood disorder, something called thrombocytopenia, she no longer enjoyed her family visits. There was always that little something that seemed to be missing when they were together. Of course, it was Shannon. Her jolly bantering whenever they were together. As the firstborn grandchild, Shannon had been the life of the party, the link in the chain that bound them together, the one who made sure that they all had wrapped gifts under the tree exclusively from her. If someone felt the least bit cranky, Shannon had always made it her job to cheer them up. Shannon had always been the life of the party since day one, when she'd wrapped the entire O'Brien family around her tiny, pink finger. So if she was completely honest with herself, and she tried to be most of the time, she was actually grateful for Donald's request. Before she had a chance to change her mind, she scrolled through her BlackBerry for Patrick's phone number.

"Hey, sis," Patrick answered, not bothering with hello.

Caller ID, Claire thought. Sometimes a good thing. Sometimes not so good. The personal etiquette of phone calls no longer existed in today's high-tech-oriented world.

"Hey, yourself," she replied, knowing she was stalling. She couldn't just blurt it out. "So, how's the family?" *Lame, Claire, lame.*

"Why do you want to know?" Patrick asked.

Darn! He was onto her already. She could hear the tell-tale indications of an inquisition in his voice.

She might as well get it over with. "You know how much I want to spend the holidays with you guys, right?" She paused, waiting for him to agree with her.

"No, but I suppose you're about to tell me?" he shot back.

"Patrick Edward O'Brien! Stop being such a shit. This is hard enough as it is. Look, I just received a call from a major client. He's near death and has requested my presence. You know, the will and all." At least she guessed it was about his will, but Patrick didn't need to know that. She held her breath as she waited for him to reply.

"Really, Claire?"

"Of course, really! I wouldn't lie about

something so important. I am ashamed of you, Patrick. You ought to know me better than that by now."

She heard his chuckle and knew she'd gotten through the worst of the conversation. "What I know is you're an attorney who, it just so happens, has a way with words. So, seriously, little sister, is your client really at death's door?"

Attorney-client privilege prevented her from explaining further. "That's what I'm told. You know I can't go into details about my clients. I really wanted to see you guys, but this is my bread and butter. If I don't hustle my rear over to Ireland, I could be out of a job."

Claire heard his sharp intake of breath. "Ireland? Did I hear you correctly?"

She couldn't help smiling. Coming from a big Irish family that had never had the opportunity to travel across the pond, she had expected precisely this reaction. "Yes, as a matter of fact, you did."

"Then I say go for it even though Stephanie and the girls are really looking forward to your visit. Stephanie has a secret, but you'll just have to wait to hear what it is."

"Stop it! I hate it when you do that," Claire said, truly meaning it. Patrick had a way of saying things that irked her to no end — or rather a way of not saying them. "Spit it out."

"No can do. You'll just have to wait until your next visit."

"I'll call Stephanie myself. I am sure she won't make me come all the way to Colorado just to hear a little secret. And for the record, I do not know what that saintly woman and those two precious girls see in you."

More chuckling across the phone lines. "They adore me, what can I say? Of course, the feelings are mutual. Seriously, Claire, can't you reschedule this trip until after the holidays? We were really looking forward to seeing you this year. I know it's hard since Shannon's death, but the rest of us seem to manage to get through the holidays."

To be sure, he was right. It had been over five years since her niece's untimely death. Claire remembered all too well the utter shock she'd felt upon hearing the news. Even worse, she'd died on the day she was due to graduate from high school. She'd be out of college now had she lived. Claire's eyes teared up just thinking of the loss that Colleen and Mark, her sister and brother-in-law must feel. Seeing how they'd suffered, Claire avoided committed relationships like the plague. Of course, Patrick had as well, but then he'd met Stephanie, a young woman with two daughters. They'd married three years ago and had yet to have children of their own.

Children of their own!

"Stephanie's pregnant!" she blurted out. "Patrick? Is this the secret you're not telling me?"

More laughter. "Hey, I'm not saying another word. When you get your client's affairs in order, come home and find out for yourself."

"That is so not fair!" Claire said, sounding as though she were still in high school. "I'm going to call her myself as soon as I hang up."

"She's been sworn to secrecy, just so you know. And Stephanie is my wife; her loyalties lie with me." More cackling across the lines.

If she thought he could see her, she would roll her eyes and stick her tongue out like she did when they were kids; but they were adults, and she would do the adult thing.

"You are an asshole, Patrick O'Brien." There, now that was the *adult* way to handle her older brother.

"Some may agree with you, but don't count my wife as one of them," Patrick cautioned her. "She's loyal to the end."

"Yes, Stephanie's a gem. She had to be to marry you. So, you won't give an inch?" Claire waited, hoping he'd cave, but her brother was as stubborn as she was. An Irish trait the entire O'Brien family shared.

"Not even a centimeter," he said.

"Then what am I supposed to tell the girls, and the rest of the gang?" Since she had planned on spending Christmas with the family, she had all their gifts wrapped and stuffed inside three extra suitcases in preparation for her flight to Colorado. Now, she'd have to mail them, and most likely, at this late date, they wouldn't arrive until after Christmas.

"The truth, just like you told me. You have a wealthy client who just happens to be dying. How convenient for you," Patrick said a bit smartly.

Damn!

"Look, this isn't funny. I have three giant suitcases stuffed with presents for the entire family. I had every intention of spending the holidays in Colorado. I miss my family. Plus, I am long overdue for a vacation."

"Look, I understand. Really I do, it's just the rest of the gang. It's just difficult for them to understand why you always seem to be too busy to spend time with them, especially the kids," Patrick said, then

16

added, "And us."

Claire wanted to choke Patrick but couldn't. Did he really believe this was her choice? Surely he remembered how terrified she was of flying? Thoughts of spending hours in the air, with nothing but miles of water between her and land, almost caused her to refuse to make the trip. But unless she was prepared to lose Donald as a client, she really didn't have a choice. Damn Patrick for making this harder than it already was.

"I'll make you a promise. The second my work is finished, I'll fly straight to Denver from Ireland. Deal?" she asked.

"You've got yourself a deal. For now, I won't tell the others you're traipsing across the pond. Is that a deal?"

Unsure of how long Donald would need her to remain in Ireland, though clearly it couldn't be more than a couple of days, she readily agreed to delaying news of her trip to Ireland to the rest of the family. "It's a done deal."

Pressing the END button on the phone, Claire could only hope to keep her promise. It was that magical time of year, a time to enjoy and to cherish those whom she loved so dearly. If she broke her promise, Patrick would taunt her for the rest of her life.

Decision made, she quickly dialed the number for the travel agency the firm used. Twenty minutes later, she had a reservation to leave for Ireland in four hours.

CHAPTER ONE

By the time she arrived in New York City, Claire was beyond exhausted and just a wee bit tipsy. She'd been so nervous on the flight from Los Angeles, she'd had one too many glasses of wine in hopes of calming her nerves. It hadn't helped.

After going through Customs, with a two-hour wait before her flight to Dublin, Claire found a vacant spot at one of the many bars at JFK. Knowing she would regret it, she hoisted herself up on the barstool and, in doing so, managed to get her shoe caught on the footrest at the bar, where she proceeded to lose her four-inch heel. Horrified because she did not have access to another pair of shoes — in her carry-on she'd packed only a book and a travel pillow for her trip — Claire crammed her foot in the shoe where the spiked heel dangled from the sole.

"What'll you have?" A twentysomething

good-looking bartender asked her as she adjusted herself on the barstool.

"Uh, something that'll wake me up."

"Coffee?"

"No, I meant something that will make me sleepy."

"Long flight?" the bartender asked.

"Yep," Claire said somewhat woozily, then hiccupped. "Just came from LA, and now I'm headed to Ireland."

"I'll fix you up then. I know the perfect drink. Once you're on board, I promise you will sleep like a baby."

"I'll have that then," Claire said, not really caring what it was as long as it knocked her out. She did not like to fly. Period. It was not natural. If humans were meant to fly, they would have been born with wings.

Two minutes later, he placed a cocktail napkin in front of her, topping it off with a tall glass filled with amber liquid and a slice of lemon. Claire immediately took a sip. "This is good. Tastes like sweet tea." She downed the glass easily, then moved it aside, motioning to the bartender for another. He laughed, shook his head, and again placed another one of the tasty drinks in front of her. "This is really good," she said after she took another drink.

"It will help you sleep," the bartender

commented as he wiped the bar down. "Just don't drink too many, or I can't promise you'll find your seat on the plane."

Claire finished the last of her drink, suddenly feeling beyond woozy. Her words came out fuzzy and slurred when she spoke. "How much ya need?" she asked as she fumbled inside her purse for her wallet.

"Forty bucks should cover you," he said.

Even in her state of inebriation, she thought the price outrageous. She smacked a fifty-dollar bill beside her empty glasses, then said, "Merry Christmas," but to her it sounded more like *Meruhkissmus.*

"Happy Holidays," the bartender called over his shoulder as he made his way over to his next customer.

"Yeah, sure," Claire mumbled as she exited the bar. Quickly scanning her surroundings for the ladies' room, she spotted it across from a Best Buy mini kiosk.

Limping through the throngs of travelers, Claire joined a long line of women waiting for their chance in the ladies' room. Too-bright fluorescent lighting along with her consumption of too much alcohol, made the room begin to swirl. Leaning against the wall, Claire closed her eyes, praying that the sudden urge to throw up would pass.

An elderly woman tapped her on her

shoulder, "Honey, it's your turn."

Claire opened her eyes just in time to see an open stall waiting just for her. She waved at the kindly woman before she skip-hobbled the short distance. Dropping her purse and duffel on the floor, not caring that the germs of the world were probably seeping inside, she dropped to her knees, wrapped both arms around the base of the commode as though she were locked in a passionate embrace, and proceeded to purge herself of the alcohol she'd just downed.

Amid the sounds of running water, the whisper of air hand dryers, the clinking of the metal locks on the stall doors, and a lowered whispered from a harried mom, Claire had a brief moment of lucidity when she heard the same woman whispering harshly to her daughter that the woman in the next stall, *her,* was a very bad example. Claire gritted her teeth and squeezed her eyes into gatorlike slits as another wave of nausea forced her to lean over the toilet once again. However this time, she neglected to hold her shiny black hair behind her. Not only did she now have vomit in her hair, but the automatic flush chose that moment to do its thing, and giant drops of toilet water splattered her in the face.

Claire came to the conclusion she was

more than a bit tipsy: She was drunk, smashed, inebriated, highly intoxicated, whatever. She should know better, she thought, as she grabbed on to the giant plastic container that held an equally giant roll of tissue and struggled to steady herself. "Shit," she muttered when the plastic surrounding the tissue fell off, landing in the toilet. More water splashed her navy skirt. Bits of vomit clinging inside the bowl flew out of the water, creating tiny polka dots on her skirt.

Still woozy from the alcohol, Claire acknowledged that she was still drunk. She hadn't been so drunk since she'd passed the bar exam, and she knew that a killer hangover loomed in her near future. Taking a deep breath, she carefully eased into a standing position, heedful as she tried to balance herself on one four-inch heel, the other heel dangling from its sole, all while carefully stretching her arm to her side so she could retrieve her purse and duffel bag.

Forcing herself to appear normal, Claire managed to unlock the stall door and tumble to the sinks. The sight of herself in the mirror almost made her throw up again. Chunks of something she didn't want to put a word to clung to the ends of her hair. The makeup she'd applied so carefully in California was smeared across her face. Her mascara had run, leaving her with two raccoon eyes. The lipstick that promised to keep her lips plump and full for twelve hours made her look more like a clown. And she had always hated clowns, thought them beyond creepy. She took another quick look in the mirror. If she weren't so pathetic, she would have laughed. Her main concern was getting to her gate. Anything more in the way of hygiene and cosmetic repairs could wait until she was safely aboard the plane. She did rinse out her mouth and rake a shaky hand through her hair. Turning around, she almost fell flat on her face before she remembered her high heel was broken. Catching herself, she stopped and removed both shoes, stuffing them in her canvas bag. Maybe she'd find a pair of slippers in one of the shops.

Taking a deep breath, Claire reunited with the throngs of travelers, ignoring the stares of the few who caught a good look at her appearance and her lack of shoes. Holding her head as high as she could without making herself dizzy, she walked what felt like ten miles before locating Gate 27. Spying one of the usual shops that sold everything from earplugs to blankets, Claire, still a bit woozy, but not nearly as drunk as she had been an hour ago, entered the shop and searched for a slipper, a flip-flop, anything to put on her feet. She perused the mini aisles and saw nothing that remotely resembled footwear of any kind. Seeing that the cashier was watching her every move, Claire took advantage of it. "Do you sell slippers of any kind? Shoes?"

The older man was dark-skinned and extremely attractive. He nodded, then motioned to the wall at the very back of the store. Claire followed his instructions and saw several pairs of children's slippers before locating the footwear for adults. "Oh." She almost said *shit* again but thought better of it as there were small children in the store. Realizing this was it, all or nothing, she grabbed a pair of Betty Boop slippers in a size seven. At the register, she paid for them, had the gentleman remove the tags, then slipped them on her feet. Warm, she thought with a smile. She hadn't realized how cold her feet were. She'd been too nauseated to pay much attention to anything else.

Slowly, she made her way back to her gate. No sooner had she sat down, preparing to relax for a bit before she boarded yet another long flight, this time across the Atlantic, she was surprised to hear the airline attendant telling those in first class to begin boarding. Taking extra care to appear steady on her feet, Claire slung her duffel over one shoulder while clutching her purse to her chest. She did not like flying. Not one little bit. Even first class.

Donald Flynn had better be on his deathbed.

She plucked her boarding pass from her purse and gave it to the attendant, then stumbled backwards.

"Are you all right, miss?" the attendant asked.

Yes, she was fine, still a bit intoxicated, but she wasn't going to mention this. "Yes, just a bit of jet lag," Claire answered, taking her boarding pass and tucking it in the side pocket of her purse.

Walking down the Jetway, Claire wanted to turn around and catch the next flight back to Los Angeles. As she stepped from the Jetway onto the Boeing 767, she mentally erased the image of sandy beaches and sunshine. She was on her way to Ireland, her ancestral homeland. A trickle of excitement inched down her spine as she located her seat. Her mother and father would've come with her had she invited them. Now, sitting here all alone, she was sorry that she hadn't invited them; but this was a business trip. She wouldn't have had enough time to spend with them. Maybe she would give them a trip to Ireland for their wedding anniversary.

With her thoughts all over the place, Claire's fear of flying took a backseat as she attempted to cram her duffel beneath the seat in front of her. Once that task was accomplished, she removed her compact from her purse. She peeped in the mirror and didn't recognize herself. That bartender surely added ten times the amount of liquor called for in whatever it was she'd drunk. Still feeling slightly woozy, she was ticked at herself for acting so irresponsibly. She rarely had a drink, and now here she was flying to another country, letting a strange guy fix her a drink without even asking what was in it. Feeling the need to right herself some way, she took a packet of wet wipes from her purse and cleaned the smeared makeup from her face. Then she ran another wipe along the length of her hair to remove the horrid smell, along with little chunks of — she didn't even want to go there. Before she changed her mind, she hit the CALL button. Within seconds, a perky blond flight attendant hovered over her. "Ma'am?"

Ma'am? Claire thought, feeling old and

dirty beside the perfectly groomed young woman.

"Ma'am? Is there something I can get you before we prepare to take off?"

"Uh, yes. Would it be possible to get a wet cloth and a cup of strong coffee?"

Chalk white teeth smiled down at her. "Absolutely. Would you like cream and sugar?"

"No, black is fine, thanks."

Minutes later, the perky flight attendant delivered a warm cloth along with a steaming cup of coffee. Claire thanked her, placed the coffee on the side table, then ran the warm cloth across her face and neck and the strands of her hair. She practically downed the hot coffee in one gulp and felt a bit better physically. Still slightly nervous, she leaned against the headrest and closed her eyes. She forced her mind to another place — her happy place, she called it. Rainbows, lots of sunshine, and warm, sandy beaches with cool blue water lapping against a creamy shore. She'd found this simple exercise quite useful when she had to fly. If only she hadn't added alcohol to the mix, she might've enjoyed the hours of forced relaxation, but she'd acted impulsively, and now her method wasn't quite as effective.

Claire continued to lean back against the headrest as more passengers made their way down the narrow aisles. Since it was a night flight, she figured all would be quiet, and she would use the time for some much-needed rest. No more had the thought flickered across her mind than she heard an infant's high-pitched cry. She sat up in her seat and turned around. A pretty redheaded woman, probably in her mid-thirties, held the baby next to her chest and bounced the child up and down as she tried to put a bag in the overhead bin with one hand. A flight attendant saw her attempt and finished the task for her. The woman and crying child sat in the aisle seat beside Claire, which meant if she had to get up to go to the restroom during the long flight, she'd have to disturb the mother and child. On an impulse, Claire turned to the woman. "Do you want to trade seats? I wouldn't want to bother you" — she nodded toward the crying infant — "if I have to go to the restroom."

"Aye, that would be helpful," she said in a thick Irish accent. "I like the window seat. I can" — she pronounced *can* like *kin* — "lean me head against the window an' have a rest if this little bairn allows me."

Claire grinned. "Boy or girl?" she asked as

she removed her duffel from beneath the seat.

"This wee one's a lad, and a mighty hungry one, I might add."

With quick precision, the young woman eased out of her seat, her grip on the baby firm, yet she still continued to bounce him up and down to soothe his now-soft cries. Claire stepped into the aisle while the woman adjusted herself in the window seat.

Relieved, Claire sat down, fastened her seat belt, suddenly glad for the young woman's company. At least she wasn't seated next to some old man who wanted to tell her his entire life history and that of his ancestors. She'd been through that scenario more than once.

"I'm Claire O'Brien," she said.

"I'm Kelly, and this is Patrick, but we've taken to calling him Paddy, an' I think it's gonna stick."

"My brother is named Patrick, though most of his friends call him Eddie."

"Must be the name no one wants to own up ta," Kelly observed as she removed a blue plastic baby bottle from her bag. "This one is hungry, an' I can't put off feedin' him any longer. I wanted to wait till we were airborne, but he's gonna start wailin' again if'n I don't."

Claire adored Kelly's accent and couldn't wait to hear the rest of Ireland's folk speak the brogue she'd wanted to hear for most of her life. She'd mimicked the accent many times, but she never sounded quite the way a true Irishman would.

"Poor little guy," Claire said for lack of anything better. She didn't have children, and though she'd been around her nieces and nephews plenty of times when they were toddlers, not too much as infants. She was as unschooled in the care of an infant as much as little Paddy himself.

"This is his first flight, and my first time flyin' with a babe. My mum tells me their ears hurt, and I should make sure he's feedin' until we reach altitude."

Again, Claire was completely out of her element and didn't know what to say, so she said the first thing that popped into her head as she observed the white liquid in the light blue bottle. "Looks like he'll be finished before we even take off."

"Aye, that's what I was afraid of," Kelly said suddenly, no longer the confident mother she appeared to be.

"I can help," Claire spurted out of the blue.

"You've experience with babes?" Kelly asked, her eyes brightening with hope.

She swallowed, then licked her lips. "Not really, but I can learn."

Kelly laughed, the sound almost magical. "He's just eight weeks. Not sure I'm even qualified to offer suggestions, but I'll manage."

The mere thought of the responsibility of caring for a child instantly sobered her up. She thought of her sister Colleen, and how she must have felt losing Shannon. And Megan, her other sister, had three sons. How *did* they manage to care for a family and do all the other things required? Claire had spent her entire adult life pursuing her career, climbing up the ladder in hopes of making partner in a prestigious law firm. Now, though she was within a year of achieving that goal at Arleo, Hayes and Ring, she thought it insignificant compared to her sisters' accomplishments. Raising a family wasn't in the cards for her. She'd be up a creek without a paddle if she were Kelly.

"If you need to stretch your legs, or use the restroom, I'll be happy to hold him." *Yes,* Claire thought, *I can do that.* She'd held babies before.

"And I might just let ya," Kelly replied. "I didn't want to travel alone so soon after having the babe, but me gran passed away, and I had to come to New York for the services."

"I'm sorry. My sister lost her oldest daughter a few years ago. It's still hard for her. Really, for all of us. Especially during the holidays. Shannon was always the bright light of the family. She was the first grandchild."

Kelly adjusted the now-sleeping Paddy to her other shoulder. "Oh that's terrible. I'm very sad for yer sister. I would die if somethin' were to happen to my babe here."

With the effects of the alcohol practically gone, Claire was glad when the captain announced they were taxiing to the runway and were third in line for takeoff. She didn't want to think about Shannon, or anything sad. Having Kelly and Paddy next to her would keep her occupied for the flight.

But deep down inside, seeing them together forced her to think of her future and just how empty it was.

CHAPTER TWO

As soon as she was through Customs, Claire saw a beret-wearing older man holding a sign with her name on it. This must be the driver Donald had promised. Not wanting to keep him waiting, she hurried to greet him. "I'm Claire O'Brien. I'm waiting for my luggage."

The old guy was red-cheeked with white tufts of hair peeking out from the side of his plaid beret. "Not a problem, Missy. Take as long as ya need. I'll be here to help ya," he said, then added, "By the way, me name is Martin. My friends call me Marty." His smile was as genuine as the accent with which he spoke.

Claire couldn't help but laugh at the old guy. A friendly twinkle in his eye, and a happy grin, she liked him instantly. "Marty, then. Give me a few minutes, and we can be on our way. I don't want to keep Mr. Flynn waiting. Will we be going to the hospital first?" she asked before checking the board to see which carousel her baggage was on.

The old man looked as though she'd knocked him upside the head. "Why in the world would you think Flynn was in the hospital?"

He truly looked perplexed. "I was told by the man himself that he'd been diagnosed with a deadly disease and it was only a matter of time before he" — she didn't want to say died to this old man because he appeared to be in a state of semi-shock — "well, he said there wasn't a lot of time left and asked that I come to Ireland immediately."

"That old coot, I knew he had something up his sleeve."

Claire stared at him. "What do you mean?"

"I'll let Mr. Flynn explain himself to ya," he replied.

Clearheaded now after a few hours of sleep and several cups of hot coffee, Claire was her old self again, yet she wondered if she'd somehow misunderstood Donald's words. No, she thought to herself, she had not. Something wasn't right, but until she met with the man face-to-face, there wasn't a thing she could do but wait and hear him out. Maybe Martin, *Marty* hadn't been told of his employer's imminent death.

She saw her flight number and the designated carousel on the board, and, lucky for her, it was just two rows down. Within a couple minutes, she spied her luggage, yanked it off the conveyer belt, then returned to follow Martin to the car.

Outside, the weather was cold and damp, the skies a slate gray. Claire shivered as she removed her jacket from her duffel bag and slipped it on while Marty took care of her luggage.

Though he was older, Marty hefted her luggage in the vehicle's trunk as though it were light as a feather. Maybe he looked older than he actually was, Claire thought. She laughed when she saw *Marty* slide into the driver's seat as it appeared completely foreign to her. "I don't think I could ever drive a car like this," she said as soon as she was settled in the backseat.

"Aye, it's what I'm used to, don't know nothin' else, Miss Claire. I've never traveled across the pond to America, and don't mean to be rude, but I ain't never wanted to. I love ma country."

"A man should be proud of his country. There is certainly no shame in that. My ancestors are of Irish descent, yet I'm the first one in my family to have the opportunity to travel to Ireland. I can't wait to see the countryside, all the shades of green."

"Aye, there's about forty of 'em, maybe more. It's a grand old place to be," he said as he maneuvered his way out of the line of traffic. "If you want to see the countryside, I'll drive as slow as I can. Though it's cold, and we'll see fog all over, it's still unlike any beauty ya've ever seen, lass."

Claire wrapped her arms around her waist, unused to the biting cold. "Is it always this cold this time of year?" she asked.

"Aye, and it'll get colder, too. Am used to it, though, as are most Irish. That's why we spend sa much time in the pubs. A tall Guinness or a hot whiskey warms the soul."

After her experience with alcohol yesterday, there was no way she was going to imbibe any form of booze while in Ireland. After all, she was here on business. At least that's what she'd been led to believe. She now suspected Donald Flynn had called her across the pond for reasons that had nothing to do with his supposed imminent death. And if he'd called her away from her family at Christmas unnecessarily, she would show him her Irish side. She grinned at the thought, but still, if Donald hadn't been truthful, she wasn't going to let him get away with it, wealthy client or not.

CHAPTER THREE

Once they were out of the city, Claire took the time to view Ireland's great beauty. Though it was foggy, she was still able to view the green farmland, some of it filled with dairy cows, others dotted with sheep, some shaved and others waiting for their turn at the shears. She'd get the family some good wool socks while she was here, she thought, as they passed yet another farm. Colorado winters were brutal.

Man-made stone walls separated areas of each farm they passed. Often, in the middle of a lavish field of green, there stood more of the man-made stone fences, with a small bit of what once might have been a small cottage, or possibly a church. Ancient cemeteries, some she knew were hundreds and hundreds of years old, dotted the countryside, with the occasional Celtic cross. Claire knew a bit of the cross's history, but in her mind now she summed it up as a cross surrounded by a ring. When and if the opportunity presented itself, Claire would return to Ireland, maybe even bring her family along, and together they could explore their homeland together as a family. Powerscourt Gardens, the Blarney Castle, and the Cliffs of Moher were just a few of the places she wanted to visit when time permitted.

"So how long will ya be here?"

Good question. If Donald Flynn wasn't dying, she might leave tomorrow, but she wasn't going to tell this to Flynn's employee. "I'm not sure at this point. I promised my family I'd be home for Christmas." And she would do her best to keep that promise.

"Aye, you don't want to be away from the wee ones, especially this time of year."

"No, I don't have children. I live in California, one of my brothers and his wife and children live in Colorado. My brother manages a ski lodge there, and I was planning to spend Christmas with them this year, or at least I was until Mr. Flynn called."

"Got that stiff-headed nephew on his back for something. Won't tell me what it's all about, but I can tell ya, Quinn Connor ain't a happy man."

Quinn Connor? She'd heard his name before but couldn't recall where at the moment.

"I'm sure Mr. Flynn will keep me informed if there is a situation," she said though now she didn't believe anything Mr. Flynn had said. If he were truly on his deathbed, would his nephew be on his back? And if he were dying, what kind of man was this nephew? Heartless? She would avoid any preconceived notions just yet. She would wait and see for herself.

"Aye, I hope so, miss, I sure hope so."

For the next hour, they traveled in silence. Claire strained to see as much of the countryside as possible through the fog, which had gotten even heavier since they left the airport in Dublin.

Breaking the silence, Claire asked, "How far to Glendalough?"

Marty glanced at his watch. "Another half hour. With this fog movin' in, I'm not wantin' to drive too fast."

"No, of course not. I just assumed it was a short distance from the airport." The roads were so small, she couldn't believe two vehicles could drive either way without scraping against one another. Twice they'd had to practically take to the ditch when a tour bus zoomed down the road as though

41

they were on the freeway. She didn't want to drive in Ireland, or at least not this trip.

"You just sit back an' relax, lassie, so when we arrive at the Flynn estate, you'll be all rested up, ready for whatever it is that old Donald's got up his sleeve."

Relax, right. She wouldn't be able to relax until she had a hot shower, a good night's rest, and at least one pot of coffee. She felt crummy because she hadn't showered in almost twenty-four hours. And how could she forget her upchucking episode at JFK? Once she'd settled in for the long flight, she spent a bit of time in the airplane's restroom. She managed to stick her hair under the meager stream of water, which she had to hand pump, then used the hand soap to wash the vomit completely out of her hair. She had managed to clean herself up a bit more with the baby wipes Kelly gave her. She'd added a bit of lipstick and combed her hair before they landed. Lucky for her, the Betty Boop slippers were an item much desired by Kelly. When they landed she'd actually offered to buy them from her. When Claire explained her broken-heel situation, Kelly whipped a pair of gently worn black leather ballet flats from Paddy's diaper bag and offered them to her. She'd gladly accepted them, giving the Betty Boop slippers to Kelly. They'd exchanged phone numbers, and again Claire made another promise to visit her before she returned to the States. She'd made lots of promises, *commitments,* and she hoped she would be able to keep them.

The soft lull of the engine and the narrow winding roads forced her to recline against the plush headrest. Her eyes were gritty from being awake so many hours. Closing them for a few minutes, she fell into a deep and troubled sleep.

"No!" she shouted in her dream, only to realize she'd screamed aloud.

"Nightmares?" Marty asked.

Claire took a deep breath, trying to clear the cobwebs from her head. She never remembered her dreams, but whatever this one was, she must've been frightened and running because her heart continued to pound even after she came fully awake. "No, not that I remember. I'm just overly tired."

"We're turning down the road leading to the estate now. You might want to have a look as we round the corner. The Flynn place is a sight ta behold, especially with the fog hoverin' above."

Claire nodded. "I'm sure it is," was all she could come up with.

Marty was right. As soon as they went

around a sharp curve, she saw the Flynn estate. The mountains behind the estate were stunning. Claire drew in her breath as they made the final round, where she had a bird's-eye view of the Flynn *estate* . . . This was not an *estate*!

"Good heavens! This is a castle," Claire exclaimed.

"Aye it is, lassie. Been in the Flynn family since the 1700s, though it's been modernized several times."

For a minute, Claire was truly awestruck. A castle. Why didn't she know this about her client? Why hadn't she been made aware of his . . . living arrangements? She was quite aware of his financial status, knew he was one of Ireland's wealthiest men. But a castle? No, she truly hadn't a clue.

"Wait till ya see it tonight when it's all lit up. It's all decorated for Christmas. People from all across Ireland drive by to have a look. Mr. Flynn even opens the gates so they can get a close-up. Old Flynn's a good fella, just a bit ornery at times."

She stared at the *castle.* She had actually been *summoned* to a *castle.* A week before Christmas. It reminded her of one of those cheesy Lifetime movies she loved to watch. No, this was real. She couldn't wait to hear what Mr. Flynn had to say. It was becoming more and more obvious that he wasn't dying. Marty didn't have a clue, and when he'd called her, he'd sounded just fine. No, there was something more going on at the Flynn estate, rather *castle,* and she planned to find out exactly what as soon as she entered. *I won't be the least bit surprised if there's a moat,* she thought, as they reached the end of the winding lane leading to the front of the castle.

CHAPTER FOUR

Even though it was the dead of winter, the grounds were a lush, deep forest green, with shrubs in so many shades of green, she couldn't count them. And the flowers she couldn't even begin to identify; she'd never seen anything like them in America, anywhere. "How do the flowers survive in the winter?" she asked, finding it odd.

"Some only grow in the winter," Marty said. "The fall is our best time for color, though. It's a mighty sight to b'hold."

Claire couldn't begin to imagine just how beautiful the grounds were in the fall. Mesmerized by the site of the castle, the mountains in the background, the complete and total enormity of this place Mr. Flynn called home, she couldn't wait to see the inside.

There was a circular drive at the side of the castle, and Claire knew full well that this hadn't been here in the 1700s, but it appeared as though it had. The stones were an exact match to those on the castle, the small garage-like area where Marty parked the car was also an exact match to the rest of the castle's stone. Claire wondered if this had been a carriage house of sorts back in its day.

Marty opened her door and took her by the hand, helping her out of the car. "Tilly will be wantin' to feed ya as soon as ya walk through the doors. She's Mr. Flynn's chef, and she's a fine one, too. But if you don't wanna eat any o' that fancy stuff she puts out, she makes a mighty fine Irish stew. I saw Quinn's motorcycle. He must've arrived while I fetched you from the airport, but don't pay him no mind either."

Claire laughed. "Does this mean I'm to ignore everyone but Mr. Flynn?" she asked, her tone light and teasing.

Marty chuckled. "I'll let ya decide that for yourself. Now let's get inside outta this cold. Me old bones are aching from the chill."

Claire couldn't agree with his proposal more.

The door they used led them to the kitchen. Claire didn't have a clue what the aroma that she smelled was, but all she knew right then and there was that she had to have whatever it was, and it was absolutely heavenly. She entered a kitchen that reminded her of something they used on *Iron Chef,* a popular TV show in America that aired weekly on the Food Network. She stared at all of the chrome appliances; pots and pans of every shape and size hung from a giant rack from the ceiling. A bay window that faced the sunshine, when there was sunshine, Claire imagined, held dozens of colorful pots filled with aromatic herbs. Rosemary, thyme, and cilantro were just a few that she recognized. She wasn't much of a cook but did appreciate a well-stocked kitchen. From the looks of it, Mr. Flynn had it all in the food department.

"Told you it was pretty nice in here," Marty said.

Claire smiled. "You did, you just didn't say how pretty it was." She walked around the kitchen amazed that she was actually inside of a castle. In all the fairy-tale books she'd ever read, castles did not have kitchens that looked like this, but she supposed that could be part of *her* fairy tale.

Claire had to remind herself that she was not in Ireland, in this castle, to admire the kitchen and call up fairy tales from her childhood. She was here as an attorney, a financial advisor to one of Ireland's wealthiest men, who just so happened to be at death's door, or so he had said. Not wanting to waste another minute, Claire spoke up. "So where is Mr. Flynn? I really need to see him." About that time, a tiny little Asian lady appeared from around the corner. Claire thought she couldn't have been much over four feet tall and *might* weigh eighty pounds, and that only soaking wet. Her jet-black hair was cut as though a bowl had been placed around the circumference for a guide. Her bangs, or at least what there were of them, were cut so short, they barely covered her forehead. Tiny, almond-shaped eyes focused on hers, then a grin as big as the castle lit up the little woman's face. *This must be Tilly,* Claire thought.

"Mr. Flynn was right," Tilly exclaimed to no one in particular. "You are perfect for the one. And you are tall like him, too." The little woman spoke as if Claire were in another room and not there to observe and listen as the diminutive woman stared at Claire as though she were an object to be admired.

"Tilly," Marty admonished the little woman. "You're here to make sure Miss Claire has a nice hot meal waiting for her as soon as she's had a chance to clean up."

Claire would've sworn Marty was giving

Tilly the evil eye. She observed the two of them together, and that is when it clicked.

Donald Flynn was not sick; nor was he dying. He was probably looming above them somewhere in this giant castle, looking down at the scene below him, laughing. Claire clinched her hands in a fist, completely ticked off.

Tilly chose that moment to acknowledge that Claire was actually in the room with them.

"You want dinner now? Or do you want to wait for the men?" Tilly asked.

Claire actually had to close her eyes for a couple of seconds. Then she opened them again just to make sure she wasn't living in some fantasy fairy tale of a dream. She looked around the kitchen. No, this was very real, too real. Could it be possible that they still lived by the rules of etiquette from another century? Possibly the seventeenth century? No, that was too much.

"So, which you want?" Tilly asked again.

Marty cleared his throat, shook his head, walked across the kitchen, and placed a caring hand on Claire's shoulder. "Tilly sometimes forgets her manners, thinks she's back in China, where women are ruled by their men."

That explains it, Claire thought. She mentally forgave the little woman her faux pas.

"And isn't that as it should be?" said a deep male voice.

Claire directed her gaze in the direction from where the words came. She blinked once, then twice, and yet again, sure what she viewed was just another part of this fantasy world that she had stepped into when her feet touched the green grass of Ireland. Because, nowhere in her world, and her world was quite the fantasy land living in Los Angeles, California, did men look like the one that bracketed the doorway with lanky yet muscular arms, extending from an equally broad chest that led to a narrow, but not too narrow, waistline. He wore faded black denim that looked as though it choked the muscular legs encased inside and clung in other places that it shouldn't. Claire felt her cheeks flame as she stared just below the man's belt. Quickly raising her eyes to his chest, she saw that it clung too tightly to a worn-out black T-shirt. When she was able to take her eyes away from his massive chest, she swallowed quickly, then turned her eyes away.

"So you're that attorney who flew all night long to get here before Donald kicks the bucket?"

Claire took a few seconds to gather herself. She had to remember she was a professional woman used to dealing with men of all kinds. "I'm Claire O'Brien," she stated firmly, confidently. "And you are?" She let her words hang in the air.

The man chose to fully show himself. He walked across the giant kitchen as though he belonged there. *It would be funny,* Claire thought, *if a man's life wasn't hanging in the balance.* Well, she didn't really know that, not yet. She reminded herself that she was about to find out. She looked at Marty and Tilly, who watched the two of them as though they were both animals about to pounce on their prey.

"I guess he doesn't speak. Possibly you're a younger version of Liam Neeson, maybe a stand-in?" Claire couldn't help but notice the strong resemblance between the two. And she would never admit it to the man who stood before her, but he was much better-looking than Liam Neeson, and certainly much younger. Raw power and a keen intelligence emanated from him, despite his good looks.

The guy had the audacity to laugh, loudly. "I hear it all the time, but no, that isn't my chosen profession. Like you, I'm an attorney."

It was then that Claire remembered Quinn

Connor and where she'd met him. "We've met before," she said, using her best attorney voice. Firm, commanding, and no-nonsense.

All six-foot-four of him walked across the room, stopping a couple of feet in front of her. He held out his hand to her. "I'm sure I would have remembered," he said with barely a trace of an Irish accent.

Claire was sure he was speaking the truth. It had been during her last year of law school, and though their introduction was only a brief one, she'd never forgotten him. And looking at him now, she realized he had only gotten better with age. Like a fine wine, maturity had only made him sexier, more appealing to the opposite sex. Now the question was, did she remind him of that long-ago meeting or should she let it go? Deciding on the latter, she spoke. "You're probably right; I must've mistaken you for someone else."

If he suddenly remembered their chance meeting, she would simply use time and age as an excuse. Though something told her, by the glint in his eye, that he knew exactly when they'd met, and where. Los Angeles, a cocktail party when, fresh out of law school, the firm at which she had begun her career, Visco, Walsh and Mack, opened a second office in a new high-rise they'd built. The managing partner had invited attorneys from across the globe, and a few of the clerks who were in their last year of law school and had been offered associate positions in the firm, Claire being one of them. Quinn Connor was the legal golden boy that day, as was mentioned numerous times throughout the evening. He had garnered a perfect score on the bar exam. She remembered watching him throughout the evening, smiling at him. The few times his eye had caught hers across the room, he really hadn't paid much attention to her, and for some reason, even now, she remembered feeling rejected by him. She wasn't the girl she'd been back then. Now she was a powerful professional woman who could hold her own against men like Quinn Connor.

CHAPTER FIVE

Claire took immediate control of the situation before it got even more out of hand. "It's been a long twenty-four hours. If Mr. Flynn is well enough to see me, I'd like to freshen up a bit before I make my appearance." Claire turned to Marty and Tilly, who watched her and Quinn as though they were a circus sideshow act.

Quinn laughed, then replied, "You do appear to be a bit rough around the edges; you look like you could use a shower and a hot meal."

Knowing he was trying to get under her skin, she lifted her chin, meeting his sexy gaze straight on. "And you, Mr. Connor, look as though a trip to a clothing store might be in order. Or is this the mode of dress attorneys affect when they're in Ireland?"

Suddenly, Marty stepped between the two. "Quinn, leave this young lady alone; she ain't used to your warped sense of humor. Right, Ms. Claire?"

Marty was wrong. She liked a good sparring partner now and then. It broke up the monotony when things got boring.

"I get his sense of humor," Claire remarked, then stepped away from Quinn's penetrating stare. Apparently he wasn't aware of the fact that she had five brothers whose sense of humor was most likely more warped than Quinn Connor's.

"I like a woman who understands a sense of humor. Actually, it's one of the main requirements for all the women I date," Quinn said teasingly.

Claire didn't believe that for a minute. With a man who looked like Quinn Connor, he needed a matching beauty, a bit of competition in the looks department. While Claire wasn't a great beauty, by any means, she'd been told on more than one occasion that she was quite attractive. She supposed when she put on makeup and did her hair, she wasn't too hard on the male eye. At five-foot-seven, with long, shiny black hair and clear blue eyes, Claire had turned a few heads in her day.

"I don't know what that is I'm smelling, but I'm dying to taste it. Tilly, Marty tells me you're the best chef in all of Ireland."

Claire watched the little woman squirm under her praise.

Tilly chuckled, her little almond eyes twinkling like the lights on a Christmas tree. "I wasn't sure what you would like, being from America and all, so I made entrées for you to choose from. I wasn't sure if you are one of those vegans or a vegetarian, whatever they call them over there, so I made a little bit of everything. I've made a cheese platter. You might like to get started on that. Ireland has some of the finest cheeses in the world. Ardrahan, has a rich nutty taste, and then there's Corleggy, a pasteurized goat cheese I get from County Cavan, some of the best in Ireland. And, lastly, I have Durrus, a creamy, fruity cheese. Of course, we have an array of breads, scones, and biscuits. I didn't know if you were one of those girls who watched their figure all the time, but apparently it looks like you don't have to, so you might want to try my potato, cabbage, and onion soup with my hearty brown bread. Made just this morning when I heard you were coming. Donald insisted I make a traditional Irish stew for you. It's good beef, lamb, lots of potatoes, and a few secret ingredients I'll never reveal. So, if you're hungry," Tilly finished.

If she weren't hungry before, she certainly

was by then. She wanted a taste of everything. "I don't know when I've been offered such a variety of foods to choose from. Would it be rude of me to want to try a bit of everything?" Claire asked, grinning. Just that moment, her stomach chose to make its state of hunger known to all who were within a few feet of her. She couldn't remember when she'd had her last meal, only that she'd had way too much alcohol in her system during the past twenty-four hours and not near enough food.

"I think you probably just made Tilly the happiest woman in the world," Marty said.

"And me, too. I just hate to eat alone," Quinn teased, then actually had the nerve to look Claire straight in the eye and wink at her. "Do you mind if I join you?"

Claire thought it a little late for him to ask for permission, but she didn't see any reason to deny him. "Not at all."

Tilly scurried about the kitchen, filling platters with cheeses and bread, ladled the thick, hearty soup into bowls, brought these to the table, a giant wooden structure that Claire would bet was hundreds of years old and had been in the Flynn family forever.

"I'll let you two get started with the soup and cheese; then, if you're still hungry, I'll serve you both up a dish of my Irish stew.

Marty, why don't you make a pot of tea for these two while I get their plates ready."

"Would it be possible for me to clean up a bit before I sit down to eat?" Claire asked, dying to remove her wrinkled skirt and Kelly's too-tight black ballet slippers.

"I'm sorry, Miss Claire," Marty said. "Donald told me where to put you."

He spoke of her as though she were a thing, something to be placed wherever he desired. Again, Claire thought, as soon as she saw Mr. Donald Flynn, she was going to give him a piece of her mind, American-style.

"If you wouldn't mind taking me there, I'd love to clean up before I eat," Claire stated firmly, letting them all know how she felt about Mr. Donald Flynn's *putting* her anywhere.

Tilly called over her shoulder as she prepared their plates of food. "Marty doesn't always remember his manners, Miss Claire. You follow him upstairs, and when you come back, I'll have your meal waiting for you." Tilly happily bustled around the kitchen, in her element. Claire couldn't help smiling as she watched her.

"I'll be right down," she said as she made her way up the winding staircase. "This is some place," she said to Marty's back. "Not sure I'd want to live in a place this size."

What she assumed were oil paintings of the Flynn dynasty decorated the stairway. Polished sconces that Claire would swear were pure gold lit up the staircase, bright red velvet ribbons hanging from them. "This way," Marty said, directing her down a narrow hall, where a giant spruce decorated with tiny white lights and angels met them.

"The tree is spectacular!"

"Donald likes his trees; there's one in just about every room."

"Must be a lot of work, but the fun kind. I always put up a tree, a small one, but it brings back memories," Claire said, then thought of Shannon, and that wasn't on her good-memory list.

He opened the door and stepped aside so Claire could enter. Delighted, she spun around the room, again thinking she had stepped right into a fairy tale. "This is gorgeous!" A set of tall windows provided a perfect view of the massive estate's gardens. It looked like a park, not someone's backyard, Claire thought as she gazed out at the beauty. This was definitely not a backyard, at least the kind she was used to. She reminded herself not to be taken in by all of this. Donald Flynn had taken her away from her family, and at Christmastime, too. Short of a real diagnosis of terminal illness, he'd best have a darn good explanation.

"There's the bath, and Tilly assured me there's all the stuff in there you'll need. Russell brought your bags up." Claire saw her luggage placed discreetly at the foot of the giant canopied bed. She wondered who Russell was and what his position was around the castle but wasn't going to ask as it really wasn't her concern. "I'll be downstairs shortly," she said to Marty, who was waiting by the open door. "Tell Tilly I'm starving."

Marty laughed, then closed the door. Finally alone, Claire opened her luggage and removed a change of clothes. She almost screamed with delight when she saw the giant claw-foot tub. A separate glass area enclosed the shower opposite the tub. She turned on the tap and quickly shed her clothes, leaving them in a heap on the floor. Standing under the hot shower, she groaned. "Oh, this is wonderful," she said out loud. She leaned back so that the warm water ran down her face. She could stay here for hours she thought, but later, after she learned why she was here, she planned to spend some time in that claw-foot tub before heading back to the States. Quickly, she found a bottle of lilac-scented shampoo. She washed her hair, rinsing away all traces of the muck from yesterday. A bottle of bath gel, along with a mesh sponge, was sitting on another shower shelf. Squirting the floral-scented wash into the sponge, Claire washed as fast as she could, then stood under the shower for a full minute before stepping out. Though she didn't want to keep Tilly waiting, she couldn't help but smile at the thought of keeping Quinn Connor waiting. She toweled off, slipped into the black leggings and a bright red sweater that hung just below her rear end. Thankful for her own shoes, she slid into her favorite black Uggs. Raking a comb through her freshly washed hair, she piled it in a topknot, secured it with a clip, and, as an afterthought, spritzed her favorite jasmine perfume on her neck.

Racing down the stairs, the enticing aroma from the kitchen made her stomach growl once again. With some food in her stomach, she would feel almost human again.

Though when she saw Donald Flynn himself seated at the head of the table, she almost fainted.

"I see you finally arrived," Donald said as he helped himself to a slice of bread.

Anger fueled Claire across the room to

the table where she stood next to Donald Flynn. "It's barely been twenty-four hours since you demanded that I come to your deathbed, and from what I can see right now, you are the picture of health. Do you mind telling me what this is all about?"

Donald Flynn didn't bother to stand up as most gentlemen would. No, he continued to spread cheese on his bread carefully as though he hadn't a care in the world. "Claire O'Brien. You're as beautiful as I remember."

Hunger overriding her anger, though only for a second, Claire sat in the chair across from Donald. "Look, I didn't come all the way across the damned Atlantic ocean to listen to compliments. You told me you were dying, that it was a matter of life and death. I rearranged my holiday to come here. Now, don't you think it's about time you tell me why I'm really here?" Claire no longer cared about manners. She reached across the table for a slice of bread and dipped it into her hot soup. If she hadn't been so ticked right now, she would have sighed with pleasure, as the soup was to die for. Marty was right. Tilly was an excellent chef.

"Brock Ettinger assured me you had no plans for the holidays. He said you rarely traveled out of California. Knowing your

Irish heritage, I just assumed you would be happy to have a chance at a vacation, especially in Ireland, and at my expense."

For a moment, Claire was at a loss for words. "Brock told you this?" She was fuming. Maybe it was time to step out on her own, walk away from corporate law and the good-old-boy system since they thought they could control her life.

"Oh come on, Claire, do tell me that this is the best offer you've had all year long. Working for a man like Brock Ettinger can't be all that exciting," Donald said between bites.

"I'm sorry I can't keep quiet any longer," Quinn said, his voice laced with anger. "Tell her the truth. Donald, tell her why you've really asked her to come to Ireland."

Claire felt as though she had been completely and utterly duped. That, she supposed, was because she *had* been completely and utterly duped. She was so mad, she wanted to toss her bowl of hot soup in Donald Flynn's face, but, frankly, the soup was too good to waste on such a sneaky old man. "Yes, why don't you tell me why so I can explain to my family why I had to back out of my Christmas plans?" Now she felt guilty when she remembered the relief she'd felt when she'd explained to Patrick that

64

she wouldn't be spending the holiday week with him and Stephanie. As soon as she finished eating, she planned to call the airlines and book a return trip home.

Donald Flynn placed his napkin in his lap, then lay his spoon next to his soup bowl. "Okay, I admit I wasn't completely honest. Though we're all going to die someday, that part was true. You see how large this estate is, and this is just a small portion of all that I have. I have no children, and, of course, no grandchildren, not even a great-niece or -nephew." Donald stared at Quinn. "He's my only living blood relative. I want to leave everything I own to him, but he refuses to be named as my beneficiary."

Claire took another sip of her soup, pulled off a chunk of bread, and washed it down with tea. "And what does this have to do with me?"

"You're an O'Brien. Let me see if I have this right, and correct me if I'm wrong. Don't you have five brothers and two sisters? There's Colleen, who married her high-school sweetheart, Mark Cunningham, they had two daughters, Shannon Margaret and Abigail Caitlin. Sadly, Shannon Margaret passed away several years ago. There's Megan, who's married to Nathan, and they have three sons. I believe their names are

Joseph, Ryan, and Eric. Your parents, Eileen and Joseph are still alive, and they've retired to Florida. And that still leaves Connor, Aidan, Ronan, and Michael."

"You're forgetting Patrick," she couldn't help but add. "Five brothers, two sisters."

"Yes, I forgot about Patrick. Isn't he the one that married Stephanie, who has two little girls named Ashley and Amanda."

Claire now knew the true meaning of feeling violated. How dare he go behind her back and bring her family into something that they weren't even aware of. She wasn't even aware of where this was going!

Quinn spoke again. "Uncle Donald here seems to think you and I, and of course your large family, would be the perfect occupants for this . . . *house he* claims to love so much."

Stupefied, Claire's jaw dropped to her chin and back. She was truly at a loss for words. Was it possible Donald Flynn was suffering from Alzheimer's? What person in their right mind would concoct such an insane plot? And why?

This was too much. "Look, I don't know why you've picked me to be your, I don't even know what you've picked me to be, but this much I do know, I want no part of this scheme. And if I find out that Brock had anything to do with this" — Claire paused, trying to come up with a plausible statement — "I'll quit the minute I see him. He can shove the firm up his ass!"

Quinn laughed. "You've got moxie, I see. I like that. Now, let me fill you in. Uncle Donald seems to think when he dies, this great castle will go to the great country of Ireland and be made into a tourist trap. So, since I'm his only living blood relative, who just so happens to be single living in California, as do you, my dear old uncle's plotting an arranged relationship, at least that's what I assume. Am I right?" Quinn asked his uncle.

Donald actually had the audacity to laugh. "You have to admit it's not a bad idea. You're both Irish, you both come from good families, not to mention you're both quite good-looking, can you imagine what beautiful children you would have together?"

Claire felt her face turned fifty shades of red. Even Quinn appeared stunned.

During this entire exchange of words, Marty and Tilly kept themselves busy washing pots and pans and banging them whenever they felt they shouldn't be privy to certain parts of the conversation.

"I'm sorry, Claire," Quinn said. "I suspected he had something like this up his sleeve when he demanded that I be here today. I returned to Ireland for the holidays, thinking I would ride my bike along the coast. Maybe take a day trip to see the Cliffs of Moher, the usual touristy stuff. I planned to kiss that Blarney Stone, too. Even though I was born here, I've spent most of my life in the States. My parents lived in America. We only spent a short period in Dublin before my father's job, he was a pilot for Aer Lingus, took him to New York. Mom loved the city, all the hustle and bustle. Me, on the other hand, once my parents died — my father was Uncle Donald's younger brother — I think I forgot to add that in here somewhere, but once they were gone, I moved out West. And now, you pull something like this." Quinn was mad, Claire could tell, but he was also hurt that his uncle had used him like this. Claire barely knew Quinn, but she saw the hurt in his eyes, heard it in his words. "Dad wouldn't have wanted this."

"Don't you think I know that? Your father didn't want this castle, didn't want all the responsibility that goes along with the family wealth. All he ever wanted to do was fly airplanes. He could have cared less about our family's fortune. Once he was out of college, he got away before our father insisted he join the family business. I, being the older of the two, didn't have a choice." Donald stopped talking and, for a minute, actually seemed ashamed of himself. "The farms, the dairies have been in the family too long to just let them go to a stranger."

"I'm a stranger, Donald. You don't really know me. All you know of me is my professional life, you know nothing of my personal life. No, forget that. Apparently, you made it your business to find out all about my family. I don't appreciate it, either. It's almost vulgar to think all the while I was looking after your finances, you were scoping out my family tree hoping to preserve your precious family castle and your fortune, which, by the way, is enough for hundreds of families. Has it ever occurred to you to use all these millions for something other than acquiring more?"

Claire held out her hand, "Don't answer that. Look, Quinn, I'm going upstairs and make a few phone calls. If you could offer me a ride back to Dublin, I'd appreciate it." With that said, she stood, took her dishes to the kitchen, where Marty and Tilly were nowhere to be found. She rinsed her bowl, spoon, and cup, then put them inside the industrial-sized dishwasher, wondering why he needed such a large dishwasher in the first place since the castle was hardly occupied.

On her way back upstairs, she passed several beautifully decorated Christmas trees that hadn't been lit up before. Reds, greens, gold, and silver sparkled throughout the parts of the castle, but Claire no longer felt any pleasure at being in her homeland. All she wanted to do now was pack her bags. No, she didn't even have to do that as she hadn't bothered to unpack. The gods were smiling on her, she thought as she entered her guest room. Digging through her purse for the cell phone that she'd never bothered to turn on since landing in Dublin, she turned it back on and saw that she had five voice mails, all from a number she didn't recognize. As she was about to listen to her voice mail, she heard a light knock on her door. Tossing her phone on the bed, she walked across the room and leaned against the door. "Yes?" She asked, unsure who was there. And if it was Donald Flynn, he could stand there and knock all night long before she would open the door.

"Claire, it's Quinn."

As soon as she heard his voice, she opened the door.

"Okay if I come in?" he asked.

Quinn Connor wasn't the ogre his uncle

was, that she was sure of. "Sure," she said, and stepped aside.

"I knew he'd put you in this room. It has the best view of the back of the estate, plus the mountains. I've spent a night or two in this room myself."

Claire wondered if he'd been alone, but it wasn't her business, and right now, it was unimportant.

"Yes, it's beautiful, and I'm sorry, but I can't stay here. I was about to call the airlines to see if there's another flight available tonight. I promised my family I would be home in time for Christmas, and from the looks of it, I'm going to be able to keep my promise."

"Look, I want to apologize for my uncle's behavior." Quinn walked across the room and stared out the window. "For the past year, he's been obsessed with keeping the property in the family."

"Apparently. I was about to check my voice mail when you knocked. Mind if I check it now? I saw several calls from a number I don't recognize. I hope it's not bad news." Claire took her phone from the bed.

"They're from me," Quinn said. "As soon as I got wind of Donald's plan, I tried calling you, but you were already on your way.

I'm sorry you had to travel so far for nothing."

Claire smiled suddenly, liking this guy a wee bit more than she had an hour ago. "Thanks, that was good of you, but I had the phone off, and to be truthful" — Claire felt the urge to spill the beans — "I got a bit tipsy on the flight from LA to New York. When I arrived at JFK, I was a total mess. I had two drinks, and I swear they tasted like sweet tea. I drank them too fast or something, I don't know, but by the time I left the bar, I was so drunk I couldn't walk. Well, no I couldn't walk because I'd managed to break the heel on my shoe, so I limped through the airport and purchased a nice comfortable pair of Betty Boop slippers, but this was after I spent a while hugging the porcelain god." Claire laughed. "I am terrified of flying."

Instead of laughing like she expected, Quinn took a deep breath, then blew it out, all the while clenching and unclenching his fists. "It's just like him to do this. Did he know you weren't fond of flying?"

Claire saw where he was going. "No, it's not something I talk about. In my line of work, I have to travel, and it's something I've learned to live with. I usually do a few relaxation techniques, and they actually work quite well. I think all the alcohol in my system just amplified my fear. Though I did have a very pleasant seat mate. I promised I'd try to visit before I left." Claire hated to make promises and not keep them, but she would call Kelly and send her a brand-new pair of Kate Spade ballet flats as soon as she returned to the States.

Curious, Quinn asked, "I take it you liked his company?"

"Actually, he was quite pleasant when he wasn't crying," Claire said.

"Crying?" Quinn asked.

"Yes. His name was Patrick, too. Though he prefers to go by Paddy. I thought the name was cute. It suited him."

"Paddy, huh?"

"I'm sure when he's older, he will grow out of the name, but until then it suits him just fine. I'm just sorry I won't be able to tell him good-bye, he was quite the guy."

Quinn stepped away from the window and sat on the edge of the bed. "So this Paddy, do you think he's someone you could have a relationship with?"

Claire couldn't help herself any longer. She laughed out loud, then sat on the bed with Quinn. "Yes, I think I could have a relationship with him. As I said, he was quite the guy. But he's too young for me.

I'm sure his mother, who traded her shoes for my Betty Boop slippers, would agree. I think he was about eight weeks old. It was his first flight, too."

He turned to face her. "You mean Paddy was a baby?"

"He was, and he had a set of lungs on him, too. Kelly, that's his mother, had to fly to New York to attend her grandmother's funeral. We hit it off, and I am truly sorry I won't get to tell her good-bye in person though I would like to call her before I leave." She glanced at the clock on the bedside table. "I suppose it's not too late to call, but I want to call the airlines first. I do not want to spend the night in this place." Claire realized she spoke a bit too harshly. "I'm sorry, I know this is your family home, or castle, but I can't help it. Your uncle took unfair advantage of me. And you, too."

"I don't want the place, trust me. It's beautiful, and grand, but it's not a home. No one lives in a castle anymore. I've told Donald for years he should turn the place over to the country, it's an historical landmark, but he refuses to let go. I think his dad made him swear on his life he'd keep the castle in the family forever, but times aren't like they were then."

"True, but I can appreciate Donald's

desire to preserve his heritage."

"I can, too, but it's more than that with him. He's obsessed. He rarely talks of anything else. You don't see that side of him. I've been more than concerned. Thank God for Marty and Tilly. They know what's going on, and we stay in contact almost daily since the change in him."

"I'm sure I know this, but right now it escapes me. How old is Donald?" Claire asked.

Quinn appeared to do a quick mental calculation. "He's turning eighty, get this, on New Year's Day."

"Wow, he's in good shape for his age, at least physically. I'm not so sure about his mental status," Claire said, then regretted it. It wasn't her place to make a medical judgment. She was an attorney. She'd best leave the medical diagnosis to the pros.

"Yes, he is, but he's been declining the past couple of years. Repeats himself. Marty says he's forever losing things, then blames him or Tilly for hiding whatever it is he's claimed to have lost." Quinn truly hated this, but it is what it is. "I guess it's inevitable. We're all getting older, and I don't know about you, but it sure beats the alternative."

Before she realized what she was doing,

she reached for his hand. His glance slipped to their entwined hands, and when he looked at her and smiled, Claire knew then and there that she was toast. About to pull her hand away, he placed his other hand on top of hers. "Don't pull away, Claire."

She didn't want to. But this would never work. She lived in California. He lived in . . . California!

What was she thinking? She smiled at him and continued to hold his hand. Wanting to stay this way for as long as possible, she knew she couldn't. "I don't think I can call the airlines without the use of my hands."

Before letting go, he took both of her hands, wrapped them in his, then before releasing them, he placed a light kiss on the palm of her hand. Her heart jolted, and her pulse pounded as though she'd just run a marathon. She took a deep breath but said nothing, as words weren't necessary.

"You finish getting your things together, and I'll call the airlines," Quinn said, his voice husky, seductive. "If that's okay?" he added.

Claire nodded, not sure she could speak. Her emotions were all over the place. Here she was prepared to dislike this handsome, intelligent Irishman, and all she could think of at the moment was the feel of his lips when he'd lightly kissed her palm. She looked at her hand, amazed that it still tingled from his lips, and his touch.

Before she lost total control of herself, she went to the bathroom and grabbed her dirty skirt, blouse, and underclothes off the floor. She hadn't used her toiletries, so there wasn't anything else to pack. She rearranged a few items in her luggage and found a plastic Target bag to put her dirty clothes in. A trick she'd learned years ago. She tied the bag into a secure knot, then tucked it beneath the shoes Kelly had so graciously traded for those silly slippers. Claire saw that the shoes were cheap and worn, which made her feel twice as bad for taking them. Maybe it was the only extra pair of shoes she owned. Claire hadn't paid too much attention to Kelly's feet, but she believed she'd had on sneakers. Yes, she would send her a brand-spanking-new pair of Kate Spades, along with a pair of warm Uggs. And a pair for Paddy. Ireland winters being as cold as Marty said, she was sure the mother and baby could use a warm pair of boots. She already knew Kelly wore a size seven, and between all her nieces and nephews, her sisters surely could advise her on a close size for baby Paddy. That settled in her mind, she listened to Quinn as he spoke on his cell phone. When she saw him reach for his wallet to remove a credit card, she practically leaped across the bed. "No! I have a return ticket," she whispered loudly.

He smiled and brushed her hand away, then grabbed it and planted a wet kiss on her index finger. Jolts of desire shot through her, settling in the middle of her body. She wanted to yank her hand away but didn't. She liked his lips, liked his kisses, no matter how slight. She smiled at him and leaned up and planted a kiss on his chin. He was too tall for her, and that was nice. She liked tall men. And she was liking Quinn Connor more by the minute.

CHAPTER SIX

Claire turned away, suddenly embarrassed. She was thirty-four years old and couldn't ever remember being so instantly physically attracted to a man. Her insides danced like Mexican jumping beans when he blew her a kiss while he continued to speak on the phone. "Yes, we'll make sure to arrive on time. Thanks," he said before clicking off.

"We're all set," he told her before pulling her into his arms. He wrapped his hands around her shoulders, and the gesture seemed familiar and comfortable. Claire lifted both arms and placed them around his neck. Before either of them could stop, Quinn's lips gently covered her mouth. Slowly, he teased her mouth with the tip of his tongue, then he traced the soft fullness of her lips with his own. Desire burned inside her, and when he pulled away and stared into her eyes, her entire being was filled with a longing unlike any she'd ever known. It was more than physical, and she knew he felt it, too, from the sensuous light that passed between them. His gaze was tender yet smoldered with passion. He took a deep, shaky breath before pulling her completely against him. When she felt his hardness, a ripple of pure lust shot through her. She wanted Quinn Connor badly. And she wanted him now. Right here in his uncle's guest room.

"Are you thinking what I'm thinking?" he whispered against her ear.

"Probably," she answered.

Lightly, he fingered a loose tendril of hair on her cheek. "If you want to make the next flight out, we have to leave now."

She touched his thick hair, wanting to plant her hands in it, wrap her fingers around the long hair at his nape, but resisted. Now wasn't the time, and maybe there would never be another time, but for now Claire cherished these few moments with this man, whom she'd thought of as an adversary only a short time ago.

"Let's get out of here before I forget I'm a gentleman," he said, then kissed her again, only this time on her cheek. Still, Claire felt hot with wanting. It would be a miracle if she didn't jump his bones on the way to the airport.

Quinn carried her luggage, while she strapped her duffel over one shoulder and her purse on the other.

"I need to tell Marty and Tilly good-bye," she said as they walked down the long hallway. Part of her felt a moment's sadness knowing she was leaving Ireland behind without really having seen all that she'd longed to see, but she made a promise to herself; she would come back, and when she did, she would bring the entire O'Brien family with her.

Marty and Tilly must have possessed a sixth sense because both waited at the bottom of the staircase. "I didn't think ya'd stay the night, an' I'm sure sorry 'bout Mr. Flynn. I don't think he's in his right mind," Marty said. Claire could see that it hurt the older man to speak such words about a man whom he admired and respected. There was probably some history between the two, Claire guessed.

On impulse, she gave Marty a quick hug and kissed his ruddy cheek. Tilly lingered behind him, though Claire saw the bag she tried to hide behind her small frame. When she saw Claire looking at the bag, she stepped forward and held it out to her. "This is for your trip. It's cheeses, and breads, with a fresh batch of cranberry

81

orange scones. I put a slab of butter in a plastic bowl, and a knife, too, but it's one of those plastic kind. I didn't want you to get in any trouble with the airlines. I see how they take stuff away from people now. It's a shame what the world has come to."

Claire stooped down and gave Tilly a tight hug. "Thank you so much, Tilly. I'm sorry I can't stay and try another of your tasty dishes, but I'll appreciate this" — she held up the bag — "on the flight home." Before she knew it, tears filled her eyes. She sniffed, then Tilly handed her a wad of tissues. "Thanks, Tilly. Would you mind if I stayed in touch with the both of you?" Claire had only known the couple for a few short hours, but she felt as though she'd known them forever.

"We'd like that," Marty said, then removed a slip of paper from his pocket. "That's our snail-mail address, and our e-mail addresses. If you want, friend us on Facebook, and we can stay in touch that way, too."

"I'd like that," Claire said.

"We better get on the road if we want to make it to the airport in time. Keep in touch with me, and if you need me here, just say the word." Quinn shook Marty's hand, then he practically lifted Tilly off the ground when he hugged her.

Dark outside, the night air damp and bitterly cold, Claire suddenly remembered Quinn rode a motorcycle. "Do you have a car?" she asked as they walked to the side of the castle where Marty had parked earlier.

"No," he said.

They were really going to ride a motorcycle to the airport? In this frigid night air? She'd be an iceberg by the time they arrived in Dublin! Or die of pneumonia!

They walked to a modern building, that looked as if it were recently built. It didn't have the stones like the area where Marty parked. Quinn removed a set of keys from a box, then unlocked the door. He flipped a light on, before Claire stepped inside. When she did, what she saw almost took her breath away. It did take her breath away.

"You said you didn't have a car."

"I don't. I have *several* cars. I had this building constructed last year when I was here. Donald had a fit, but he loves these cars as much as I do. He kept them in a specialty garage in Dublin and never drove them. I finally convinced him the cars would be useless in a few years if he didn't drive them. So, take your pick." Quinn gestured to an array of vehicles.

"Should I ask which you prefer?"

"I like them all," he said as he walked her through the rows of cars.

"How many?" she asked.

"Fifteen here, and three more in Dublin undergoing repairs."

"So, you're telling me you have eighteen cars? Here in Ireland?"

Quinn threw back his head and laughed. "I am."

She could only nod. "So, you pick. I know absolutely nothing about cars other than they get me from point A to point B."

"Stick with me, and I promise to teach you a thing or two," Quinn said. Claire caught the double entendre.

"The roads might get icy. I think we'd better take the Range Rover. It has four-wheel drive, too."

"Wait! I can't leave yet. I have to call Kelly," Claire suddenly remembered.

"Okay, but you do know you can call her from the car? We've got cell towers here in Ireland, too," Quinn teased as he unlocked a black Range Rover. He took her luggage and duffel bag and placed them in the back of the car, along with Tilly's doggie bag.

Unlocking the passenger door, he helped Claire climb inside. Once they were settled and their seat belts fastened, Quinn pressed a button, and an automatic door opened.

"Nice," Claire said.

"Yes, building this was one of the best things I've done for myself in years," Quinn said as he backed out of the garage.

Claire supposed it was if you were a car buff but didn't voice her thoughts.

"I'll call Kelly now, if you don't mind."

Quinn handed her his cell phone. "Use mine. It's local."

"Sure," Claire said as she searched through her purse for the paper with Kelly's number and address. As soon as she found it, she punched in the number.

" 'Ello?"

"Hi, Kelly, it's Claire. From the plane," she added, just in case Kelly had forgotten she'd given out her phone number.

"Oh, Claire, it's mighty fine ta hear ya voice. I was hopin' you'd call."

She couldn't help but smile hearing her heavily accented voice. "It's hard to believe, but I'm on my way to the airport now. My business . . . only took a couple of hours." And she wasn't even bothering to spend the night? Claire realized how crazy she must sound. It'd been close to thirty-two hours since she'd slept in a bed.

"Aye, that was fast, I must say. Are ya sure ya can't stay? Paddy would love to see ya again."

Claire heard the laughter in her voice. "And I would like to see Paddy as well, but I have to rush home. I promised to spend Christmas with my family."

Though Claire had spent several hours with Kelly, she suddenly realized that all she knew about her was that her grandmother had passed away, and she had a newborn son. Come to think of it, Claire hadn't heard her mention the baby's father. She'd spoken of her mother, but never mentioned a husband, if she had a career or anything remotely personal.

"That's nice ya know. Family and Christmas. I was gonna decorate a tree this year, but aye, they're so expensive. Paddy's too wee to know about Christmas just yet," Kelly said, her voice sounding far away and sad.

What the heck was wrong with her? Was Claire so self-centered that she couldn't assess a situation that wasn't connected to her or her legal life? Yes, she was, she thought, as Kelly told her about Paddy's first giggle.

"I would've loved to hear that. I'm coming back to Ireland, though I'm not sure when. I'll make sure to come for a visit. Stay in touch, okay?" Claire said. Kelly promised she would. When Claire punched the END button, she felt sad. Seeing the scrap of paper with Kelly's address, she read it to Quinn. "Are you familiar with the area?"

Quinn looked in the rearview mirror, adjusted it before answering. "It's Dublin's worst possible area. Drugs, prostitutes, murders. You name it, it happens there."

"I can't leave without seeing her, Quinn. She's a young woman, and I think she's in need of a friend and maybe some financial help." Claire really didn't know what to do.

"You'll miss your flight, you do realize that?"

"Yes, yes I do. Never mind. Let's just get to the airport. I'll figure out a way to help Kelly and Paddy."

"I have an idea," he said, a grin showing his white teeth in the darkened car.

"Let's hear it."

"How would you like to play Santa Claus?"

"Well for starters, I would need a sleigh, along with eight reindeer, about a hundred extra pounds, a white beard, and a red suit, but I'm game. I'm all ears."

"It'll take a bit of work, but I think I can make sure that Kelly and Paddy have a Merry Christmas."

"Go on," Claire prompted.

For the next half hour Quinn explained what he would do as soon as they arrived in the States. It took Claire a minute or two before his words registered. "What do you mean, when *we* arrive in the States?"

"I'm going home, too. A bit earlier than planned, but with such a sexy traveling companion, I couldn't resist."

Claire was at a loss for words. "But . . . why? You have all those cars, and your uncle is here. He's not well, Quinn. Someone needs to keep an eye on him."

"Marty and Tilly are highly qualified. Not only is Tilly an amazing chef, when she lived in China, she was also a doctor — an internist, I think."

"You're not joking, are you?"

"I wouldn't joke about that."

Claire realized she hardly knew Quinn Connor, yet she knew she could trust him, knew he was a man of his word. Plus, he was a really good kisser, and beyond good-looking. And an attorney, too. She couldn't have handpicked a more suitable match for herself, but she'd keep those thoughts to herself. At least for now. When Colleen and Megan heard about him, the matchmaking would never end. She'd keep him a secret for a while.

"Does Donald know this?"

"I think he has an idea, but as long as she prepares gourmet meals, he doesn't really give too much thought to anything else she does. Or Marty. Though Marty's been working for my uncle since I was a boy, so there's a story there. And they're really good friends even though Marty works for him. He's very well-off, and doesn't need to work, but he seems to believe Donald couldn't get along without him."

"Then Marty and Donald must be about the same age," Claire stated.

"Marty's in his early seventies. And Tilly just turned sixty-seven. She made sure to remind me that I missed her birthday this year."

"She hardly looks a day over fifty."

"She's a very intelligent woman. She's never told anyone why she left China, but it can't be good. Whatever her reason, I'm glad we have her. And so is Marty. They've been more than friends for a number of years."

"I guessed as much. They make a cute couple."

Quinn reached across the bucket seat and placed his hand on her upper thigh. "I know someone else who would make a cute couple, too."

Claire grinned.

"Who would that be?"

"That's for me to know and you to find

out," Quinn said, then squeezed her thigh, sending shocks of desire through her.

And Claire would find out.

CHAPTER SEVEN

They arrived at JFK on time. Claire had never been so happy to get off an airplane in her entire life. The return flight home was much longer, and they'd had seats in coach by the toilets. Between the passengers' coming and going, not to mention the smell that seeped out every time the door opened, Claire never slept a wink. By now it'd been close to forty-eight hours since she'd had any real sleep. Her eyes were gritty, her teeth felt like she hadn't brushed them since they'd come in, and on top of everything else, she felt like she was coming down with a cold.

Once they passed through Customs and retrieved their luggage, Quinn made a phone call. Twenty minutes later, they were picked up in a black Lincoln and whisked off to a private airport.

"Where are we going?" she asked, though truly she didn't care. As long as it was away from that terrible smell.

"I thought you wanted to spend the holidays with your family," Quinn said. "I am making it my personal mission to see that you arrive safely. I've chartered a private jet to take you to Colorado."

"Tell me you're kidding."

"I would, but I'm not."

"I don't know what to say, other than thank you." Claire was too tired to think straight. All she wanted to do was sleep. If Quinn wanted to hire a private jet to take her home, it was fine with her. As long as she could sleep, and the plane didn't smell like urine, she was good. She didn't even think about being afraid. And she hadn't been afraid on the return flight from Ireland. Quinn had entertained her, they'd watched two movies, shared the goodies Tilly sent, and talked about everything and nothing. By the time they landed on American soil, Claire felt as though she'd known him her entire life. Quinn told her about his law practice. He was a defense lawyer but devoted much of his time to the down and out. She wanted to ask him how he managed to earn a living, but she knew he'd inherited half of his father's fortune when he'd died. Quinn Connor was a very rich man but Claire didn't care. She liked him, maybe a bit more than liked, but again, she would keep those thoughts to herself. For now, she was content to let him take charge of her life even if it was only for a few hours.

"You don't mind if I come along for the ride?" he asked, as they climbed aboard the luxurious Beechcraft Super King Air B200.

"Not at all, but I can't promise to keep my eyes open much longer," Claire said, then immediately yawned. "I am tired."

Quinn helped her get settled in her seat, showed her all the fancy buttons, and as soon as they were at a safe altitude, he explained to her how her seat reclined. He removed a soft pillow from the overhead bin, along with an equally soft blanket that smelled like Downy fabric softener. "You sure know how to make a girl happy."

He sat in the seat facing her. "You ain't seen nothing yet."

It wasn't long after takeoff that Claire fell into a sound, restful sleep. When she awoke, she was surprised to learn she'd been asleep for almost five hours. Her eyes didn't feel gritty, but her mouth felt horrible. Quinn was sipping a cup of coffee and reading *The Wall Street Journal.* He must have sensed her watching him because he tore his gaze from the paper, and when he looked at her, Claire truly felt her heart skip a beat. She smiled at him.

"Have a nice nap?"

"Beyond. That coffee smells luscious."

"I knew you'd want a cup, so I made sure to save some for you." Quinn had to stoop as he walked to the small galley at the back of the aircraft, but when he returned with a cup of strong black coffee in a real china cup, Claire felt as though she'd died and gone to heaven. She sipped the hot brew, relishing every drop. When she finished, Quinn poured her a second cup, this time bringing her a wrapped blueberry muffin and a paper plate with a knife and fork. "Sorry about the paper plate. Jack forgot to pack the good china plates."

"Hey, this is the most luxurious plane I've ever seen. And you know what?" she asked as she opened the cellophane-wrapped muffin. "I'm not even remotely nervous, or afraid. If I could travel in a plane like this, I don't think I'd be nearly as fearful. Is that crazy or what?" she asked, then took a bite of her muffin.

"Not at all. Now do you want to hear about Kelly and Paddy's surprise? While you were sleeping, I made a few phone calls. It seems that Kelly's husband died in a motorcycle crash right after she learned she was pregnant. Her mother barely gets by, but Kelly didn't have much choice after her husband died, so she moved in with her. It's public housing, which isn't so bad, but the area is Dublin's worst. Apparently, Kelly works as a full-time housekeeper for a well-to-do family. They bought her and Paddy's tickets to New York."

"How do you know all this?"

"First, and foremost, I am an attorney with contacts across the globe. Secondly, I have access to the Internet and a telephone. Now does that answer your question?"

He grinned, and once again, Claire felt her heart skip a beat or two. "Has anyone ever told you what an amazing man you are?" She couldn't help it. This guy was almost too good to be true. And like him, she, too, had her contacts. As soon as she was able, she just might have a look-see into his past, just to make sure there wasn't anything . . . what, she thought? Bad? A juvenile record? An unwanted child? No, she would not do this. She trusted him, and she trusted her gut instinct as well. Quinn Connor was the man she thought he was. Decent, giving, and kind. Not to mention good-looking, brilliant, and, yes, she might as well add rich to his long list of growing attributes. And he was an excellent kisser. If his skills in the bedroom were anything like the rest of him, then Claire knew making love with Quinn Connor would be life-changing.

"Claire?"

She jerked herself out of her reverie. "Sorry, I was fantasizing."

"About me? Us?" he asked, all traces of humor gone.

Claire wasn't sure how to answer him. Did she tell him the truth? Or was she willing to be just another woman in a string of many? Someone to toy with until he grew tired of her? Was all of his kindness and concern for others nothing but an act? No, no, no! She had to stop second-guessing herself. She had feelings for this man. Real feelings that had nothing to do with his looks, his financial status, or the number of cars he owned. She just clicked with him, pure and simple.

"Claire, did I say something to upset you?" Again, he was serious.

She shook her head. "No, I'm just not sure why the sudden change of mood. One minute you're teasing me, and when I tell you I am fantasizing, you're suddenly serious. Did I say something to upset you?"

"No, you didn't. So tell me what you're thinking? Please," he added, a trace of his earlier humor in his words.

"I'm thirty-four years old, Quinn, not

some young cutesy girl that you can discard as soon as you tire of me." There, she'd said it. Now all she had to do was wait for him to explain that he really liked her, and yes they were going to enjoy one another, but that's as far as he was willing to go.

What the hell happened to her? The Claire that needed no one. The Claire that was self-reliant and independent? The woman who vowed to remain footloose and fancy-free? She didn't know. Maybe she'd left that woman behind when she'd crossed the Atlantic. Whatever it was, she wasn't Super Claire anymore and didn't want to be.

More than anything, Claire O'Brien wanted to be loved. And she would accept nothing less. And that was the old dynamic Claire talking. She grinned.

"Want to tell me what's so funny because right now, I don't seem to see the humor in what you just said. And for the record, Claire, I'm almost forty years old. I am not looking for some 'young cutesy girl' to have a fling with. I thought we had something. Was I mistaken? Am I moving too fast? Tell me, I want to know."

The old stubborn Claire was up and running, putting her foot in her mouth. The new, softer Claire was glowing inside just knowing that Quinn might have more than lust on his mind.

"I was fantasizing about sleeping with you, when you asked why I was grinning. Then I decided that you're way too handsome, way too accomplished, and way too rich to want . . ."

"— what?"

"A relationship." There it was out. She barely knew the man, and she wanted a commitment from him. Sort of.

"Do you think I make a habit of traipsing across the globe to help damsels in distress? Is that the kind of man you want to be with?"

"No and yes," Claire replied.

"I suppose I have to ask if that was answered in the order in which the questions were asked?"

Claire smiled, she couldn't help it. She needed to learn to stop putting words in the mouths of everyone she came in contact with. It was truly a bad habit, one she wanted to rid herself of, but it wasn't going to be easy.

"Now you're laughing at me," Quinn commented, but he, too, had a slight grin on his face and a twinkle in his eyes.

"I would never laugh at you, Quinn, but I promise I will laugh *with* you."

"I like that answer. And let me say something before we land, because something tells me it might be a while before we're alone again. But before I say anything else, I just want you to know that Kelly and Paddy, and, of course, her mother now have a brand-new home, courtesy of Flynn Financial. That's the name of my private company. And Kelly will no longer be cleaning other people's homes to earn a living. A little bird told me she's always wanted to go to school to become a nurse, and, of course, I made sure that this will happen. I did save that for Christmas Day, though. I thought the house was enough for now. And Paddy. He'll never have to worry about a college education because that's been taken care of, too."

Claire was truly at a loss for words. And here she thought sending Kate Spade shoes and Uggs was a grand gesture. A house? An education for Kelly *and* Paddy? No, she didn't even want to try to top that. Stunned that he'd managed to accomplish all this while she slept, and aboard an airplane! If ever there was a true Santa Claus, it was Quinn Connor.

"You know what? From now on, I think I'm going to call you *Mister Christmas.*"

CHAPTER EIGHT

When they arrived in Denver, Claire called Patrick as soon as they were on their way to the city. "Bet you don't know where I'm at?" she asked as soon as Patrick picked up the phone.

"Now, let me guess. Kissing the Blarney Stone? Having a Guinness? No, scratch that, you wouldn't like that. Too strong for a wimpy kid like you. Let me see, maybe you're about to jump off the Cliffs of Moher?"

She laughed. "Wrong on all accounts." She placed her hand over the phone. Whispering to Quinn, she said, "He thinks I'm still in Ireland."

"What did you say?"

"Oh for crying out loud, Patrick, I'm back in the States. As a matter of fact, I'm about to head out to I-70 tomorrow. Wanna give me a road update?"

She heard her brother laughing. "Seriously? You've been to Ireland and back in two days? I take it the place wasn't up to your standards?"

"It's beautiful there, but I had to leave. I'll explain it to you when I see you. Tomorrow. I'm spending the night in a hotel tonight. I've hardly slept since I last spoke with you. Make sure to tell Stephanie and the girls that I'll see them tomorrow, okay? And the rest of the gang, too. They'll all be there right?"

"Yep."

"Good, because I'm bringing a guest along. Someone special that I want to introduce to my family. Okay, I'm about to lose what's left of my battery. See you tomorrow." Claire clicked END, then turned her phone off before it rang again. Knowing her brother, he was probably calling the rest of the gang right about now. Since there were so many, Claire knew it would take at least half an hour for the news to spread throughout the O'Brien family. Once the news was out that she was bringing someone for them to meet, her cell phone would never stop ringing. She explained all this to Quinn. "And that's why I won't turn my phone on until we arrive."

"And you say they're in Telluride?" Quinn asked as he exited off the interstate.

"Yes. Where are we going?" She assumed they would stop at a motel along the way, share some private time together, maybe she'd jump his bones, but apparently he had other plans. He drove down Sheridan Boulevard and pulled into a McDonald's. "I have a confession to make. I'm addicted to Big Macs. I treat myself once a week, no more, but it's been almost two weeks since I've had one. Do you mind?"

She busted out laughing. "I learn something new about you by the minute. And for the record, I like a fish sandwich from Mickey D's myself now and then. Minus the cheese, though. A large fry, extra ketchup, and a large Dr Pepper."

"Now that we have that out of the way, let's go inside. I'm starving."

Claire was tired to the bone but in a good way. She'd slept on the plane, and it'd been a good, deep sleep, but she still longed for a bed, a hot bath, and a steaming mug of Earl Grey tea. But for now, she planned to enjoy every minute of her time alone with Quinn.

Inside, they placed their orders. As soon as the food was ready, they sat by the window overlooking the parking lot. It wasn't much of a scene outside. It had snowed in Denver two days ago, but now the sun had melted it, and it was nothing more than brown slush. Cars with rust from the salt on the roads were parked haphazardly throughout the lot. Snowdrifts were banked against the curb. A few kids jumped around in the play area, and Christmas tunes could be heard from hidden speakers. A fake tree decorated with empty french fry boxes and the paper boxes they now used in place of the styrofoam ones for the variety of sandwiches they carried hung from the tree. Cookies and the tiny toys that came inside the kids' meals were strung across the branches. It wasn't much of a tree, Claire thought, but it was quite appropriate for McDonald's.

Silent for a change, they were both focused on eating when Claire suddenly had an epiphany. "This is the first time we've been out to dinner together."

Quinn raised his eyebrows in surprise. "I believe you're right. Now my Big Mac cravings will be even more meaningful. And I'm serious, Claire. This isn't a joke, or small talk. You've become very special to me, and I hope you feel the same about me."

Claire's heart did another dance, the rumba, from the way it was beating out of control. "I do, Quinn. It's just a bit unexpected, that's all."

"Why? You never planned to fall in love?"

More rumba dancing in her chest. "I'd always hoped to, I just never met the right person. Trust me, I tried; it just didn't happen for me."

"And this means?"

"That it's happening for me. Hard and fast." *Crap! I didn't say that, did I?*

"And it will be the first time. After that, it's slow and easy, all the way."

Good grief, Quinn was verbally seducing her in McDonald's! She almost choked on her french fries. She felt her face turn red, glad the few customers in the place weren't mind readers. "If you keep talking to me like that, I will not be responsible for my actions," Claire stated, then dipped a fry in her pile of ketchup.

"I'll hold you to that." He wiped his mouth with a paper napkin, then stuffed it inside his empty Big Mac box. "You told your brother you were staying in a hotel tonight. Did you have a particular place in mind?"

More rumba from the dancers in her chest. "Not really. I usually stay with my family when I'm here, and they're in the mountains. Except for Colleen and Mark. They live in Washington State, but they'll be here. They're the ones who lost a daughter, my niece, Shannon. They're always sad during the holidays, but it's to be expected. We all are in our own way, but we try to make each other happy. I really should warn you, though. They're a great group of people, but my sisters are incredibly nosy, and my five brothers, well, they take protecting their sisters seriously. Mom and Dad, they're the best. You'll like them."

"They raised you, so how could I not?"

"If I didn't know better, I would think you were trying to butter me up." Claire ate the last of her french fries. She neatly wrapped her empty boxes together, then added Quinn's pile to her own. She watched him as she did this. Togetherness.

"Actually, there is something I want you to know. It's nothing major, but I should have told you."

Here goes the bomb, she thought. "What's that?" She wanted to appear calm, as though nothing he might tell her could affect her, but she knew better, and so did he. They'd moved fast and furious, but whatever it was, it was very real for both of them.

"That Beechcraft belongs to me."

"What?"

"The airplane. It's mine."

"That's it?"

"I'm afraid so," he said, a smile in his eyes and a grin the size of the moon on his handsome face.

"Somehow, I think I can live with that."

"How would you feel about flying to Telluride rather than us driving? I don't want to force you to do something you're not comfortable doing, but you did say you weren't afraid."

"Oh. I don't have a problem, as long as you're with me," Claire said.

"Then let's fly. We can surprise your family."

Claire had never been excited about flying in an airplane. Ever. Until now. She was sure it had something to do with the man and not the plane.

CHAPTER NINE

They all agreed to meet at Snow Zone at ten o'clock. Claire's entire family plus a few extras had all accepted her invitation when she asked them to come skiing last night. Part of her was beyond excited for her family to meet Quinn, and another part of her was afraid they wouldn't like him. She hadn't told them about his wealth, and she certainly hadn't mentioned they flew to Telluride on his private jet.

On the slopes, everyone was having a good time. Claire assumed Quinn could ski since he knew how to do most everything else, and he hadn't said otherwise. The downside: He'd insisted they have separate hotel rooms when they arrived yesterday. She'd told him about Max's owning the resort. Though she'd fantasized about spending the night in Quinn's arms, it would wait. And they both decided it wouldn't look good if someone were to catch them sleeping in the same hotel room. Claire had thought it old-fashioned and courtly. She hadn't met a man quite like Quinn, and she didn't want to take a chance on anything. If he wanted to wait a while before they took their relationship to the next level, she was perfectly fine with it, however much her hormones said otherwise.

So here she was, all decked out in the latest ski fashions, courtesy of Stephanie and Patrick. When she realized she was planning a ski meet with no gear, they'd opened up the shop after hours and let her choose whatever she wanted and insisted it was on the house. She seemed to be getting a lot of things on the house lately.

But now here she was. Almost ten o'clock, and there was no sign of Quinn or her family members. Had she said ten o'clock? And they were all supposed to be here at Snow Zone. She went inside, expecting to see Stephanie but saw a young girl working the register. She must be Candy Lee. Amanda and Ashley talked nonstop about her whenever she spoke with them on the phone.

Bing Crosby billowed throughout the ski shop. The scent of warm chocolate filled the air. A giant Douglas fir was decorated with mini skis, tiny scarves, and hats. Red and green lights twinkled on the tree. Claire took a deep breath, inhaling the scent of fresh pine. This was almost too perfect, she thought as she walked up and down the aisles. All the jackets and ski pants were perfectly stacked in neat piles. Mittens, hats, and the usual ski supplies filled up the shelves next to the register. Claire knew the office was in the back of the store. But it wasn't much larger than a closet, so there was no way everyone could fit in the office. And why would they be in there in the first place? There was no reason for any of them to hide. She'd simply got the time mixed up. She was a few days shy of her normal sleep pattern, plus the high altitudes. She'd spend her time looking at all the goodies the place had to offer. Briefly, she thought of purchasing a few gifts while she was here, but no one would appreciate them since they all had their own gear, and it was always top-of-the-line. She wished she could send for those three suitcases packed with gifts, but she'd have to wait and send them when she returned to California.

The thought actually depressed her. For the first time in her legal career, she wasn't excited about her work. While she would always practice law — it was in her blood — she didn't want to go back to work for Brock Ettinger. He'd betrayed her when he'd given out her personal information to Donald Flynn. There was no way she would work for a man like him anymore, not the new Claire.

As she poked around the shop, she suddenly realized that Quinn's last name was different than his uncle's. Shouldn't they share the same last name if his father was Donald's brother? She really hadn't thought that much about it until now. She was sure there was a reasonable explanation for the difference in their names. Checking her watch, she saw that it was already ten thirty. Taking her cell phone from her pocket, she called Patrick since he seemed to be the one who always answered his cell.

"What's up, Claire?"

"Aren't we supposed to be meeting this morning? I thought I said ten o'clock."

Silence. Unusual for her brother. "Patrick."

"Uh, yeah, you did."

"Then where is everyone? I'm usually the one who's late." Claire felt the first stirring of fear. Something wasn't right, she could feel it in her gut. It couldn't be good if her entire family was missing.

"I take it you haven't seen the news."

She'd slept in, not bothering with the television. "Patrick, if you don't tell me what's going on right now, I'm going to kick your ass. You're scaring me."

His intake of breath sounded raspy as though he were congested, or maybe he'd been . . . crying? "Okay, some whack job is in the main dining hall right now. Look around you."

She did. The lifts weren't running. The usual array of skiers who dotted the mountainside were gone. As a matter of fact, the only person she'd seen since she'd been up was Candy Lee. "Hold on, Patrick." Claire went to the girl, who sat behind the register reading Suzanne Collins's latest. "Aren't you Candy Lee?"

The girl looked up from her book. "Yes, sorry I just get so involved when I'm reading. Is there something I can help you with?" she asked.

"Where is everybody?"

Candy Lee glanced out the front of the store. "Wow, no one is out there today. I wonder what gives?"

"Patrick, you better tell me what's up. There is absolutely no one on the slopes, the lifts aren't moving, and the only person I've come in contact with since I got up at nine thirty is Candy Lee. I want to know what's going on, and I want to know right now! If you guys are playing some kind of silly prank, then just quit it because I don't like this. I have a very bad feeling."

"We were supposed to meet at ten, you're right. Candy Lee was late getting to work. Stephanie and the girls called and said for me to have everyone meet in the main dining hall. I'm still at the house, Claire. The rest of the family is in that dining hall, and there is a man in there. He has a gun. No one has been hurt, but you need to stay inside. The police have the place surrounded. It's on the news. Tell Candy to turn the TV on. Go on, do it now."

Claire's hands shook uncontrollably. "Turn the TV on now!" she screamed.

Candy Lee practically jumped off the barstool she was sitting on. "Jeez, give me a sec." She found the remote and clicked the portable television set on. The scene on the monitor instantly became familiar. Candy Lee placed her hands over her mouth, her book dropping to the floor.

"This is here! What's happening? Oh my gosh!" Candy's eyes filled with tears.

Claire looked at the screen and saw several police cars with their lights flashing yet the sirens were off. It was eerily silent. Her hands continued to shake, but she knew she had to get control of herself. She and Candy were the only two, as far as she knew, who were free right now. Though the anchor-woman's mouth moved, Claire couldn't hear what she was saying. "Turn the volume up."

Candy did as instructed.

"Patrick, are you still there?"

"I'm here, I'm listening. Hang on."

Claire listened to the anchorwoman, who stood in front of the main dining hall at Maximum Glide.

"Jeb Norris was fired from his job last night at this exclusive ski resort. Manager and operator Patrick O'Brien caught Jeb Norris with cocaine and other drugs though we cannot confirm what they were at this point. All we know now is that when the resort opened this morning, Norris entered the main dining hall, where he had worked in the kitchen. He was armed with an automatic weapon, and we're still unclear as to the model at this time, but we do know the dining hall was full when Norris began firing his weapon. We have no information on the injured at this point, and we're not clear if there are any injured, but we want to make it very clear, Jeb Norris has fired at least six shots inside the main dining hall. A negotiator is arriving now."

"Oh my God." Claire was stunned. Here, in Telluride, at this small but luxurious ski resort. "What happened, Patrick? Why did you fire this guy?"

"First Max has a zero drug policy. If you're caught with anything, you're history. No second chances. Last night, when I went to the kitchen to meet with the night manager, I saw Jeb acting strange, like he was trying to cover something up. He was using the table we use to roll out our bread dough to snort coke. He had a mirror and two lines of coke all nice and straight, ready to go right up his nose. When I asked him what he was doing, he looked at me and said what the F do you think I'm doing? I fired him on the spot and slapped the damned mirror where he'd laid his drugs, the coke went flying, the mirror broke. I told him he had two minutes to get off the property before I called the police. He left, and now it seems he's returned. God, I could kick myself for not calling the cops when I had the opportunity. If something happens to those people in there, and most of them are our family, it's all my fault. Stephanie and the girls are inside. Mom, Dad. Mark and Colleen, their boys. You and I are the only two, besides Candy Lee, who aren't in the building. Quinn is there, too, you know that, right?"

Claire could only shake her head. "I assumed he was when I didn't find him at

Snow Zone. Of all days for Candy Lee to be late for work." Claire lowered her voice when she said the last words. It wasn't her fault, but had she arrived at work on time, maybe her family wouldn't be trapped inside with that madman. "Have you heard anything from anyone inside? They all have cell phones. Has anyone tried to contact you?"

"No, and I thought they would at least try, but we don't know what that crazy bastard's likely to do. He may have taken their cell phones. Most likely that's what's happened. I just bought Amanda and Ashley cell phones to be used in an emergency. Stephanie and I both told them if they ever found themselves in trouble and couldn't call, we made sure they know how to send a text message. I've checked my phone repeatedly, and there's nothing." Patrick sounded defeated, as if the very life had been sucked right out of him. Claire understood, as she felt the same way. Though she was new to this love thing, that didn't make it any easier.

"So we wait? Isn't there something you can do? A back door the cops can use to slip inside? Something that kook in there isn't aware of?"

"Not that I know of. Give me a minute,

let me think."

Claire watched the anchorwoman, but she simply repeated what she'd just said minutes ago. There was nothing new to report. She hoped and prayed that was a good sign.

How could such a perfectly good plan go awry? Claire was having a tough time comprehending the sheer insanity of the situation, the odds of something like this happening here, in Telluride. Candy Lee shook with sobs, and Claire wanted to comfort her, but she was afraid to put her phone down for fear she'd lose her connection with Patrick. She knew he could talk, text, and answer incoming calls on his iPhone. She hated her old outdated Black-Berry just then and wished she'd purchased something new when it was all the rage. What a stupid thought to have at a time like this. Though she'd heard somewhere that when people were under extreme stress, their thoughts tended to be a bit haywire. She totally understood that now.

"Claire, are you still there?"

"I'm here."

"I think there might be a way for the police to get inside without Jeb's knowing."

"Then hang up and call them now! Hurry!"

"I'm going to put you on hold, don't hang

up, okay?"

"I won't," Claire said, her eyes focused on the TV. Something was happening. The anchorwoman kept messing with her earpiece like she was having trouble hearing something, or someone. She turned around to look behind her. Claire and Candy Lee both stared at the scene unfolding live on the air.

"Oh my Gawd, that's him!" Candy Lee said, pointing at the television set. "That's that insane psycho, Jeb Norris!"

Captivated by the scenario Claire almost had a heart attack when she saw her mother and father being held at gunpoint out in the parking lot by the madman! The anchorwoman raced to get as close to the scene as the police would allow.

Jeb Norris couldn't have been a day over twenty if that. He was medium height but much too thin. Claire saw the signs of drug abuse all over his face. The sunken cheeks, dark circles under his eyes, the manic way he stared into the camera. "Listen up!"

They did. The television, while live, was totally silent.

"These two are gonna be the first to go. I'm startin' with the oldest ones first."

Claire watched in horror as her father was shoved to the ground. Her mother tried to help him up, and when she did, the madman slapped her hard, sending her flying to the ground, her back slamming against the icy pavement. Tears fell from Claire's eyes. She could not watch her parents die. Someone had to do something, and from what she could see, no one was doing a damned thing. She laid her phone on the countertop. "Stay on the line. If Patrick comes back on the phone, tell him I'm going for help. I can't just sit here and watch my parents die on live television!"

Before Claire had a chance to reconsider, she flew out the door. She didn't know what she would do, but she had to at least try. She raced around to the parking lot, where the fired ex-employee had her parents. Several police cars surrounded the area.

"Ma'am, get down!" a police officer called out to her. "This is a hostage situation. Stay where you are!"

Claire dropped down on the wet, icy pavement. "Do not move!" came another voice.

She wasn't going anywhere, and now she realized the folly of her impulsiveness. She had to try, she told herself as she lay on the cold concrete. She couldn't live with herself if something were to happen to her parents.

"Claire." A loud whisper came from an area beneath the steps that led to the back door of Snow Zone. She turned to find

Patrick huddled under the stairs. "What the frig are you doing out here? I told you to stay inside! Damn it, Claire, you don't always have to be the one in control of things. You're going to get us both killed lying out here in the middle of the parking lot where that nut job can see you!"

Tears fell from her eyes. He was right. She had always wanted to be in control. Of everything. Why, she didn't know, and now it didn't matter. She should've listened to her brother.

"Try to slide over toward me, okay?"

She nodded, then carefully moved her body like an inchworm until she was just a few feet away from the back entrance. Jeb Norris was still standing in the middle of the main hall parking area, and from what she could hear, her parents were still on the ground, unharmed at this point.

A loud voice, which sounded like it was coming through a megaphone, filled the air. The negotiator, Claire guessed.

"Jeb, if you give up now, you can walk away from this. You haven't injured anyone yet. There is no need for you to keep the other hostages inside. Let them go, and you and I will talk."

Claire breathed a massive sigh of relief; and then she prayed, something she hadn't done in a very long time. She tried to catch Patrick's eye. She did and saw that he'd heard what she had. No one was injured at this point. Thank God. But who knew what this drugged-out crazy kid would do before all was said and done.

"I want to talk to that son of a bitch Patrick O'Brien. This is between me and him! This is all his fault!"

"Listen, son," the negotiator said. "This isn't anyone's fault. From what I've been told, you've got a bad cocaine habit. I can get you some help, but in order for me to help you, you have to help me out. You can start helping both of us by letting all the hostages go."

Claire strained to hear, but nothing was being said.

"How do I know you won't try to shoot me?" Jeb Norris said. Claire knew this was a good sign. He was beginning to ask for help in his own sick way.

"I am a man of my word. If I tell you I will see that you get help for your addiction, then that's exactly what I will do. But you have to help me, too, remember? You can help us both right this very minute, Jeb. All you have to do is let all those innocent people leave. They've done nothing to you, right?"

Claire and Patrick waited for him to respond.

"I don't trust you," Jeb called out.

"Jeb, listen to me. I am all you have right now. I'm the man that's keeping you alive. As soon as I give up on you, they will, too. We have professionally trained sharpshooters. They can take you out right now if I give the order, but I'm not going to do that because I know you've got problems, and I know that you need help. Take it while I can still offer it, Jeb. I'm just doing my job, you understand? I don't want to see anyone hurt. I don't think you do, either. It's Christmas. You know that there are kids inside that dining hall right now, don't you? Kids who still believe in Santa Claus? Kids whose lives you'll be responsible for ruining if you don't let them go home to their mothers and fathers. Where's your mother, Jeb? Think she's watching this on TV right now? I bet she is, and I bet she's crying her heart out. What do you think?"

"My mom ain't got nothing to do with this! You leave her out of this, you hear me?" Jeb's voice was trembling now.

"I'm running out of patience, Jeb. Seriously. My boss tells me I've got ten minutes, after that . . . well, remember what I said about those sharpshooters. They can take you out in a split second. And I think some of them want to. They've got kids, and they don't like to see little children frightened or threatened in any way. You think about that, Jeb? Okay, I want you to think about it."

A loud crashing noise, then the sound of crying as Jeb Norris dropped to his knees. Before he had a chance to make the slightest move, he was handcuffed and lifted off the ground, then escorted to a cruiser.

The next hour was pure pandemonium. Claire rushed to her parents' side. They were unharmed, thank God. One by one, the police officers escorted the remaining hostages out of the dining hall. When Claire saw Quinn, she ran toward him and threw herself in his arms. "I was so afraid for you," she said, as they walked arm in arm to the temporary tents the police had set up. There were twenty-three people who'd almost lost their lives. It was going to be a very long day for all of them.

CHAPTER TEN

The night before Christmas Eve . . .
Claire lost count of the cookies after the twenty-third dozen. Her entire family was gathered at Hope House, a shelter for battered women where Max Jorgenson, his wife Grace, and their daughter Bella held their annual cookie bake-off.

This was the first time Claire had attended, and she knew without a doubt that she would return next year. She was having so much fun, no wonder Tilly had chosen to be a chef over her career as a medical doctor. Donald Flynn, the old coot, was getting his way in spite of all the trouble he'd created last week when he demanded Claire come to Ireland where he supposedly lay on his deathbed. Though she wanted to stay angry at him, she couldn't. He would be eighty years old in a matter of days. Claire and Quinn were waiting until then to tell him they were a couple now. With every passing minute, she knew she'd made the right decision when she let Quinn Connor into her life, and into her heart. Connor was his mother's maiden name, she'd discovered. She hadn't wanted Quinn to be burdened with the Flynn name and had chosen to use her maiden name instead. While "Flynn" was close to "Trump" in Ireland, here in the States, it was just another Irish name.

"Can we call you Uncle Quinn yet?" Amanda asked.

"I'd be delighted if you did," he replied.

"So you're gonna marry Aunt Claire?" Ashley asked as she slopped gooey red icing on her Santa cookie.

Quinn looked at Claire. "I plan to."

"But don't you have to ask her first?" Ashley asked again.

Stephanie chose that moment to enter the kitchen, carrying another tray of cookies to the table to be decorated. Something both girls were quite good at.

"Are they being nosy?"

"No, they're just being girls," Quinn said, and winked at Claire.

There were cookies in every possible Christmas design. Angels, stars, Santa's of all shapes and sizes, reindeer, Christmas trees and snowflakes set on cooling racks on the dining room table. This was the cooling station. Grace had them all set up in assembly-line fashion. The messiest job, the decorating, was done in the kitchen.

Claire's mother and dad helped to mix the batter. Once the dough was chilled, and they had lots of dough, the kids — Amanda, Ashley, and Bella, and Megan and Nathan's boys — Joseph, Ryan, and Eric — helped to roll out the dough. Abigail, Mark and Colleen's remaining daughter, supervised the young kids.

Later that evening, they would take the cookies to local nursing homes and hospitals. Claire knew there was a big surprise coming up, but she kept it to herself. She and Patrick had decided she wouldn't even hint that she knew what that surprise was.

When the adults returned from delivering the cookies, they all gathered in the formal living room, where Grace served them cookies and hot toddies, and cocoa for those who didn't wish to imbibe. Claire was definitely in the latter group. After the episode at JFK, it would be a very long time before she had another alcoholic beverage.

When the adults were settled, and the younger children put to bed for the night, they watched Bryce, Grace's brother, set up his new Apple computer. They made a big production of turning the computer on, then Bryce clicked the mouse a few times and a face appeared on the screen.

"Claire, I think you should look at this," Quinn said, seeing that she was engaged in a conversation with Melanie, Bryce's wife.

"Look at what?" she asked, then before Quinn had a chance to answer, Claire squealed with delight. "Kelly! Oh my gosh, I can't believe it!"

"Aye, these computers are quite amazing, huh? We can Skype now that Quinn gave me a computer. I can't tell ya how excited I was when he tol' me and mother we were gettin' a new place to live! And Paddy loves his new boots." Claire had just sent them three days ago, but she'd sent them overnight air, so she knew they'd receive them before Christmas.

"I'm glad he likes them. Wait until next year, he'll be walking in those boots. No, he'll be too big. I'll make sure to keep little Paddy supplied with boots, and his mom with shoes."

"Aye, the Kate Spades were ta die for! Thank ya so very much."

Claire knew Quinn had a few more surprises for Kelly. She couldn't wait to see the expression on her face. "Kelly, Quinn wants to have a peep, is that okay with you?"

She laughed. "Of course it is!"

Quinn leaned close to the microphone so Kelly could hear him. "A little birdie told me you wanted to go to school to become a nurse."

"Aye, it's always been a dream o' mine."

"Beginning in January, your tuition is paid in full at the university. And Paddy's, too, though I know it will be a while before he heads off to college, but Claire and I just wanted to make sure he had that opportunity."

Tears rolled down Kelly's face. "I don't know what ta say, except thanks to ya both; my life, me mum's life, and Paddy's life are better for knowin' ya, all of ya."

"Kelly, there is one more thing," Quinn said, his voice full of happiness. He looked at Claire, and she raised her brows. She didn't know what else he had up his sleeve, but whatever it was, she knew it would be life-changing.

Quinn Connor was a giver, a doer, and a life changer, for all those who were lucky enough to have him as a friend.

"I don't know of anything else, I have everything I could possibly want."

"When I told you the house was yours to live in as long as you want, I meant it. The deed is now in your name, and the house is yours, free and clear."

Claire looked at Quinn, then back at the computer monitor, where she saw Kelly crying her eyes out. She blew her nose on one of Paddy's diapers, then laughed when she looked into her camera. "There's nothing ta say, Quinn, nothing left to say, except thank ya, you changed me life."

No one said a word. They were all lost in their own thoughts, their own reasons for being especially thankful on this blessed night. They'd all survived during the hostage takeover, each had their wounds, but all had a new appreciation for all that was good in their life.

The computer monitor went black, and they all clapped and congratulated Quinn on his generosity.

Patrick chose that moment to clap his hands. "Listen up, folks. I've got a bit of good news I'd like to share with you while we're all together."

This was Stephanie's clue to join her husband. "Amanda, Ashley, would you come here just for a minute. We have something we want to say, and since you're both big girls now, and don't have to go to bed for at least" — Patrick looked at his watch — "another fifteen minutes, your mom and I thought you should hear this."

Claire wanted to tell him to hurry up and share their good news, but this was special and deserving of those few extra words as it was a life-changing event for them all.

Patrick rubbed the palms of his hands together, excitement brightening his handsome face. He looked at his wife, then wrapped his arm around her shoulders. "Go on, Stephanie, tell them."

"Yeah, tell us."

"Come on, don't keep us in suspense."

"Spit it out, bro, I need to . . ."

"Okay, okay. Stephanie, the honor is yours."

She grinned, her big brown eyes shining like jewels. "Patrick and I recently learned we're going to have a baby!"

Shouts of joy, backslapping, hand clapping, and tears flowed like a fine wine. Joseph and Eileen were just as thrilled with this news as they were when Colleen had told them she was pregnant with Shannon. Though the eldest granddaughter wasn't there in body, somehow the grandparents knew she was there in spirit.

Max shook Patrick's hand. "It's about time, my friend. Grace and I were starting to worry about you."

"Bull," Patrick said.

"Watch your mouth, there are kids in this

house," Grace called out, and they all laughed.

Everyone continued to offer Patrick their congratulations. Amanda and Ashley were so excited, the adults knew it would be quite some time before they settled down.

"Is it a boy or a girl?" Amanda asked.

"Yes, do you know yet, or is it too soon?" Claire asked.

"No, we haven't had the ultrasound yet. Don't we have this scheduled for next week? I plan to make a full day of it. Taking the girls with us, too."

Stephanie cleared her throat loudly, hoping to focus the attention on herself. "I hate to be the one to bring up bad news, especially tonight when we're all together as a family for the first time in a very long time, but I don't think there's going to be a more appropriate time, so please" — she paused — "hear me out."

When she saw she had everyone's undivided attention she continued, her voice quiet but strong. "When Jeb Norris held us in the dining hall the other day, I prayed for all of us. I prayed for my girls and my husband, and I also prayed for my unborn child. But as some of you know, being a mother is so much more than a name or an act. It's who I am, what I do best." She smiled when both girls took a bow. "As you can see, I've raised two hams. However, as I was saying, a mother is the greatest joy in life, at least it has been in mine." They all knew there was time in Stephanie's life when she lived in fear for her daughters' life and her own. But those days were in the past, and nothing more but a faded memory. "When we all escaped without injury, the mother in me couldn't relax until I knew my unborn baby was safe. So, I pulled a fast one, and Patrick, please don't be upset with me for going behind your back, but I had to. I had an ultrasound the day after, and I know the sex of our child. I hope you're okay with this?" Stephanie's eyes filled with fear, but only for a moment. She was safe with Patrick and knew he would never lash out at her in anger.

"Sweetie, I could never be upset with you for wanting to protect our child." He kissed her lightly on the lips. "But I will give you a great big hickey in front of my entire family if you don't tell me, tell us if we need to paint the nursery pink or blue."

Again, all eyes were focused on the couple, and their two girls. "Maybe striped. Because you see, there seems to be one of each. So to answer your question" — Stephanie beamed — "we're having twins. A boy and a girl."

More whoops and hollers, and tears. Congratulations were said again and again.

Claire watched her brother and her sister-in-law and prayed that she and Quinn would always be as happy as they were at this exact moment.

When the excitement died down, and plans for baby showers, new baby furniture, and names dominated the conversation, Quinn grabbed Claire and whisked her outside.

"It's freezing out here! Have you lost your mind?" Claire asked, though she was teasing and thrilled to be alone with him even if it were only for a few minutes.

"I have not lost my mind, at least not yet, but I have lost my heart. To you. Donald got his wish after all, and he really didn't need to do a thing."

"Well, poor old soul, he loves his castle and his country. What more can a man want?"

Quinn gathered her in his arms, tilting her chin up so she could look into his eyes. "You, Claire. I want you."

She smiled up at him. "I'm all yours."

"No, I mean for always and forever. I want to share the rest of my life with you. Will

132

you do me the honor of becoming my wife?"

Claire had expected anything, but not a proposal, but then she remembered who she was dealing with. "I would be honored to spend my life with you, *Mister Christmas.*"

Quinn kissed her with such passion, Claire's rumba dancer's went wild.

"I love you, Claire O'Brien."

"And I love you, Quinn Connor."

"Let's go inside and tell the rest of the family we're all going to Ireland Christmas Day."

Claire's heart swelled with love.

Life was good. Very, very good.

■ ■ ■ ■

THE YELLOW ROSE
OF CHRISTMAS

MARIE BOSTWICK

■ ■ ■ ■

CHAPTER ONE

Miss Velvet Tudmore, Executive Director of the Too Much Texas Historical Society lifted her chin proudly as she concluded her story.

"And that, boys and girls, is how Too Much, Texas, got its start: on the conviction of a strong-willed woman and the indolence of a handsome but shiftless man." She paused, sighed and shook her head regretfully. "Which . . ."

". . . pretty well describes the makeup of our population to this day!" the teenagers circled around her chorused before breaking into laughter.

Miss Velvet, not in the least annoyed by this interruption, smiled. "Oh, you've heard the tale of my illustrious ancestor before, have you?"

Seventeen-year-old Noel LeFaver, president of the senior class of 1985 and one of the brightest girls in town, answered for them all. "Of course we have, Miss Velvet.

Everybody has. You've told the story of how Flagadine Tudmore founded Too Much to every fifth grade class since . . . How long has it been, Miss Velvet?"

"1944. That was the year I started working at the historical society. In that time, I've shared the history of our town not just with you but with your older and younger siblings, your aunts and uncles, mothers and fathers. And, because the residents of Too Much possess an ill-advised propensity to rush headlong into romance and reproduction, I've even told the story to some of your grandmothers and grandfathers."

She sighed again. Velvet could not understand why her fellow citizens should be so peculiarly subject to the more primitive impulses but accepted that there was nothing to be done about it. It was a flaw that ran through many of the families in Too Much, particularly her own, a Fatal Flaw. At some point in their lives, nearly all Tudmore women allowed lust and biology to overcome morality and reason and, as a result, ended up tied to some shiftless man for the rest of their lives. All because they lost their heads in a moment of passion. Such a shame.

But Miss Velvet didn't blame them for their weakness. It was something in the bloodline. The Tudmore women just couldn't seem to help themselves. Of all her clan, she alone had escaped the curse and consequences of the Fatal Flaw and, on the whole, considered herself a happier woman for it.

If she'd gone off and gotten married at a tender age, or even in middle age — not that anyone had asked, but if — would she be Executive Director of the Too Much Historical Society today? Would she have had the opportunity to acquire, document, and preserve the important relics of their town's past now displayed in the society's collection? Would the proud history of Too Much have been so faithfully recorded and passed on to future generations? Doubtful.

Marriage left women little time for such important work. From what she'd observed, men were demanding creatures and, more often than not, unworthy of the time and regard that women lavished upon them. Especially the men of Too Much. Shiftless. All of them.

However, now that she was in her middle sixties Miss Velvet had to admit that the prospect of spending her final years alone made her feel a little melancholy. It wasn't that she regretted the choices she'd made. After all she had her work to keep her busy and her family, her niece Taffy and Taffy's husband, Dutch, her great nieces Mary Dell and Lydia Dale, plus their four children to love, not to mention her sister and very best friend, Silky, for company. Still, she sometimes wondered what it would have been like to have had a man in her life, someone to talk to at the end of the day, someone to grow old with, someone who knew her likes and dislikes and secrets, who coupled her name with a private endearment that made her blush when he said it, someone who loved history and Texas and holding hands and her, not necessarily in that order. What might it have been like, she sometimes asked herself, to have had a grand romance? To have been someone's darling? Pursued and ensnared by love? Just once . . .

Well . . . whatever *may* have been had not been. At her age, romance was a ship that had sailed. But . . . it might have been nice. On the other hand, it might not. Either way, there was no point in dwelling on it. Velvet was not the sort of person who went around feeling sorry for herself.

"For nearly forty years, I've been privileged to share the history of our town with you and your families," she told her young listeners. "There are worse ways a woman could spend her life, much worse. So if you've heard the story of Too Much so often that you can tell it yourselves, I make no apologies for it. How many other towns in Texas were founded by women? Precious few, if any. A history as proud and unique as ours bears repeating. And I *will* repeat it, for as many times as it takes to pound it into those thick, adolescent skulls of yours," she said with mock-solemnity, earning another round of laughter from the teens.

"But Mr. Delacorte hasn't heard the story before. He's new in town." Noel turned toward her teacher, a man with full head of thick white hair, a neatly trimmed beard and mustache, and eyes so blue and bright that they fairly twinkled.

Miss Velvet, who had purposely avoided looking at Mr. Delacorte up to this point, now glanced in his direction.

"Miss Velvet?" Noel asked, moving quickly to her side, as if worried that the older woman might faint. "Are you all right? Your face has gone all red."

"I'm fine," Velvet assured her, gripping the edge of a table to steady herself. "Perfectly fine. It's just too warm in here."

Chapter Two

If he hadn't been so tall and skinny, six-foot-four with a thirty-two inch waist, Thaddeus Delacorte would have been a natural stand-in for Santa Claus. In fact, he'd already been recruited to fill that post at the town's annual Christmas Eve ball, a gala charity event organized by the Too Much Women's Club. Marlena Benton, president of the women's club and a member of the school board to boot, had dragooned him into service during his job interview.

"Wilfred Owens was our Santa for years but he up and died of an aneurysm last week," Marlena said with a cluck of her tongue, making it clear that she considered Mr. Owen's sudden demise not only inconvenient but disloyal. "Fortunately, the Women's Club owns the costume, so everything will be fine."

Sitting in the center of the panel of interviewers, she looked Mr. Delacorte up and down. "You're awfully lanky to play Santa, but we're desperate. We can add some padding around your middle and take down the hem of the costume. If you stay sitting most of the time, your height won't be so noticeable. Yes," she said with finality. "You'll do. You're hired."

And that was that. Mr. Delacorte was engaged, not just to play Santa Claus but also to serve as history teacher at the high school for the coming year, filling in while Mrs. Ryland took maternity leave. Miss Velvet, who looked upon the imparting of history to future generations as a sacred trust, was present to observe Mr. Delacorte's interview. She was furious that he had been hired without Marlena or the other members of the panel asking him a single question about his experience or qualifications but she wasn't really surprised.

Earlier in the week, Velvet had attended a meeting of the city council to request one thousand dollars to fund an oral history project which would document the memories and experience of the town's older citizens. As Miss Velvet envisioned creating a booklet of the histories which would be sold to offset much of the costs involved, the project didn't require a great deal of seed money and she anticipated that her request would be granted without much fuss. It likely would have been, had not Marlena Benton come up to the microphone after Velvet finished her presentation and made a speech about the need for belt tightening and not wasting taxpayer money on frivolous projects. She didn't mention Miss Velvet or the oral history project by name but her meaning was clear. Velvet's request was defeated unanimously. After the vote was taken, Marlena, who was seated in the front row of the chamber, turned around and gave Velvet an icy smirk, reveling in her victory.

Velvet was livid! Marlena Benton wasn't interested in fiscal responsibility but she was deeply interested in making life as difficult as possible for anyone named Tudmore. The feud between the Tudmores and Bentons was almost as old as the town of Too Much and things had only gotten worse in the last couple of years.

The marriage of Marlena's only son, the worthless Jack Benny, to Velvet's niece, Lydia Dale, had marked the beginning of a tenuous, ten-year truce between the two families. But since the couple's ugly divorce and Marlena's humiliation when Lydia Dale's twin sister, Mary Dell, outflanked

Marlena and bought the old Waterson's Dry Goods building, the only commercial building in Too Much not already in Benton hands, to open her new quilt shop, Marlena was on a rampage, unleashing her fury on any Tudmore that had the misfortune of crossing her path, including Miss Velvet.

Nobody in Too Much, the Tudmores excepting, dared to stand in the way of Marlena Benton. The Bentons were too rich to challenge, at least by Too Much standards. It wasn't that the Bentons owned *everything* in Too Much, just everything that was worth owning. Even, it seemed, the high school history department.

Things being the way they were, Miss Velvet was naturally suspicious of the new teacher. In her position, who wouldn't be? But her suspicions waned a bit when Mr. Delacorte sought her out after the school board meeting.

"Miss Tudmore?" he called, quickly crossing the room to catch up with her.

"Yes?"

Velvet turned at the sound of his voice, looked into his brilliant blue eyes and was struck by a strange and unfamiliar sensation. Her heart started to race. Little beads of perspiration popped out on her forehead. She experienced a tingling on her scalp and a sudden flush of heat that began at her breastbone and spread quickly upward to her neck and face, turning them red. She tried to speak but her voice caught in her throat. She closed her eyes, swallowed, and tried again.

"Yes, Mr. Delacorte."

She opened her eyes and looked at him but shifted her gaze to a spot over his right ear when the strange sensations returned.

"What can I do for you?"

He frowned, looking concerned. "Are you all right, Miss Velvet?"

"I'm fine. It's a little warm. Too many people packed together in too small a space. And no matter the temperature, come November, Mr. Purdy, the town custodian, turns the radiators up as high as they'll go. If the council was truly concerned about the budget, they *might* start with getting Jed Purdy to turn down the heat a notch or two. *That* would save them a thousand dollars and then some! In any case," she said quickly, aware that she was rambling and that this newcomer likely had no clue what she was talking about "what can I do for you, Mr. Delacorte?"

"Well, I was thinking that there might be something I could do for you," he said, then cleared his throat and amended his state-

146

ment. "Or rather, something I could do for the historical society. I was at the council meeting earlier in the week, sitting in the back. I thought it might help me get a better sense of the town. In your project proposal, I noticed that the bulk of the funds you requested would have gone to pay for people to conduct the interviews."

"Yes. I can't close the doors to the society while I conduct the interviews so I planned to hire some history majors from the community college in Waco to do it for me."

"Well, I was thinking that perhaps we . . . I mean, you . . . might be able to use volunteers instead, high school students."

Miss Velvet gave him a doubtful look.

"Only the seniors," he rushed to assure her. "And only students from the honors class. It would make an interesting class project. And I would give them special training beforehand, according to your standards and requirements, of course."

Mr. Delacorte inclined his head just slightly as he said this last and rested his hand momentarily on his chest, almost as if he were bowing to her. Miss Velvet smiled to herself. She couldn't fault him for lack of manners, that was certain. He was almost courtly in his demeanor, a real gentleman. Quite different from the standard grade of shiftless men one met in Too Much. And far better looking. His eyes. His smile. His hair, as white and shining as strands of new-spun silk . . .

Velvet shook herself, wondering how such a silly thought could have popped into her head. The effects of the overheated room must still be with her. And she'd yet to have her supper. Clearly, this was having an impact on her blood sugar.

Obviously, Velvet thought, speaking to herself in the most business-like tone she could muster, Mr. Delacorte was a well-intentioned man and kind, but she had real concerns about allowing teenagers to take on so important a project. She was about to explain this to the handsome history teacher when her sister, Silky, peeked her head around the door of the room.

"Velvet? Are you all right? I've been waiting out by the curb for ten minutes."

Velvet jumped, startled by her sister's sudden appearance. "I'm sorry. I was just chatting with Mr. Delacorte, the new history teacher. This is my sister, Silky."

Mr. Delacorte inclined his head once again. "Very nice to meet you, ma'am."

"Likewise. Velvet? Are you ready? *Dynasty* starts in five minutes."

"Coming," Velvet answered and then

turned to Mr. Delacorte. "I have to run. My sister is addicted to her programs. But perhaps you'd like to call me at the historical society so we can discuss this further?"

"Yes, ma'am," he said. "I surely would."

As they walked to the car, Silky asked, "Are you feeling all right, dear? You look a bit flushed."

"The chamber was too hot."

"Mr. Purdy," Silky said with a disapproving shake of her head.

"Exactly," Velvet replied.

Mr. Delacorte called her at the historical society the very next morning. They discussed his idea and worked out a specific training program that would teach the members of the honors class how to conduct a professional and scholarly oral history.

The strange symptoms which beset Velvet during their face-to-face encounter did not re-occur during their telephone conversation, which was a relief. And, in spite of her initial doubts, Velvet became convinced that the students, with proper instruction, would be able to record the interviews. She also became convinced that Mr. Delacorte was a fine history teacher. Her suspicion toward him began to thaw.

And now, as he turned his twinkling blue eyes in her direction and spoke in that deep voice of his with its slight Texian twang, a voice as smoky and rich as barbeque slow-roasted over mesquite, what remained of those suspicions melted entirely. Or was it her knees? Either way, when he looked at her with those beacon-blue eyes, she felt suddenly overheated and flushed, just as she had upon their earlier meeting. Unfamiliar with the chemical and physiological manifestations that accompany a physical attraction to another person, Miss Velvet made a mental note to write a memo to the mayor about Mr. Purdy and his flagrant waste of heating oil.

"Noel is quite right," Mr. Delacorte said in a dignified tone. "This is the first time I've had the opportunity to hear Miss Velvet tell the story of her celebrated ancestor. But I did have the pleasure of reading an account of it in the state historical society newsletter several years ago."

Miss Velvet's eyes went wide. She felt little beads of sweat popping out around her hairline. "You read my article?"

Mr. Delacorte nodded solemnly. "Yes, ma'am. At least a dozen times. Impeccable research. And your writing . . . so vivid. The way you described Flagadine Tudmore, exhausted, dehydrated, and half-starved because of her husband's ill-considered, late-season start from Arkansas to Austin, yet still a tower of strength, standing there with her feet spread and her arms crossed, informing him that it was all too much — the sun, the heat, the wind — and that she refused to budge one-inch further . . ."

Delacorte blinked and swallowed hard, as if trying to keep his emotions in check.

"I felt like I was standing right there myself, witnessing the whole thing. You made the story come alive for me, Miss Velvet, which is what a truly skilled historian does. But to actually *hear* the tale, told in your own words, has been a real pleasure."

Miss Velvet pulled a linen handkerchief from her pocket, one she'd embroidered herself with French-knot flowers, held it briefly to her nose and then dabbed it daintily and, she hoped, nonchalantly, against her damp brow.

"Oh. Well. You're too kind, Mr. Delacorte. Much too kind."

"However," she said, adopting a more business-like tone and quickly turning her gaze from the teacher to the gaggle of teenagers who were staring at her with more than usual interest, "I do agree with your teacher that the oral tradition is a vitally important component of the full historical record. That's why I'm so glad you're will–

ing to help collect and transcribe these oral histories."

She walked to her desk, picked up a stack of papers, and began handing them out to the students.

"I'm giving each of you a list of interview questions along with the names and vital information for five of our older citizens. Mrs. Murphy, the music teacher, has said she'll lend tape recorders to anyone who needs one. Be sure you pick those up from her before the start of the Thanksgiving holiday.

"Now, some of the folks you talk to may tend to ramble a bit. I know that will mean more work for you when you type up the transcriptions but please resist the urge to cut them off or lead them in any way. I don't need the transcripts back until January, which leaves you all of the Thanksgiving and Christmas holidays to complete the project. Also, as you look over your list of inter-viewees, may I suggest that you begin with the oldest first? Many of these folks are getting on in years and in the case of Vida Wynne Henderson and George Plank . . ."

Miss Velvet looked up at the students. "Who's got Vida Wynne and George?"

Noel LeFavre and Buck Swanson raised their hands.

"Well, I suggest you interview them immediately, this afternoon if you can manage it. Vida Wynne is ninety-nine and George is one hundred and two. There's no time to waste. Oh, and Buck? When you go to Mr. Plank's house, be sure to stop by the Tidee-Mart first and ask the butcher for a bone."

Buck's forehead creased, signaling his confusion.

"For the dog," Miss Velvet said in as patient a tone as she could muster, even while wondering if she should entrust so important a task to a boy who was obviously slow-witted. "When you get to Mr. Plank's gate, Buster is going to lunge and snarl at you. But if you take that bone and throw it as hard as you can across the yard, he'll chase it. Then, while he's busy with that, you run to the front door and get inside quick. Understand? Good. Are there any other questions?"

Buck, who was wondering how he was supposed to make the trip from the front door back to the safe side of the gate after the interview without getting his leg torn off by Mr. Plank's dog, started to raise his hand but before he could speak, Wanda Joy Cleary, Too Much's cranky, gum-cracking postmistress, opened the door and stomped into the society's main gallery.

"Mail!" she bellowed.

Miss Velvet's mouth flattened into a line. "There's no need to shout," she said, walking toward Wanda Joy, holding out her hand to accept a small pile of envelopes. "I'm standing right here. Why didn't you just leave it in the box outside?"

"Believe me, I'd-a ruther. Two days to Thanksgiving but I'm already up to my earlobes delivering cards and packages and I don't know what all. Gets worse every year. Last thing I have time to do right now is play Cupid's messenger."

Miss Velvet frowned. "Cupid's messenger? What are you talking about?"

"This!" Wanda Joy barked. She pulled a white vase containing a single yellow rose out of her mailbag and plunked it unceremoniously onto the nearest table.

"Somebody left it at the postal counter with two dollars to cover delivery and a note saying to send it to you here at the historical society. The dang thing is too tall to fit into the mailbox so I had to take the time to park the truck, haul my biscuits in here, and deliver it personal. Plus, the dang water from the dang vase spilled in my bag and smeared the ink on one of my letters so bad that I can't tell if it's going to one-oh-seven Republic Road or one-oh-nine. I'm going to have to guess. And if I guess wrong, then next thing you know people are calling up the post office and complaining about bad service and the price of stamps."

Wanda Joy chewed her gum faster and drew up her nose in disgust, as if she'd suddenly smelled something bad. "Two days to Thanksgiving and here I am, playing Cupid's messenger. And do I get any thanks for it? No, ma'am. I do not."

Seemingly deaf to Wanda Joy's tirade, Miss Velvet walked toward the table and bent her head low over the vase, breathing in the rose's sweet scent.

"But," she asked, lifting her head, "who in the world would send me a yellow rose?"

Velvet glanced toward Mr. Delacorte but when she saw the warm blue of his eyes turn suddenly flat and cool, she quickly looked back to Wanda Joy. "Was there a return address?"

"No, ma'am. Just that letter," Wanda Joy replied, tilting her head to indicate the stack of mail that Miss Velvet held in her hand and a large, yellow-gold envelope on the top. "There's no return address there either, just your name."

Wanda Joy smirked, scratched her left ear, and moved her enormous wad of chewing gum to her right cheek. "That's why I say

I'm playing Cupid's messenger. If I didn't know better, Miss Velvet, I'd say you've got yourself a secret admirer."

"A secret admirer? At my age? Don't be silly . . ."

Feeling another sudden flush of heat, Miss Velvet dabbed her forehead with her handkerchief once again. Standing behind her, Noel and the other members of the class of 1985 looked at each other with gleeful eyes, clamping their mouths tightly closed to keep from laughing out loud.

CHAPTER THREE

Texas is a state known for producing beautiful women who are strong of body and spirit but the Tudmore women were among the strongest of all, and the most unusual.

Flagadine Tudmore, the ancestor whom Miss Velvet took such justifiable pride in, outlived her pioneer husband by several decades and founded, not just the town of Too Much, but also the twelve hundred acre F-Bar-T ranch. The ranch had been passed down from mother to daughter, as a strictly matrilineal inheritance, for six generations. Though not an especially large spread by Texas standards, the F-Bar-T sat on the best grazing land in the county and the most beautiful, with waves of gently rolling hills and a thin blue ribbon of sweet water running through the middle. It was like an oasis in the desert, a precious pocket-sized kingdom, a realm ruled by women.

And so, though Dutch Templeton sat at

the head of the table and carved the turkey, his position as family leader was symbolic rather than actual, gained by virtue of being the only adult male present at the family's Thanksgiving feast.

Dutch was not bothered by this. He was an affable but unambitious fellow, who loved his wife and daughters and understood what he was getting into when he married a Tudmore. However, since his sons-in-law had walked out the year before, he felt outnumbered, like a lone rooster living among the hens. Sometimes he enjoyed flapping his wings and having a good crow, just for the sake of stirring things up, seeing his womenfolk clamor and cluck in response. This was one of those times.

Dutch pushed himself to a half-standing position, leaned across the table for a second helping, spearing an entire leg from the turkey, and said in a loud voice, "So, Velvet? What's this I hear about you having a secret admirer?"

"Dutch!"

Taffy gasped and delivered a cautionary kick to her husband's shin, giving every appearance of being horrified by the bluntness of his question. But her shock and dismay were feigned.

Two days before and less than two hours

after the incident took place, Taffy had gone to the Tidee-Mart to buy groceries for the Thanksgiving feast and overheard young Buck Swanson telling the butcher about Miss Velvet and the rose. Though she'd never have blurted it out quite like Dutch did, Taffy had been dying to ask her aunt the exact same question.

Velvet dropped her fork onto her plate with an impatient clatter. "Oh, for heaven's sake! Do the people in this town have nothing better to do than gossip and spread rumors?"

Silky, just a year older than her sister and so like her in appearance that they might have been twins, grinned. "Not really. In a town of two thousand, there's never much news to share but what news there is, gets out quick. Especially in a week when half the population is stopping by the meat counter to pick up their turkey."

Velvet growled with disgust and mumbled something about hammering the butcher with his own meat mallet on her next visit to the Tidee-Mart.

Lydia Dale and Mary Dell, who *were* twins, though fraternal rather than identical, and who were so busy supervising their little ones dinner that they'd barely been able to converse with the other adults at the

table or eat more than a mouthful themselves, now jumped into the conversation,
delighted that the subject they were so curious about had been thrown open to discussion.

"Don't be mad, Aunt Velvet," Lydia Dale
said while lifting an eyebrow at the eldest of
her three, ten-year-old Jeb, who quickly
removed his elbows from the table. "You
can't blame people for being interested.
After all, when's the last time somebody in
Too Much got a dozen yellow roses!"

Mary Dell, who was holding her infant
son, Howard, in one arm and trying to cut
her turkey with the other, looked up in
surprise. "A dozen? I heard it was two."

Velvet let out an exasperated growl. "It
was one! One rose! Not one dozen! One
single rose. That's all. Nothing worth getting worked up about."

"Well, do you know who it was from?"
Lydia Dale asked. "Did he send a message?"

"I heard there was a card," Mary Dell said.

Silky, who shared a little cottage in town
with her sister, confirmed this. "There was.
But she won't let me read it."

"Must be juicy if you're keeping it secret
from Granny," Mary Dell said, raising and
lowering her eyebrows meaningfully. "You
tell her everything."

Velvet rolled her eyes. "Don't be ridiculous. There was nothing juicy about it. If you must know, the note was practically illegible. I've never seen such poor handwriting or grammar, like something a child would write. Probably a child *did* write it, one of those silly boys over at the high school, thinking it would be a fun prank to play on an old spinster."

"Who cares about the handwriting?" Taffy asked eagerly. "Tell us what it said!"

"Just a lot of nonsense. I can't remember it now. I threw it away as soon as I finished reading it."

Taffy clucked her tongue with disappointment. "Threw it away? Really? So you don't have any idea who might have sent it?"

Miss Velvet picked up her fork and started to work on the tiny mound of sweet potatoes that occupied the lower right quadrant of her dinner plate. She'd always had a dainty appetite.

"It might have been that hulking Buck Swanson," Velvet said. "I wouldn't put it past him. He was awfully quick to run to the Tidee-Mart and report everything to Bob Baker, probably counting on the fact that Bob would pass it along with every pound of poultry he sold that day. I don't like that scheming Buck Swanson. Never did. I can't imagine how that boy got himself into the honors history class. He's as dull as a rusty ax."

Dutch, who was still chewing, said through a mouthful of turkey. "Well, wait a minute, Velvet. Is the boy scheming or is he stupid? Don't see how he could be both."

Velvet ignored the question.

"Seriously, how does a boy like that get into honors history? Mrs. Ryland must have signed off on his placement before she went on maternity leave, knowing she wouldn't have to deal with him. I can't imagine that Mr. Delacorte would have approved it."

Silky, who had been listening to this exchange without comment, though paying careful attention to her sister's vocal tone and facial expressions, took a casual sip of sparkling cider from her glass and asked, "How is Mr. Delacorte working out anyway? Is he as bad a teacher you thought he'd be?"

Velvet picked up her knife and began methodically cutting her tiny portion of turkey into tiny bites, each a half-inch square, keeping her eyes on her plate as she spoke.

"I never said I thought he was a bad teacher. I had no way of knowing whether he was or wasn't. Neither did the school board; that was my beef. The board didn't lift a finger to find out about his qualifications! They let Marlena Benton run roughshod over them, just like she always . . ."

Velvet, receiving a pointed look from Lydia Dale, stopped herself in mid-sentence.

Since the divorce, Miss Velvet sometimes forgot that Lydia Dale's children, Jeb, Cady, and Rob Lee, were half-Benton and that Marlena Benton was their grandmother. Though her former mother-in-law had treated her like dirt since the divorce and Jack Benny had treated her worse, even spreading a rumor that the baby, Rob Lee, wasn't his, Lydia Dale would not allow her children to be exposed to any disparaging talk about their father or their Benton relatives. She was right, of course, and Velvet knew it. But sometimes it was hard to restrain herself.

It was just like she always said; taken as a group, men were disappointing, most of them not worth the time it took to throw them over. Oh sure, now and then you'd find a decent one. Dutch was all right. A typical Too Much male, handsome and shiftless, but he loved his children and grandchildren. And, for reasons that Velvet found hard to fathom, her niece being a little spoiled and self-centered, Dutch worshipped the ground Taffy walked on. Yes, Dutch was a decent enough sort.

But just look at what had happened to poor Lydia Dale; left high and dry with three little children to support when Jack Benny left her for that floozy! After all Lydia Dale had been through, Velvet found it hard to believe that she was willing to take the plunge again. Not that Velvet had anything against, Graydon, Lydia Dale's fiancé. He doted on her children, had done a good job as their ranch manager, and gave every appearance of being steady and hard-working. Even now, he was off in Montana, investigating some new and supposedly hardier breeds of sheep. But appearances could be deceiving.

Mary Dell's husband, Donny, had seemed steady and devoted, too. But for their inability to have children, Velvet would have said Mary Dell and Donny were as happy as any couple she'd ever met. But when Mary Dell was finally blessed with a baby boy, Howard, who was born with Down syndrome, Donny just couldn't cope. He went out to pick up some groceries at the Tidee-Mart and never came back.

Donny wasn't a cheating louse, not like that horrible Jack Benny, a Benton if ever she'd seen one, but he wasn't as strong as he appeared to be. In fact, in comparison to Mary Dell, who, quite rightly, considered that sweet little Howard to be a gift from heaven, Donny was downright weak. It was such a shame. But, that was the way it was with men. Yes, indeed. Appearances could be deceiving.

"Well, from what I can tell so far, Mr. Delacorte appears to be a good teacher. His students seem to like him well enough. But I don't know if that signifies much. However," she said, smiling a little as she recalled his comments about her newsletter article, "he does have a finely tuned appreciation of history. That I know for sure."

Silky nodded. "He's such a nice-looking man, too."

"Do you think so?" Velvet asked absently. "I hadn't noticed. Can't say as I care much for that beard. A full beard always makes me think a man is trying to hide something . . . a personal insecurity. Or a weak chin."

"Mr. Delacorte isn't using his beard to hide a weak chin," Dutch said as he ladled more gravy onto his mashed potatoes.

Taffy turned toward her husband. "How would you know? You've never even met him."

"Yes, I did. Yesterday. He was coming out

165

of the hardware store carrying two wooden poles and twenty yards of white canvas. When I introduced myself and asked him what he was up to with all that stuff, he told me that he's one of those historical re-enactors. Plays the part of a general in the Texas Army, back in the days of the republic. Just on the weekends and such, for fun. But he's sure excited about it. He went on and on. I don't think I've ever met anybody who gets that worked up about Texas history. Present company excepting," Dutch said, nodding in Velvet's direction before loading his fork with potatoes. "Anyway, that's why he has the beard. It's part of his character."

"Really?" Velvet asked. "A general, you say?"

"Uh-huh. Oh, Mary Dell, I almost forgot. Mr. Delacorte needs some help sewing his tent. When I told him that you owned the quilt shop, he asked if you might know somebody who could make it for him."

Mary Dell, who had given up trying to eat and was playing peek-a-boo with Howard instead, looked up at her father.

"I don't know anybody that does that kind of work." Mary Dell shifted Howard in her arms. "But, why don't you tell Mr. Dela-corte to bring everything to the quilt shop. I

166

don't know if I can sew a tent or not, but I'm willing to give it a try."

"Try stitching it on my old Feather-weight," Silky advised. "That should do the trick." Almost everything that Mary Dell knew about sewing, she had learned at her grandmother's knee.

"Do you really think so?" Mary Dell asked doubtfully. "Canvas is so heavy and your machine is so old. I'd hate to break it."

"Bah!" Silky said, dismissing her grand-daughter's concerns. "Those Featherweights were built to last! You can sew anything from silk to leather on those old Singers. Not like these new machines. From the prices they'd charge, you'd think they were made of gold but most of them are pure plastic. Don't worry, honey. You can't break my machine. My momma sewed all our clothes on it when we were little, everything from dresses to dungarees. Isn't that right, Velvet. Velvet?"

Velvet, who was dissecting her half-inch squares of turkey into even smaller quarter-inch bites but had yet to eat a single one of them, jerked, startled at the sound of her own name.

"What? Did you ask me something, Silky? I'm sorry, I wasn't paying attention."

Silky grinned and waved her hand. "That's

all right. We weren't discussing anything all that earth-shattering. What were you thinking about, anyway?"

Velvet shook her head, pulled her napkin from her lap, and dabbed it daintily against her lips and then against her brow.

"Oh. Nothing. Nothing important. Just the . . . the oral history project. Yes, that's right. I was thinking about the oral history project. And George Plank. I hope Buck Swanson followed the script I gave him and didn't try to cut him off. You know how George can ramble."

"At George's age," Dutch said, "he's earned the right to ramble. I bet it turned out fine but if you're so worried, Velvet, why don't you go over and see George tomorrow? Check on him yourself."

"We've got a ham bone in the refrigerator," Dutch said. "You can take it with you to give to Buster."

"That's a good idea. Thank you, Dutch."

"You're welcome."

"So," she said, looking at her nephew-in-law, "a general, you said?"

Dutch nodded. "Yes, ma'am. That's what he told me."

Velvet pressed her lips together for a moment before finally spearing a sliver of turkey meat with her fork.

"A general," she mused. "Well, it stands to reason, doesn't it? You can tell just by looking at him."

CHAPTER FOUR

The F-Bar-T ranch was located just six miles from downtown Too Much but it took Silky and Velvet a full fifteen minutes to drive back to their little shotgun cottage on Houston Street. Silky believed that any speed above thirty miles per hour would tax the engine of her 1964 LeSabre. After dark she insisted on driving even more slowly, concerned about the possibility of hitting any stray cattle that might have escaped through a broken fence and wandered onto the road. Velvet felt this was a remote possibility but she wasn't the one driving so she kept her opinions to herself. After a lifetime of living together, she and Silky were tolerant of each other's foolishness and idiosyncrasies.

When they pulled into the driveway, Velvet hopped out of the car without being asked and raised the door of the garage, a single-stalled, detached structure that had once served as a small stable. With the car turned off and shut up safely for the night, the sisters went inside and, without saying a word, set about their nightly routine.

Velvet brought in the cat, Mr. Bowie, named for the famous frontiersman who died at the Alamo, and gave him a bowl of kibble and a little leftover turkey as a treat. Then she took the milk carton out of the refrigerator, filled two glasses and set them on the kitchen table. Meanwhile, Silky put a kettle of water on the stove, then went around and made sure all the doors and windows were locked before returning to the kitchen and sitting down to drink her milk. When their glasses were empty, at almost the exact moment the tea kettle started to whistle, Silky rose from her chair and took two red rubber hot water bottles out of the cupboard.

"I don't believe I'll need one tonight," Velvet said. "I've felt overheated all afternoon."

"Are you sure? It's going to get awful cold. Forty-degrees, the paper said. If this keeps up, maybe we'll have ourselves a white Christmas."

"That would certainly be one for the history books," Velvet said. "It hasn't snowed in Too Much since December 16, 1911."

Silky smiled as she poured steaming water carefully into her own hot water bottle. She never ceased to be impressed by her sibling's ability to keep important historical milestones cataloged in her head.

"Last chance," she said, looking at Velvet before pouring the rest of the water down the sink.

Velvet shook her head. "I'm fine. If anything, I'm too warm."

"Could be the change," Silky suggested.

"Don't be silly. I went through that ten years ago. Maybe I'm coming down with something?" Miss Velvet touched her forehead. It was cool.

"Well, I'm sure I'll be fine in the morning. Good night, Silky. Happy Thanksgiving."

"Happy Thanksgiving, Velvet."

Mr. Bowie followed Velvet to her room and hopped up onto the bed, kneading the blue and white "Sister's Choice" quilt, which Silky made as a Christmas gift for Velvet years before, into a state of optimal comfort before curling up into a ball and closing his eyes.

Miss Velvet took off her gray, calf-length dress and hung it up in the closet next to similarly shapeless frocks of black, charcoal, and navy blue, before changing into her white flannel nightgown. Next, she went into the bathroom, brushed her teeth, washed her face, unpinned and unwound the braided coronet of her hair, unplaited it, gave her gray, waist length locks fifty strokes with a brush, and plaited it again, letting the braid hang loose down her back, before walking to the bedside and kneeling down to say her prayers, thanking her Maker for his many mercies and blessings.

Velvet climbed under the quilt, inadvertently bumping Mr. Bowie who opened one eye and glared at her.

"Pardon me, sir. It might help if you didn't insist on sleeping smack dab in the middle of the mattress."

The cat went back to sleep. Miss Velvet pulled the covers up to her chest and turned out the bedside lamp only to turn it on again a minute later. She pushed herself into an upright position and pulled a yellow-gold envelope out of the nightstand drawer.

Miss Velvet had lied about throwing the note away, but not about the quality of the handwriting or the primitive literary prowess of the writer. The lettering was scrawled and every sentence sloped downward and to the right, as if the entire missive were in danger of sliding off the page. The phrases that declared her beautiful were short, choppy and full of misspellings. In fact, the word "beautiful" was missing an "a." And the word "cornflower," contained within a sentence suggesting she would look even more "beutiful" were she to wear a dress of that color, was spelled "cornflour."

"Cornflour? Maybe he meant cornstarch." She chuckled to herself and slid the stationary back into the envelope. "Maybe I should buy young Mr. Swanson a dictionary for Christmas. What do you think, Mr. Bowie?"

Hearing his name, the cat yawned, but made no comment. Miss Velvet placed the envelope back in the nightstand, turned out the light, and went to sleep.

In the morning, Velvet awoke at six-thirty, just as she always did. She said her morning prayers, got dressed, ate breakfast with Silky, and walked to work. She didn't expect many visitors at the historical society on the Friday after Thanksgiving and so planned to spend the day cleaning the glass display cases and carefully dusting the collection of historical artifacts.

Striding at a brisk pace and following the most direct route to Too Much's tiny commercial center and town square, it normally took Miss Velvet exactly twelve minutes to get from home to the historical society. But today she strolled instead of strode around the square, taking time to enjoy the three-foot high red-and-white striped plastic candy canes, newly purchased by the town council, that decorated each lamppost, and peer into the display windows of each business, already decked out for Christmas.

The window of Pickens Hardware held a collection of bright red power tools resting on a bed of "snow," really a mixture of pulverized Styrofoam and silver glitter, each tied with an enormous green bow. Hilda, the proprietress of Hilda's House of Pie, who had something of an artistic streak, had painted her window with a chubby, apple-cheeked Mrs. Claus, standing under a sprig of mistletoe and looking expectant. A poster resting on the windowsill declared that anyone who gave Hilda a Christmas smooch would get a free cup of coffee with their pie. Velvet didn't consider this a particularly appealing offer but it seemed to be effective. Looking through the window, she could see that every stool at Hilda's counter was occupied by a man who was eating pie and drinking coffee.

The window of the Patchwork Palace, Mary Dell and Lydia Dale's recently opened quilt shop, contained an artfully selected and arranged display of fabrics, not in the expected reds and greens of the season, but in rich shades of gold, ruby, emerald, amethyst, and sapphire set against a drape of black velvet, like gems in a jewelry shop.

Velvet knew that every woman in town, quilter or not, would stop to admire those fabrics and a goodly percentage of them, quilter or not, would go inside and end up buying some, perhaps signing up for one of Mary Dell's classes so they could learn what to do with all that luscious fabric. It was a stunning display. Velvet also knew just who had come up with the idea and put it all together: Lydia Dale. Lydia Dale could hardly sew a stitch but she had exquisite taste and incredible color sense.

Mary Dell, on the other hand, had no more taste than a hothouse tomato but she could perfectly match the points on an eight-pointed star blind-folded and with one hand behind her back. More importantly, she could teach other people how to do the same thing. Mary Dell and Lydia Dale were two sides of the same coin. Velvet was so proud of them and happy that the quilt shop was turning out to be a success. She thought about popping inside and telling them so but changed her mind after looking at her wristwatch. In forty years working at the historical society, she had never called in sick and never been late to work. Not once.

She scurried past the windows of the Five-And-Dime, the Feed-And-Seed, and the Primp 'n Perm without so much as a second glance. But as she approached Antoinette's Dress Shop, Velvet stopped dead in her tracks and stared at the mannequin in the front window.

"Cornflower blue," she whispered.

Antoinette knocked on the door of the dressing room. "Miss Velvet? Does it fit all right? Or do you need me to find another size?"

Miss Velvet's voice, sounding uncharacteristically high-pitched and nervous, came from the opposite side of the flowered curtain that separated the dressing room from the dress shop.

"Oh . . . I don't think so. It . . . ummm . . . doesn't look as good as I thought it might. And I think it's too small. Too tight. Definitely too tight."

"That should be your size, Miss Velvet. Maybe we just need to take it out a little bit. Let me see."

"No!"

Antoinette swept the flowered curtain aside. Miss Velvet squealed and clutched her arms over her chest, as if she'd been caught skinny-dipping.

"Oh, my!" Antoinette laid her hand over her heart as if she felt a palpitation coming on. Her eyes became dewy.

"Oh, Miss Velvet! That color! It's perfect for you! Do you know something? Until just this minute, I never realized you had cornflower blue eyes. You look beautiful."

"I do?"

Velvet loosened her grip on herself, not dropping her arms completely, but relaxing just a little, not resisting when Antoinette took her firmly by the shoulders and turned her around one-hundred and eighty degrees to face the mirror.

"But . . . don't you think it's too tight?" Velvet asked, tugging at the blue fabric on the bodice and waistline. "Maybe if we got rid of the belt."

"Absolutely not," Antoinette declared, gently pulling Miss Velvet's arms down from her body like she was peeling the rind from an orange. "See? It's perfectly smooth over the chest, hips, and waist. Not a pucker or pull anywhere. Miss Velvet, I never knew you had such a tiny waist. In fact, I never knew you had a shape at all! Where have you been hiding it all these years?"

Antoinette made a tsking sound and answered her own question, speaking to

Velvet's reflection as she looked over the older woman's shoulder and into the mirror.

"Underneath all those gray and black feed sacks you've always insisted on wearing, that's where. I swear, it's bad enough that you make all your own clothes . . . I mean, how would I ever feed my children and make my car payment if everybody in Too Much did that? Hmm? But, Miss Velvet, as talented as you and your sister are with a needle, didn't it ever occur to you to sew up a dress that looks at least a tiny bit fashionable? Never mind. You're here now and that's what counts. You look beautiful."

Velvet lifted her hand and swatted away the compliment. "Stop saying that. I am *not* beautiful. I'm a dried up old spinster and we both know it! Don't make fun of me. And don't go telling tales just so you can sell me a dress, Antoinette."

"Dried up old spinster?" Antoinette rolled her eyes. "Please. How old are you, Miss Velvet? Sixty-five?"

"Sixty-four."

"Sixty-four is a long way from dried up. My granny Boone buried her third husband when she was seventy-seven, married her fourth at eighty, and buried him two weeks later! The poor man couldn't keep up with her, I guess. Had a heart attack on their honeymoon."

"Well, if I'd been your granny Boone's fourth husband, I'd have had a heart attack too," Velvet muttered.

Antoinette put her hands on her hips.

"Miss Velvet, I am not telling you a tale. You look lovely in this dress. Beautiful even. You truly do. I tell you what; if you'd dye your hair, put on some lipstick and earrings, get rid of those nasty old orthopedics," she said, curling her lip as she peered at Miss Velvet's thick-soled lace-ups, "and buy yourself a nice pair of heels, every white-haired bachelor in this town would be following after you like a lovesick pup." She winked. "Maybe even a few of the married ones."

Once again, Velvet waved off the shop owner's compliment, though not quite as vehemently as she had the first time.

"Now, you stop that," she said with a smile. "I never heard anything so silly."

"Well? What do you say, Miss Velvet? Can I wrap it up for you?"

Velvet dropped her arms to her sides and took a good long look in the mirror, turning to the left and right, studying her reflection at all angles.

"It is pretty," she admitted after a moment. "The color and all but . . . I just don't know. It's such a change. And really, so close to Christmas and with so many gifts to buy, I don't think I should be spending money on myself. I'll tell you what . . . let me think about it for a day or two. All right?"

Antoinette smiled woodenly and nodded. She was sorry to lose the sale but sorrier still that Velvet Tudmore simply refused to see how well she looked in that dress. Maybe not beautiful, though Antoinette always felt that beauty lay in the eye of the beholder, but unquestionably pretty. Such a shame. For a moment, she'd been so sure that Velvet was going to take the dress but now, in spite of the older woman's hedging words, she knew that the moment had passed. In the language of retail, "let me think about it" means that the buyer had already thought about it and decided against it but didn't want to be impolite by coming right out and saying so. Velvet Tudmore was not going to buy the beautiful blue dress that so perfectly matched her eyes, not today and not tomorrow. In fact, Antoinette never expected Velvet to cross the threshold of her dress shop ever again. Such a shame.

Clad once again in her shapeless black

181

dress, and later than she'd ever been on a workday, Miss Velvet jogged to the end of the block, huffing and puffing as she crossed the street to the center of the square, zipping past the bronze monument where Flagadine Tudmore, arms crossed defiantly over her chest, stared toward the horizon with frozen resolve. When she reached the sidewalk that led to the courthouse, Miss Velvet looked up and saw that the municipal clock was set to strike ten in just a few seconds. Breaking into a flat out run, she sped around the side of the building to the door of the basement, where the historical society was housed.

For the second time that day, Miss Velvet stopped dead in her tracks, transfixed by an unexpected sight, staring at the single yellow rose which someone had tied to the doorknob with a red ribbon.

Three minutes later, the door to the dress shop flung open and Miss Velvet ran in, flushed purple as a plum and nearly gasping for breath.

Antoinette was standing on a chair in high heels while she changed a burnt out light bulb. Certain that Velvet was having a heart attack, she scrambled down from her perch so quickly that she twisted her ankle.

"Miss Velvet!" she cried, limping as quickly as she could to the older woman's side. "Are you all right? Do you need a doctor?"

Still gasping, Velvet moved her head from side to side in an exaggerated motion and held up her hand, indicating that Antoinette should let her catch her breath.

"I'm fine," she puffed after a moment. "But . . . I've changed my mind. I've decided to take the dress after all. And a tube of lipstick. And a pair of heels. Size eight-and-a-half wide."

CHAPTER FIVE

Antoinette stood in front of the class sample with a skeptical expression. "You really think you can teach *me* how to make this? I was the girl who flunked lanyard making at Sunday school, remember?"

Mary Dell laughed. She'd known Antoinette since she was a little girl and she did remember. Poor Antoinette's lanyard had been a tangle of blue, yellow, and red plastic cording, like something created by an electrician who had taken to drink.

"That wasn't your fault, hon. When it came to crafts, Mrs. Pickens just wasn't a very good teacher. But I *am*," she said confidently. "And this quilt isn't nearly as hard as you think. It's all just straight lines, really. Tell you what; if you're not able to finish the project or you aren't happy with how it comes out, I'll give you your money back. How about that?"

Antoinette chewed on the edge of her

thumbnail and stared at the quilt, trying to make up her mind. Mary Dell was right; the jewel-tone on black quilt, which included variations of the Rail Fence block with some Nine Patch blocks in the borders, both beginner's blocks, wasn't very complicated. But to someone who'd never sewn, it seemed a daunting project. Antoinette had never had the least interest in quilting or any other crafts. Her experiences in Mrs. Pickens Sunday school classroom had convinced her that she had not even a drop of artistic talent. But when she'd walked past the Patchwork Palace window that day and seen those delicious gem-colored fabrics, she simply had to go inside and have a closer look.

Antoinette's eyes moved up and down, left and right over the patches of emerald, ruby, and sapphire. "I can't believe I'm even thinking about doing this," she said, half to herself and half to Mary Dell. "Think I can get it done by the 23rd?"

"Well, I don't know about the quilting and binding," Mary Dell said. "But you'd certainly be able to finish the piecing by then. If it's a Christmas gift, you could take it back after whoever you're giving it to opens it, just so they can see it, and let them know you'll get it back to them as soon as it's finished."

Antoinette's face fell. "Oh. Well, I was really hoping I'd be able to finish the whole thing by Christmas Eve. I wanted to donate it to the silent auction at the Christmas Ball. I usually bring something from the dress shop. The cardigan I donated last year didn't bring much and Marlena made a wisecrack about it — said if I hadn't just grabbed any old rag from the sale rack, maybe people would have bid on it." Antoinette's face clouded over as she recalled the incident and Marlena's cutting comment.

"She practically accused me of using the auction as a way to get rid of shopworn goods and then write it off my taxes for full price. Marlena is so nasty! That sweater had come in only the week before and it was beautiful. I ordered three others for the shop and they all sold!" Antoinette said defensively.

"Nasty doesn't even begin to cover it," Mary Dell said with a mixture of sympathy and disgust. "The only words you can use to describe Marlena are the ones your momma used to wash your mouth out with soap for saying. I like most everybody and the few I don't like, I can tolerate. But Marlena? I can't stand her."

"She's not real wild about you either,"

Antoinette said with a little laugh. "You should have heard her at the last meeting of the Women's Club, going on and on about how having the Patchwork Palace as a sponsor was going to lower the whole standard of the ball, and how she didn't want a table full of those low-class Tudmores and Templetons sitting up at the front of the ball-room . . . It was just crazy! Even for Marlena. What'd you ever do to make her hate you so, Mary Dell?"

"Well, for starters, I was born. The feuding and fussing between the Bentons and Tudmores goes way back. And, of course, when Lydia Dale and Jack Benny got divorced, it kind of stirred things up again. But, the real reason Marlena hates me so much is because I bought this building out from under her."

"Sure wish you'd have bought my building while you were at it," Antoinette said. "You wouldn't believe what Marlena is charging me for rent. If I dare to complain about it or even to look at her sideways, she raises it. So I've got no choice but to put up with it." She spread her hands in resignation. "It's not like I can move my shop to another location. The Bentons own the whole of downtown Too Much. I sure wish I could tell Marlena what I really think of her, just once."

Mary Dell patted her on the shoulder. "Well, you can't do that. Not unless you'd like to see your rent double. But I tell you what you can do; you can show Marlena and everybody else in town how creative you are. You can piece a beautiful quilt and I will quilt it for you and bind it in time for you to donate to the auction. How about that?"

Antoinette grinned. "Really? All right, Mary Dell. If you're game, so am I!"

The beautiful sample quilts that hung on every wall of the shop were part of what made the Patchwork Palace such a special place. Customers were inspired by what they saw and wanted to re-create those lovely quilts for themselves. But Mary Dell and Lydia Dale were adamant that every quilt should be a distinct reflection of the quilter who made it, so while they did offer a few kits complete with patterns and pre-cut fabrics, no two of those kits were exactly alike. The wall hanging that Antoinette wanted to make was not offered as a kit at all. And so, with a little guidance from Lydia Dale, Antoinette considered and selected a unique combination of jewel-toned fabrics that were inspired by the sample quilt but not identical to it.

After making her selections, she brought the fabric bolts to the counter so Mary Dell could cut the yardage and Lydia Dale could ring it up on the register.

"With the scissors, thread, ruler, and your new customer discount, that comes to thirty-nine dollars and ten cents," Lydia Dale said.

"All right," Antoinette replied as she pulled two twenty-dollar bills from her wallet. "Guess I can pay for it out of what I made on your aunt Velvet today."

"Aunt Velvet was in the dress shop?" Lydia Dale asked. "And she actually bought something?"

"She must be trying to get her Christmas shopping done early," Mary Dell commented.

Antoinette moved her head slowly from side to side. "No, ma'am. She bought a cornflower blue dress. And earrings, high heels, and a tube of lipstick — powderpuff pink. For herself."

The sisters stared at her with open mouths.

"Earrings?" Lydia Dale said after a moment's pause. "And high heels?"

"Powderpuff pink lipstick? Are you sure you're talking about Aunt Velvet?" Mary

Dell questioned. "Our aunt Velvet?"

Antoinette nodded and smiled, practically beaming with pride. She took as much pleasure in making a formerly dowdy woman look pretty as Mary Dell did in teaching a woman who had never learned to thread a needle to make a beautiful quilt.

"Impossible! Aunt Velvet doesn't wear store bought clothes."

"That's right," Lydia Dale confirmed. "And she'd never wear cornflower blue. Even in high summer at a hundred and ten degrees, I've never seen Aunt Velvet dressed in anything brighter than dove gray."

"Well, at ten minutes after ten o'clock this morning, all that changed," Antoinette reported smugly. "She bought a whole new outfit. She even bought a pair of pantyhose. I told her she is forbidden to pull another pair of support hose on those lovely legs of hers."

"Lovely legs? Now I *know* you can't be talking about Aunt Velvet," Mary Dell said. "Maybe you're hallucinating. Did you fall and hit your head or something?"

"You don't believe me? Fine," Antoinette said with a self-satisfied shrug. "Take a peek out your front window. Here comes Miss Velvet right now."

Mary Dell and Lydia Dale simultaneously

190

turned toward the street-side window. Sure enough, Velvet was walking past — actually, as she had not yet become accustomed to heels, her gait could more accurately be labeled a totter than a walk — wearing a bright blue dress with a narrow black belt cinched around her waist and a hem that fell just above her knees.

As if drawn by some magnetic force, the twins walked slowly to the front of the shop until their faces were practically pressed against the window glass. They stood still as statues, eyes glued to the foreign but strangely familiar figure in blue.

"I never knew Aunt Velvet had such a little waist," Lydia Dale said with amazement. "Or such a cute figure."

"I never knew she had *knees*," Mary Dell said.

Had such a remarkable transformation occurred to anyone but their dear maiden aunt, a stalwart woman who had spent a lifetime not only ignoring the trends of fashion but actively eschewing even the most minor attempts at enhancing her appearance, the sisters would have immediately identified the cause. But as it was, it took a few seconds for Mary Dell and Lydia Dale to recall the events of the last few days, sort out and add up clues, and find the solution to the equation. When the answer came, it hit them like a flash and at exactly the same moment.

"Oh my gosh!" Lydia Dale cried. "Do you think there really *could* be . . ."

Mary Dell bobbed her head vigorously, simultaneously finishing and answering her sister's question.

". . . a Secret Admirer!"

As if still unable to trust their own conclusion, they ran to the front door and stuck their heads outside, eyes following the figure in cornflower blue until she rounded the corner and disappeared from sight.

The Templeton twins were not the only people in Too Much who stood witness to this spectacle. Three doors down, several male patrons of Hilda's House of Pie, some in cowboy hats, some in feed caps, one with a full head of handsome white hair, rose from their counter stools and stood at the window staring as Miss Velvet tottered past.

CHAPTER SIX

Throughout the remainder of November and first ten days of December, Velvet daily received a single yellow rose from the Secret Admirer but no further notes. Sometimes the rose was found sitting in a vase on the porch of the cottage. One Sunday morning, as they were heading to church, she even discovered a blossom lying on the seat of Silky's LeSabre. But usually, the Secret Admirer tied his offering to the door of the historical society.

Though she refused to discuss the possible identity of her admirer with anyone, not even Silky, Velvet felt certain that the flowers were coming from Mr. Delacorte. It just stood to reason, didn't it?

For sixty-four years, no male inhabitant of Too Much had shown her even a hint of romantic interest. But suddenly, just weeks after Thaddeus Delacorte, an undeniably good-looking man of exactly the right age who shared her passion for history, moved to town, she was being showered with roses! And the sort of attention she'd never known before. Everyone in Too Much was talking about Velvet and the roses.

A part of her, especially at first, found the whole situation a little embarrassing but another part of her liked being such an object of interest. And much to her surprise, as she had discovered when she strolled past the window of the pie shop in her blue dress on that Friday after Thanksgiving, she liked feeling pretty. So much so that she'd purchased two more dresses from Antoinette's shop — one in a rich shade of royal blue and one in a bright pink. Also, and again to her surprise, she discovered she liked receiving admiring glances from men, Thaddeus Delacorte in particular.

Out of the corner of her eye, she'd caught a glimpse of him at Hilda's window that day, had seen the expression of longing in his eyes, had wished she could stop right there and speak to him, saying, "I know it's you. I know you're the one, the only man who ever bothered to look close enough to realize that my eyes are the color of cornflowers, the only man who ever sent me a gift. I know. And this is my gift back to you, the time and trouble I took to buy a new dress and put on lipstick and stockings, not because I want others to think I'm pretty, or because I think so myself, but because you do. Because you are a good and kind man, and I would like to be the woman whom you have imagined I am. Because I want to give you back a little bit of the gift you have given me, the gift of your regard and sincere admiration . . ."

But she couldn't bring herself to say any such thing.

She couldn't bring herself to speak to him at all, or acknowledge that she knew it was he who left her the roses. Of course, knowing he was a teacher, historian, and very intelligent, she found it a little curious that the one and only note she'd received from him was so poorly written. That was a puzzle. But after a day or two, she concluded that he was shy and that the terrible spelling and cramped handwriting were just attempts to disguise his identity. How silly. How sweet. As if she would have been fooled. She was sure that Mr. Delacorte was her admirer. Who else could it be?

The roses were lovely, such a thoughtful gesture. Never in her wildest dreams could she have supposed that something so remarkable and . . . well . . . romantic might happen to her! But, after a few flower-filled days, it was hard not to wish that he would reveal himself. Or at least send her another note. She longed for a word from him and to know with absolute certainty that her secret Romeo was truly who she supposed him to be.

She tried going to work earlier, hoping to catch him in the act of tying a yellow blossom to the doorknob but without success. Every day, the rose was either already in place or, if not present, would show up in some unexpected spot — the porch, the LeSabre, the newspaper box — at some other time in the day. Just the rose. No note. Not until a full two-and-a-half weeks after she'd received the first.

Doubtless realizing what an inappropriate and unromantic messenger Wanda Joy Cleary made — after all, Mr. Delacorte had witnessed that embarrassing spectacle firsthand — the Admirer chose a much more charming and discrete individual to deliver his second missive. Arriving home from work one evening she was greeted, as usual, by Mr. Bowie, who had a piece of paper rolled up like a scroll tied to his neck with a yellow ribbon.

When she looked down at the big old tomcat, winding around her legs and meowing for his dinner, Velvet couldn't help but smile at the Admirer's ingenuity. What a clever way to get the message to her. But she was glad that Silky had gone out to the F-Bar-T to help Taffy with some holiday baking that day. If her sister had come upon the cat before she had, untied the note from the ribbon, and read the contents, it would have been just too awful. And too embarrassing!

She scooped the cat up in her arms, went into her room, sat on the edge of her bed with the door closed and locked in case Silky returned unexpectedly, and read the letter. The handwriting was just as hideous as before, the spelling just as inept but if those rightward sloping sentences had been lines of sonnet penned by Shakespeare himself, the contents could not have thrilled her more, or caused her heart to beat any faster.

He still thought she was "beutiful," even more than he'd known before since he'd seen her in the gown of "cornflour" blue. He'd even written a little poem about it.

Roses are yellow,
Cornflours are blue,
That fancy new dress,
Sure looks fine on you . . .

It was a joke, of course. He was poking fun at himself. A man of letters such as Mr. Delacorte could easily compose far more sophisticated verse if he desired to do so but it was sweet just the same. No one had ever written a poem for her before, not even in jest. She was charmed by his teasing doggerel and read the lines through three times, smiling wider each time. She was touched and a little breathless when he wrote of how he spent whole nights lying awake thinking of her, picturing her in the blue dress, and the pink, and the royal, and imagining how lovely her long hair might look, unwound from the coronet at the back of her head, unloosed from its braid . . .

Oh, my.

Just reading those phrases, though more plainly expressed than Miss Velvet had translated them in her mind, caused her to blush. It was only a discussion of hairstyle but the image of unbound locks seemed to hold deeper and more intimate implications.

Oh, my!

Miss Velvet's heart pounded like a Congo drum in her chest as she continued reading and her cheeks flamed pink, especially when she got to the last paragraph and the words she had longed most to see, words that spelled out the Admirer's plan to reveal his identity to Miss Velvet.

The next morning, Saturday, Silky and Velvet got up, ate their breakfast, put on an album of Johnny Cash Christmas carols on the record player, and began decking the halls of their little cottage.

Humming along with "O Little Town of Bethlehem," they began the task of decorating, as they did every year, by removing the ceramic Nativity figures hand-painted by their dear mother back in the 1920s, from the nest of newspaper and scraps of cotton quilt batting where they had slumbered for so many months, and arranging them carefully on the oak mantel above their seldom used fireplace. Next, they replaced the white wax candles in their collection of brass candlesticks with new tapers, red in color and cinnamon scented, then placed the musical angel, family of snow people, knee-high tall figures stuffed and sewn by Silky when Taffy was a little girl, antique snow globe, and other seasonal ephemera onto tables, floors, shelves, and sideboards, in the exact same spots they'd occupied the year before. After that, they hung a red-ribboned wreath on the front door, wrapped the porch banister with strings of white lights, plugged them in and, though it was a little hard to get the full effect so early in the day, stood at the edge of the yard to admire their work before going back inside to complete the last task on their to-do list.

While Silky made cocoa and put ginger-snaps on a plate, Velvet started tree record over again and set a skinny but fragrant ranch-grown pine up in the tree stand. Working together, the sisters wrapped the tree with five strings of lights, added some tinsel to fill in the bare spots, and hung the branches with antique glass balls passed down through the generations, as well as a cherished collection of handmade ornaments made by Mary Dell and Lydia Dale when they were little girls.

This annual decorating ritual, performed with little variation for almost as long as they could remember, was something they looked forward to every Christmas. But it seemed to Silky that her sister was enjoying herself even more than usual this year. Velvet positively beamed as she went about her work, not only humming along with the crooning Mr. Cash but actually singing aloud with "Joy to the World." And when Silky came into the living room carrying the tray of cocoa and cookies, she spied Velvet holding the largest of the stuffed snowmen in her arms, waltzing around the tree to the strains of "Blue Christmas."

Velvet was Silky's first and best friend, the person she felt closer to than anyone in the world. It was wonderful to see her sister so happy, so filled with life and love and hope. And yet, this whole business with the roses and Secret Admirer made her feel a little anxious as well.

To the outside world, Velvet appeared confident, intelligent, and self-controlled, and she was all of those things. But Silky alone knew that she was also innocent and tender of heart. She hoped that Mr. Delacorte really was the one who was secretly sending those roses every day and that his intentions were exactly what they appeared to be — a sweetly romantic way for a shy but sensitive bachelor to woo and win the heart of an equally shy and sensitive maiden lady. If her dear sister suffered any embarrassment because of this or had her heart broken by an insincere suitor, Silky's heart would break as well. But, she told herself, she was probably worrying about nothing. Velvet was so good and kind; who could possibly want to embarrass her? And having lived a whole lifetime in Too Much without exciting the romantic interest of any of the local swains, who besides the new man in town would pursue Velvet? Especially in such an obvious way? Yes, surely it was Mr. Delacorte who sent the roses. It had to be. Velvet was the perfect match for a high school history teacher. And he was perfect for her. Look how happy he made her!

After they finished their work and their cookies, Silky put the empty cups and napkins back onto the tea tray.

"Can you turn the record player off?" she said as she picked up the tray. "We'd better get a move on if we want to make it out to the ranch by lunch."

Velvet followed her into the kitchen. "Oh. Yes. You know, I was thinking I might skip lunch today."

"But we always have lunch at the ranch on Saturday," Silky said as she unloaded the dishes into the sink. "And, anyway, I've got to measure Jeb and Cady for their pageant costumes. Mary Dell can't make the costumes for every child in the church, not now that she's got the quilt shop to run and a baby to take care of."

"I know but . . ." Velvet interrupted herself, racked by a sudden and wholly unconvincing fit of coughing. "I'm afraid I might be coming down with something. A cold. I'd hate to give it to the children, especially so close to Christmas. I think it would be better for everyone if I stayed home."

"Bless your heart," Silky said, endeavoring to look sincerely concerned over the state of her sister's health. "You sound just awful. I'm going to call Taffy right now and tell her we can't make it today. You go back to bed and I'll make up a pot of hot lemon tea with honey. Poor thing."

"Oh, no. You don't have to do that! I mean . . . I'd hate for you to miss lunch on my account. I don't think it's serious. Just a little cold . . . that's all. You go on to the ranch without me. I'm just going to stay here and have a little nap. That should fix me up."

Silky wasn't in the least fooled by her sister's sudden pretense of illness, especially when she noticed Velvet craning her neck and pulling at her dress collar. From the time she was a little girl, Velvet had never been able to tell a fib without feeling short of breath. Silky was amused by her sister's transparent efforts at untruth but decided not to push too hard.

Maybe Velvet wanted to do a little secret Christmas shopping downtown. Or maybe she and Mr. Delacorte had planned a rendezvous. She hoped it was the latter. The roses were lovely but the sooner the Secret

Admirer ended his secrecy and declared his intentions, the better.

"If you're not feeling well then rest is the best medicine. I don't mind staying and keeping you company."

Velvet lifted her hand. "No, no. I can take care of myself. After my nap, I'll pull the vaporizer out and sit in the steam." She lifted her hand to her mouth and coughed again, but not as forcefully as before.

"Well," Silky said slowly as she put on her coat and slipped her purse over her arm, "if you're sure you'll be all right . . ."

Velvet stood watching at the window until the LeSabre pulled out of the driveway and drove slowly to the end of Houston Street before disappearing around the corner. Five minutes later, she changed into her pink dress and, the weather being appropriately chilly for December, put on a cream-colored coat before leaving the house.

CHAPTER SEVEN

Miss Velvet had always "done" her own hair, or, more accurately, done nothing to it, and so she was not a regular client at the Primp 'n Perm.

She did come in twice a year to get the calluses pumiced from her feet but she had completed this procedure in October and wasn't scheduled for another appointment until April. So it was understandable that Hazel Dawn, the owner of Too Much's only full-service beauty parlor, looked up from the reception desk with a surprised expression when Velvet came through the door.

"Well, hey, Miss Velvet! Cute shoes! What can I do for . . ."

Hazel Dawn's greeting was interrupted by the ringing of the telephone. She gave Velvet an apologetic glance and answered it.

"Merry Christmas from the Primp 'n Perm, your holiday hairdo haven. This is Hazel Dawn. May I help you? Hey, Mrs.

Pickens! How are you? Today? Oh, I don't know . . . Let me look."

Velvet began looking around the walls of the shop, feigning interest in the posters of elaborately coiffured women. She didn't want to appear to be eavesdropping on the conversation, though it was hard not to. Hazel Dawn had to practically shout into the phone to make herself heard.

Every styling chair, hood dryer, and washing station in the Primp 'n Perm was occupied by women in various stages of washing, cutting, curling, teasing, spraying, dying, and drying and every single one of those women, as well as the other beauty operators who oversaw these renovations, were talking. The din of their collective voices, competing to be heard over the whine of blow dryers and a plodding version of "The Little Drummer Boy" coming from the radio, was beginning to give Velvet a headache.

Maybe this wasn't such a good idea after all. She started to move quietly toward the door but Hazel Dawn saw her and lifted her index finger, signaling that she'd be with Velvet in just one minute. And so Velvet waited. It would have been rude not to.

Hazel Dawn flipped a page in her big appointment book and scanned the page, frowning.

"I'm sorry, hon, but we just can't today. I know. But we're booked solid. We could squeeze you in on Tuesday — or almost any day besides Saturday."

Hazel Dawn wrote something in the appointment book and nodded sympathetically while the person on the other end of the line talked.

"Yes, I know. This time of year, everybody has the same idea. I know. Don't worry. We'll get it done in time for the Christmas Ball. Uh-huh. Sure thing. Yes, I'll call you back if anybody cancels before then. All right, Missus Pickens. Yes, ma'am. We'll see you Thursday at 11:00. Thank you!"

Hazel Dawn put the phone down. "I'm sorry, Miss Velvet. Saturday is always our busiest day of the week, but Saturdays in December are just crazy! Every female in the county wants her roots done and her perm freshened in time for the big ball and they *all* want it done on Saturday. But we've only got four chairs. And I've only got two hands! And the receptionist called in sick so, on top of everything else . . ."

Hazel Dawn lifted her hand and let it flop. "Anyway, you didn't come in here to listen to me gripe. Are you out doing your Christmas shopping? I'm sure Mary Dell and

Lydia Dale would love a couple of gift certificates. Were you thinking of a manicure or a full-out day of beauty?"

"No. I . . . well . . ." Miss Velvet said, backing away from the counter. "I was really hoping to get an appointment for myself. But . . . another time. You're so busy."

Hazel Dawn made a sympathetic face. "Are your calluses bothering you, Miss Velvet? It's the heels. They're murder if you're not used to them . . ."

"No, it's not that . . . It's just that . . ." Velvet took a deep breath. "Mary Dell bought a table to the Christmas ball, a gold sponsorship for the Patchwork Palace."

"Is that right?" Hazel Dawn said innocently, though she already knew all about the stir this had created and was not at all displeased to see Marlena Benton outflanked by Mary Dell. She knew all about the Secret Admirer, too, and why Miss Velvet was wearing a pink dress and pumps. But she would never dream of commenting on either subject.

Hazel Dawn was the closest thing to a therapist that most women had in Too Much. They told her everything about themselves and their families, things they wouldn't have dreamed of sharing with their closest relatives or best friends. Hazel Dawn wasn't sure why — perhaps the sensation of having the scalp lathered and massaged helped people relax, or maybe the smell of permanent wave solution acted like a truth serum on certain parts of the brain — but she knew from experience that even the most tight-lipped women will open up to their hairdresser more willingly than to their minister, and that the styling chair is not far removed from the confessional. And though there is no code of secrecy or silence required on the part of hairdressers, Hazel Dawn behaved as if there were. She heard a lot of gossip but she never repeated it. The secrets of Hazel Dawn's clients were safe with her and they knew it. Her discretion, coupled with her ability to re-create any celebrity hairdo found in *People* magazine just by looking at the picture, was what kept the Primp 'n Perm in business.

"Yes," Velvet replied. "So I'll be going to the ball this year, the whole family will. And, I was thinking that, maybe, since we'll be sitting up front and all . . . Maybe I should . . . but . . . Never mind. You don't have time today."

Hazel Dawn stepped out from behind the desk, rested her fingers gently on Miss Velvet's bony shoulder. "Never mind what, Miss Velvet? You can tell me."

Velvet shrugged, nonchalantly. "I was just thinking about getting my hair trimmed and colored, that's all," she said and then tried to go on, to explain that it wasn't really important and could wait for another day, but she didn't have the chance.

Hazel Dawn let out a whoop of joy and wrapped her arms around Miss Velvet's thin frame, actually lifting her from the ground.

"Stop that! Put me down, Hazel Dawn!" Miss Velvet cried, squirming and repeating her demand until the overjoyed hairdresser turned her loose.

"For goodness' sake," she grumbled, running her hand over the skirt of the pink dress to smooth out the wrinkles. "What are you getting so worked up over? You'd think you'd never done anybody's hair before."

"I've never done *your* hair before, Miss Velvet! But I've been dying to, for years and years!" Hazel Dawn placed her hands on Velvet's shoulders and steered her into the salon. "Right this way, darlin'."

"But," Velvet protested, "I thought you didn't have time for another customer today. I thought you said you couldn't squeeze in one more person . . ."

"I did," Hazel Dawn replied. "But to get my hands on that head of yours, Miss Velvet, I'm willing to squeeze a little tighter. Now you just sit right down here and make yourself comfortable. And let me ask you something; have you ever thought about going red?"

Miss Velvet would not consider the possibility of going red, or even auburn. But she did allow Hazel Dawn to return her coloring to the soft chestnut brown of her youth. And, after several minutes of consultation and coaxing, she also consented to having her tresses cut, rather than trimmed, to remove the scraggly ends and extra weight.

When Hazel Dawn went into the back room to mix up her color, Velvet waited nervously in the styling chair. She felt so conspicuous sitting there and worried that the other customers of the Primp 'n Perm would go home and tell tales about old Miss Velvet's foolish and hopeless attempt at beautification. When she realized that the woman sitting under the hood dryer with her eyes closed was Marlena Benton, she considered getting up and walking out the door. But Hazel Dawn returned just then, applied a coat of brown-colored paste to her roots, and started combing it through so Miss Velvet had no choice but to stay put. She couldn't very well run into the street with a half-dyed head of hair.

The dye smelled awful but the application was painless and Velvet realized it felt nice to be fussed over a bit. Hazel Dawn worked quickly and efficiently, keeping up a steady and distracting stream of chatter. After a few minutes, Velvet started to feel less nervous. No one was paying her any mind, she realized. They were all too absorbed in their style magazines or conversations with their own hairdressers to notice her. And Marlena, still sitting under the dryer and lulled by the steady white whoosh of warm air in her ears, seemed to have fallen asleep.

"Happens every time," Hazel Dawn informed her. "Two minutes under the dryer and she's out like a light, dead to the world. I'll have to give her a good shake to wake her up but she'll be under there for a good while yet. Marlena has the thickest head of hair in Too Much. Takes forever to dry.

"Speaking of people with good hair," Hazel Dawn said casually, while guiding Velvet to the washing station, "have you met that nice Mr. Delacorte yet? Well, of course you have, him being the history teacher and all. He's a handsome thing, don't you think?"

Velvet had not had her hair washed by someone else since her mother had done it when she was a little girl. Reclining in the wash chair, soothed by the streams of warm water, the clean scent of shampoo, and the gentle massaging of Hazel Dawn's fingers on her scalp, she felt her body relax and her tongue loosen. Before long, she was telling Hazel Dawn all about the Secret Admirer, which was not news to the hair-dresser or anyone else in town, and also about his most recent letter and the manner by which he would reveal his identity to her on the night of the Christmas Ball.

The last part, of course, *was* news to Hazel Dawn, and to Marlena Benton, who, with eyes still closed and feigning sleep, quietly switched off the hair dryer and reached up with stealthy fingers, raising the hood to a spot just above her ears, enabling her to hear every word Miss Velvet said.

CHAPTER EIGHT

The more pious citizens of Too Much took great pride in the fact that their town had only one bar, the Ice House, but four churches, Baptist, Methodist, Episcopalian, and Catholic.

The Catholic congregation was the oldest, the Baptist the most numerous, and the Episcopalian the wealthiest. But it was the Methodists who hosted the town's annual outdoor Christmas Nativity, partly because they thought of it first and partly because the church stood adjacent to a vacant lot. This was essential because of the considerable square footage required to accommodate the temporary stable, the animals, the Holy Family, plus as many shepherds, drummer boys, and angels as there were children between the ages of three and twelve in the Methodist congregation, not to mention the crowd of onlookers who came to sing "Silent Night" and be reminded of the original Nativity as well as the many commemorative ones they had observed and celebrated in that same place in that same way, for as many years as they could remember.

As lifelong Methodists and one of the church's founding families, the Tudmore-Templeton clan had always been instrumental in organizing and staging the Nativity, sewing costumes for the cast and loaning livestock for the stable. And this year, the three youngest family members would actually take part in the tableau. Jeb, Lydia Dale's eldest son, would be a shepherd. Her daughter, six-year-old Cady, was a junior angel. Mary Dell's baby, Howard, would play the part of the Holy Child, an honor bestowed upon him by virtue of being the infant most recently born among the Methodists.

Given this, it was understandable that Mary Dell and Lydia Dale arrived on the scene an hour early, wrapped up in sweaters and scarves, carrying a thermos of cocoa and three cameras, to claim a spot in the front row and secure a little extra room for Silky, Velvet, and Taffy, who would arrive later, bringing baby Rob Lee with them.

"I wish they could have had two Baby Jesuses this year," Mary Dell said to her

215

sister. "It doesn't seem fair that Rob Lee isn't part of the Nativity. After all, he was born just a few hours before Howard. You don't mind, do you?"

"Of course not," Lydia Dale said sincerely. "And who better to play the miracle baby than Howard?"

Mary Dell smiled, her features softening and eyes glistening, as they so often did when she thought of her baby, the child who after thirteen years of prayer and tears, of hopes raised and dashed again and again, seemed like a gift from above to her. Others might look into Howard's little face, with those almond eyes and slightly flattened features, characteristics of a child born with Down syndrome, and see nothing but his disability but when Mary Dell looked at her baby, she saw the answer to her prayers. She never looked at Howard with anything less than complete pride and unquestioned love.

"Well, I know he's not *the* miracle baby," she said softly, "but he's *my* miracle baby."

Lydia Dale put one arm around her sister's shoulders and gave her a quick squeeze.

"Besides," she said, "Rob Lee doesn't know the difference. And it isn't like he won't get his chance. He'll have eleven whole years to be part of the pageant."

Lydia Dale grinned. "Remember how sick

we got of it when we were little? I couldn't wait to turn thirteen! And how cold we used to get? You got bronchitis that one year, remember? You had to spend the whole of Christmas in bed."

"That's because the angel costumes were so thin," Mary Dell said, "nothing but white cotton sheets and cardboard wings with glitter. I added some white flannel lining to them this year, but it doesn't help much. The shepherds have it easier. They just put on a bathrobe over their blue jeans and they're good to go."

"Well, you won't convince Jeb of that," Lydia Dale said. "He's only ten but he did *not* want to be a shepherd this year. After Graydon talked to him, he settled down, but until then? No, ma'am. He wanted no part of it."

"Graydon sure is good people," Mary Dell said, touching her sister lightly on the shoulder. "He really makes you happy, doesn't he?"

Lydia Dale nodded and smiled. "And the kids are just as crazy about him as I am. Jeb would do anything for him, which is a good thing. That boy can sure be a handful. I don't know what gets into him sometimes. Must be those Benton genes."

"Speaking of which," Mary Dell said, casting her eyes to the far side of the crowd, her voice suddenly ominous, "Don't look now, but I see your in-laws."

Lydia Dale craned her neck and saw Jack Benny, with a cigarette dangling from his lower lip and his arms crossed over his chest, glaring at her. Marlena was standing next to him, wearing a fur coat. She smiled acidly and raised her hand when she spotted Lydia Dale looking at them.

"Ex-in-laws," Lydia Dale muttered. "And thank heaven for that. Do you see that smile? You could freeze ice on Marlena's face. What do you think they're doing?"

"The same thing we are," Mary Dell said, stamping her feet in a fruitless attempt at keeping her toes warm. "Freezing our keisters off and waiting to see our kids in the Nativity. You may be divorced, but Jack Benny is still the children's father. And Marlena is still their granny."

"I don't mean what are they doing *here;* I mean what are they *doing*? Marlena is up to something. She's been going around telling everybody in town about Aunt Velvet and the Secret Admirer; how he's supposed to unmask himself by coming to the ball with a yellow rose in his lapel and then asking Aunt Velvet to dance."

"So what? I mean, it wasn't nice of her to

eavesdrop when Aunt Velvet was talking to Hazel Dawn but half the women in Too Much would have done the same if they'd had the chance. Everybody in town is talking about Aunt Velvet's Secret Admirer. And Marlena has always been a gossip. There's nothing new about that. It isn't like she's been mean about it or made fun of Aunt Velvet. She just tells the story like it's kind of sweet — which it is."

"I know. And that's what has me worried. Marlena doesn't have a sweet bone in her body."

Mary Dell shrugged. "It's Christmas; maybe she's trying to turn over a new leaf."

"Marlena doesn't have new leaves," Lydia Dale replied, shaking her head. "She is nasty from bark to trunk. Seriously. If she was saying anything mean about Aunt Velvet, or making fun of her new clothes and hairstyle, that would make sense. At least for Marlena. But being all sweet and saying how precious Aunt Velvet looks . . . that's not like her. Marlena's up to something. I'm sure of it."

Mary Dell rolled her eyes. Lydia Dale always did have a dramatic streak.

"Only you would be worried because somebody *wasn't* acting nasty," Mary Dell said.

Mary Dell looked at her watch, and then rose up on her toes to see if Velvet, Silky, or Taffy were coming their way. The crowd was starting to press in on them. They wouldn't be able to reserve the extra space much longer.

"Aunt Velvet does look precious and everybody knows it," Mary Dell continued. "The clothes were one thing, but the hair? Never in a million years would I have thought Aunt Velvet would cut her hair and wear it loose, but those waves around her face make her features look so much softer. And she looks about ten years younger with the gray gone, don't you think?"

"Yes," Lydia Dale concurred. "Not even Marlena can deny it, but . . . I don't know. It makes me nervous. You don't know how vindictive my dear old ex-mother-in-law can be. She never did like me, but since the divorce . . . I'm telling you, Mary Dell. There are no depths that Marlena wouldn't stoop to if she thought it would hurt or embarrass our family."

"Well, even if that's true, I don't think Marlena is up to anything this time. Everybody in town knows that Mr. Delacorte is the Secret Admirer." Mary Dell grinned. "You remember how cute he was when he came in the shop and dropped off the canvas for his tent, don't you? How he kept talking about that article Aunt Velvet wrote and saying how much he admired the work she'd done with the historical society and all?"

"But is admiring a person's work the same thing as admiring the person? And I still say Marlena's up to something. Look how happy she looks," Lydia Dale said, looking to the opposite side of the lot. "Marlena is only ever truly happy when she's about to make somebody else miserable."

Mary Dell, who was starting to become worried that her mother, aunt, and grandmother were going to miss the start of the Nativity and baby Howard's big debut, let out a happy hoot when she saw Silky pushing her way through the crowd, and waved her arms over her head.

"Yoo-hoo! Granny! We're over here!"

Silky saw her, waved back, and headed toward her, looking a little irritated.

"Hey, Granny. Where's Momma and Aunt Velvet?" Mary Dell asked, pulling her camera out of its case. "They'd better hurry up or they'll miss the start. I can see the kids lining up around the back of the church."

"They're still at the car. Your momma is trying to figure out how to unfold the baby

221

stroller and Velvet is putting on more lipstick." She sighed. "It sure was easier to get places on time before my sister got to be such a fashion plate. How're you two? Probably about half-frozen after standing here all this time."

"We kept warm arguing about Marlena," Mary Dell said. "Lydia Dale thinks she's up to no-good."

"That's a bet worth taking any day of the week," Silky replied. "When has Marlena Benton been up to anything else?"

"But Lydia Dale thinks that Marlena is in cahoots with the Secret Admirer, hatching some kind of scheme. Which is silly," Mary Dell said, giving her sister a pointed look, "because Mr. Delacorte is much too nice a man to do anything like that."

"Assuming Mr. Delacorte is the Secret Admirer," Silky said.

Mary Dell clicked her camera to test the flash and made an exasperated sound.

"For goodness' sake! You and Lydia Dale are just too suspicious. Mr. Delacorte is obviously crazy about her. And anyway, who else could it be?"

At that moment, as if in answer to her question, Thaddeus Delacorte came wending his way through the crowd, murmuring his apologies as he made his way to the front row of onlookers.

"Miss Silky! I thought it was you!" he said with a grin, then inclined his head toward Mary Dell and Lydia Dale. "Ladies. Nice to see you. And . . . the rest of the Tudmores? Miss Taffy? And . . . uh . . . Miss Velvet? Will they be joining you?"

Mary Dell tossed her sister and grandma a knowing little smile.

"They're here somewhere. Momma is having a little trouble with the stroller and Aunt Velvet is with her. Mr. Delacorte," she said sweetly, "you're so much taller than me — can you look back and see if they're coming this way? I'd hate for them to miss the start of the pageant."

At the mention of Velvet's name, Mr. Delacorte's bright blue eyes became even brighter and bluer. He pulled himself up as tall as possible, which was very tall indeed, turned around and scanned the faces of the restless audience.

"There she is!" he cried, the tips of his ears coloring slightly. "I mean, there *they* are. Toward the back on the far right side. Allow me to go get them, Miss Mary Dell. Your mother is having a hard time getting the stroller through the crowd. I'd hate for them to miss the procession."

"Oh, would you?" Mary Dell smiled,

sincerely charmed by the older gentleman's obvious eagerness to see her aunt and sincerely grateful that he would go out of his way to make sure that Velvet and Taffy wouldn't miss Howard's moment in the sun. "Thank you so much, Mr. Delacorte."

"My pleasure," he replied and began elbowing his way toward the back of the audience, begging people's pardon and waving to get Velvet's attention.

"What did I tell you?" Mary Dell said. "Look at him, pushing his way to the back. Oh, isn't that sweet? He offered Aunt Velvet his arm. Such a gentleman," she said with a satisfied sigh, then gave her sister and grandmother a challenging look.

"Now will you both quit worrying? Of course Mr. Delacorte is the Secret Admirer. Who else could it be?"

Silky and Lydia Dale looked at each other and shrugged, acknowledging the logic of her conclusion. Mr. Delacorte's admiration for Velvet was obvious and sincere.

Just then, eleven-year-old Hooty Capshaw marched to the north side of the church and tootled a not-quite-on-key fanfare on his Boy Scout bugle, signaling the arrival of the Archangel Gabriel. Gabriel, a part always played by the Methodist minister, dressed in a white supplice, topped by his most elaborate and richly embroidered liturgical stole, welcomed the audience as well as a group of young boys, Jeb among them, who appeared to be strolling by, leading a couple of sheep on ropes, and told them not to be afraid and to get themselves down to the stable in Bethlehem just as quick as they could.

The boys replied in unison that they would and began circling toward the far side of the still-empty stable at a somewhat slower pace than they'd planned. Their progress was impeded by the largest of the sheep, who was more interested in munching grass than in making haste to Bethlehem. The boys began tugging on his tether as hard as they could but the sheep refused to budge, which brought forth a wave of laughter from the crowd.

Another blast of the bugle marked the beginning of the Holy Family's journey to Bethlehem. Joseph held the donkey's tether and Mary walked alongside, holding the baby in her arms. This was, of course, not quite true to the biblical text, Mary having given birth in the stable after their arrival in Bethlehem, but the church had always done it this way. It was easier to stage and nobody felt comfortable about showing a twelve-year-old girl heavy with child, not even for the sake of scriptural accuracy.

When they approached the stable, the girl playing the part of Mary placed Baby Howard, who was well wrapped up, not in swaddling clothes but in a quilt of his mother's making, into the manger, then knelt down next to Joseph.

At that point, Mary Dell, who had been fighting to keep hold of her emotions, lost the fight and burst into tears. The women of the family, including Taffy and Velvet, who had joined the rest of them shortly after the shepherds left, patted her shoulders and tried to comfort her.

"It's all right," she assured them with a sniffling whisper, "I'm just so happy."

Silky dug a packet of tissues from her pocket, handed one to Mary Dell, then pulled out another for herself. Silky loved Christmas — the scenes, the gifts, the music, the traditions — but more than that, she loved how the season filled her with gratitude for God's goodness, reminded her of the magnitude of the gift given to the world on that long-ago day in Bethlehem, and gave her the opportunity to share that joy with her family. They were so very fortunate in so very many ways.

Hoping no one in the family would notice, or accuse her of becoming sentimental in her old age, Silky turned her head to one side and furtively dabbed her eyes.

As she did so she saw Marlena Benton, staring at them with a smile on her lips and a face that could freeze ice.

CHAPTER NINE

Silky spent the next few days engaging in a bit of espionage, trying to confirm the identity of the Secret Admirer.

She went to the Tidee-Mart in search of yellow roses, thinking that she might be able to quiz the clerks about who might have been purchasing a large number of those kinds of flowers recently, only to be told that the market didn't sell any roses but red, and then only in February and May, for Valentine's and Mother's Day. If she wanted yellow roses, she was informed, she'd have to drive to the florist shop in Waco.

Next, she tried putting Mr. Delacorte under surveillance, parking the blue LeSabre a block away from the high school and waiting for the dismissal bell to ring. When he left the building and got into his car, she followed at a discrete distance. She was excited when she realized his route was taking him right by the historical society and saw his vehicle slow to a crawl as he passed the building, but he didn't stop. After he turned the corner, he increased his speed to a heart-pounding forty-two miles per hour so Silky had no choice but to give up the chase.

Finally, with just two days to go until the Christmas ball and feeling more and more worried by the daily arrival of roses and her sister's steadily-increasing happiness and anticipation as the night of the ball approached, Silky decided to take more drastic measures.

That night, at nine-thirty, after drinking their milk and completing their usual bedtime ritual, Silky said good night to her sister and retired to her bedroom, just as she always did. But she didn't undress or put on her nightgown. Instead, after thirty minutes, she crept into the kitchen and across the hall and laid her ear next to Velvet's bedroom door. Hearing the soft and regular whoosh of her sister's slumbering breathing, she crept quietly out of the house and got into the LeSabre. With the headlights off for the first block to make sure they didn't shine through Velvet's bedroom window and wake her, Silky drove downtown. She parked the car across and a bit down the street from the historical society, turned off the ignition, scrunched down in the seat, and waited.

Settling down for what she supposed might be a very long and possibly pointless wait, Silky opened her big purse and pulled out her sewing, a nearly-finished needlepoint Christmas stocking, one of two she was making to commemorate her great-grandbabies' first Christmas. The moonlight was dim and Silky's eyesight wasn't as sharp as it once had been, so she squinted as she worked, stitching out the word "Howard" in forest green needlepoint yarn.

Silky never went anywhere without a bit of handwork tucked into her purse. Like so many generations of Tudmore women, she was an expert needlewoman. She made clothing, quilts, luscious needlepoint tapestries, sweet cross-stitched samplers, and delicately embroidered handkerchiefs and pillowcases. She particularly enjoyed handwork. It helped distract her from worries and organize her thoughts. Just then, she was sorely in need of both.

Mr. Delacorte was a lovely man. Nothing would have pleased Silky more than to know that he was, in fact, the Secret Admirer. But, in spite of Mary Dell's assurances and the worthy gentleman's obvious interest in Velvet, she wasn't entirely convinced the flowers were coming from him.

Silky had lived almost the whole of her life in Too Much and so had known Marlena Benton from childhood onward. Like Lydia Dale, she knew that Marlena was never truly happy unless she was about to make someone else miserable. Try as she might, she simply could not erase the image of Marlena Benton's icy smile from her mind.

There was certainly no love lost between any of the Tudmores and Bentons and Velvet had done nothing to hurt Marlena. But when Mary Dell managed to purchase the last remaining piece of commercial property not in Benton hands, it had been a huge defeat and humiliation for Marlena. It seemed entirely possible that she wanted to return the favor, doing whatever she could to harm or humiliate any Tudmore that came into her sights, even the most innocent of them.

Velvet, bless her, truly was an innocent, more tender and timid than anyone knew, so steeped in the history, ideals, and mannerisms of an earlier time that she seemed not quite a part of the present age. Yes, innocent was the perfect word to describe her sister. Velvet was innocent in the ways of love, incapable of intentionally harming another, and far more fragile than most people realized.

In these last few weeks, basking in the warmth of the first romance she'd ever known, Velvet had truly blossomed. She had opened like the petals of the roses she'd been showered with, becoming beautiful with every passing day, not because her beauty was something new, the product of store-bought clothes and a bottle of hair dye, but because, for the first time, Velvet had begun to believe it was true.

Silky sincerely hoped that all those flowers *had* been sent by Mr. Delacorte. The two of them would make a darling couple. He seemed just as courtly, and shy, and sweetly old-fashioned as Velvet. But, if he wasn't the one who had sent the roses and notes, if he didn't show up at the ball with a yellow rose on his lapel, if he didn't ask her sister for the pleasure of a dance, if someone had decided to play a cruel joke on the town spinster, Velvet's heart would break. Withering with embarrassment and shame, she would shrink back into her shell, shed her pretty petals, and become a wallflower once again.

For weeks, Silky had longed to sit Velvet down and talk to her about this whole situation, to caution her, to protect her from getting her hopes set quite so high, but she couldn't do it. In spite of the daily delivery of roses, for the first time in her life, Velvet had not confided in her sister. She had not shared the contents of the notes with her or even discussed their existence, though, thanks to Marlena's eavesdropping ears and flapping tongue, she had a pretty good idea of what they contained. And, though she'd lived her whole life in Too Much and knew how even the most inane bits of gossip can spread like wildfire in a small town, Velvet seemed truly unaware of the rumors and speculation that swirled about regarding herself and the Secret Admirer. Obviously the rose-colored glasses her sister was wearing had impaired her vision, making her unable to see or think about anything besides this secret that was anything but.

Because of this, Silky couldn't discuss the situation with Velvet, not unless Velvet brought it up first. If she did so, if she gave even the barest hint that she wasn't entirely convinced that the Secret Admirer was who and what Velvet believed him to be, Silky knew her sister would be wounded, and begin to doubt herself, to worry that everyone was laughing at her. Silky couldn't and wouldn't do that to Velvet, not unless she was one hundred percent sure she was right.

Even if it meant staying awake and keeping watch through the whole of the cold December night, she simply had to find out the truth!

Silky kept her unwavering vigil but saw nothing. The streets of Too Much were dark and silent. No one walked or drove past the door of the historical society.

As the first fingers of dawn began to creep over the horizon, Silky's concerns mounted. The ball would take place that very night. This was her last chance to catch the Admirer in action but he had failed to appear. Unless, perhaps, he decided to leave his offering at the house as had been the case on one or two other occasions? Or maybe he'd spotted her car and been scared off?

It was nearly five o'clock. Silky had to return home and sneak back into the house before Velvet woke up and started asking questions. Frustrated by her failure but finally admitting defeat, Silky sighed and clutched the car keys.

She was about to turn over the ignition when, across the street, she saw movement in the branches of the crepe myrtle tree that flanked the entrance to the historical society. Silky watched, hardly daring to breathe, as a figure moved out from behind the tree.

There was only a little light in the sky and so it was impossible for Silky to see the face or features of the man who emerged from the bushes, but Silky recognized the beat up cowboy hat and arrogant swagger, the indolent slope of the shoulders that had always been too light for heavy work, the curling lip with the ever present Marlboro hanging from it.

Her heart sank. She had so hoped that her suspicions would turn out to be unfounded, that her surveillance would prove Mr. Delacorte to be the real Secret Admirer. Now that she knew the true identity of the pretended admirer, she wasn't really surprised, except on one count. She'd never have guessed Jack Benny Benton was capable of rising so early in the morning.

For a moment, Silky considered getting out of the car and confronting him, calling him every shameful name in the book but then thought better of it. Jack Benny was incapable of shame. Her words would bounce off him like rain off a rooftop. She might, by confronting him, put a stop to any further plan he and his hateful mother might have hatched to embarrass Velvet at the ball but, either way, the damage was done. And if word got around town of the

Bentons' cruel joke and Silky's hapless attempts to stop it, she might make the situation even worse.

If she kept silent for now, she had the advantage of surprise. Jack Benny didn't *know* that she knew. That might buy her some time and give her a chance to turn the tables in their favor. Though, as she watched him slink off into the darkness, she could not honestly imagine any way in which this could be accomplished.

As Jack Benny disappeared around the far corner of the building, Silky made a fist and pressed it to her lips.

What could she do? How could she tell Velvet the truth without breaking her heart and wounding her pride? It seemed an impossible task, because it was. But Silky had to do it. There was no other choice.

CHAPTER TEN

When she got ready for bed on the night before the ball, Miss Velvet was more excited than she could recall feeling since she was five years old and had tried to stay awake on Christmas Eve, hoping to catch a glimpse of Santa Claus and the reindeer.

She climbed beneath the quilts, scooted Mr. Bowie from the middle of the mattress, and closed her eyes, sure that sleep would evade her. She was wrong. The events of the previous month, the roses, the notes, the building anticipation as the day of the ball drew near, had been more taxing than she'd realized. She fell into a sound sleep only minutes after her head hit the pillow and didn't stir until the alarm on her nightstand clock rang the next morning.

Heedless of the cold, Velvet threw back the quilt and all but leapt from bed, humming to herself as she went into the bathroom to wash her face and fix her hair.

Since her visit to the salon, the latter operation took somewhat longer than it used to but Velvet was becoming more adept in the use of curling irons, teasing combs, and hair spray, and so she was coiffed and ready to dress at five minutes before seven o'clock.

Mr. Bowie, who was eager for breakfast, purred and curled around her nylon-clad legs.

"Just a minute," she said to the hungry feline. "I've got to decide what to wear. What do you think? The blue? The pink? Or maybe the gold?"

One by one, Velvet pushed her inventory of colorful frocks, which had continued to grow so that, by this point, there was hardly a hint of black, gray, or navy in her wardrobe, from the left to the right side of the closet rod, trying to make up her mind.

When she came to the last dress in the row, a purchase she had made secretly and in response to a third and final note from the Admirer only two days before, she sighed happily.

"Of course, it'll have to wait till tonight but I wish I could put this one on right now. Mr. Delacorte . . . Thaddeus . . ."

She blushed as she recalled their encounter at the church Nativity, the way he had sought her out in the crush of people, the little thrill that had run through her when, at his invitation, she had rested her fingers upon his strong forearm as he escorted her to the front of the crowd, the way her heart had pounded in her chest when he, responding to her thanks and best wishes for a Merry Christmas, had asked her to please call him by his first name.

Thaddeus. Thaddeus Delacorte. Such a perfect name for such a perfect gentleman. She sighed again.

"Thaddeus will love this color," she informed the cat. "It's exactly the shade he described in his note."

Mr. Bowie meowed impatiently, making it clear that he didn't care what she put on as long as she did it quickly and fed him his breakfast.

"Oh, all right," she said, taking the gold dress from the hanger and buttoning it up quickly before stepping into a pair of brown shoes with a stylish but comfortable one-inch heel, then clipping on a pair of gold earrings. After quickly making the bed, she scooped the cat up in her arms and walked to the door. But she paused just before opening and looked at the door of her closet, which was still ajar.

Her new dress was meant to be a surprise, but after so many weeks of silence . . . well, not complete silence. She had opened up to Hazel Dawn that day at the Primp 'n Perm but, aside from that one lapse, she hadn't shared her secret with anyone, not even Silky. And, as Mary Dell had correctly observed on Thanksgiving, Velvet always told Silky *everything.* Until now.

It wasn't that she didn't trust Silky with her secret, far from it. But at first she really had believed it was a prank pulled by a teenager making fun of an old spinster and though she'd tried to laugh it off as exactly that, she'd felt a little embarrassed about it. Even when the roses continued to arrive, and then the notes, and she began to dream of whirling around the dance floor, wearing a beautiful gown, encircled by Mr. Delacorte's strong arms, she couldn't quite bring herself to believe it truly would happen. Every day when she found yet another rose, a part of her supposed it would be the last, that she'd allowed herself to get caught up in a dream, a foolish dream imagined by a foolish old woman. And so, even though the flowers continued to arrive, she didn't talk about them, not even to Silky.

But in spite of her fears, the roses kept coming, the calendar kept advancing and she had not woken up one morning to discover that it had all been a too-beautiful dream, and that she'd been transported back to the cold world of gray dresses and tresses, the lonely future that had once been hers. But now! At last! The long-dreamed of day really had come! In just a few more hours she would be dancing with Mr. Delacorte . . . with Thaddeus. Soon everyone in Too Much would know their secret.

She couldn't bear to keep it to herself any longer. If she didn't share her excitement with someone else she was sure she'd burst! And who better than her very best friend in the world? Who better than her sister?

Velvet entered the kitchen with Mr. Bowie tucked in one arm, a zippered dress bag from Antoinette's shop in the other, and a smile on her face. Silky was standing at the stove with her back to her sister, making breakfast.

"Good morning!" Velvet chirped.

"Good morning," Silky responded as she turned around, holding a cast iron skillet filled with scrambled eggs.

Velvet gasped when she saw the big bags under her sister's eyes. "My goodness, Silky! You look awful. Are you coming down with something?"

"I'm fine. Just didn't sleep very well, that's all." She smiled wearily as she shoveled eggs onto the plates. "You look like you had a good night though."

Velvet draped the dress bag over one of the kitchen chairs before filling Mr. Bowie's dish with kitty kibble and retrieving a pitcher of orange juice from the refrigerator.

"I did," she said, setting the pitcher down on the table before getting the silverware out of the drawer. "Best night's sleep I've had in ages. With all the excitement around here lately and then the ball tonight, I was worried I wouldn't be able to sleep a wink. But, I dropped right off."

"That's nice."

"Maybe you should try to take a nap before tonight," Velvet said as she laid out the forks, knives, and napkins. "It'd be a shame if you weren't able to enjoy the ball."

Silky, who had just finished pouring their coffee, pulled out a chair and sat down at the table.

"Velvet," she said slowly, "about the ball. There's something we should talk about . . ."

Velvet's face lit up and she held up one hand, interrupting her sister.

"I don't mean to be rude," she said with a laugh, "but . . . me first! There's something I've just been dying to show you."

Silky looked up at her with a pained

expression, protesting that they really did need to discuss something, but Velvet wasn't listening. She snatched the dress bag from the back of the chair, unzipped it, and pulled out a floor length evening dress, simply but elegantly cut, with a scoop neck and smooth bodice, and six inch wide pleats at the waist that fell gracefully into a sweeping but not overly full skirt, made from a rich, lustrous satin in the exact red of a Christmas poinsettia.

Velvet's eyes sparkled like a girl's as she held the gown against her chest. "Isn't it beautiful!"

"Oh, it is," Silky said quietly.

Velvet was beaming, so happy that she failed to notice her sister's somber expression.

"You don't think it's too much?" she asked, then went on without waiting for an answer, so excited she fairly tripped over her own words.

"I just love it! Of course, I'd never have dreamed of wearing something so bright, not until now. But . . . and I hope you'll forgive me for not telling you sooner, Silky . . . but you know all those roses I've been getting? I mean, of course, you do." She laughed. "You couldn't have missed them, could you? Well, they really *did* come

243

from a secret admirer! I think I know who it is, at least, I'm pretty sure I do but I still don't want to say because . . . well, he wants it to be a surprise. You don't mind do you?"

"No, Velvet. Of course not, but maybe you should . . ."

Velvet clapped her hand against her chest, as if immensely relieved by this.

"I'm so glad you understand. It wasn't that I didn't trust you. I just didn't want to talk about it before, not to you or anyone, in case it wasn't really true. But it is! And *he* is!

"Tonight, he'll be wearing a yellow rose in his lapel, so I'll know for sure that it's him. Isn't that the most romantic thing you ever heard of? And I'll be wearing this! Of course, he doesn't know that. It's a surprise. But in his last note to me — there were only three and this one came just a few days ago — he said how much he'd love to see me in a dress as red as a poinsettia. And the next day, when I was walking to work, what did I see in the window of Antoinette's dress shop but this! Isn't that amazing?"

Silky nodded and rubbed her forehead. "It is. It's amazing. But, Velvet . . ."

Velvet frowned. "Silky, are you all right? Do you have a headache? Maybe you should go lie down. I can take care of the dishes."

"No, dear. It's not that but . . . I've been trying to tell you . . ."

Velvet clapped her hand over her mouth, covering her grin, then quickly removed it.

"Forgive me." She laughed. "You can't get a word in edgewise today, can you? I'm sorry. I don't mean to be chattering on so but I can't seem to help myself. I feel . . . giddy! Like a schoolgirl going to her first dance! Not that I have any actual knowledge of what that would feel like," she said with a self-deprecating smile. "As you probably remember — I certainly do — I was never invited to dances when we were in school."

Velvet paused to look down at the gown and run her hand over the lustrous red satin.

"But tonight will be different," she said quietly, her grin softening into a smile, the smile, not of a giddy schoolgirl, but of a lovely woman, mature and secure in her beauty, confident of her worth. She looked up at her sister.

"Tonight I'm going to the ball. And I'm going to dance every dance."

Silky's eyes filled. She pressed her lips together and swallowed hard.

"Yes," she said. "Yes, you are. And you're going to have a wonderful time."

Velvet laughed softly and laid the red gown over the back of the chair. She leaned down to embrace her sister.

"You are the best, dearest sister in the world. You truly are," she said, squeezing her tightly.

Silky squeezed her back. "So are you."

"Well!" Velvet said, wiping a small tear from the corner of her eye as she finally took her seat at the table. "Aren't I just getting to be a sentimental old thing? Now, what was it you were trying to say, Silky? You'd better spit it out before I go off and interrupt you again."

Silky shrugged a smile and picked up her fork. "I can't remember now. It must not have been all that important."

CHAPTER ELEVEN

Velvet was surprised when, as they were washing the breakfast dishes, Silky asked if she wouldn't mind meeting her at the ball rather than driving together.

"I promised Mary Dell and Lydia Dale I'd go over to the quilt shop and help out for a bit," she said. "They've got so many last minute Christmas shoppers coming in. And then I've got a pile of errands to run, picking up some last minute items for the silent auction, and then I have to get over there early and set it all up."

"You're helping with the silent auction? But you've never done that before. Shouldn't somebody from the Women's Club be in charge of it? It's their fund-raiser."

"I know, I know," Silky said as she handed one of the wet plates to Velvet, who wiped it dry with a dishcloth. "But it's for a good cause, the children's toy drive and all. And

I'm not in charge. I just said I'd help. That was the thing I meant to tell you before, but it kept slipping my mind."

Velvet frowned. It wasn't like Silky to forget things.

"Are you sure you're not coming down with something? I really think you should go back to bed and get some rest," she said. "You know, if you gave me a list of what you need to pick up and from where, maybe I could take the afternoon off from work and take care of it for you. I'm worried about you overdoing it."

"And let you drive my car? Certainly not. You've got a lead foot. And anyway, I've got to go all the way to Waco and back. But I'm fine. I've already got my second wind."

Velvet looked at her sister, who did appear much more animated and energetic than she had before breakfast.

"All right," she said grudgingly. "If you're sure. I'll just bring my clothes to work with me, change there, and meet you at the ball."

Velvet glanced at the kitchen clock.

"Oh dear. I'd better get a move on. I've got to pack my dress, underthings, shoes, jewelry, makeup, and all that hair who-ha." She wiped her hands on the dishcloth and hurried toward the door.

"Being female certainly requires a lot of

advance planning and equipment," she muttered as she grabbed her dress from the
back of the chair. "Sometimes I wonder if
it's worth it."

Silky untied her apron and smiled.

"See you tonight."

Though the deadline she'd given to the
students in Mr. Delacorte's honors class
was more than two weeks off, nearly all of
the students had already turned in the
transcripts of their oral history interviews.
The only exception was Buck Swanson,
which didn't surprise Velvet one bit. The
boy may not have been the prankster she'd
supposed him to be but she still couldn't
understand how he'd talked his way into
honors history.

Velvet had plenty of work to keep her
busy. She began reading through and edit-
ing all those transcripts, correcting the spelling and such, and then started the process
of cataloging each of them according to
name, family connections, dates, events,
locations, and the like. Even so, she'd never
known a day to pass so slowly. But, finally,
it did pass.

At five o'clock on the dot, Velvet put out
the closed sign, locked the door, and went
into the ladies' room to change into her red

evening gown. She was so nervous that she over-teased her hair and had to comb it out and start over but by six o'clock she was ready to go.

As she walked through the galleries and to the front door, she turned out the lights room by room, catching a glimpse of herself reflected full-length in the glass of the largest display case. She stopped for a moment, turned left and then right.

"Not bad," she murmured before putting on her shawl and heading out the door. "Not bad at all."

The Too Much, Texas Christmas Ball always took place on December 23rd, and was always held in the fellowship hall of the Episcopal Church, which had more gathering space than the other congregations and more elegant surroundings, with wood floors, beamed ceilings and rows of narrow, arched stained glass windows on either side of the room.

The members of the Women's Club always went out of their way to make sure that the decorations for the ball were similarly elegant, hanging the doors with ropes of fresh, fragrant greens, gathered from local pines, and placing fresh arrangements of pine and pillared candles in the center of each table and on the sill of each stained glass window. It always made for a charming and festive atmosphere — at least, that was what Velvet had been told. She'd never gone to the ball before but she was looking forward to seeing the decorations she'd heard so much about. Not as much as she was looking forward to dancing with Mr. Delacorte, of course, but she counted this as a little icing on the cake of what she anticipated would be a perfect and perfectly memorable evening.

This year, some bright and eager new member of the club suggested they step up the decorations and add luminarias, which, in spite of their exotic sounding name, were really just white paper bags partially filled with sand to anchor them and a votive candle to make them glow. Velvet hadn't heard about this addition to the decorating scheme and so, when she rounded the corner onto Austin Street, she gasped, delighted by the sight of hundreds of flickering white lanterns lining both sides of the street from the corner all the way to the church and then up the walkway to the door, like a ribbon of light leading the way home.

Velvet handed in her ticket at the door and loitered in the church vestibule for a few minutes, scanning the faces of the people who were milling about the crowded lobby, trying to find a member of her family. She felt very conspicuous standing there, alone and unescorted. Where was Silky? Or Dutch? She didn't want to go into the ballroom all by herself.

Noel LeFavre, who was helping staff the coat check table, spotted her on the other side of the room and walked over.

"Merry Christmas, Miss Velvet! May I hang up your shawl? Your sister and nieces are already inside."

Velvet's pulse started to race and she was suddenly overcome by a wave of doubt and a fear that red was, in fact, *not* her color. But it was too late to turn back now so she reluctantly allowed the girl to slip her shawl from her shoulders.

"Oh, Miss Velvet! You look beautiful. You really do!" Noel exclaimed, her voice a mixture of shock and admiration, as if she'd never imagined saying such a thing to the old lady who haunted the dusty galleries of the historical society.

Noel's observation was neither subtle nor soft. The sound of her exclamation caused heads to turn and a murmur to spread through the other party-goers. Miss Velvet's cheeks flamed as crimson as her gown. For a moment, she considered snatching her shawl back from the girl and running out of the building but Father Winston, the rector of the church, who was standing just outside the fellowship hall turned ballroom, shaking hands with the arriving guests, came to the rescue.

"Miss Velvet!" he called, lifting his hand. Abandoning his post, he crossed the room to greet her. "Merry Christmas. Your sister told me we'd have the pleasure of your company this year. I'm so pleased. Shall we go in?"

He held out his arm. Miss Velvet accepted it with a grateful smile and, together, they walked toward the door. Perhaps sensing her anxiety, the priest slowed his steps as they reached the entrance and, with his eyes focused front, whispered to her out the side of his mouth.

"Don't forget to smile. Ready, then? Big breath. Here we go!"

Following his advice, Velvet bowed her lips into a smile, took a deep breath, and stepped across the threshold.

The hall was redolent of pine and glowed with the light of a hundred candles. An enormous Christmas tree, at least twelve feet tall, perhaps taller, covered in white lights and decorated with glass ornaments and matching ribbons of crimson, emerald, and gold and topped with a golden-winged angel, stood in the center of the opposite wall. A double row of round tables, covered with white, floor-length cloths, set with silver and glassware that shone like fine sterling and crystal in the flicker of candle-light, ringed the three remaining walls, leaving space for dancing in the center. A few couples were already on the floor, dancing to the strains of "I'll Be Home For Christ-mas," presented by the band, consisting of a keyboard player, a bass guitar player, a drummer, and a man who doubled as lead singer and fiddle player, that occupied a platform on the far left corner.

It was a beautiful room, a magical scene, and just as Velvet had imagined it but even better, because she wasn't just imagining anymore. At long last, it was truly happening. She was in the room, at the ball. And in the next moments or minutes, she would meet her admirer face-to-face and dance in his arms, free from the farce of secrecy.

Though he was standing in a corner, engaged in what appeared to be a somewhat heated exchange with Marlena Benton, it took only a moment for her searching eyes to spot Mr. Delacorte. Dressed in full Santa regalia, he was hard to miss.

Of course, Velvet knew he was to play the part of St. Nicholas that evening, she'd known that from the first moment she'd seen him. But she was slightly taken aback when she saw he wasn't wearing a suit, which was the picture she'd painted in her mind.

Nor was he wearing a yellow rose.

Mr. Delacorte looked up suddenly, as if he felt her staring at him. Their eyes locked, but only for a moment. He gazed at her with an expression of embarrassment and regret until Marlena, frowning even more deeply, poked a finger into his chest. Mr. Delacorte glared at Marlena, his eyes blazing and his jaw set. After another short and seemingly sharp exchange, he stormed off, disappearing through a back door. Marlena marched after him.

The crimson flame reignited in Velvet's cheeks. She didn't fully understand what was going on or what had transpired between Mr. Delacorte and Marlena Benton but it didn't matter. What she did understand was that Thaddeus Delacorte had not sent the roses, or the notes. He was not her secret admirer. Probably no one was. She understood that. And understood that she'd been made to look foolish.

Velvet removed her hand from Father

Winston's arm, preparing to flee, but was prevented from doing so by the firm and manly grip of Dutch Templeton, who took her by the shoulders and planted a kiss on her cheek.

"Merry Christmas, Aunt Velvet. May I have the pleasure of this dance?"

Velvet looked from his warm eyes to his navy blue, western-cut suit, and the yellow rose that was pinned on his lapel.

"And I'd like to claim the next, Miss Velvet. If you'd do me the honor."

Velvet turned toward the sound of Father Winston's voice who smiled as he finished pinning a yellow bloom to the lapel of his black jacket. Velvet looked over the shoulder of the priest and spotted Bob Baker, Harold Pickens, Graydon Beebe, all smiling at her, all dressed in their holiday best, all sporting yellow rose boutonnieres on their lapels.

In fact, she realized as her eyes scanned the perimeter of the hall, moving from right to left around the sea of familiar faces that, except for scowling Jack Benny Benton who sat glaring at her from a table in the corner, every man in the room, from young Buck Swanson, dressed in the ill-fitting suit he'd borrowed from his father, to ancient George Plank, seated in his wheelchair, was wearing a yellow rose and a smile, and gazing at her with undisguised admiration.

Velvet's eyes filled. But before she could give way to tears, the fiddle player lifted his instrument to his shoulder and the band swung into a countrified version of "Jingle Bell Rock." Dutch grabbed her by the hand.

"Come on, Aunt Velvet! Let's cut a rug!"

CHAPTER TWELVE

Before Velvet could lodge any protest, Dutch pulled her into the middle of the floor and began dancing — at least Velvet supposed that's what he was doing; she'd never seen anything quite like it. Dutch clapped his hands, stomped his feet, and gyrated his hips in time to the music, then held his hands, palms up, and wiggled his fingers in a come-hither gesture, indicating that Velvet should do the same.

Velvet hadn't danced with a man since she was a very little girl, when her father had let her stand on the tops of his shoes and guided her through a jerking and stiff-legged waltz at a cousin's wedding. And she'd certainly never, not even in her imagination, tried to dance to "rock and roll" music. She was sure she'd look like a perfect fool dancing to such wild music. Dutch certainly did but he didn't seem to care. Neither did any of the other couples on the floor, most of whom were jumping and twisting in ways that made Velvet think they'd been goosed with a cattle prod. Did they know how silly they looked?

On the other hand, she reasoned, they couldn't look any sillier than she did, standing stupidly still in the middle of a dance floor.

Velvet tapped her left foot, then her right, rocking cautiously from side to side along with the music. Dutch grinned and bobbed his head approvingly. "That's it, Aunt Velvet! You've got it!" Velvet, feeling a little less self-conscious, grinned back at him and waggled her hips a bit. She was, she realized, actually enjoying herself.

But enjoyment turned to alarm when Dutch grabbed her right hand, let out a whoop, spun her around in a circle, then under his arm before bringing her back in toward his torso, then unwound his grip on her like a yo-yo on a string before reeling her back in, grabbing her about the waist, and making her bob up and down in tandem with him for a couple of seconds before repeating the entire series of movements. Velvet's initial response to Dutch's exuberant gamboling was one of shock and panic. Her mind raced as she tried to anticipate his next move. But before long, once she realized that she didn't have to figure out what Dutch was going to do next, only to follow his lead, panic turned to pleasure, then to heart pounding giddiness as she spun and twirled and clapped and stomped, her grin growing wider with every passing measure of music until, almost before she knew it, the song was over and everyone was clapping and hooting their approval of the band.

"My goodness!" Velvet exclaimed, practically shouting to make herself heard above the applause. "That was fun! Thank you, Dutch. I'm so dizzy, I feel like I've taken fifty trips on a Ferris wheel. I'd better sit down a minute and catch my breath."

Dutch laughed. "Oh, I don't think you'll have a chance of that, Miss Velvet. Not tonight."

Dutch was right. Even before he finished speaking, Velvet found herself encircled by a ring of men with yellow roses on their lapels, congratulating her on jitterbugging skills and asking for the honor of the next dance. Father Winston responded on her behalf, informing the assembled gentlemen that he had already reserved a spot as Miss Velvet's next partner and suggesting they draw numbers to work out the order for the rest of the evening.

The next dance, much to Velvet's relief,

was a waltz. Not that she had done much waltzing, not besides that one time with her father, but she'd watched *The King and I* on television often enough so she understood the general principal. It was a struggle, at first, not to count the steps — one, two, three, and — or look at her feet but she soon discovered that, as with the jitterbug, all she really needed to do was relax and follow her partner's lead. Father Winston was a good dancer and Velvet told him so.

"Thank you. So are you, Miss Velvet. Very graceful. And, may I say, quite lovely."

"Oh, well . . . thank you."

She had been about to tell him that he didn't have to say things they both knew weren't so, but she didn't think it would be very nice to accuse a clergyman of telling an untruth, even if he meant it kindly.

And the truth was, at that moment, in the soft glow of candlelight, floating on a cloud of music and rustling red satin that swished and swirled about her feet as she glided and turned in three-quarter time, she *felt* graceful. And lovely. And, she supposed, there was nothing so very wrong in that. Even if it was an illusion, as fragile as a fairy tale, an artifice brought about by a fairy godmother, her sister, a spell that would, like a glass slipper or pumpkin coach, disappear

261

before morning.

Which meant there was all the more reason to enjoy it for as long as it lasted. And Velvet did.

She danced every dance, feeling not an ounce of regret for the temporary nature of her transformation, so busy enjoying the music and the dancing and the company of her partners, that she didn't feel Marlena's laser sharp glare upon her, or notice the argument that erupted between her and her husband, Noodie. When he too, pinned a yellow rose to his lapel and joined the line of men waiting to dance with Miss Velvet, Marlena stormed off, leaving the ball early with Jack Benny slouching along in her wake.

The only moment of melancholy Miss Velvet felt during the entire evening came when she looked at the Santa throne that sat empty next to the Christmas tree, the chair that should have been occupied by Mr. Delacorte, whom she had already ceased to think of by his Christian name. She was sorry that she would not be able to dance with him and sorrier still that now, after having learned of how his name had been connected with this cruel prank and how she'd behaved like an addled schoolgirl, imagining that a man she barely knew had harbored a secret affection for her, she would likely never see him again, not as admirer or even as a potential friend. Jack Benny had tried to make fools of them both. It was one thing for him to have done this to Velvet but quite another to have involved Mr. Delacorte. He was too fine a man to be made fun of.

For a moment, Velvet considered the possibility of going to see him and apologize, or perhaps even just sending him a note, but quickly dismissed the idea. She didn't want him to think she was chasing after him. No, the best thing, the most dignified thing, would be to leave things as they were. Any attempt to contact Mr. Delacorte would only serve to make a bad situation worse.

And, aside from that, it really wasn't a *bad* situation, not entirely. Velvet thought back to that wish she'd made just before Thanksgiving, really more of a passing thought than a wish, that just once, she'd have liked to know what it felt like to have a grand romance, to be admired and pursued by a man. It occurred to Velvet that her wish had come true, after a fashion. No, she had not *had* a grand romance but she knew now what it might have been like if she had. She was glad. She'd never had such a splendid evening.

And when, near the end of the night, the band struck up the strains of the tune so dear to the heart of every true Texan and everyone lined up on the floor to dance the Cotton-Eyed Joe, Velvet had another revelation.

Velvet told Silky that she'd never been to dances when she was younger but that wasn't quite true. She'd never been asked to a dance in her schoolgirl days but she'd attended a few, spending her evening miserably manning the punch bowl or hiding out in the ladies' room, embarrassed to be a wallflower. And, of course, when she'd gotten older she'd been to weddings and a few parties where there was dancing but had never actually danced, preferring instead to hide behind the refreshment table or sit safely among the other spinsters, matrons, and dowagers, keeping a dignified but disinterested eye on the festivities. But her disinterest was feigned. She paid much closer attention than anyone would have suspected and, after so many years of watching line dancing, Velvet had memorized every single step of the Cotton-Eyed Joe, even though she'd never put this knowledge into practice. Until now.

Without waiting for her next partner,

young Buck Swanson, to issue the invitation, Velvet scrambled to the center of the ballroom and lined up with the others, grinning when she saw that Silky had scurried to take the spot to her left and Dutch to her right.

As the fiddler sawed his bow back and forth across the strings and the singer declared that had it not been for the Cotton-Eyed Joe, he'd have been married a long time ago, Velvet took steps forward and backward and turned and repeated the sequence, executing the dance without error or hesitation, moving in perfect unison with everyone else, as though she and her neighbors were of one mind, one heart, one heritage.

And that was the moment it came to her, the revelation, the gift, the realization that turned out to be of more value to Miss Velvet than all the yellow roses in Texas.

For years and years that added up to a lifetime, she'd been sitting on the sidelines, hiding behind her intelligence, her dowdy clothes and orthopedic shoes, her spinster status, hiding behind anything she could find, because she'd been afraid of being rejected, or getting hurt, or looking foolish. How much she had missed in all that hiding! And how silly she had been because, of course, in spite of everything, she *had* been rejected, been hurt, looked foolish. Everyone had! These were the unavoidable consequences of being human and drawing breath.

But the loneliness she'd known, the sense of not quite belonging, at least not entirely, to her community . . . this was a self-imposed sentence. She had done it to herself. Just as anyone, single or partnered, could jump in and dance the Cotton-Eyed Joe, anyone could participate in the life of the community — *fully* participate. The only one standing in Velvet's way was Velvet.

Until tonight, she hadn't believed that anyone outside of her family felt she mattered much. She'd been wrong. Just look at the way her family, friends, and neighbors had taken her part, refusing to see her humiliated, standing up for her even in the face of Marlena Benton's wrath! Would they have done so much for someone they considered a woman of no consequence? No.

Velvet Tudmore had lived her entire life in Too Much, Texas but that Christmas, for the first time, she felt like she was home, where she belonged. It was a night she would never forget and a feeling that would never desert her, not ever again.

CHAPTER THIRTEEN

Miss Velvet forgot to set her alarm clock when she went to bed.

She slept through the hours of seven and eight, and even through Mr. Bowie's insistent purring and head butting, not stirring until a firm knock on her bedroom door announced the presence of her sister, who brought her breakfast on a tray.

"Merry Christmas, Cinderella," Silky said as she came through the door. "Or maybe that should be Sleeping Beauty."

Velvet opened one eye, closed it again, and mumbled, "Either way the ball is definitely over. Probably a good thing. My feet are killing me. What time is it?"

"Nine-fifteen."

"Really?" Velvet blinked a few times, yawned, and slowly pushed herself into a semi-sitting position, wedging a pillow behind her back and reclining against the headboard. "I've never slept this late in my life; not unless I've been sick."

"I know," Silky said, settling the breakfast tray on Velvet's lap. "That's why I figured I'd better get in here and make sure you were still breathing. I also figured you'd need some sustenance. Bet you burned a pile of calories with all that dancing."

"Oh, Silky," she said as she looked down at the breakfast tray. "Thank you. I don't deserve you. I truly don't."

Silky waved her hand dismissively. "Don't go starting that again. You thanked me enough last night. I'm just happy you had a nice time. And you really did, didn't you?" she said, her statement more comment than question.

"I did," Velvet confirmed, feeding a morsel of crisp bacon to Mr. Bowie, who was purring loudly and rubbing against her arm.

"Of course, the evening didn't quite turn out the way I'd envisioned it," Velvet admitted, "but, except for the part where Bob Baker kept stomping on my feet, I did enjoy myself. Who knew that these shiftless Too Much men would turn out to be so smooth on the dance floor? I'm almost starting to understand what the women around here see in them."

Silky arched her eyebrows in disbelief and Velvet laughed.

"Almost!" she reiterated, raising a caution-ary finger.

Silky settled herself on the edge of the bed. "Well, I think they had as much fun as you did. Wasn't it something? Did you see the way George Plank maneuvered that wheelchair around the dance floor?" Silky let out a low whistle. "Even with gout, he's still got some moves. And an eye for the ladies."

"Yes. He certainly does," Velvet said. "Do you know that he pinched me?"

"No! He did not!"

Velvet gave an exaggerated nod. "He most certainly did. Right in the middle of the Hokey Pokey, when we were turning our-selves around, he reached up and pinched me! Right on the behind!"

"No!" Silky exclaimed again, and started to laugh. "I can't believe it. Why that old codger!"

"I tell you what!" Velvet hooted. "Good thing he's stuck in that chair. If he could have reached up any higher, who knows what he might have pinched?

"Anyway . . ." she continued, when their laughter subsided. "It was sweet of you to talk all those men into putting on flowers and dancing with me."

"Don't be silly. I didn't talk anybody into

anything. They were more than willing, every one of them. Mr. Delacorte included. He wanted to put a rose on his Santa suit but then Marlena stuck her nose into it and said he'd better not, and then Mr. Delacorte got his back up and walked out on the job."

"Is that what they were arguing about when I came in?" Velvet asked. "I wondered."

It was kind of Mr. Delacorte, especially being so new in town, to have stepped up for her that way. And she never minded seeing anyone thwart the machinations of Marlena Benton but, of course, this didn't signify anything. Mr. Delacorte was just trying to do the gentlemanly thing.

"Well, it was nice of him. And them. Nice of everyone."

"Nice, nothing," Silky protested. "Those men all but lined up around the block to get a rose and a dance with you . . ."

". . . Once you explained what a lowdown, dirty trick Jack Benny tried to play on me. Silky," she said flatly, giving her sister a knowing look. "Let's not go around pretending that a new dress and a bottle of hair dye suddenly transformed me from the spinster historian to the Queen of the May. But it *was* nice of them to do it, and nice of you to arrange it all. Really. You didn't just save my evening, you saved my dignity."

Velvet squeezed Silky's hand and Silky squeezed it back, silently acknowledging and accepting her sister's gratitude.

"And *then,*" Velvet said in a lighter and brighter voice, "as if all that weren't enough, you bring me breakfast in bed!" She picked up her fork. "Look at all this! You thought of everything — bacon, eggs, biscuits and gravy, coffee, juice. All my favorites."

She lifted the napkin from the tray, found a yellow rose hidden beneath, and pressed her hand against her lips, too touched for words.

"Oh, Silky . . . I really *don't* deserve you. You are so thoughtful."

"Don't look at me," Silky said, raising her hands in denial as she got to her feet. "I just cooked the breakfast. That's why I came in here. The poor man has been sitting in our living room for one solid hour, hoping you'd finally wake up."

Velvet sat straight up. "What poor man?"

Silky strolled toward the door, taking her time. "The one who brought the rose, of course. The secret admirer. Who else could it be?"

Velvet pushed the breakfast tray to one side and scrambled out from under the

271

quilt. Mr. Bowie, seeing his chance, moved immediately to the abandoned tray and started gobbling Velvet's scrambled eggs.

"What! He's been waiting for a whole hour? Why didn't you tell me before?"

"Because I'm telling you now," Silky said simply. "It's good to let men wait a little. Keeps 'em humble. And coming back for more. But you better get dressed now. I'll go keep him company until you're ready."

Velvet flung open the doors of her closet and searched through the rack of dresses, pushing the hangers frantically from right to left on the rod, then suddenly stopping cold. She turned to her sister with a slightly panicked expression.

"Wait! And is it . . . you know . . . him?"

"Yes, it is," Silky said as she opened the door. "And, by the way, the cornflower is nice but he likes you best in the green."

Silky sat on the sofa and watched Mr. Delacorte pace. She was beginning to wish she'd gone in to wake her sister sooner. The poor man was getting more anxious by the second. If Velvet didn't come out soon, he might wear a hole in her carpet.

"Are you sure you won't sit down, Mr. Delacorte?"

"No, no," he said, halting his pacing, but

272

only briefly. "I'm fine. Thank you. Are you sure she's all right?"

"Yes. She's just doing her hair. It takes a little time. Women don't just wake up looking beautiful," she said with a chuckle, trying to lighten his mood. "It takes a little effort to look this good."

"I can believe that of most women," he said seriously, "but not your sister. From the first day I arrived in Too Much and on every occasion since, I've never seen Miss Velvet looking anything less than perfect."

He slowed his pacing, realizing the broader implications of the first half of his commentary.

"Pardon me, Miss Silky. No offense intended."

"None taken, Mr. Delacorte."

He nodded, looking a bit relieved, and took another lap around the rug.

"Mr. Delacorte, I hope you won't mind my asking, but if you've admired my sister for so long, why didn't you declare yourself until now?"

"I would have but I was present when the first rose was delivered to her, remember? I believed that someone else had beaten my time. A woman as fine as Miss Velvet undoubtedly receives all sort of attention from gentlemen; I felt certain there was no point in pressing my suit since, obviously, she already had a beau."

Silky smiled. What a sweet man he was. He and Velvet would do very well together; she'd thought so from the first.

"Mr. Delacorte, do you have any plans for Christmas Eve? If not, we'd love for you to come out to the ranch and join us for dinner."

Mr. Delacorte stopped in the middle of his circuit. His face lit up. "Well, no! I don't have any plans. I'm new in town, you know. And . . . you don't think she'd mind?"

"I'm sure I can speak for my sister and my whole family when I say that we'd love to have you as our guest for Christmas."

"Well! I'd enjoy that very much. Thank you, Miss Silky! Let me ask you something . . . I'm supposed to take part in the reenactment of the battle of San Jacinto this spring. Do you think your sister might like to accompany me?"

"That certainly sounds like the sort of thing she'd enjoy, Mr. Delacorte." Silky got up from the sofa. "But why don't you ask her yourself?"

Mr. Delacorte turned around and stared at Velvet, who stood in the doorway wearing a dress of emerald green and an expression of joy that perfectly mirrored that of her handsome, white-haired suitor. For a long moment, neither of them said a word. It was almost as if they'd forgotten to breathe.

But when Silky, impatient for this romance to finally begin, cleared her throat, Mr. Delacorte's shoulders jerked, as if he'd just remembered where he was and why he'd come. He walked quickly to the sofa, retrieved the bouquet of yellow roses he'd left lying there, and, with a respectful inclination of his head, presented them to Velvet, holding them out to her with both his hands, like a courtier offering a scepter to a lady of high rank.

"Merry Christmas, Miss Velvet. These are for you."

Velvet accepted his gift, cradling the roses in the crook of her arm, burying her nose in the fragrant blossoms.

"They're lovely. So lovely," she murmured.

She looked up at him with a smile that washed over him like clear water, making everything new, blessing him like a benediction.

"Thank you . . . Thaddeus. And Merry Christmas."

■ ■ ■ ■

Nightmare on Elf Street

Laura Levine

■ ■ ■ ■

CHAPTER ONE

You'd think after all I've done for my cat — the belly rubs, the back scratches, the endless cans of Fancy Feast — you'd think she could at least wear a pair of reindeer antlers for three minutes while I took her picture for my annual Christmas card. But, no, Prozac, the little drama queen, had decided that the fuzzy felt antlers I'd ordered online were emissaries from the devil and was determined to avoid them at all costs.

"Pumpkin face," I pleaded. "Just think how adorable you'll look."

But she just glared at me balefully.

I'm already adorable. And don't call me pumpkin face.

I was on my knees that late November morning, begging her for the umpteenth time to let me put the antlers on her stubborn little head when the phone rang.

Wearily I picked it up to hear:

"Fabulous news, Jaine! I've just spent the

past forty-five minutes fondling the feet of a fabulously wealthy Malibu blonde."

No, you haven't stumbled on a foot fetish novella. The voice on the other end of the line was my neighbor Lance Venable, who happens to fondle feet for a living as a shoe salesman at Neiman Marcus.

"She wound up buying five pair of Jimmy Choos," Lance was saying. "And guess what? It turns out her husband owns that new mall out in Santa Monica — Conspicuous Consumption Plaza."

Of course that wasn't what it was really called. I've changed the mall's name to protect the innocent — namely *moi* — from a lawsuit.

"It seems they're looking for someone to write their ads, and I told her all about you and your award-winning campaign for Apple computers."

"But Lance, I've never worked for Apple. My biggest client is Toiletmasters Plumbers. And the only award I've ever won is the Golden Plunger from the L.A. Plumbers Association."

"A mere technicality, honey. The bottom line is you've got an interview with their HR gal tomorrow morning at ten o'clock."

I have to admit I was excited. How nice it would be to have something glamorous to write in between toilet bowl ads.

"Oh, Lance. You're an angel!"

"Try to remember that when shopping for my Christmas present — Oops. Gotta run. Trophy Wife over by the Ferragamos. Damn. Looks like she's got bunions."

I hung up the phone in a much better frame of mind than when I'd picked it up, my head spinning with visions of all that a new job could buy: A high-def TV. New slipcovers for my sofa. Maybe even a lifetime membership in the Fudge-of-the-Month Club.

"Fabulous news, Pro!" I said, whirling around in a happy glow. "I've got a job interview!"

To which she merely rolled over on her back, her paws poised daintily in the air.

And I've got a belly that needs scratching. So hop to it.

"No belly rubs for you, young lady," I said, marching straight past her to my bedroom. "Not after your churlish behavior with those felt antlers."

Okay, so I didn't march straight past her.

I may have stopped to give her belly a teeny scratch. But I swear it wasn't for more than two minutes. Five, tops.

Okay, twenty, if you must know.

■ ■ ■ ■

Conspicuous Consumption Plaza was an upscale mall with valet parking, froufrou boutiques and stocking stuffers that cost more than my Corolla.

To fool the Human Resources gal into thinking I actually belonged there, I showed up in my one and only Prada suit and one and only pair of Manolo Blahniks. I'd blown my mop of unruly curls reasonably smooth, and was now clacking along on the mall's travertine marble floors on my way to the executive offices. Shiny baubles glistened in shop windows, lush garlands hung overhead, and the air was redolent with the scent of cinnamon spice and new money.

All the glitz came to a screeching halt, however, when I walked through the door to the staff offices. Suddenly everything was linoleum and fluorescent lights.

I found Molly Grover, the head of Human Resources, in a no frills cubicle down at the end of a corridor.

I'd been expecting a kamikaze fashionista straight from the pages of *Vogue,* but instead I found a somewhat frazzled thirty-something woman in a wrinkled pantsuit.

She gazed up from a pile of papers, her

face pale and pasty, her mousy brown hair hanging in limp clumps on her shoulders.

"Have a seat." She gestured vaguely to a cracked plastic visitor's chair. Then, with a hopeful smile, she said, "I hear you've written for Apple."

Oh, gulp.

"I'm afraid there's been a bit of a mix up. I haven't actually handled any computer accounts. Although some of the septic tanks sold by one of my top clients, Toiletmasters Plumbers, do come with a computerized control panel."

"Is that so?" she said, her smile rapidly fading. "Well, let me take a look at your samples anyway."

I handed her my book of writing samples, and she began leafing through them. Every once in a while she paused to gaze at me intently, then back to the book.

Finally she slammed the book shut, shooting me one last penetrating look.

"You're perfect!" she exclaimed.

Wow. Talk about your dream interviews.

I'd been there less than five minutes, and already I'd landed the job.

"Here." She reached down under her desk and pulled out a shopping bag. "Try it on."

"What is it?"

"Your elf suit."

"My elf suit?"

"Yes, one of my Santa's elves just quit and I'm in desperate need of a replacement."

"But what about the writing job?"

"Oh, that. I like your samples, very impressive. You're definitely on the short list. But let's just say you'd be a lot higher up on that list if you helped me out and worked as Santa's elf for a few weeks."

"In other words, you're bribing me."

"Not in other words. In those words. Put on the elf suit," she commanded, suddenly tough as a marine drill sergeant, "or you don't have a snowball's chance in hell of getting the writing gig."

Well! If she thought I was the kind of person who would sacrifice my dignity and self-respect just to better my chances at landing a job — she was absolutely right. It had been a long time between toilet bowl ads, and I needed the bucks.

"So how about it?" she asked. "Are you game?"

If I'd known what was in store for me, I would have grabbed my sample book and skedaddled straight to the food court. But I knew nothing of the disastrous events waiting in the wings. So with hope in my heart, and a pair of curly-toed shoes in my hands, I said yes.

A mistake, I would soon learn, of monumental proportions.

Chapter Two

I got my first hint of how truly ghastly my days as an elf would be when I hustled off to the employees' ladies' room to try on my elf suit. I still shudder to think of that hideous costume. The green velvet tunic, piped in gold, wasn't too horrible, if you didn't mind looking like Peter Pan on estrogen. Nor was the stocking cap with the fuzzy pompom at the tip. Or the green curly-toed shoes.

But those godawful red and green striped tights! That was truly the fashion accessory from hell. Those damn stripes added at least five extra pounds to my thighs — which had all the poundage they needed, thank you very much.

But on the bright side, I reminded myself, I'd actually managed to squeeze into an elf costume. For those of you who don't know me, I am not ordinarily considered the elfin type. Far from it, as my scale will be the

286

first to assure you.

To tell the truth, when Molly said I'd be perfect for the part, I'd actually been a tiny bit flattered. But my bubble was quickly burst when, back in Molly's office, she looked at me and beamed, "Oh, marvelous! The costume fits you so much better than it fit Kenny."

"Kenny?"

I was wearing a *guy's* elf suit?

"Yes, the elf you're replacing. He quit to concentrate on his Weight Watchers classes."

I was wearing a *fat guy's* elf suit?

Ouch.

At which point, there was a knock on Molly's cubicle door and a truly elfin elf waltzed in. A tiny pixie of a thing with a pert little nose, enormous brown eyes and waist the size of my red and green striped thigh.

"Hi, Molly," she said, looking adorable in her elf costume. "You wanted to see me?"

"Yes, Gigi. Say hi to Jaine Austen, our new elf. Jaine, this is Gigi Harris."

The pixie and I exchanged hellos.

"Would you mind taking Jaine around and showing her the ropes?"

"Not at all."

Gigi shot me a friendly grin. And, grabbing my sample book, I followed her tiny tush out into the hallway.

■ ■ ■ ■

My first shift did not officially start until
the next day. So thank heavens I was allowed to change out of my elf suit before
returning to the mall. As Gigi explained
while I struggled out of my hideous tights
in the employees' ladies' room, she and I
were the two weekday elves, working Mon-
days through Fridays, taking turns with the
day and night shifts. Working alongside us
were two weekday Santas, while a whole
other crew took over on the weekends.

"We get minimum wage," she said, popping a wad of gum in her mouth and sending a blast of Juicy Fruit my way. "Plus a
twenty percent employee discount. Of
course, the discount doesn't help much with
the ridiculous prices they charge around
here. The real reason I'm working at Conspicuous Consumption is the exposure."

"Exposure?"

"Sure. A lot of show business insiders
shop here. A gal never knows when she's
going to get discovered."

"So you're an actress?"

"Couldn't you tell?" she asked, batting her
saucer eyes. "Practically everybody who
works in Santa Land is in the biz. Or trying

to break in, anyway. Scotty, one of the Santas, has done a Taco Bell commercial, and Barnaby, the other Santa, used to play Shakespeare on Broadway."

By now I'd changed back into my civvies, and Gigi led me to a fluorescent-lit employees' locker room.

"The lockers are co-ed," she explained, "which is why we have to change into our costumes in the ladies' room. Here's yours." She pointed to a rusty cubbyhole against the wall. "It's right next to Barnaby's. He's a real sweetie. Scotty, on the other hand, can be a bit of a handful."

That, as I was about to discover, was putting it mildly.

"Well, c'mon," she said, popping her gum. "Time for you to see Santa Land."

Conspicuous Consumption's Santa Land was an extravaganza of the highest order — the highlight of which was a ginormous Christmas tree sitting on a bed of fake snow, its boughs bedecked with glimmering baubles. Nearby a lifesized Rudolph with a blinking red nose stood watch over a sleigh piled high with ornately wrapped presents. Off to the side was a miniature cottage with a sign on the door that said "Santa's Workshop." And meandering through it all was a candy cane lane leading up to Santa's chair, a rococo gold affair straight out of Versailles.

The only thing missing from Santa Land was, in fact, Santa.

Several kids were lined up in their Tommy Hilfiger/Ralph Lauren finest, asking the bewildered Hispanic maids who had been delegated to schlep them to the mall, "*Donde esta* Santa?"

"Damn!" Gigi muttered as she surveyed the scene.

Then she plastered on a bright smile and turned to the children waiting on line.

"Santa must be busy wrapping presents in his workshop. I'll go get him."

"Darn that Scotty," she muttered as she stomped over to the workshop. "He's on another bender."

She opened the door to Santa's workshop, and poked her head inside.

"Wake up, Scotty!" she hissed. "You've got kids waiting."

Peering over her shoulder, I saw a guy in a Santa suit sprawled out, clutching a bottle of tequila.

"Tell 'em Santa's got a hangover," he mumbled.

"Are you crazy?" Gigi snapped.

"Okay, okay." Reluctantly he got up and started to crawl out the door, his Santa's beard dangling from his neck. Just before he pulled it up, I took a look at his face, and realized that he was one heck of a handsome Santa. Small but deep blue eyes, fabulous cheekbones, and pouty Brad Pitt lips. He had Out Of Work Actor written all over him.

Blearily he glanced over at me.

"Who the hell are you?"

"The new elf," Gigi said. "Kenny's replacement."

"She's supposed to be an *elf*?" he said, with a none too flattering glance at my thighs.

Taking a deep breath, he walked over to his throne and muttered to Gigi, "Bring on the brats."

The heart melts, *n'est-ce pas*?

I watched as Gigi led a skinny little girl over to his lap.

"Ho-ho-ho!" he boomed, practically melting the tot's eyebrows with his tequila breath. The kid started to whimper, and Gigi quickly whisked her off Scotty's lap and into the safety of her nanny's arms.

As another, much braver, kid took her place and whipped out a spread sheet printout of the gifts he expected Santa to bring him, Gigi sprinted over to my side.

"I better stick around," she said, "otherwise Lord knows what hell will break loose."

"Is he always this bad?" I asked.

"Pretty much. Just remember. When you work with him, never loan him money. Don't let him flirt with the pretty moms. And whatever you do, try to keep him away from his 'hot chocolate' thermos. It's filled with tequila."

"Yikes. How come he hasn't been fired?"

"Because he's dating Molly, that's why."

My mind boggled at the thought of mousy little Molly with the soused Santa.

"Well, thanks for showing me around," I said.

And with the sound of some poor tyke wailing on Scotty's lap, I scooted off, about to begin My Life as a Santa's helper.

Or, as I'd soon come to know it, Nightmare on Elf Street.

I headed for the Conspicuous Consumption parking lot, my elf costume in a garment bag, dreading the thought of wearing the damn thing in public. As I tossed it in the backseat of my Corolla, I prayed that somehow it would morph into a tasteful Eileen Fisher pantsuit by the time I got back to my duplex in the slums of Beverly Hills.

(Contrary to popular belief, not every street in Beverly Hills is studded with mansions and Mercedes. There are quite a few humble pockets in town — none quite so humble as the duplex-and-Toyota lined street that I call home.)

Driving along, I shuddered at the memory of how I'd looked in my elf suit, my thighs glowing like giant neon barber poles.

But then a ray of hope dawned on my horizon. Maybe the mirror at the mall was a "fattening" mirror — one of those distorted mirrors I so often find in department stores when I'm trying on bathing suits.

That was it. I bet I'd look much thinner in my mirror at home!

And so, filled with a desperate burst of optimism, the minute I got back to my apartment, I raced to my bedroom and tried on my elf costume again, hoping the Conspicuous Consumption mirror was all wrong.

And indeed, it was.

As it turned out, my striped tights did not add another five pounds to my thighs. No, siree. In my mirror at home, they added another *ten* pounds.

I was standing there groaning in dismay when there was a knock on my front door.

"Open up, Jaine. It's me. Lance. I want to hear all about your job interview."

I trudged to the door to find Lance on my

doorstep, spiffed up in his Neiman-Marcus work togs, his blond curls moussed to perfection.

He took one look at me and gasped.

"My God, Jaine. What happened? You look like you were mugged by a leprechaun."

Wearily I told him how Molly had offered me a chance at the Conspicuous Consumption writing gig, but only if I agreed to be a Santa's elf.

"The pay stinks, the hours are awful, I get a twenty percent discount on things I can't begin to afford, and worst of all, I have to work with a Santa from hell."

"You poor thing," Lance tsked soothingly. "You can't possibly be seen in public in that outfit. You're going to have to quit."

"You think so?"

"Absolutely! But not before you use your twenty percent discount to get me a Hugo Boss tie for Greg."

"Greg?"

"The most adorable guy at work. I pulled a few thousand strings and I'm his Secret Santa! I saw the perfect tie for him at your mall the other day."

A tiny alarm bell went off in my head.

"How much does this tie happen to cost?"

"About two hundred bucks. But don't worry. I'll pay you back as soon as I get my

Christmas bonus in December. No, wait. I might need that money for last minute gifts. How about early January? Possibly February. April at the latest."

"Forget it, Lance. I'm not laying out two hundred bucks so you can impress a guy you barely know. Besides, Secret Santa gifts are supposed to be inexpensive. This Greg guy will think you're coming on way too strong if you hit him with Hugo Boss."

"You're probably right," he said, with a pensive scratch at his curls. "But I've got to get him the perfect gift. I'll start making a list tonight. Don't quit your job, hon, until I know for sure what I'm getting him. I may need your discount."

How gratifying to know he had my best interests at heart.

While Lance trotted off to his apartment to work on his Secret Santa list, I headed back to my bedroom and began struggling out of my tights. I was in the midst of yanking them off my hips, flushed from the effort, my elf hat askew on my head, when Prozac wandered in and stopped in her tracks.

She looked up at me with what I can only describe as a smirk on her face.

And I thought I looked silly in my antlers.

CHAPTER THREE

As much as I was tempted, I was not about to throw away my chance at a lucrative copywriting gig.

I'd be an elf if it killed me.

And my first day on the job damn near did.

I can't tell you how mortifying it was standing there in that moronic elf suit. The bright green tunic top barely covered my striped tush, leaving my neon thighs on display for all the world to see. There was no getting around it. I was a hot elfin mess — from the top of my pointy green hat to the tips of my curly toes.

Somewhere in time, I was convinced, some medieval court was missing its jester.

Not five minutes into my shift a towheaded tyke in a tiny blue blazer and red bow tie looked me over with the soulless eyes of a future hedge fund manager.

"I thought elves were supposed to be

skinny," he sneered, much to the delight of the other kids on line, all of whom broke into a most humiliating round of giggles.

Where's a lump of coal when you need one?

But the truly hellish part of the day was working with Scotty.

The guy was lazy, rude, egotistical and mean spirited.

And those were his good points.

It was clear from the moment he came swaggering down Santa Lane that he hated working there.

"I can't believe I'm wasting my talents like this," he muttered, taking a swig from his "hot chocolate" bottle.

Good heavens. Was he actually drinking tequila at nine o'clock in the morning?

"I'm up for a starring part in a TV pilot," he told me, "and the minute I get it, I'm outta here."

That day could not come a moment too soon, as far as I was concerned.

Mr. Showbiz couldn't be bothered to remember my name, so he called me Elf #2. (Gigi, apparently, got top billing as Elf #1.)

And I was lucky that's all Scotty called me. He was capable of worse. Much worse — as I would find out when a large, ruddy-faced woman in a mall security uniform walked by Santa Land speaking into her walkie-talkie.

Scotty looked up from the kid who was on his lap and called out, "How's it going, Porky?"

The woman flushed and, gritting her teeth, walked on, ignoring him.

"Her real name's Corky," he said. "What a tub of lard, huh? I love to get a rise out of her."

By now, I was ready to strangle the guy, and I hadn't even been there an hour.

As for his duties as Santa, Scotty was one sly son of a gun. When kids showed up with a nanny or a low-income parent, he barely gave them the time of day, whipping them off his lap with lightning speed.

But if a little tyke was holding the hand of a well-heeled parent, Scotty was all smiles and ho-ho-ho's.

And if that parent happened to be a pretty blonde, he was in full-tilt flirtation mode.

"What can Santa get *you* for Christmas, pretty lady?" he'd leer.

The really aggravating thing was that most of the women fell for it. He was a good looking dude, and those deep blue eyes of his made the designer moms giggle with adolescent glee.

Elf #2, I can assure you, was ready to puke.

He refused to wear any padding, and when kids asked him why he wasn't fat, his standard reply was, "Santa's been working out."

Then, with a snarky glance in my direction, he'd add, "His elf, not so much."

In slow periods when there were no kids on line, he was off like a shot to Santa's Workshop to guzzle tequila or take a nap.

Frankly, those were the highlights of my day.

It was during one such lull, just as Scotty was about to scoot off for a nap, that Molly from Human Resources showed up.

He quickly sat back down in his chair, all smiles.

"Molly, babe." He grinned. "How's my favorite boss?"

I looked down and saw his hand on her fanny.

Like the designer moms, she burst out in giggles.

"Really, Scotty," she said, reluctantly removing his hand from her tush. "People are looking."

And indeed, over by a roasted chestnut cart, Corky the security guard was glaring in Scotty's direction.

"Let 'em look," Scotty said. "You're my main squeeze, and I don't care who knows it."

With that, he shot her his idea of a sultry look.

Somehow Molly restrained herself from jumping on his lap and turned to me.

"So how's your day going, Jaine?"

"Great," I lied. "Just great."

"Isn't Scotty a terrific Santa? He's so wonderful with the children."

This time I could barely manage to nod my head.

Talk about love being blind.

Eventually Molly tore herself away from Scotty and headed back to her office. The minute she was gone, he zipped over to his workshop for a nap.

The rest of the day dragged by, with Scotty barking orders at me in between naps and nips of tequila. At one point, he actually snapped his fingers and said, "I'm hungry, Elf #2! Go get me some donuts at the food court."

Like I was his own personal servant or something.

"Get your own damn donuts!"

Okay, I didn't actually say that. Mainly because I was sort of hungry myself, and a donut sounded like a pretty good idea at the time.

Needless to say, I counted the milliseconds till the end of my shift, and practically kissed the toes of her curly shoes when Gigi showed up to relieve me.

Thank heavens I'd made it through Day One.

Only twenty-eight to go.

But who's counting?

Thoroughly exhausted, I changed into my civvies and headed for the food court for an espresso latte. (Okay, and another donut.)

I'd just paid for a chocolate-glazed beauty when I turned and saw Corky, the security guard Scotty had been taunting all day. She sat at a table by herself, a bag of fries and a can of Coke in front of her.

At that very moment, she glanced up and caught me looking at her.

I smiled feebly and waved. To which she just nodded curtly and shoved a fry in her mouth.

Somehow I got the feeling she didn't like me. Maybe she thought I was laughing at her when Scotty called her "Porky."

The last thing I wanted to do was hurt her feelings, so I walked over to her table to make amends.

"Hi," I said, with my brightest smile. "I'm

Jaine, the new elf."

"I know," she said, dunking a fry in some ketchup. "I saw you in Santa Land."

For such a hefty gal, she had a surprisingly childlike face: big baby blues, button nose, and pale blonde hair scraped back into a sparse ponytail.

"I'm so sorry about what happened today," I said. "I hope you don't think I had anything to do with Scotty's stupid comments."

"Nah," she said with a shake of her ponytail. "He's been calling me Porky ever since he started working here. What a prince, huh?"

"The worst!"

At last she broke out in a tentative smile.

"Mind if I join you?" I asked.

"Help yourself," she said, gesturing to an empty chair.

I plopped down, and without any further ado, chomped into my donut.

"Yum!" I exclaimed after my first heavenly bite.

"You should try the cheesecake donut," Corky advised. "And the chocolate with sprinkles. They're fantab."

Clearly I'd met my junk food soul mate.

We soon launched into a discussion of the best places to go for soft ice cream; Corky extolling the joys of Carvel, me mounting an impressive campaign for Dairy Queen. I was in the middle of a paean to Dairy Queen's Blizzard when I was interrupted by a loud, braying laugh.

I looked up to see Scotty walking by with Molly, looking annoyingly handsome in his street clothes, laughing his silly head off. How irritating that he was in such a good mood after all the hell he'd put me through.

"There goes Satan's Santa," I muttered. "I don't know how you've put up with him all these weeks."

"Oh, he doesn't bother me," Corky said with a shrug. "Not one bit. I'm used to fools like him."

Her angel face was calm as could be, but when I looked down at her fist, I saw she'd smashed her Coke can tighter than a trash compactor.

He bothered her, all right. More than a bit.

I'd bet my bottom Blizzard on it.

CHAPTER FOUR

All I can say is thank heavens for Barnaby.

I'll never forget the morning I met him. I'd just changed into my elf suit and was walking into the employees' locker room to lock up my purse, when I heard a deep plummy voice intone:

> She walks in beauty like the night
> Of cloudless climes and starry skies
> And all that's best of dark and bright
> Meet in her aspect and her eyes.

I looked over by the locker next to mine and saw a skinny guy in a Santa suit several sizes too big for him.

At first I thought he was making fun of me with his "she walks in beauty" crack; after all, I was a woman in striped tights and curly-toed shoes.

But no, there was a warm smile on his face as he said, "You must be the new elf Gigi told me about, the lovely Jaine. A pleasure to meet you, my dear."

With that, he took my hand and actually kissed it.

"Allow me to introduce myself. I'm Barnaby King."

"Nice to meet you," I said, wondering how this skinny little guy with a face like Mr. Magoo had actually landed a job as a Santa.

"It seems as if we're working together today," he said. "I so look forward to it. Wait for me while I finish getting ready and then we can walk out together."

I sat down on the locker bench and watched as he took a giant hunk of padding from his locker and strapped it around his waist.

"Oh, that this too too solid flesh would melt!" he said, fluffing it up with a wink.

First Lord Byron. Now Shakespeare. Obviously a former English major.

Once his tummy was in place under his Santa jacket, he reached into his locker and took out a makeup brush and began dotting his cheeks with blush. After which he donned a white bushy beard, wire-rimmed glasses, and finished off his ensemble with a Santa hat perched rakishly over his wisps of curly gray hair.

Before my very eyes, Mr. Magoo had

become St. Nick.

"Well, how do I look?" he asked, turning around for my approval.

"Like you've just come down a chimney."

"Oh, my dear. I can tell we're going to have such fun together."

And we did.

Compared to Scotty, Barnaby was heaven to work with. Of course, compared to Scotty, the Marquis de Sade would have been heaven to work with.

And the kids adored him.

His favorite shtick was to surprise them by knowing their names before they even sat on his lap.

"Well, well!" he'd cry out. "If it isn't Courtney!"

Courtney's eyes would grow wide with wonder, and Barnaby would tell her how just last night he'd seen her name on his list of Good Little Girls.

I, of course, was his accomplice in this magical feat, asking the kids their names as I led them up Candy Cane Lane, and whispering their answers in Santa's ear.

And what a fuss he made over them.

"Why, I bet you're the prettiest little girl I've seen all day!" he'd whisper confidentially, so the other girls on line wouldn't hear. "I bet you're a movie star, aren't you, sweetheart?"

Inevitably, the little girl would blush with pleasure. The plainer they were, the more they soaked up his praise.

Occasionally, this being Conspicuous Consumption Plaza, the kid actually *was* in show biz and would tell Santa about her most recent parts. Sometimes, she'd even show Barnaby her head shots.

With the tiny tots, the ones who tended to cry on Santa's lap, Barnaby was gentle, whispering a soothing, "There, there," before handing the child back to his parent.

With the older kids, Barnaby zeroed in on what they wanted — or needed — to hear.

The plain girls were all beautiful princesses.

The shy boys were all action heroes.

And the bratty ones, the ones with their Excel spread sheet gift lists, those were the ones he always asked, "And what are you *giving* for Christmas?"

The kids would inevitably sit there, blinking, for the first time considering that the world did not revolve around them.

Every once in a while, he'd break out in a Shakespearean fit of fancy. Especially if I brought him a girl whose name sounded anything like "Juliet."

"But soft!" he'd cry. "What light through

yonder window breaks? It is the east, and Juliet (or Julie or Julianne) is the sun!"

"Do you know who Juliet (Julie or Julianne) was?" he'd ask the little girl on his lap, re-writing Shakespeare a bit if need be. "A beautiful maiden who lived a long time ago, so beautiful she shone brighter than the sun! And you know what?" he'd say. "You look just like her younger sister!"

Usually little Juliet/Julie/Julianne would squirm in delight.

And the kids weren't the only ones whose egos he bolstered. He insisted I looked "cute as a button" in my elf suit, that he was sick of all the "skinny minnies" he saw on TV and the movies. "Some of these mothers," he would say, shaking his head at the designer moms in their size zero jeans, "look like they could use some intravenous Quarter Pounders."

In those moments, my neon stripe thighs didn't seem so bad, after all.

When it was slow, we chewed the fat and snacked on roasted chestnuts from a kiosk next to the Christmas tree. I told him about my life as a freelance advertising writer, and he told me about his career as an actor — starting out playing Lady Macbeth in his all-boys prep school, going on to do Shakespeare in the park in New York City, and

308

starring as Tevye in the national touring company of *Fiddler on the Roof.*

"My acting days are pretty much over," he told me during one such gabfest. "Except for some community theater and my Santa gig. And there's the Tiny Tim Project, of course."

"The Tiny Tim Project?"

He pointed to a large plastic bin right outside Santa Land.

"We collect toys for underprivileged kids. I started it a couple of years ago when I realized how many children never even get a gift on Christmas."

What a welcome change from the insufferable Scotty, whose favorite charity was, no doubt, himself.

CHAPTER FIVE

And so the days passed as I dragged myself through my shifts with Scotty, the hours flying by with Barnaby.

It was on one of those days from hell with Scotty when I was listening to a twelve-year-old explain why she needed a pair of diamond studs from Tiffany that I heard my name called out.

"Jaine Austen! Is that you?"

I turned to see a mucho attractive guy with jet black hair and a crooked smile, carrying a Godiva shopping bag.

Omigod. I'd know that smile anywhere. It was Jason Nicoletti. I'd had quite a crush on him back in high school in Hermosa Beach, when we worked together on our school newspaper, the *Hermosa Herald*.

From the first day I saw him in our editorial offices (which we shared with the janitorial supplies), my heart melted just a tad.

Much to my delight, Jason had taken a

liking to me, too. Working at adjacent desks, we shared our teenage angst and took great pleasure in making fun of the "A" listers who ruled our school with despotic glee.

The more we kidded around, the more I liked him, and the more I was convinced he liked me, too.

Then one day, he turned to me. For once looking quite serious, he said, "Jaine, there's something I need to ask you."

Omigosh! This was it. He was going to ask me out on a date.

"Go ahead!" I said, grinning like a maniac. "Ask."

He cleared his throat nervously and then quickly blurted out: "Do you think I stand a chance with Becca Washton?"

My maniacal grin froze.

Becca was a cheerleader, an insanely popular redhead, a prominent member of the Reign of Terror we always made fun of. My heart sank. Surely Jason couldn't possibly be interested in her? All along I'd assumed he was the kind of guy who looked past the superficial and saw the true beauty inside a person with slightly generous hips.

But clearly I'd been wrong.

"So?" he asked eagerly. "What do you think? Do I have a shot with Becca?"

"Sure," I managed to say. I had no idea if

Jason stood a chance with Becca, and I didn't care.

Somehow our friendship was never the same after that, and I'm ashamed to confess that I took great pleasure when Jason asked Becca to the prom and she turned him down.

And now here he was all these years later, looking more attractive than ever. The soft lines of adolescence were gone, replaced by craggy cheekbones and sharply etched laugh lines.

In spite of myself, I felt a jolt of excitement.

"Jason!" I said. "How've you been?"

"Great. Just great. I'm a creative director over at Saatchi."

Yikes. Saatchi & Saatchi was one of the world's biggest ad agencies.

"And what about you?" he asked. "What have you been up to?"

Oh, Lord. It suddenly dawned on me that I was standing there in my elf suit, my striped thighs glowing like spandex flares.

How mortifying. I couldn't possibly let him know that I'd been reduced to going on donut runs for an out of work actor.

"I'm a freelance writer," I said.

At which point, Scotty barked out, "Oh,

Elf #2! Santa needs an espresso latte. Now!"

I shot him an angry glare and turned back to Jason who was no doubt wondering why a freelance writer was hanging around Santa Land in a cheesy elf suit.

And then I thought of the most marvelous explanation. True, it was a bit of a whopper, but it was all I could think of at the time, so I went with it.

"Actually," I said, "I'm writing a piece for *L.A. Magazine* on what it's like to work as a Santa's elf."

His eyes lit up.

"You write for *L.A. Magazine*? Very impressive."

Yes! He bought it!

"Gosh, Jaine," he said. "We used to have so much fun together at the *Hermosa Herald,* didn't we?"

He shot me that crooked smile, the same smile that first melted my heart next to the janitor's mops.

"You know," he said, staring deeply into my eyes. "I've never forgotten our time together."

Was it my imagination or was he interested in me? Had he finally grown up and realized what he passed up all those years ago?

"I'm throwing a little Christmas party,"

313

he said, "and I'd love for you to stop by."

"Sounds wonderful."

Indeed it did.

"What's your number?" he asked. "I'll text you an official invite."

"My phone number?"

Oh, darn. His smile had me so rattled, it had totally slipped my mind.

"My phone number. Of course. It's right on the tip of my tongue."

When at last I finally remembered my own phone number, Jason typed it into his phone.

"Can't wait to catch up," he said, blasting me with another killer smile.

"Me, too," was my witty rejoinder.

Then he headed off to do some Christmas shopping while I proceeded to zoom straight up to Cloud Nine.

Looked like Santa had just brought me an early Christmas present.

Later that night, I was stretched out in my bathtub, up to my neck in strawberry-scented bubbles. Perched across from me on the toilet tank, Prozac was deep in sleep, her pink mouth slightly open as she snored.

We'd just spent a rather vigorous half hour running around my apartment, me chasing Prozac with my camera, trying desperately to get her to stay still for one millisecond while I got a shot of her for my holiday greeting card. I had long since given up any notion of sticking felt antlers on her head. All I wanted at this point was a plain old photo, and even that was proving impossible.

I'd taken at least twenty-five shots of her, one blurrier than the next.

"How can one cat be so aggravating?" I'd finally wailed, tossing my camera on the sofa in defeat.

She looked up at me with huge green eyes. *It's not easy, but I try.*

Soon the hot bubbly water began to work its wonders and ease away my stress. (The glass of chardonnay perched on the edge of the tub didn't hurt either.)

And my thoughts drifted back to Jason Nicoletti. I told myself not to get my hopes up, but I couldn't help it. I saw the way he'd been looking at me. He was interested. Most definitely.

Clearly he'd outgrown his shallow Becca Washton days and realized that flaming red hair and skinny hips did not a soul mate make.

I couldn't help thinking that our chance encounter at the mall might be the start of something big.

Before long I was lost in a fantasy, walking down the aisle with Jason on a beach in the Bahamas, then settling down in a Santa Monica cottage and raising a passel of adorable moppets while writing my Great American Novel. I was in the middle of telling our future grandkids how Jason and I made our love connection at Santa Land when I heard a disembodied voice float through the air.

"Hey, you've been in that tub long enough!"

No it was not the voice of my conscience, but Lance, whose X-ray hearing allows him to hear toilets flushing in Pomona.

"I need to talk to you!" he called out, banging on our paper thin walls. "On an extremely urgent matter!"

Lance's idea of an urgent matter is a BOGO sale at Old Navy, so I took this with a grain of salt. Nevertheless I dredged myself out of the tub and fifteen minutes later I was perched across from him on my living-room sofa, a bowl of pretzels between us.

"So what's this urgent matter?" I asked, helping myself to a pretzel or three.

"Russian River Pinot Noir or Singing Chihuahua?" he asked.

"What on earth are you talking about?"

"I've narrowed Greg's Secret Santa gift down to two choices. A bottle of Russian River Pinot Noir, or a mechanical Chihuahua that sings 'Feliz Navidad.' "

"A Chihuahua that sings 'Feliz Navidad'?"

"It was either that, or a moose that pooped M&M's."

Remind me never to go gift shopping with Lance.

"The Pinot Noir says I'm an urban sophisticate, suave and debonair. While the singing Chihuahua shows him my fun side, the zany, madcap me. So which one should I choose?"

He bit into a pretzel, eagerly awaiting my answer.

"I'd go with the Pinot Noir."

"But the Chihuahua is pretty darn funny. I mean, a sense of humor is very important in a relationship."

"Okay, then go with the Chihuahua."

Lance's brow furrowed in doubt.

"But then Greg might think it's silly. I'm probably better off playing it safe and going with the Pinot."

"That's what I think."

"Really?"

"Really. That's what I think."

"Then I'll stick with the Chihuahua."

"What???"

317

"C'mon, Jaine. Let's face it. You don't exactly have the greatest track record winning over the opposite sex."

"For your info," I said, whipping the bowl of pretzels from his hands, "my track record with the opposite sex is about to take a gigantic leap forward."

"Why?" he asked, perking up at the scent of some hot news. "What's up?"

I told him all about my chance encounter with Jason, how cute he looked in his jeans and blazer, carrying his Godiva shopping bag. I told him how we'd met all those years ago at the *Hermosa Herald* and how he was now a big cheese advertising man and how we locked eyeballs over Candy Cane Lane and the next thing I knew he was asking me to his Christmas party.

"Omigod!" he cried, jumping up. "That's fantastic! Just fantastic!"

How nice that he was so excited for me.

"That's what I'll get Greg! Godiva chocolates!"

"What??"

"They're sweet and sensuous at the same time. Just like me. So what do you think? Should I get him milk chocolate or dark?"

Like a fool, I said, "Dark."

"Then milk chocolate, it is."

One of these days, I've got to stop answering my door.

CHAPTER SIX

I knew I was in for trouble when I showed up at Santa Land the next day and saw Scotty sprawled out in his Santa chair, his beard in his lap, grousing to Molly.

"Those fools wouldn't know acting talent if it bit them on the fanny," he whined.

I remembered him telling me he was up for a role in a TV pilot. From the pout on his pretty boy lips, it looked like he hadn't gotten it.

"They were idiots to turn you down, honey," Molly said with a placating smile. "But I'm sure a much better part will come along soon."

"Like what?" he sneered. "The Easter bunny?" He waved his beard in disgust. "God, I hate this crummy job."

What an ingrate. He was damned lucky to have this gig. If I were Molly, I would've sent him packing on the spot.

But I was not Molly. She was actually in

love with the creep.

"I'd better get to work," she said, checking her watch. "Love you," she added, clearly waiting for him to echo her sentiment.

But all she got in reply was an abrupt, "Yeah, right."

She walked away with a worried look in her eyes, and Scotty took out his "hot chocolate" thermos for his morning slug of tequila.

Then for the first time he noticed me standing there.

"Not you again," he moaned. "Why the hell do I always get stuck working with you?"

The feeling, I can assure you, was mutual.

But not wishing to set off the powder keg I sensed was brewing under his Santa cap, I merely replied, "And a good morning to you, too."

By now the mall was open and a few kids were heading over to Santa Land.

"Better put on your beard," I told him. "And pop an Altoid. You don't want the kids passing out from the tequila fumes."

"Fooey on you."

(Technically he didn't use the word "fooey." But this is a family novel, so I'll spare you the real F-word involved.)

After another slug from his thermos, he muttered, "Bring on the brats."

Fasten your seat belts, kids, I felt like saying. *It's gonna be a bumpy sleigh ride.*

And indeed it was. The kids were on and off Scotty's lap so fast their little heads were spinning. He was in such a foul mood, he didn't even bother flirting with the cute moms.

He refused to pose for any photos, snarling, "Santa's having a bad beard day."

One of his favorite gags, when the kids would tell him what they wanted, was to say, "Sorry, we're out of that this year. Elf #2 was supposed to make them, but she's too lazy, so it ain't gonna happen."

"Santa's only kidding," I'd hasten to assure them, glaring at Scotty. "He's going to try his very best to get you your gift, aren't you, Santa?"

"Oh, all right," he'd pout.

A couple of hours of this nonsense had passed when, with a redheaded tyke perched on his knee, Scotty looked up and saw Corky walking by.

She'd already walked by several times that morning, and each time he saw her, he'd called out, "How's it going, Porky?"

Each time she'd gritted her teeth and

ignored him.

This time, however, Corky was not alone. She was walking with a fellow security officer, a young hunk with muscles the size of ham hocks. They were laughing about something, and from the way Corky was looking at her coworker, I sensed she had a bit of a crush on him.

She was punching him on the shoulder playfully when, in a booming voice, Scotty called out his familiar refrain:

"How's it going, Porky?"

Corky stopped in her tracks, her face flushed.

Then she left Mr. Ham Hocks and marched up Candy Cane Lane, fire burning in her eyes.

She gently lifted the little redhead off Corky's lap and, with bulging biceps, grabbed Scotty by the collar of his Santa suit.

Up close I could see a knotted vein throbbing in her forehead.

"You call me Porky one more time," she hissed, "and you're a dead man."

By now, her grip was so tight, Scotty was gasping for air.

"Corky!" I cried. "Cut it out! You're strangling him."

"Am I?" she sneered. "What a shame.

Next time," she practically spat in Scotty's face, "I'll finish the job."

Then reluctantly, she let go and marched off.

Scotty sat there hacking for a few seconds. Then, hands trembling, he screwed open his thermos to take a slug of tequila.

"Fat cow," he muttered when his breathing had returned to normal. "She doesn't scare me."

Like hell she hadn't.

From that point on, Scotty was a train wreck, guzzling tequila and barely talking to the tots. It got so bad that, after a while, *I* was the one the kids were telling what they wanted for Christmas.

The hours dragged by and at long last we reached the end of our shift. Outside Santa Land I saw Barnaby and Gigi waving to us in their street clothes, having come to relieve us.

"Thank goodness you guys are here!" I said, racing over to them.

"Bad day?" Barnaby asked.

"The worst. Scotty got turned down for his TV pilot and has been on a rampage ever since."

We looked over to where a gawky little girl was sitting on Scotty's lap, whispering in his ear.

"A Barbie doll?" we heard him sneer. "Better ask Santa for a nose job, sweetie. That's what you really need."

A long-limbed moppet with wide doe eyes, the little girl would probably grow up to be an Audrey Hepburn lookalike, but at this stage in her life, her nose was large for her face. With cruel accuracy, Scotty had zeroed in on her weak spot.

Her hands flew up to her face, covering her nose. Tears welled in her eyes.

Next to me, Barnaby gasped in disbelief and scooted over to the little girl, who had left Scotty's lap, sobbing.

"Honestly," I muttered to Gigi, "sometimes I feel like strangling Scotty with his own sleigh bells."

Barnaby now kneeled down to talk to the little girl.

"You're beautiful, sweetheart," he said. "And your nose is just fine. Santa didn't mean what he said. In fact, he's not really Santa. He's just an out of work actor." He turned to glare at Scotty. "And a bad one at that."

At which point, Scotty bolted out of his chair and marched over to Barnaby.

"You're calling *me* a bad actor?" he fumed. "Why, you two bit fraud. You may have everybody else fooled, but I know all about you. You never did Shakespeare in the Park. Or toured with *Fiddler on the Roof.* The closest you ever got to Broadway was the TKTs booth in Times Square. You're a joke, that's what you are. A joke!"

With a colorful expletive, not at all suitable for little ears, he kicked Rudolph in the shins and stormed off.

I turned to the crowd of astonished kids and their parents.

"Well, kids," I said. "Santa's imposter has gone to his anger management class. But if you wait just a few minutes, the real Santa will be here to talk to you."

And as I walked off with Barnaby and Gigi to the employees' locker room, I prayed that Scotty had at last gone too far, and that Molly would be forced to fire him.

CHAPTER SEVEN

Days passed, and much to my disgust, Scotty did not get fired. I don't know how many strings Molly had to pull, but somehow he kept his job.

What's worse, Molly clearly hadn't read him the riot act, because he was as obnoxious as ever. Although I couldn't help noticing that now, whenever Corky walked by, he was dead silent.

As for Barnaby, he was the same jolly Santa he'd always been. If he'd been upset by Scotty's tirade, he showed no signs of it.

It wasn't until one day after our shift when Barnaby and I were sitting on one of the mall benches, munching on roasted chestnuts, that he brought up the subject.

"Remember what Scotty said the other day?" he said, cracking open a shell. "About me being a phony?"

"I didn't believe him for a minute," I assured him.

"He was right, Jaine."

I blinked in surprise.

"He was?"

"I never did play Shakespeare in Central Park. Or Tevye in *Fiddler on the Roof.* But I've done some community theater. And I *was* Lady Macbeth in prep school," he added with a wry smile.

"Actually, I was a high school English teacher for thirty-two years before I retired. I don't know why I lied about my past. I guess I just wanted to live the dream I never had the courage to pursue. After a while, I got to believe it myself. It was fun being a professional actor. Even if it wasn't true."

He looked up at me sheepishly.

"I hope you don't think any the less of me."

"Oh, no! I totally understand."

I looked over at him and for the first time I saw sadness behind those twinkling blue eyes.

Popping a chestnut in my mouth, I hoped I'd lead the kind of life that wouldn't require a re-write.

If you happened to have walked by Casa Austen later that night, you would not have seen me sipping eggnog. Or writing out my gift list. Or belting out jolly Christmas

328

carols. No, you would have found me hiding in my hall closet, crouched among my boots, my vacuum cleaner jammed into my ribs.

My latest ploy in the Battle of the Christmas Photo.

Up until then, I'd tried everything to get Prozac to sit for a picture. I'd tried kitty treats. I'd tried squeaky toys. I'd even tried attaching feathers to my camera, hoping she'd think it was a bird.

All to no avail.

But this, my latest plan, the Candy Cane Caper, felt destined for success.

I'd cleverly placed a candy cane smeared with Minced Mackerel Guts on my living-room coffee table. Surely Prozac would not be able to resist this holiday treat.

It was just a matter of time before she came wandering in from the kitchen where I'd left her meowing for her dinner.

Her little nose would twitch at the scent of the fetid fish, and before I knew it I'd be snapping hilarious photos of Prozac licking a candy cane. Perhaps I'd even send them in to one of those photo contest web sites.

Honestly, sometimes I surprise myself with my creativity.

I sat in the closet, thinking of how cute my Christmas cards would be, and not incidentally about the moo shoo pork I'd picked up for dinner, waiting for Prozac to take the bait.

Five minutes passed. Then ten. Then fifteen. Then twenty. Where the heck was she? And why the heck wasn't she howling for her chow?

Hunched over with that damn vacuum cleaner still jammed in my ribs, every one of my muscles were now aching at full throttle.

Finally, when me and my muscles could stand it no longer, I conceded defeat. Hobbling out of the closet, I headed for the kitchen, eager to pour myself a glass of chardonnay and dig into my moo shoo pork.

You know where this is going, right?

You know what I saw the minute I stepped into the kitchen:

Prozac sprawled out on the kitchen counter, belching up the remains of my Chinese dinner.

Somehow she'd clawed open the carton, and now just a few shards of pork lay scattered around her on the counter.

She was kind enough to leave me the fortune cookie, though.

Covered with cat spit.

What a disaster that had been, I thought, rinsing mackerel guts off the candy cane before I ate it.

The next day I shared my woes with Barnaby. We were at the end of our shift, waiting for Scotty and Gigi to show up, and at the moment there were no kids on line.

"I've had it with that cat," I said. "I guess I'll just take the easy way out and send e-cards."

"Have you tried the Cat Whisperer?" Barnaby asked.

"The Cat Whisperer?"

"Yes. A fellow named Ernie DeVito. He owns a shop right here in the mall called Picture Perfect. He specializes in photos of children and animals, and I hear he works wonders with cats."

"Really?"

Suddenly I was filled with hope. Maybe this Cat Whisperer could somehow wrangle Prozac into submission. Maybe he could even get her to wear those reindeer antlers!

A designer-clad kidlet now showed up with her Conspicuous Consumption mom in tow.

As I trotted over to greet them, I heard Mom say, "Now, remember, sweetie. No biting Santa like you did last year!"

I led The Biter over to Barnaby and plopped her on his knee, hoping no rabies shots would be required. She then proceeded to give him detailed instructions about exactly what kind of pony she wanted for Christmas.

"All white. No spots. Pure bred. And not smelly."

Barnaby reminded her about the needy kids who couldn't afford ponies and got her off his lap with admirable finesse.

"Poor kid," he sighed when she'd gone. "With expectations that high, life's not going to be easy for her."

I, however, was not thinking about The Biter's future.

My mind was still on the Cat Whisperer. I was dying to hustle over and make an appointment. But Scotty and Gigi had still not shown up to relieve us.

"Where the heck are those two?" I sighed.

"You go ahead, Jaine," Barnaby said. "I can handle the kids."

"Are you sure?"

"Of course."

"Thanks, Barn. You're a doll."

Happily I trotted over to the employees' locker room to change, visions of Reindeer Prozac floating in my head.

My visions came to a screeching halt, however, when I turned the corner to my locker and saw Scotty locked in a steamy embrace.

At first I could not make out his embrace. But then I caught a whiff of Juicy Fruit gum and recognized that pert little figure.

Omigosh. It was Gigi! It looked like she really was Scotty's #1 Elf!

And all along I assumed she hated him just as much as the rest of us.

I stood there, boggled, as she clamped her lips on his.

And I was not the only one to witness this touching scene. After a second or two I realized I was not alone. I turned to see Molly standing behind me, fury oozing from every pore.

"Scotty!" she hissed, her fists clamped in tight balls at her sides.

The lovebirds flew apart, Scotty's eyes darting like a trapped rat.

"Molly, babe," he cried. "This isn't what it looks like."

"Oh? Then what is it? Mouth to mouth root canal?"

I could practically see the wheels spinning in Scotty's brain trying to tap dance his way out of this mess. But then Gigi spoke up.

"It's no use, Scotty," she said. "You've got to tell her the truth."

The truth was clearly a novel approach for a guy like Scotty, but apparently he decided to go with it.

"I didn't mean for this to happen, Molly," he said with his idea of a penitent look. "I fought it, really I did." Then, placing his arm around Gigi, he dealt the *coup de grace.* "But Gigi and I are in love."

"Well, goody for you," Molly said, dripping sarcasm.

"I suppose this means we're fired," Gigi said, her voice practically a whisper.

"No, I'll never be able to replace you this close to Christmas. You can keep your jobs. Just don't ever talk to me again. Either of you."

Gigi had the good grace to look ashamed as Molly turned on her heel and started for the door.

"Molly, babe," Scotty called after her lamely. "I'll make it up to you somehow. I promise."

She whirled around, fire burning in her eyes.

"You want to make it up to me, Scotty? Drop dead."

Whaddaya know? It looked like the mouse had claws, after all.

CHAPTER EIGHT

By the next day I'd forgotten all about the drama in the employees' locker room.

That's because I'd managed to set up an appointment with Ernie DeVito, aka The Cat Whisperer. He was squeezing me in that very morning to take Prozac's photo. Which would give me plenty of time to bring her in before reporting for work on the night shift.

"My gosh, Pro," I said as I brushed her fur to a glossy shine. "Isn't this exciting? We're going to the photographer who took the original head shots for the Taco Bell Chihuahua!"

(I'd looked up Ernie on the Internet, and his credits were quite impressive.)

Prozac, I regret to say, was not nearly as stoked as I was.

She spent the entire drive over to the mall yowling at the top of her lungs.

The humane society is going to hear about this!

"Oh, please. Do you know how many cats would kill to be photographed by the Cat Whisperer?"

But Prozac just hissed.

The only thing I'd kill for right now is a new owner.

At last we arrived at the mall and I made my way over to the Cat Whisperer's studio, Prozac yowling every inch of the way.

Help! Police! Someone report this woman to the ASPCA! — Whoa! Is that a corn dog you're eating, mister?

What can I say? She's easily distracted.

I headed into Ernie's studio and announced myself to the receptionist — a middle-aged woman with a blunt cut brown bob and an *I ♡ My Cat* pin on the lapel of her polyester suit jacket.

"Mr. DeVito!" she called out. "Ms. Austen is here."

And then the great Cat Whisperer himself came out from behind a curtain that separated the reception area from his photo studio.

I must admit I was shocked.

You'd expect a guy named Ernie DeVito to be short and stocky with more hair in his ears than on his head. You would not expect him to look like he'd just stepped out of a *GQ* fashion spread. Tall and sinewy, with patent leather slicked-back hair and smoldering bedroom eyes, Ernie was one suave signor indeed.

"Ah, Signorina Austen," he said, "what beautiful eyes you have. So big and round, like the Taco Bell Chihuahua. I took his head shots, you know."

"Yes, I know," I said, wondering if he expected a round of applause. "I read all about it."

"And who do we have here?" he said to Prozac, who had mercifully stopped wailing and had confined herself to merely shooting me dagger looks.

He took her carrier from me and set it down on the reception counter.

"Be careful," I warned him, as he started to open the latch. "She's in a terrible snit. She'll probably scratch."

"Oh, no. Not this bella principessa."

When he reached in to get her, I fully expected the fur to fly, but much to my amazement, she took one look at Ernie and began purring like a buzzsaw.

Hubba hubba, hot stuff!

"Ciao, bella!" he said, scratching the sweet spot behind her ears.

She lay nestled in his arms, much like Scarlett O'Hara on her honeymoon with Rhett, as Ernie carried her past the curtain into his studio, where a bank of cameras were set up across from a raised platform.

"Aren't you the most beautiful kitty in the world?" Ernie cooed, still scratching her sweet spot.

She gazed up at him dreamily.

That's what I've always thought.

"I can't wait to take your picture, *cara mia!*"

Ernie kept on scratching. Prozac kept on purring. It was quite a love fest. In fact, I was almost tempted to tell them to get a room, when he finally carried her over to the raised platform, on top of which was a pedestal draped with black velvet.

"Cats like to be high up," he explained, perching Prozac on the pedestal. "It makes them so much easier to work with."

Oh, yeah? Just wait till he took out his camera. Let's see how easy to work with she was then.

"Once she sees your camera," I warned him, "she's going to be impossible."

Prozac looked up at him with innocent green eyes.

Don't listen to her. I'm very easygoing. She's the impossible one.

"I don't suppose you could get her to wear these?" I whispered, showing Ernie the fuzzy reindeer antlers I'd shoved into a shopping bag.

"Of course!" he beamed. "You are looking at the man who once got Vin Diesel's pit bull to wear a tutu."

He took the antlers from the bag and headed over to Prozac.

At this point, I expected her to leap up and fly off the pedestal, but she barely moved a muscle as he put the antlers on her head and tied the straps under her chin.

Then she cocked her head at a coquettish angle.

Ready for my close up, Mr. DeVito.

I blinked in amazement. Suddenly she was Heidi Klum with retractable claws.

"Why the heck couldn't you do this for me," I muttered, "the woman who's fed you and scratched your belly for the past umpteen years?"

She shot me an impatient glare.

Move it, willya? You're blocking my view of his tush.

By now, Ernie had his camera in his hand. I feared that once Prozac saw it, all would be lost. But no. She kept on purring and posing like a pro.

It looked like Ernie really was a miracle

worker! I'd be getting the holiday photo of my dreams, after all.

And then, just as he raised the camera to take his first shot, disaster struck.

At that moment a toddler, whose name I would later find out from the news reports was Wesley Thorndal III, was being wheeled in his stroller past Ernie's studio. His nanny had just bought him a corn dog from the food court.

Now you must remember Prozac is a cat who can smell food cooking in Beirut.

At the first whiff of that corn dog, Ernie's charms were totally forgotten and Prozac was off her pedestal like a rocket, bounding out the studio at the speed of light.

Where she then proceeded, as Wesley's nanny told the Eyewitness News reporter, to nab the corn dog straight out of little Wesley's hand and sprint off down the mall.

I, of course, was in hot pursuit, chasing Prozac past startled shoppers as she sped by, reindeer antlers on her head, a corn dog in her mouth.

Before I knew it, I'd chased her all the way over to Santa Land, where Scotty and Gigi were on duty.

Prozac, the fickle hussy, took one look at the ginormous Christmas tree on display, and forgot all about Operation Corn Dog.

Because there, standing before her, were at least a hundred shiny ornaments, all of which she could destroy.

It was her fondest Christmas dream come true!

I raced over to get her before she could do any damage, but, alas, I was too late.

Just as I was about to reach out and grab her, she leaped up into the tree, flying past screaming kids and a terrified old lady in a holly berry scarf.

"Omigod!" the old woman cried out. "It's a bat. Somebody call animal control!"

"It's not a bat!" I said. "It's just a cat in reindeer antlers."

"A cat in reindeer antlers?" huffed an indignant mom. "What sort of person puts a cat in reindeer antlers? Everybody knows cats hate costumes."

Well, excuse me for trying to get into the holiday spirit with a simple little photo.

"Some people shouldn't be allowed to have pets!" sniffed PETA mom, whose own tyke at that very moment was busy kicking another kid in the shins.

I was hoping that Santa would say something to calm down the crowd, but Scotty, in his usual helpful way, just took a big snort from his thermos.

At which point, Corky came huffing on

the scene.

"What's going on here?" she asked.

"There's a bat in the Christmas tree!" the old lady screamed.

"It's not a bat!" I snapped. "It's a cat in some perfectly pet-friendly reindeer antlers."

Catching sight of my antlered darling on one of the Christmas tree branches, Corky sprang into action, lunging for Prozac, who nimbly sprinted to a higher branch. Corky lunged again, hurling her rather hefty bod against the tree.

A major mistake.

Because this time she rammed into the tree with just a little too much force.

The massive tree teetered for an agonizing second and then began to fall. We all watched in horror as, on its way down, the tree toppled the umbrella from the nearby roasted chestnut stand. Which in turn landed smack dab in the chestnut cooker. Seconds later, the umbrella was up in flames. Which, naturally, triggered the sprinkler system.

Bedlam ensued as water gushed from the ceiling.

I rushed over to the felled Christmas tree, my heart pounding, afraid Prozac might have been injured in the fall.

But no, there she was, keeping dry under the shelter of some branches, happily batting around a glass ornament like a hockey puck.

The minute I realized she wasn't hurt, a wave of anger came washing over me.

"Bad kitty!" I tsked, sweeping her up in my arms. "Look what you've done."

I gestured to the chaos around us.

She preened with pride.

I know. Isn't it great?

By now the sprinklers had shut off and when I looked over at the crowd, I saw that Molly had shown up.

Which meant it was time for me to make tracks.

Lest you forget, I desperately wanted that copywriting gig, and the last thing I needed was for Molly to find out my cat was at the epicenter of this little fiasco.

No, I'd quickly slink away and avoid any possible collateral damage.

And so I was tiptoeing out of Santa Land when I happened to pass Scotty's chair.

How odd. He was just sitting there like a lump, his thermos in his lap.

Was he so drunk that he slept through this whole disaster?

"Wake up, Scotty!" I hissed.

But he didn't move a muscle.

I went over to shake him awake, and that's when I saw it — the sharp metal snowflake ornament plunged in his heart.

For once, Scotty wasn't dead drunk on the job.

This time, he was just dead.

CHAPTER NINE

So much for keeping a low profile.

Before I knew it, the cops had shown up on the scene, and I soon found myself sitting in the mall's security office, shivering in my wet clothes, Prozac snoozing peacefully on my lap. Across from me sat a freckle-faced young cop who looked less like an officer of the law than a boy scout on steroids.

"So you're the one who first discovered the body," he said.

"Right," I replied, staring at a rebel cowlick popping up from his copper colored hair. First the freckles. Now the cowlick. Good heavens. I was being questioned by Huck Finn.

"Notice anyone else near the deceased before you walked over?" Huck asked.

"No, nobody."

"Can you think of anyone who wanted to kill him?"

Could I think of anyone who *didn't* want to kill him, would be more like it.

But I wasn't about to get an innocent person in trouble. Surely, the Conspicuous Consumption security department would have the whole crime captured on their security cameras.

"Nobody liked Scotty," I said, "but I wouldn't go so far as to accuse someone of murder."

"What about you?" asked my freckle-faced inquisitor. "How would you describe your relationship with the deceased? Were you on friendly terms?"

"Not exactly," I confessed.

Now Huck started rifling through a small pad, brows knit in concentration.

"According to your co-worker, a Ms. Gigi Harris," he said, reading from his notes, "you were quoted as saying, in reference to the deceased, *I'd like to strangle him with his own sleigh bells.*"

Oh, for crying out loud.

That's what I'd told Gigi the day of Scotty's meltdown.

I couldn't believe she actually felt the need to share that little tidbit with the authorities.

I was sorely tempted to rat on her in return, but unfortunately, she was the only one I could think of at the moment who actually seemed to like Scotty. Loved him, in fact.

"It's true I said I wanted to strangle Scotty, but I didn't really mean it. It was a figure of speech. And besides, Scotty was killed with a Christmas ornament. Not sleigh bells."

"Uh huh." Huck nodded dubiously, making a note on his pad.

"On another matter," he said, "is it true that your cat is responsible for the mess over in Santa Land?"

At the sound of her name, Prozac's eyes fluttered open.

"Well, yes," I confessed. "I should have never taken her in to get her photo taken. It's just that I thought she'd look so cute in those reindeer antlers —"

"You put antlers on your cat? Don't you know cats hate wearing costumes?"

Prozac shot him her patented Little Orphan Annie look.

You can't imagine how I suffer.

"What a little sweetheart," he said, reaching over to scratch her under the chin.

My God, was there no one on this planet who could see her for the demon feline she was?

"You can go now," Huck said. "But from

now on, take care of your cat."

Prozac wiggled happily in my arms.

That's telling her, officer!

"And one more thing," he added as I got up to go. "Don't leave town."

Don't leave town??

Oh, hell. Isn't that what they tell murder suspects?

Prozac was an absolute angel that night — rubbing herself against my ankles and gazing at me goo-goo eyed. Stuff she normally saves for strangers.

She knew she'd been a bad cat and was desperately trying to ease her way back into my good graces.

Usually all it takes is the touch of her soft fur against my shins for my heart to melt. But not that night.

I was steamed. I mean, here I was — a murder suspect. All because of Prozac.

Whoever killed Scotty clearly had taken advantage of the fiasco in Santa Land to plunge that snowflake in Scotty's heart. A fiasco that never would have happened in the first place had it not been for the antics of my mischievous feline.

"Honestly, Pro," I muttered as I climbed into bed. "Sometimes I wonder why I ever adopted you."

She hopped in bed right after me, eyes wide as saucers.

Hey, I know what'll make you feel better. Rubbing my belly for the next half-hour or so.

She rolled spread-eagled on her back, waiting for the rubbing to begin. But she waited in vain. Ignoring her belly, I reached for the remote and turned on *House Hunters*.

Finally she got the hint and shot me a dirty look.

Well, if that's the way you're going to be —

With that, she leaped down from the bed and stalked off to the living room.

Usually in these little tiffs of ours, I'm the first to crack, jumping out of bed and running after her, begging her forgiveness with ear scratches and kitty treats.

But not that night. That night I was just too darn mad.

I watched TV for a while, then after the 3,768th couple in the history of *House Hunters* had chosen a three-bedroom, two-bath house with an open floor plan, granite countertops and stainless steel appliances, I turned out the light.

Without Prozac cuddled next to me, it was hard to fall asleep, but I'd be damned if I went running after her.

I'd finally managed to drift off when out

of nowhere I felt someone shaking my arm.

My heart began beating like a bongo.

Someone had broken into my apartment!

"Lance?" I called out, hoping it was him and that he'd used the key he knows I keep under my flower pot.

"No, it's not Lance," a woman's voice replied.

Suddenly the light snapped on and I saw the old lady in the holly berry scarf from the mall. The one who thought Prozac was a bat. There she was, standing at the foot of my bed. Wearing the same velour jog suit she'd worn that afternoon.

"Who are you?" I asked. "And how did you get into my apartment?"

"I," she said with a toss of her scarf, "am your fairy godmother."

"What?" I blinked in disbelief.

"But you can call me Hazel."

"My fairy godmother??"

"Hey, some of us wear jog suits and bunion pads. Live with it."

Yikes. Somehow this nutcase had followed me home and broken into my apartment. I tried to reach over to call 9-1-1, but my hand felt like lead. I simply couldn't get it to move.

"You said you wondered why you ever adopted your darling kitty," Hazel was saying. "Well, now you're about to find out what your life would be like without her." She snapped her fingers. "Voilà! You are now a cat-free woman."

Honestly, the old gal was certifiable.

"Let's go see what life is like without Prozac, shall we?"

With that, she took me by the hand, and led me to my living room.

I looked around and, indeed, Prozac was nowhere to be found. Not snoring on the sofa. Not curled up next to P.G. Wodehouse on the bookshelf. Not trolling for leftovers in the kitchen.

"Where is she?" I whirled around to Hazel. "What have you done with her?"

"I haven't done anything with her. You never adopted her, remember? And I'm sad to say, it hasn't seemed to work out very well. See for yourself."

She pointed over to the sofa.

Holy cow. I almost fainted when I saw myself, sitting on my couch, staring dully into space.

"Life's pretty lonely for you now," Hazel said, "with only your philodendron for company."

She pointed to a wilted philodendron on my bookshelf.

"You call it 'Phil' and pet its leaves, but

it's not the same. It's not Prozac. You're so lonely, you've even started naming your socks."

I looked over at Lonely Me on the couch. And damned if she wasn't right. I was talking to my own socks!

"Hi, Jack! Hi, Jill!" I heard myself saying. "How's it going?"

Oh, Lord. This was beyond pathetic.

"Let's get out of here!" I wailed. "I need to see Lance."

I ran out of the apartment, Hazel puffing to keep up with me, and banged on Lance's door.

Seconds later, he opened it, a puzzled look on his face.

"Yes? Can I help you?"

"Lance. It's me. Jaine!"

But he just stared at me blankly.

"Don't you see?" Hazel crooned in my ear. "You never made friends with Lance, because Prozac wasn't here to dig up his geraniums. So he never came knocking on your front door to complain. And you never invited him in to make amends over margaritas."

"Lance and me — not friends?"

At which point he slammed the door in my face.

"Apparently not," Hazel said. "C'mon,

I've got some other things to show you."

Suddenly I found myself on the sidewalk outside my local dry cleaners.

"What're we doing in front of Jiffy Clean?" I asked.

"Look closely," Hazel said.

"Omigosh. The windows are all boarded up."

"A shame, isn't it?" Hazel tsked. "They went out of business because you weren't there to bring all the clothes Prozac threw up on."

"But Mr. Jiffy was such a nice man!"

"Oh, well," Hazel said with a bright smile. "What does it matter? At least you're saving on dry cleaning bills. Now c'mon. Let's go shopping."

And with a snap of her fingers, we were in my local supermarket.

"What are we doing here?"

"Just follow me," Hazel said, leading me to the cat food aisle.

"Look," she said, pointing to the rows and rows of cat food. "Notice anything missing?"

"Omigosh! There's no Fancy Feast."

"They went belly up years ago, what with Prozac not around to eat their inventory."

"Poor Fancy Feast!" I moaned. "Poor Mr. Jiffy! Poor Prozac!" I burst into tears. "To think, she was never even born!"

"I didn't say that," Hazel said, wagging a finger in my face. "I just said you never adopted her."

"You mean, Prozac's alive somewhere?"

"Indeed she is."

"Can I see her?"

"Are you sure you want to? You might not like what you see."

Oh, God, what if my poor little angel was being mistreated somewhere? I'd find some way to bring her back to safety!

"No, no! I must see her. Take me to her right now."

"Okay, if you say so."

Another snap of her fingers, and we were walking up the path to an enormous Spanish hacienda styled estate.

"Where are we?"

"Bel Air, California. Birthplace of the one percent."

Suddenly we were in what I can only describe as a designer showcase bedroom, replete with pink satin linens, priceless antique side tables, and Persian rugs on gleaming hardwood floors.

And there, perched on a pink silk chaise longue, was Prozac, noshing on a Limoges plate of bacon bits and caviar.

"Prozac!" I cried out.

But she didn't even look up.

"She can't hear you," Hazel reminded me.

"Her new owner must be awfully rich," I said, "to have such a fabulous bedroom."

"Actually, this is Prozac's room."

"She has this room all to herself?"

"And a personal maid, too." Hazel nodded.

Just then, an impossibly tall blonde with a flawless complexion and figure to match, came drifting into the room on a cloud of designer perfume.

"Tinkerbelle, sweetie!" she cooed. "How's mommy's little angel?"

"Tinkerbelle?" I cried. "She doesn't have a silly name like Tinkerbelle! She has a perfectly sensible name — Prozac!"

But once again, I was not heard, as the blonde joined Prozac on the chaise longue and scooped her up in her arms.

"Was the caviar fresh enough for you, sweetums?"

Prozac let out a satisfied belch in reply.

"Are you happy, darling?"

Prozac looked up at her with loving eyes.

Am I ever! Thank God I'm living here with you and not in some crummy duplex with a part time Santa's elf!

"Prozac," I cried, "you can't mean that! Think of all the fun times we had together!

Think of the furniture you clawed, the pantyhose you ruined. Think of the back scratches, the belly rubs, the hairballs in my slippers!"

But Prozac just went on purring in her new owner's arms.

"Oh, Prozac!" I wailed. "Prozac! Prozac!"

Suddenly I was choked with tears, so choked I could hardly breathe.

And that's when I woke up from what had to be my worst dream ever and realized Prozac's tail was draped across my nose.

Gently I removed it, and swept my precious kitty in my arms.

"Oh, Pro, honey. I didn't mean what I said. Adopting you was the happiest day of my life!"

Prozac looked up at me with enormous green eyes that could mean only one thing:

Yeah, right. Whatever. So when do we eat?

Then she tucked her furry little head under my chin and began to purr. And I knew then that all was right with the world.

Except for that pesky little murder, of course.

CHAPTER TEN

It took them two days to restore Santa Land to its former glory, and when it was up and running again, Barnaby had taken over Scotty's shift, working from nine in the morning till nine at night. Which he didn't seem to mind at all.

"What can I say?" Barnaby confided to me between ho-ho-ho's. "I love performing, even if half my audience is still teething."

Needless to say, Scotty's absence wasn't missed a bit, and Barnaby reigned happily over a tension-free, tequila-free Santa Land.

In the bad news department, however, it turned out that, due to faulty wiring in Conspicuous Consumption's electrical system, the security cameras were short-circuited by the sprinklers when Scotty was killed.

Which meant there were no surveillance tapes of the murder. Or the murderer.

Zippo. Nada. Nothing.

Which meant I was still a suspect, still unable to leave town.

As much as my parents drive me crazy at times, I was not about to pass up my annual visit to see them in Florida for a week of coddling, cuddling, and fudge on tap 24/7.

And who knew how long it would take the cops to wrap up the case? So I made up my mind to stick around and give them a hand. They didn't know it (and you might not, either), but I happened to have solved quite a few murders in my day, action packed tales of adventure and Chunky Monkey binges listed at the front of this book.

And so the morning after the murder, I was ensconced on my living-room sofa, chomping on a cinnamon raisin bagel, going over my list of suspects.

There was Molly, Scotty's scorned lover. And Corky, who'd threatened to kill Scotty if he called her "Porky" one more time. There was also Gigi, Scotty's secret squeeze, but for the life of me, I couldn't see why she'd want to knock him off. (Unless she'd caught him cheating on her with some other elfin cutie.)

Finally, as much as I hated to consider it, there was Barnaby. After all, Scotty had exposed him as a fraud in front of a whole crowd of Christmas shoppers. Barnaby had laughed it off, but maybe he was more upset than he'd let on.

You can imagine how distressed I was my first day back at work when I saw him talking with Detective Huck Finn.

My heart sunk. What if Barnaby was about to be arrested?

Sidling up to where they were chatting in the employees' locker room, I heard Huck tell Barnaby, "You'll be happy to hear we checked out the movie theater, and several witnesses confirmed seeing you there the morning of the murder."

Yay! Barnaby had been at the movies at the time of the murder!

"Looks like you're in the clear," Huck said.

"But you're not," he said to me as he walked by. "So don't leave town."

It was all I could do not to yank on his cowlick.

With Barnaby safely off my Suspect List, I turned to my two top contenders:

Corky and Molly.

I decided to start my investigation with Scotty's spurned lover. I remembered how Molly told Scotty to drop dead in the employees' locker room.

Now I wondered if she'd turned her suggestion into a reality.

Before I could think of an excuse to stop by her office, I was summoned to see her on my lunch break.

"It has come to my attention," she said, looking up from a stack of papers on her desk, "that it was your cat who was responsible for the disaster at Santa Land the other day."

"Yes, I'm so sorry. I should have never brought her to the mall to have her picture taken."

"It wasn't easy," she said, "but I talked Mr. Halavi out of suing you."

"Mr. Halavi?"

"The man who owns the roasted chestnut concession. Thank heavens his insurance paid for a new umbrella. But I'd steer clear of roasted chestnuts for a while if I were you."

"Absolutely!" I assured her. "And I just want you to know that this little incident does not at all reflect my work ethic. If you hire me as a copywriter, I can guarantee you it will never happen again."

"I should hope not. Just be sure to leave your cat home on Bring Your Pet to Work Day," she added with a wink.

It suddenly occurred to me that she was

awfully chipper for someone who'd just had an employee stabbed on her watch.

In fact, never had I seen her hair quite so shiny or her skin so radiant.

Death (Scotty's, that is) certainly seemed to have agreed with her.

At which point, I remembered my mission and switched to part-time semi-professional P.I. mode.

"I still can't believe what happened to Scotty," I said, shaking my head.

"I can believe it," she replied, steely-eyed. "The way he lived his life, he was just asking for trouble."

Then she sat back in her chair with a sigh.

"I won't pretend I'm heartbroken that he's gone. You saw for yourself how he was cheating on me. I suppose deep down I knew all along he was using me, but I was too much of a wuss to face the truth.

"I wasted way too much of my life on that bum," she said, shaking her head ruefully. "I should've stuck with my old boyfriend. I didn't know a good thing when I had it."

Then she sat up straight again, back in bizgal mode.

"Well, if you'll excuse me, I've got work to do. Insurance reports to file for the damage in Santa Land."

I cringed at the thought of all the havoc

Prozac had caused.

"Thanks again for everything," I said.

She nodded and reached for her phone. As she did, I noticed something very interesting. There on her arm were a bunch of scabbed-over scratches.

She must have seen me staring because she quickly piped up:

"You're not the only one with a cat. I've got a mighty frisky feline of my own. Got these the other night," she said, pointing to the scratches, "giving her a bath."

Maybe, I thought, as I headed out the door.

Or maybe she got them from Scotty, trying to defend himself as she stabbed him to death.

CHAPTER ELEVEN

After my tête-à-tête with Molly, I made a beeline for the food court for a quick corn dog. And, if you must know, a side of fries. (Okay, two sides. A gal can build up quite an appetite working as an undercover detective elf.)

I was just chowing down on my last fry, when I glanced up and saw Corky, strolling side by side with the muscle-bound co-worker I'd seen her with the day she blew up at Scotty.

Now her ruddy face was flushed with pleasure, her sparse ponytail bobbing merrily behind her. I watched as she gazed into Mr. Muscle's eyes with the kind of gooey-eyed adoration normally found in puppy dogs and Viagra commercials.

She was in love, all right.

I couldn't help thinking that with Scotty and his nasty comments out of the way, her romance could proceed unimpeded.

Indeed, she and Mr. Muscle looked quite chummy strolling along, Mr. Muscle's hand just millimeters from Corky's ample tush. Finally, he gave her a pat on said tush and stepped on the escalator, bidding her a fond adieu.

Which was my cue to leap into action.

"Hey, Corky," I cried, scurrying to her side. "I wanted to thank you for trying to rescue my cat the other day."

"No problem," she replied. "That's some little monster you got there."

Hey! I'm the only one who's allowed to call my little monster a monster. But somehow I managed to rein in my annoyance.

"So how's it going?" I asked.

"Pretty good," she replied. "Except for the damn shoplifters. They're out in droves at Christmas. Figure they can get away with it, with the stores so crowded. Gotta watch for the ones with the big totes," she said, eyeing a tiny brunette with an enormous purse.

"Just yesterday I caught some gal with a KitchenAid mixer in her bag. Said it must've fallen in when she wasn't looking. She actually expected me to believe her. And here's the crazy thing. Turns out she was married to some gazillionaire movie director out in Malibu. Can you beat that? She could've bought seventeen of those mixers without batting an eye.

"The worst offenders," she said with a knowing wink, "are always the rich ones."

"Speaking of crime," I said, in an effort to wrench the conversation away from mall theft, "I still can't get over Scotty getting killed the way he did."

At the mention of Scotty's name, Corky's spine stiffened.

"Couldn't have happened to a more deserving guy."

Spoken like a woman who might have done the job herself.

Once again I remembered her threat to Scotty:

Call me "Porky" one more time, and you're a dead man!

Had Scotty called her "Porky" one more time? And had Corky made good on her threat?

"Don't get me wrong," she said, as if reading my thoughts. "I didn't kill him. I sure as heck wanted to. But I'm no murderer."

"I don't suppose you have any idea who did it?" I asked.

"Not a clue."

"Did you notice anyone near him after the sprinklers went off?"

"Just you."

Gee, thanks for the vote of confidence.

"Sure you didn't see anybody else?"

"Say, what's with all these questions, anyway? You some sort of reporter?"

"Actually, I'm a private eye."

"You? A private eye?"

She blinked in amazement. Can't say I blamed her. Standing there in my pointy elf shoes and striped tights, I was not exactly the image of a hard boiled dick.

"I work part-time, semi-professional," I explained.

"Wow." She gazed at me with new-found respect. "I've always wanted to be a detective. I tried to join the L.A.P.D. But they turned me down because of the time I spent in juvie."

"You were in juvie?"

Now it was my turn to be shocked. Corky, our genial security guard, had once done time in a kiddie correctional institution!

"Yeah, I had some anger issues when I was growing up. I've always been on the chubby side. Got bullied a lot in school. One day some kid went too far, and I beat the stuffing out of him. Just my rotten luck I busted a couple of his ribs. Spent six months in juvie. They sent me to a shrink to help me get a handle on things.

"But that's all behind me now," she added with a toss of her ponytail.

I wasn't so sure about that. For all I knew, history had just repeated itself in Santa Land.

By now, we'd reached the employees' locker room, and I followed Corky as she headed for her locker.

"I'm just grateful Molly gave me a break," she was saying, "and hired me here at Conspicuous Consumption. It's not easy getting a job when you've got a record."

She opened her locker, revealing a monumental stash of M&M's on her top shelf, as well as a locker door plastered with photos.

There was a picture of Arnold Schwarzenegger in his Pumping Iron days. Another of Bruce Lee. And another of Corky, decked out in a kimono, assuming a karate pose.

Clearly the woman had a thing for brute force.

"So you know karate?" I said.

"You bet." She nodded.

No doubt about it. Corky certainly had the strength to have rammed that snowflake in Scotty's heart.

"I graduated second in my class at the Kung Pow Academy of Martial Arts," she said, pointing to another picture, a group shot of about a dozen men and women, all in karate garb. Sure enough, Corky was in the back row, grinning with pride.

And then I noticed someone standing in the row in front of her. A thin wiry woman with mousy brown hair.

"Wait a minute," I said, squinting at the photo. "Is that Molly?"

"Sure is. She's the one who graduated first in the class. You should see that woman chop her way through a cinder block."

Holy Moses. First those scratches on Molly's arms. Now this.

Just a few seconds ago, I was convinced Corky was my Number One Suspect.

But now, thanks to the Kung Pow Academy of Martial Arts, it looked like Molly was back in the running.

Later that night I was at my dining room table, writing out my Prozac-free Christmas cards. Alongside me on the table was a mug of hot chocolate and a plate of Oreos. Well, technically there was no plate. I was munching on them straight from the bag. Things tend to be a tad informal here at Casa Austen.

Somehow I'd managed to nibble my way through a frightening number of the chocolate beauties, and I now decided to save the last one as a reward for when I finished my cards.

I spent the next twenty minutes diligently

sending XOXO's to friends and relatives and was just putting the stamp on my last card, when I heard Lance's familiar knock on my front door.

"I've been meaning to stop by for days," he said, breezing in, "but it's been crazy busy at work — Mmm, an Oreo!"

Without so much as a "Do you mind?" he scooped up my Reward Oreo and shoved it in his mouth.

"Hey! I was going to eat that!"

"You'll thank me in the morning, hon. I've just saved you scads of unsightly calories which would've gone straight to your thighs. Whereas I, on the other hand, will zap them away at the gym before they even know what hit them."

He did not lie. The man spends so much time at his gym, they've practically named a StairMaster in his honor.

"So," he said, plopping down next to Prozac on the sofa. "I heard some nutty cat set fire to your mall —"

Prozac sat up and preened.

That would be moi.

"— and that one of the Santas got killed."

"I know," I sighed. "I was there when it happened."

"Omigosh!" His eyes lit up with excitement. "Tell all! Don't leave out a single detail!"

I told him. How Prozac stole the corn dog and jumped on the Christmas tree. How Corky knocked the tree over onto the roasted chestnut stand. How the umbrella caught fire and set off the sprinklers. And how someone had taken advantage of the pandemonium to kill Scotty with a Christmas tree ornament.

"Wow," Lance said when I was through. "A Christmas tree ornament, huh? I thought about getting one of those for Greg for his Secret Santa gift."

"Forget about the damn Secret Santa gift, Lance! The point is, a murder has been committed, and the cops won't let me leave town till the case is solved. Technically I'm one of the suspects."

"Oh, sweetie," he said, "I'm sure they'll find the killer. If worse comes to worst you can always spend Christmas with me and my family and watch my uncle Delmar fall head first into the candied yams after his fifth martini. That's always good for a chuckle."

"Sounds delightful," I replied with a wan smile.

"Try not to worry, hon," he said, taking my hand. "Everything's going to be okay.

Just promise me you won't go chasing after the killer yourself. Really. That stuff is dangerous."

"Yes, but —"

"But nothing! I know how you get the minute you sniff a corpse. You're like a bloodhound in elastic-waist pants. For once, promise me you'll leave everything to the police."

"I promise," I lied.

"That's my girl," he said, wrapping me in a hug. "And remember. You've always got my dysfunctional family to come home to at Christmas."

Lance may be a royal pain at times, but when I'm in a fix, he's always there for me with a hug.

"By the way, honey," he said, "I've got a weeny favor to ask."

I should've known there was a catch to that hug.

"Neiman's having a crisis down at their Newport Beach store. A couple of their top shoe salesmen got food poisoning at a Christmas party. I need to go down there to pitch in for the next few days. So would you mind taking in my mail while I'm gone?"

"Is that all? No problem."

"One more thing. I need you to watch over Greg's Secret Santa gift."

"You need me to watch over a box of Godiva chocolates?"

If you remember, class, when last we left Lance, that's what he'd decided to buy.

"Oh, no," he said, with a dismissive wave of his hand. "I didn't get chocolates. That's so passé. I thought of a much better idea. Wait! I'll go get it."

He zipped out the door and minutes later returned with a canvas-covered dome.

"What on earth is that?" I asked.

"The perfect Christmas gift!"

He whipped off the cover and revealed an ornate wrought iron bird cage. In the center of which was a bright green and orange parrot.

Prozac looked up eagerly from the sofa.

Oh, goody! Dinner!

I blinked in amazement. "You're giving a parrot as your Secret Santa gift?"

"Not just any parrot. A Christmas parrot! Look. His wings are red and green!"

"They're orange and green."

"Close enough. Anyhow, his name is Bogie. I bought him on Craigslist for only thirty bucks! His owner says he talks, but so far he hasn't said a thing."

"I can't keep a bird here, Lance. Not with Prozac."

"Don't be silly. The bird's in a cage. What

harm can Prozac possibly do?"

Prozac's nose twitched with anticipatory glee.

Don't worry. I'll think of something!

"Just cover the cage at night so Bogie can sleep."

Then he dashed outside, only to come back seconds later with a bag of bird seed and a stand for the cage.

"Thanks, Jaine, sweetie! You're an angel."

"But, Lance —"

Before I could get in another word, he was off and running.

Gritting my teeth at the prospect of guarding Bogie the Parrot for the next few days, I put the birdcage the one place I knew Prozac was least likely to go — inside the bathtub. She has not ventured inside that tub since the one and only time I tried to give her a bath — a harrowing experience featuring much hissing, scratching, and decibel shattering wails.

(And Prozac wasn't too crazy about it, either.)

Bogie fluttered his wings a bit, then gazed at me with bright beady eyes.

"If you want anything," I said, striking a pose against the doorjamb, "just whistle. You know how to whistle, don't you, Bogie? Just put your upper and lower mandibles together, and blow."

Then, after that very poor Lauren Bacall impersonation, I returned to the living room where Prozac was staring dreamily off into space.

I knew just what she was dreaming about.

"You leave that bird alone," I warned her. "For your information, parrots happen to be one of nature's most treasured creatures."

She looked up at me with sly green eyes.

Especially with ketchup.

Chapter Twelve

Gigi was subdued in the days following Scotty's death. Gone was the spring in her step and the sparkle in her eye. She led her charges up to Santa's chair with all the *joie de vivre* of a condemned man tootling off to the electric chair.

Rumor had it she was seeing a shrink.

I tried to question her about Scotty's murder, hoping she could provide me with a valuable clue. After all, she was on duty with him when he was killed. But every time I tried to talk to her, she seemed to be in a hurry somewhere — to her acting class, to her gym, to her aromatherapist . . .

If I didn't know better I'd say she was avoiding me.

Well, she wasn't going to lose me that easily.

With a quick trip to Molly's office, and a fib about wanting to send Gigi a Christmas card, I was able to obtain her address.

I planned to pay her a visit in person. Nothing like a face-to-face chat to wring the truth out of a witness.

I waited till the following Saturday when the weekend Santa Land crew had taken over and neither of us was working. Then I called her to make sure she was home, using a pay phone at the public library so she wouldn't see my name on her caller ID.

She answered the phone with a weary "hello," and I immediately hung up and dashed to my car — eager to zip over to her apartment for our long-delayed chat.

Gigi Harris lived in Westwood, in one of the many courtyard buildings that dot the neighborhood around UCLA. I walked up the front path to a security gate, and peering inside, saw a tiny pool, surrounded by rusty lounge chairs. An abandoned volleyball bobbed forlornly in the turquoise water.

Unwilling to ring Gigi's buzzer and risk having her blow me off, I waited at the gate, examining the names on the intercom, until at last one of the tenants came out, a lanky guy toting a backpack and wheeling his bike. After he pushed the gate open, I held it out for him, and then scooted inside.

Safe in the courtyard, I trotted over to Gigi's apartment and knocked on her door.

"Who is it?" she called out.

"It's me. Jaine Austen, from work."

I heard footsteps shuffling and then the door opened a crack.

Gigi peered out at me with glazed eyes, her uncombed hair sticking out in messy spikes. Yet somehow she still managed to look cute.

Life's sure not fair, is it? When my hair sticks out in messy spikes, I look like Medusa on uppers.

"How did you get past the security gate?" she asked.

"It was open," I fibbed.

"Well?" she said, making no move to let me in. "How can I help you?"

"Look, I know you're unhappy about what happened to Scotty, but I really need to talk to you. Can I come in for just a minute?"

"Oh, all right," she sighed.

She opened the door, and I almost gasped when I saw that she was standing there in a long, white wedding dress, nipped in at the waist, with acres of tulle cascading from her slim hips.

"Scotty bought this for me," she said, doing a halfhearted pirouette. "Today was supposed to be our wedding day."

I followed as she led me to her tiny living room, furnished in Early Starving Actor —

377

rump-sprung sofa flanked by worn director's chairs, steamer trunk coffee table, and cinderblock book cases. Up on the wall above her sofa, Gigi had sandwiched a framed glamor shot of herself in between posters of James Dean and Marilyn Monroe.

At least she was aiming high.

She picked up a bottle of opened champagne from the coffee table.

"Want some?" she asked, holding it out to me.

Not at 10:30 in the morning, I didn't.

"No, thanks. I'll pass."

"All the more for me," she said, slumping down onto her sofa and taking a big slug.

"Sit." She gestured for me to take a seat in one of the director's chairs.

"Round about now," she said, checking her watch, "I was supposed to be picking up Scotty. We were going to drive to Vegas and get married in one of those corny Elvis chapels. The best laid plans, huh?"

Another slug of champagne.

I looked over and saw that about half of the bottle was gone. Gigi was well on her way to being snockered. I needed to hurry and get in some questions while she was still lucid.

"I'm so sorry about what happened to

Scotty," I tsked. "Such a tragedy."

Of course what I really wanted to tell her was that she was better off without him, that he was a sleazebag of the highest order, and that he'd only have made her life miserable in the end.

But of course I said none of this.

Instead I just murmured, "I know how unhappy you must be. And I'm sure, more than anyone, you'd like to see the killer brought to justice."

She nodded in agreement, picking at the foil on the neck of the champagne bottle.

"So I was wondering if I could ask you a few questions about the murder."

"Go ahead. Shoot. Corky tells me you're some kind of detective."

"Part-time, semi-professional."

"Who woulda thunk it?" she said, shaking her head in disbelief.

I get that a lot. For some strange reason, most people tend to underestimate the investigative skills of a woman in elastic-waist pants and a *Cuckoo for Cocoa Puffs* T-shirt.

"Like I told the police," Gigi said, "I didn't see a thing that day. I was too busy trying to calm down the kids, what with the Christmas tree falling and the sprinklers going off."

"Are you sure you didn't see anybody approach Scotty at the time he was killed?"

"I'm pretty sure," she said, a note of doubt creeping into her voice.

"Think back to the scene. Try to remember anyone, anyone at all, going near Scotty's chair."

"Okay."

She leaned back against the sofa, closing her eyes to concentrate. I waited for her to speak, but she said nothing. At first, I thought she was lost in thought. Until I heard her start to snore.

Oh, hell! She'd passed out.

A fat lot of good this interview was getting me. I got to question her for a whole thirty-two seconds.

I was just about to get up and leave when I glanced down and saw the spine of a book peeking out from under one of Gigi's sofa cushions — as if it had been shoved there hastily before she'd answered the door.

I reached over and began to slowly ease it out.

At one point my heart lurched as I saw her eyelids flutter. But thankfully she kept on snoring.

At last I'd pulled the book free, and I now saw that it was a high school yearbook.

I flipped the pages until I came to the H's,

looking for Gigi's picture.

I blinked in disbelief when I found it. There she was, listed as Virginia Harris, a chubby girl with clunky dark-rimmed glasses. A far cry from the elfin Gigi of Santa Land. But there was no doubt about it. Underneath all those extra pounds, that chubby girl scowling out at the camera was indeed Gigi.

Talk about your amazing transformations.

I continued to flip the pages until I saw something that made me stop dead in my tracks. There under the class officers, voted "Most Handsome" was a picture of Scotty. A younger version of the same handsome, cocksure Scotty who had driven everybody crazy in Santa Land.

So he and Gigi had gone to high school together.

Had they known each other? Had they been friends?

I sincerely doubted it. First, because Scotty didn't strike me as the kind of guy who would have been friends with a chubby, unattractive girl in high school.

And mainly because Gigi had slashed a big X across his photo.

What's more, she'd crossed out the word "Handsome" from his "Most Handsome" caption, and written "Loathsome" in its place.

Clearly Gigi had hated Scotty's guts back then.

Had she held on to that hate all these years and taken it out on him with a Christmas tree ornament?

But that was impossible.

After all, she was going to marry the guy. Wasn't she?

Suddenly from the depths of my reverie I heard a snort. I looked up and saw that Gigi was awake and staring at her yearbook clenched in my hands.

"I see you found my yearbook," she said. "A treasured memento of my golden high school years."

Her voice fairly dripped with sarcasm.

"I suppose you're wondering why I defaced Scotty's photo."

"Sort of."

"Would you believe I hated him back in high school but fell madly in love with him when we met again in Santa Land?"

"No, frankly, I wouldn't."

"Good for you. Go straight to the head of the class." She stopped to take another swig of champagne. "You want the truth, Jaine? I hated Scotty then. I hate Scotty now. I'll always hate Scotty."

"Then why on earth were you going to marry him?"

"Oh, but I wasn't. I was going to do to him what he did to me back in high school. Back then, I was a fat pimply senior and he was a golden boy on the track team. I didn't think he even knew I was alive. But then one day when I was sitting in the cafeteria — alone, of course — he came and sat next to me. He told me that he'd seen me in a couple of classes and thought I had really pretty eyes. Then he said he'd just broken up with his girlfriend and was wondering if I'd like to go to the senior prom with him. I was foolish enough to think he actually meant it. I didn't know it was just a joke, a crazy prank he'd thought up with his stupid buddies.

"I ran out and spent every penny in my savings account on a prom dress. My parents were so excited for me; at last their unpopular daughter had a boyfriend! They couldn't wait to meet him. He said he'd pick me up at seven. Seven came and went. So did eight. And nine. By ten o'clock I got into my pajamas and cried myself to sleep.

"I later found out he'd gone to the prom with his girlfriend, that he'd never broken up with her. Every time he saw me after that, he'd snicker, 'Wanna go to the prom?'

"God, I wanted to kill him. Then, all these years later, we wound up working together at Santa Land. He didn't recognize me, of course. I'd lost all that weight. My face had cleared up. And I'd started calling myself Gigi. So he had no idea who I was.

"But I remembered him, all right. A guy that awful, you never forget. I wanted to puke when he started coming on to me. I wanted to kick him in the groin and tell him exactly what I thought of him. But then I had a better idea. I'd do to him what he did to me. I made him fall in love with me. Lots of guys do, you know."

I believed her. The new improved Gigi was one hot cookie.

"True," she said, "I had to let him touch me." She gave a tiny shiver of disgust. "It made me sick, but it was worth it. Before long he asked me to marry him. He even went and bought me this silly dress. All this lace and tulle. So romantic. If he only knew how much I detested him.

"Like I said, I was supposed to pick him up this morning and drive him to Vegas for our wedding. But I was never going to show. I was going to keep him waiting hour after hour, just like he kept me waiting all those years ago. I wanted him to feel what it was like to have his heart broken. Oh, that was going to be so much fun.

"But then somebody killed him and spoiled everything. Scotty died thinking I actually loved him."

She shook her head ruefully and slugged down the last of her champagne.

"I should've kicked him in the groin when I had the chance," she sighed. "Oh, well. Gotta look on the bright side. At least he won't be around to insult any more fat women.

"Now if you'll excuse me," she said, getting up on shaky feet, "I'm going to pass out in my bed where it's nice and comfy. Let yourself out, will you?"

I walked past the volleyball bobbing in Gigi's tiny pool, my mind buzzing with the story she had just told me. Not for one second did I doubt that Scotty had played that awful trick on her in high school. And not for one second did I doubt that Gigi had been out for revenge. Maybe all she planned at first was to stand him up at the altar.

But who's to say she didn't change her mind and stab him in the heart with a Christmas tree ornament instead?

Just something to think about between Christmas cookies.

Chapter Thirteen

Back home, I found my answering machine blinking. My heart did a flip flop when I pressed the Play button and heard Jason Nicoletti's voice.

Hi, Jaine. Jason here. Just calling to remind you about my holiday party on Tuesday. Really looking forward to reconnecting. See you then!

In the sturm und drang of Scotty's murder I'd forgotten all about the party. But now Jason and his crooked smile came roaring back into my consciousness.

He was interested in reconnecting. With *moi*! All too exciting for words.

I hurried to my bedroom where I spent the next hour or so trying on potential outfits. After piling my bed high with clothes, I came to the perfectly logical conclusion that I had nothing to wear and raced over to Nordstrom where I found a divine Eileen Fisher outfit — hip-slimming black velvet elastic waist pants and matching black beaded sweater.

Even on sale, it was way too rich for my anemic budget, but I bought it anyway — vowing not to buy another thing for myself till after Labor Day at the earliest. Not one thing. Except maybe a fabulous Very Berry lipstick in Cosmetics. And a darling pair of chandelier earrings on sale in Costume Jewelry.

I headed home, exhilarated from the hunt. Nothing gets a gal's endorphins flowing like black velvet and dangly earrings.

My good mood came to a screeching halt, however, when I picked up my mail from where my mailman had tossed it on my front step, just in case there were any burglars in the area who needed to know I was out shopping.

There among the bills and flyers was a particularly galling invoice from Ernie, the Cat Whisperer. Would you believe he was charging me $100 for our photo session? A hundred buckeroos — and he hadn't snapped a single picture of Prozac!

I was on the phone in a flash.

"Picture Perfect Photo Studio. Edna speaking," Ernie's receptionist answered.

"This is Jaine Austen calling."

"Oh, yes. The lady with the crazy cat."

I opted to take the high road, and let that slip by.

"I believe your billing department has made a mistake, Edna. I just got a bill for $100."

"That was no mistake," Edna informed me.

"But Ernie didn't take a single picture."

"I'm sorry, but we booked an hour of studio time for you. And that's one hundred dollars."

"That's outrageous!" I fumed. "Simply outrageous. I demand to speak with Ernie."

"I'm afraid he's busy right now."

"Have him call me back as soon as possible," I said in my most authoritative voice.

Needless to say, I didn't hear a peep from Ernie that day. Or the next. So on Monday when I got back to work, I decided to pay him a visit in person.

I strode into the Cat Whisperer's studio in full tilt Tough Gal mode. Which wasn't all that easy considering I was wearing my elf suit at the time. Let's just say that a gal in a pointy green hat and curly-toed slippers does not exactly scream "I am woman; hear me roar."

"May I help you, Ms. Austen?" asked Edna, gazing up at me from behind the reception counter.

"I need to speak with Ernie about this," I said, waving my invoice in her face. "Now!"

"I'm sorry," she said icily, "but he can't be disturbed."

That's what *she* thought. I wasn't about to be put on hold for one moment longer.

Seething with righteous indignation, I started for the curtain that separated the reception area from the photography studio. As I did, Edna sprang out from behind the counter.

Whoa. When I met Edna the day of Prozac's photo shoot, she seemed like an ordinary middle-aged woman, the kind you see squeezing cantaloupes in the produce section. But now, as she came out from behind her reception counter, I realized she was a rather intimidating gal. In fact, if I'd met her in a dark alley, I would've sworn she was a linebacker for the Green Bay Packers.

Yes, along with her *I* ♡ *My Cat* pin and Easy Spirit Walkers, she had quite an impressive set of muscles on display.

But if you think for one minute that I was going to be the least bit intimidated by a mere show of brute force — you're absolutely right.

"Guess I'll come back later," I said, me

and my curly-toed slippers skedaddling out the door with lightning speed.

Okay, so I've got to work on my Tough Gal act.

After several hours hoisting kids on Santa's lap, I took a break from my elf duties and headed back to Ernie's studio.

It was after six and I was hoping maybe Edna had left for the day, but no, there she was, still on guard, just waiting to tackle interlopers.

How on earth was I going to get past her into Ernie's inner sanctum?

Then I had an idea. A rather clever one if I do say so myself.

I put in a call to Lance in Newport.

Luckily he deigned to pick up his cell phone.

"Lance, you've got to do me a favor. Call the Picture Perfect Photo Studio in L.A. and keep the receptionist on the line as long as possible."

"Can't it wait, Jaine?" he whined. "I'm in the middle of a very important Happy Hour. Martinis are only three bucks."

"Lance!"

"Okay, okay. I'll call."

I waited impatiently outside Ernie's studio as Lance tore himself away from his martinis to make the call. Finally I saw Edna pick up the phone. Which was my cue to march on over.

"Yes, of course," I heard her say as I approached the entrance. "Mr. DeVito photographs events. What sort of event are you planning?"

I scooted over the threshold.

"Your cat is getting married? To the poodle next door?"

Oh, for crying out loud. Couldn't he have thought up something more believable than that?

But for some reason, the gargoyle was buying it.

"Yes, I'll be happy to take your credit card to reserve the date."

Once I saw her writing what I was certain was Lance's bogus credit card number, I strode inside and sailed past her with a jolly wave.

I could see she was tempted to leave the phone, but the lure of a big booking was simply too great to resist. Gritting her teeth in frustration, she allowed me to slip past the curtain into Ernie's studio. Which was empty at the time.

Then I looked around and saw the door to what I assumed was an office in the back where Ernie was probably hard at work overcharging other innocent customers.

I stormed across the room and was just about to barge in when I heard voices coming from inside.

"Oh, Ernie. I'm so sorry I ever broke up with you."

Wait. I knew that voice. It was Molly.

"I must've been crazy to fall for a bum like Scotty," she was saying. "Can you ever forgive me?"

"Of course, *cara mia,*" Ernie crooned in reply. "It wasn't your fault. Scotty had you under his spell. But I knew somehow, some way I'd win you back."

Yikes. Molly had mentioned something about an old boyfriend. But I never dreamed it was Ernie, the Cat Whisperer! Was it possible Ernie had decided to win back his old love by getting rid of his competition — permanently?

My head was spinning with the idea of the Cat Whisperer as the killer — not to mention Molly as a femme fatale — when I looked around and for the first time I noticed a Christmas tree Ernie had set up in the corner of his studio — a plump, artificial affair, studded with tinsel and gold balls.

I almost gasped when I saw it.

Not because of the tinsels. Or the gold balls.

But because of the dozen or so snowflake ornaments hanging from its branches.

Good heavens. It was the exact same kind of ornament that had killed Scotty!

Had Ernie looked out his shop the day of the murder and, seeing the pandemonium in Santa Land, pocketed a snowflake from his own tree to plunge into Scotty's heart?

Maybe the murder weapon didn't come from the tree in Santa Land, but from right here in the Cat Whisperer's studio!

My musings were interrupted just then by Edna, charging in and yelling, "Exactly what do you think you're doing, missy?"

Before I got a chance to answer, the lovebirds came out of Ernie's office to see what the ruckus was about.

"She slipped right by me," Edna sputtered, "just as I was booking another cat-poodle wedding."

They'd actually done this cat-poodle wedding thing before??

Only in L.A.

"That's all right, Edna," Ernie assured her. Then he turned to me with a suave smile. "How may I help you, Ms. Austen?"

"For starters, you can tell me if you knocked off Scotty with one of your snowflake ornaments."

Of course I didn't really ask him that. But oh, how I wanted to.

Instead I launched into an indignant complaint about my bill, how a hundred dollars was a bit much for what had amounted to only about ten minutes of his time.

All the while I was yakking, I couldn't help staring at his hands. For such a slim guy, he had the hands of a dockworker. How easy it would have been for those hands to have plunged a sharp metal snowflake into Scotty's chest.

Undoubtedly trying to show Molly what a good sport he was, Ernie agreed to charge me only twenty-five bucks, and I headed back to Santa Land with a seventy-five dollar savings — and a hot new murder suspect.

CHAPTER FOURTEEN

I was lying in bed that night, Prozac sprawled across my chest, watching *Diners, Drive-Ins and Dives.* Well, Prozac was watching (she has a thing for Guy Fieri). I was busy thinking about my murder suspects, wondering which one of them could have plunged that snowflake into Scotty's heart.

Was it Molly, his scorned lover? She certainly had the strength, what with her black belt in karate. And there were those scratches on her arm, possible evidence that Scotty had put up a fight as she stabbed him to death.

What about Corky? She had, after all, threatened to kill Scotty if he called her Porky one more time. Had she carried out her threat in a moment of insane rage? There was also Gigi, who'd been nursing a grudge against Scotty ever since high school. Was it true that all she planned to do was ditch him at the altar? Or had she upped the ante and decided to kill him instead?

Finally, there was Ernie, the Cat Whisperer. I couldn't stop thinking about what I overheard him saying to Molly that afternoon:

I knew somehow, some way, I'd win you back.

Had he found the way — with a snowflake ornament from his own Christmas tree?

I laid there, pondering these questions, and whether or not I had the energy to get out of bed for a couple of Oreos.

I opted to forgo the Oreos. (Alert the media.) As much as I wanted them, I simply didn't have the strength to move. My days as a part-time, semi-professional P.I./Santa's Elf had been draining, to say the least. Juggling murder suspects and kiddies on candy cane highs was exhausting work.

So I turned off the TV and drifted off into an uneasy sleep. Before long I was deep into nightmare territory, dreaming about a toddler stabbing Santa in the heart with a snowflake ornament while I stood by helpless, eating a Double Stuf Oreo.

Suddenly I was jolted awake from this hellish vision by the sound of a deep male voice saying:

"Stick 'em up, or I'll shoot."

Omigod. It was Ernie! He was the killer! I

should have known all along. There was something about his oily charm that screamed homicidal maniac. Besides, anyone who could get Prozac to sit still for the camera had clearly made a pact with the devil.

I remembered those dockworker hands of his. Oh, Lord. Any minute now, they'd be pulling the trigger and blowing me to kingdom come! I peered into the darkness, but I saw no one. He had to be hiding somewhere.

"I swear, Ernie," I said, bolting up in bed, my hands high in the air. "Just because I saw the murder weapon in your studio doesn't mean I think you killed Scotty to get him out of the way so you could get Molly back.

"Honest," I lied, "that's the last thing on my mind!"

But all I heard in reply was:

"Stick 'em up, or I'll shoot."

Whoa. It suddenly occurred to me that the guy didn't have an Italian accent. So it couldn't be Ernie. Then who the heck was it? Yikes! It was probably a burglar!

"Look, I don't have much," I called out. "Just a gold locket from my parents, and a supposed diamond engagement ring from my ex-husband, the Blob, but knowing my

ex-husband, I'm sure it's just cubic zirco-
nia. Oh, yes, and a darling pair of dangly
earrings I bought on sale at Nordstrom for
a Christmas party I'm going to on Tuesday.
Old friend from high school, says he wants
to reconnect."

I tend to babble when I'm nervous.

"You can have everything," I said, "including the twenty dollars in the Pringles can
on top of the refrigerator. Just don't hurt
my cat."

I waited for what seemed like an eternity,
my arms aching. It felt like I'd been holding
them in the air for hours.

Then I heard the voice again:

"Stick 'em up, or I'll shoot."

But this time it was accompanied by an
extremely screechy: *Awwwwwk!*

Oh, for crying out loud, it was Bogie,
Lance's silly parrot!

I'd been taking care of him for the past
few days, running myself ragged moving
him from room to room, keeping him out
of Prozac's striking zone.

Lance said he knew how to talk. Apparently "Stick 'em up, or I'll shoot" was what
he knew how to say. Picked up, no doubt,
from one of the real Bogie's early gangster
movies.

I turned on the light, and sure enough

there were no intruders in my bedroom. Just me and Prozac.

I clambered out of bed and hurried to the bathroom, where Bogie was happily awwking away.

No wonder he'd been making such a racket; I'd forgotten to cover his cage.

"Stick 'em up, or I'll shoot," he said by way of greeting.

"Oh, Bogie," I sighed. "Of all the duplexes in all the towns in all the world, why did you have to wind up in mine?"

To which he just blinked his beady eyes and let loose with a fairly hefty poop.

Guess he wasn't much of a *Casablanca* fan.

CHAPTER FIFTEEN

Lance came home from Newport early the next afternoon, and wasting no time, I hustled over to his apartment to return Bogie, lock stock and birdseed.

"Was he much trouble?" Lance asked.

"A lot, actually."

"Aw, thanks, hon. You're a true friend. Greg and I will name our first parakeet after you."

Leaving Lance to his fantasy relationship, I headed off to Conspicuous Consumption.

I was working the three to nine o'clock shift that day, which was a shame, since Jason's party was that night. I'd tried to get Gigi to switch shifts with me, but she had an audition she had to go to, so I was stuck.

I just hoped the party wouldn't be over by the time I got there.

Somehow the day crawled by. I led the kids up to see Santa, my head in the clouds, mentally mapping the shortest route to Jason's house in the Hollywood Hills and deciding whether to wear my hair loose and flowing or swept back in an elegant updo.

Finally eight o'clock rolled around. Just one more hour to go.

Usually after eight o'clock, the line at Santa Land died down; most kids were home getting ready for bed. But wouldn't you know, at eight thirty that night there was a line of kids snaking halfway down the mall.

After about the 367th time Barnaby saw me checking my watch, he asked me what was up, and I told him about Jason's party.

"A Christmas party? With your old high school crush? Don't just stand there, girl. Go!"

"But I can't leave you alone."

"Of course you can."

"Are you sure you'll be okay?"

"I'll be fine. Just have fun."

What a doll. I really had to remember to buy a toy for his Tiny Tim Project.

"Santa's elf," he announced to the crowd, "has to go help Mrs. Claus wrap presents, so she's going to say good night to you now."

I waved good-bye to the kids and, blowing Barnaby a kiss, raced off to grab my stuff from my locker. Then I hurried out to my car and roared out of the parking lot — only to be caught in the kind of hellish traffic that descends upon Los Angeles every year during Christmas party season.

I inched home gritting my teeth and cursing, my knuckles white on the steering wheel.

By the time I got back to my apartment, it was after nine.

Having silenced Prozac's indignant howls with a bowl of Hearty Halibut Guts, I dashed into my bedroom where I threw on my new Eileen Fisher black velvet elastic-waist pants set. I was in such a hurry, I didn't even bother taking off my striped elf tights, rolling them up at the ankles so they wouldn't show under my pants.

After slapping on some makeup, I took a quick pass at my bangs with the blow dryer. (So much for that glam updo.) Then I slipped on my dangly earrings, spritzed on some perf, and I was out the door.

"Wish me luck," I called out to Prozac.

She gazed up from where she was sprawled on the sofa, belching hearty halibut fumes.

Yeah, right. Whatever. Bring back leftovers.

Wending my way over to the Hollywood Hills, "Feliz Navidad" blaring from my radio, I fairly buzzed with anticipation, wondering if that spark I'd felt with Jason way back in high school was about to be ignited.

I found Jason's house — an ultra-modern concrete and glass affair — on a winding road deep in the hills. When I got there, the narrow street was jammed with cars. In a clearing I saw a valet in a red vest. Normally, I'd rather die than fork over money to a valet, but I couldn't afford to waste another minute, so I pulled up alongside him.

He peered in at me through my passenger window.

"You here with the cleaning crew?"

I get that a lot in my ancient Corolla.

"No, I'm a guest," I said, stepping out of the car and brushing an Almond Joy wrapper from where it was clinging to my thigh.

(Okay, so I had a teeny snack on the way over.)

Then I tossed him my keys and, with as much dignity as I could muster, I headed up the steps to Jason's party.

From the open front door, I could hear the sounds of laughter and tinkling glasses, a jazz rendition of "Jingle Bells" playing in the background.

I stepped inside, and suddenly my svelte new Eileen Fisher outfit seemed a lot less svelte than it had just two seconds ago. Everywhere I looked, I saw people far hip-per than *moi.* Way too many willowy blondes in size zero cocktail dresses.

Oh, dear. Maybe this reconnection thing hadn't been such a good idea.

Then I spotted Jason across the room, chatting with a tall, aristocratic looking fellow in a tweedy blazer.

Jason caught sight of me and flashed me his crooked smile.

And just like that, my insecurities vanished.

My heart skipped a beat or three as he made his way through the crowd to my side, looking tres adorable in jeans and a bright red sweater.

"So glad you could make it, Jaine!" he said, wrapping me in the most divine hug.

Where's the mistletoe when you need some?

I was standing there, fantasizing about the two of us celebrating future holidays together, bingeing on Christmas fudge, when suddenly I was brought back down to earth with a resounding thud.

"Guess who's here?" Jason said, releasing me from his hug. "Jim Nelson." He pointed to the tall guy in the tweedy blazer. "The features editor at *L.A. Magazine.*"

"That's nice," I said with a vague smile, wondering why he thought I'd be so excited to see a magazine editor. And then it all came flooding back to me — that whopper of a lie I told about writing an article for *L.A. Magazine.*

"I figured you two would have plenty to talk about since you're writing that story for him. Let me go get him."

Oh, hell. I couldn't possibly talk to this Nelson guy and have him unmask me as the fake that I was.

My first thought was to jump back in my Corolla and race home. But I'd already given it to the valet. And lord knows where he'd parked it. Probably somewhere in West Covina. It could take ages for him to bring it back. What if Jason spotted me out front and came trotting after me, with his editor friend in tow?

No, there was only one sensible thing to do:

Hide until the party was over and then sneak out in the dead of night.

Quickly, I nipped up a nearby stairway to the second floor and ducked into the first room I saw, closing the door behind me. It was dark inside and, unable to see where I was going, I stumbled over something in my path. Something big and hairy with sharp pointy teeth. A Doberman to be precise, as I discovered when I flipped on the light. And he was not alone. A fellow Doberman stood beside him.

(For the purposes of this narration and to avoid confusion, I shall call the first Doberman "Abbott" and the second Doberman "Costello.")

"Nice doggies!" I said, with a sickly smile.

Sadly, Abbott and Costello were not in the mood to be chummy.

On the contrary, they bared their pointy teeth and growled most menacingly.

"Well, nice meeting you," I said, starting for the door.

But Abbott and Costello were not about to let me go.

Like a flash they were at the doorway blocking my exit, fangs bared, massive jaws dripping with drool.

How I yearned for the good old days of Edna the receptionist.

Now they started advancing on me, backing me into the room, which seemed to be some sort of guest bedroom. Any minute, they'd be pinning me to the bed, lunging at my neck, going for the jugular.

Frantically I looked around for an escape route.

And then — hallelujah! — I saw two French doors leading out onto a balcony.

If I could make it outside, I'd be safe.

My heart in my throat (better there than in Abbott and Costello's jaws), I started sprinting across the room. But I hadn't taken two steps when one of the Dobermans, I believe it was Abbott, clamped down on the leg of my expensive new Eileen Fisher pants.

Oh, hell. He had the velvet in his iron jaws and refused to let go.

Desperate to break free, I slipped out of the pants (thank heavens for elastic waists!) and let him have them.

I hated to lose them, but it was clearly all for the best, since Abbott, now busy chomping on Eileen Fisher, had forgotten all about Yours Truly.

Which left me free to dash over to the French doors.

Unfortunately at that juncture, Costello, heretofore busy sniffing at Abbott's tush, sprang into action and came lunging at me.

Or, I should say, at my Eileen Fisher beaded top.

I quickly pulled it off and tossed it at him.

Apparently Costello was an Eileen Fisher fan, too, because seconds later he was next to Abbott on the floor, both of them happily noshing on my new outfit.

Grateful it was not me under their grinding teeth, I raced out onto the balcony, shutting the door firmly behind me.

I stood there, breathing an enormous sigh of relief, when suddenly flood lights snapped on from the garden below.

"Jaine?"

I looked down and saw Jason standing with the guy from *L.A. Magazine.* They were both staring up at me, mouths gaping. And I suddenly realized I was standing there wearing nothing but a wonderbra and striped elf tights.

"This is Jim Nelson from *L.A. Magazine,*" Jason called up. "He says he's never heard of you."

Oh, gulp.

"And this," he said, putting his arm around one of the size zero blondes I'd seen earlier that evening, "is my fiancée Dawn."

Uh-oh. Time to cancel that mistletoe.

CHAPTER SIXTEEN

"Oh, Lord. What a disaster!"

It was the next day during one of our lulls in Santa Land, and I was baring my soul to Barnaby.

"There I was practically naked out on that balcony, everybody staring at me."

It's true. Soon after I was discovered in my elf tights and wonderbra, the whole party had trotted outside to see what the commotion was about.

Eventually Jason came upstairs and called off the dogs. And I slunk off in disgrace, my Eileen Fisher outfit shredded to bits and soaked with Doberman drool.

"How could I have been so wrong about Jason?" I sighed. "It was like high school all over again. I'd convinced myself he liked me when all he wanted was to be friends. When will I ever learn?"

"You're being too hard on yourself, kiddo," Barnaby said. "This Jason character talked about reconnecting and didn't mention Word One about a girlfriend. It's no wonder you thought he was available."

"I guess you're right," I said, sucking on a candy cane I'd nabbed from the Conspicuous Consumption Christmas tree. "But still, when I think of myself out on that balcony in nothing but a wonderbra and elf tights, I want to die."

"I've got an idea," Barnaby said, a Santa-like twinkle in his eye. "After work tonight, why don't we go over to Ben & Jerry's and drown your sorrows in a hot fudge sundae? My treat."

If he were twenty years younger, I would've asked him to marry me.

"Sounds wonderful," I said.

"Uh-oh," he said, fluffing his beard. "Here come some kiddies. Better put on a happy face."

We resumed our roles as Santa and loyal elf until closing time at nine when we headed off to the locker room together.

"I think I'll order the Brownie Special," Barnaby said, opening his locker door. "A warm brownie topped with ice cream, hot fudge sauce, and a mini-mountain of whipped cream."

"I'm feeling better already." I grinned.

"See? By tomorrow you'll have forgotten

all about Jason."

He reached into his locker to get his street clothes, and as he did something fell to the floor.

"I'll get it," I said, bending down to pick it up.

And suddenly all thoughts of Brownie Specials evaporated into the ether.

There lying on the floor was a bright red scarf. With a holly berry pattern. I'd seen that scarf somewhere before. On the day of Scotty's murder. I remembered the old lady who screamed in terror when Prozac leaped onto the Christmas tree — the crazy dame who'd insisted Prozac was a bat. That old lady had been wearing a scarf just like this.

Omigosh. Was it possible that the old lady in the mall hadn't been an old lady — but Barnaby in disguise?

Barnaby was a diminutive guy. With the right makeup, he could easily pass for a woman. Hadn't he said he'd played Lady Macbeth in prep school?

According to witnesses, Barnaby was supposed to have been at the movies when Scotty was killed. Had he somehow slipped out of the theater and nipped across town to plunge a lethal snowflake in Scotty's heart?

I so did not want to believe that my

cherubic co-worker was the killer, but something was telling me he was. Namely, that holly berry scarf, still lying on the floor between us.

But I couldn't let Barnaby see that I suspected anything. I had to be bright and cheery and act like nothing was wrong.

Alas, it was too late. When I got up to hand him the scarf, I found myself looking smack dab into the nuzzle of a snub-nosed revolver.

"Oh, dear," he tsked, grabbing the scarf from me. "I should have burned it. But I hated to give it up. The Crazy Mall Lady was one of my favorite roles."

"So it was you at the mall that day," I said, my heart plummeting.

"I was quite magnificent, wasn't I?" he asked, the revolver now aimed at my gut.

I nodded woodenly, determined to keep him talking. Surely the Conspicuous Consumption security cameras would pick up this little scene, and before long someone would come racing to my rescue.

"But I don't understand," I said. "Why did you kill Scotty? Just because he told everyone you'd never been a big time actor?"

"Heavens, no. That was most annoying. But it's not why I killed him. You see, when

Scotty said I was a fraud, he wasn't just talking about my acting. He was talking about the Tiny Tim Project."

"The Tiny Tim Project?"

"It's a complete scam, sweetie. I keep every dime I collect from my corporate sponsors. And I sell the toys on eBay." He actually seemed proud of himself. "Somehow Scotty found out about it and was threatening to turn me over to the cops."

His bushy brows furrowed in consternation.

"I couldn't let that happen, could I? After all, nobody wants to see Santa go to jail. Think of how disappointed all the kiddies would be."

"Absolutely." I nodded, hoping to get on his good side with a little faked sympathy. "I understand totally."

"So I went to the movies and made a point of talking to the ticket taker and the other people on line. I purposely chose a movie I knew wouldn't be crowded. Once in the theater, I sat in the back row by myself and slipped on a wig and a jacket I'd brought along in a shopping bag. Then I sailed back out again, a completely different person, and hurried home to disguise myself as the Crazy Old Lady. So many costume changes that day. My, it was fun!"

"I'll bet," I said, doing my best to fake a smile.

For crying out loud, the guy was practically telling me his life story, and still no one had come to my rescue. Where the hell was the Conspicuous Consumption security team?

"C'mon," he said. "Time to take a little trip to Santa Land."

With his gun lodged firmly in my back, he shoved me out into the mall. So bright and festive during the day, at night, with the people gone and the lights dimmed, it now had the antiseptic look of a hospital corridor.

"My original plan," Barnaby said as he prodded me over to Santa Land, "was to slip a little poison into Scotty's 'hot chocolate' thermos, but when your cat went ballistic, I decided to take advantage of the chaos and stab Scotty in the heart instead.

"Much more satisfying," he added with a happy nod.

By now we'd reached Santa's Workshop.

"Get in," Barnaby said, nudging me with his gun.

Oh, dear. I didn't like the looks of this. Not one bit.

"Whatever you're planning, Barnaby, you'll never get away with it. There are security cameras all over the place," I said, waving at the cameras, hoping that whichever idiot was asleep at the wheel would finally wake up and notice me.

"Forget it, hon. The security cameras got fried by the sprinklers the day of the murder and they've never been fixed."

"They've never been fixed?" I blinked in disbelief.

"Unfortunately the gentleman who owns Conspicuous Consumption has made some rather unwise investments and is in dire financial straights. He can barely pay the light bills, let alone fix his high tech security system.

"That's what Corky told me, anyway, on one of her many snack breaks. Everyone always seems to confide in me. I'm so darn likeable, aren't I?"

He smiled at me, the twinkle in his eye no longer a twinkle, but a manic gleam.

"Now get in the damn workshop!" he growled, waving the gun in my face.

I crawled into the small hideaway where Scotty had enjoyed so many tequila breaks, sick with fear. I was about to die at the hands of a nutcase Santa, all because I'd been trying to land a job at a mall that couldn't afford to hire me in the first place.

Then Barnaby crouched in the doorway

and, much to my surprise, dropped his gun.

Frantically, I grabbed it.

"Won't do you any good, Jaine. It's just a prop."

"Just a prop?"

I pulled the trigger, and sure enough, all I heard was a harmless click.

"Stole it from a community theater production of *Sleuth.* I played the Larry Olivier part. Got fantastic reviews. Personally, I thought I gave old Larry a run for his money."

Dammit. I'd let myself be conned by a silly prop!

"But *this* murder weapon is very real, my dear," he said, whipping out a switchblade knife from his Santa boot. "Souvenir of an impromptu performance I did in a back alley in Koreatown. An ugly story. I won't bore you with the details."

Oh, God. The maniac was going to eviscerate me. Here — in Santa's Workshop! And no one was coming to help.

How the hell was I going to get out of this mess?

And then I saw it. My salvation:

An empty tequila bottle, left over from one of Scotty's binges.

As Barnaby ducked his head to crawl into the workshop, I was ready for him. The minute he came through the door, I whacked him over the head with Jose Cuervo's finest. A satisfying crack rang out as the glass made contact with his skull. He crumpled to the ground, groaning.

Kicking him aside, I began scrambling out of Santa's Workshop, screaming bloody murder. I'd just gotten to my feet when I felt a hand clamp down on my calf.

Oh, crud. I hadn't knocked Barnaby out; I'd just stunned him. Now I peered down into the workshop and saw he was reaching for his knife with his other hand. Why the hell had I left it in there?

I tried to shake myself free of his grasp but it was like a manacle. Any minute now he'd be slashing my legs to ribbons.

Then suddenly I remembered The Biter — the little girl who'd come marching in to see Santa to demand a pony. I remembered how her mother had pleaded with her not to chomp down on Santa.

Pulling a page from The Biter's book, I bent over and sunk my teeth into Barnaby's bony arm. Chunky Monkey, it wasn't. But it did the trick. With a piercing wail, he released his hold on me.

Taking no chances, I then stomped on his hand, and seconds later when he came crawling out from the workshop, I was waiting for him with the *Giant Book of Mother Goose Nursery Rhymes*, a hefty tome I'd snatched from the Tiny Tim toy bin.

As Barnaby crawled into view, brandishing his knife, I whacked him on the bean with every ounce of strength I had. Jose Cuervo may have let me down, but Mother Goose did the trick. This time Barnaby was out for good. How fitting, I thought, that he was felled by a gift from his own scuzzy charity scam.

At which point, Corky finally came rushing over.

"Jaine! What's going on?"

"Quick!" I cried. "Call the police. Barnaby's the one who killed Scotty!"

"Sweet little Barnaby?" she asked, peering down at his crumpled body. "Really?"

"Yes, and he just tried to kill me, too."

"Wow," she said, shaking her head in disbelief. "This sure hasn't been our year for Santas."

Corky got on her cell phone and minutes later the place was swarming with cops. After I told them my story and showed them Barnaby's switchblade, they hauled the psychotic Santa off to the medical wing of USC county jail.

Somehow I managed to drive myself back to my apartment, vowing that from that day forward I would do all my Christmas shopping online.

Home at last, I collapsed onto my sofa, Prozac nestled on my chest.

"Prozac, honey. You won't believe what happened. I was almost stabbed to death in Santa's Workshop by a deranged Santa Claus, but thank heavens I managed to bop him over the head with a tequila bottle and a book of nursery rhymes before he could eviscerate me."

Yeah, right. Whatever. Is that brownie I smell on your breath?

Okay, so I stopped off for that Brownie Special.

(With extra whipped cream, if you must know.)

I woke up the next morning to find a message on my answering machine.

What with my near death experience, I hadn't noticed it blinking the night before.

I pressed the play button, and almost choked on my morning coffee when I heard:

Hello, Jaine. This is Jim Nelson calling from Los Angeles Magazine. We . . . um . . . sort of met the other night at Jason's party. Anyhow, Jason told me about your Christmas Elf idea, and I think it would be a great story for the magazine. Why don't we get together for lunch to talk over the details? Or dinner, if you're free. Give me a buzz.

Holy Moly. It looked like it was going to be a Merry Christmas, after all.

ONE MORE THING

It turns out that Greg, Lance's Secret Santa crush, is allergic to birds. So if anyone wants a parrot who can say, *Here's looking at you, kid,* just let me know.

Dear Reader,

I hope you enjoyed reading about Jaine and her rascally cat, Prozac. If so, there are plenty more Jaine adventures on tap.

So far, in her crime-fighting past, Jaine has dealt with Bridezillas, Trophy Wives, Fanatic Fashionistas, Diet Nazis, Sitcom Scoundrels, Cruise Ship Lotharios, and Neighborhood Witches. (None of them quite as scary, however, as Prozac at feeding time.)

And coming in January 2014, just in time for Valentine's Day, Jaine will get a job writing advertising copy for a Matchmaker from Hell — a ghastly gal with a penchant for lying, cheating, and chocolate truffles. Charging outrageous fees for services rarely rendered, it's no surprise when the chiseling cupid is murdered on Valentine's Day, bumped off with one of her own poisoned chocolates.

When the cops zero in on Jaine as a suspect, she sets out to find the true killer, all the while fending off the advances of a billionaire septuagenarian who's fallen madly in love — with Prozac!

Will Jaine find the killer? Will Prozac find true love with her billionaire AARPster? Will anyone ever send Jaine flowers on Valentine's Day so she doesn't have to keep sending them to herself?

Stay tuned to find out in *Killing Cupid*!

Laura

P.S. Don't forget to join me on Facebook (Laura Levine Mysteries) for exciting Jaine newsflashes and free book giveaways!

ROOM AT THE INN

CINDY MYERS

CHAPTER ONE

White was not Barbara Stanowski's color. As a pale blonde, white washed her out and made her look like a ghost of herself.

White didn't look so good on the rest of the world right now, either, she thought as she squinted into the swirling snow that engulfed the car. White land, white sky, white air. "How can you even tell where the road is?" she asked her husband, Jimmy.

Jimmy hunched over the steering wheel, the premature gray in his still thick hair making him look as if he'd been dusted with the same snow that covered everything else. "I can't," he said. "All I can see are the taillights of that truck ahead of us. If he drives off the side of the mountain, we do too."

"Don't even joke about a thing like that." She pulled her mink coat (vintage, left to her by Jimmy's late mother) more tightly around her and stared at the dull red glow of the truck's taillights, faint beacons in the swirling snow.

"Who says I'm joking?"

She pressed her lips together and inhaled deeply through her nose. *Think calming thoughts.* Wasn't that what her yoga teacher always told her? Not that Barb paid much attention; she took yoga for what it did for her body, not for the spiritual aspects. Though maybe that explained while she still couldn't stand on her head.

Still, this seemed like a good time to remain calm and positive. She and Jimmy had made it all the way to Colorado from Houston with no problems — the weather had been perfect until just a couple of hours ago. And Jimmy was doing great, considering he'd never driven in snow before. In a little while they'd be in Eureka, with her best friend, Maggie, having lunch at The Last Dollar Café and laughing about the Texas flatlanders' first adventures driving in a Colorado snowstorm.

"Uh oh."

"Uh oh what?" She sat up straighter, bracing herself — for what, she didn't know.

"We're stopping."

The car, which had been moving at barely a crawl, had indeed stopped, though the swirling snow still gave the unsettling impression of continued movement. The red

428

taillights of the eighteen-wheeler they'd been following since Gunnison glowed only inches from their front bumper. "Why are we stopped?" she asked.

"I have no idea." Jimmy switched off the key and reached into the backseat for his coat. "I'll go find out."

But before he had shrugged into the heavy wool overcoat that smelled of mothballs, a dark figure loomed out of the snow alongside the car and tapped on the window. Barb gasped.

Jimmy turned the key and let the window down. Icy air and needles of snow assaulted them. A black man, a gray watch cap pulled down to his eyebrows, bent to look in at them. "Road's closed ahead," he said. "Too much snow."

"Any plans to get it open?" Jimmy asked.

The man pursed his lips and turned his face up to the snow beating down. "They'll probably keep it closed until this storm passes. The wind's drifting the snow and visibility is poor, and I hear there's avalanches in the mountain passes. It's not safe to travel."

"What are we supposed to do?" Barb asked. "We're headed to Eureka for Christmas."

"You might not get there," the man said.

He leaned closer to look into the car. "You got water and blankets, in case you have to spend the night out here?"

"Spend the . . ." Barb's voice failed her.

"We'll be okay," Jimmy said, as if he'd spent the night in a snowed in car many times. "We've got water and snacks and enough clothing for an Arctic expedition."

"Most likely someone will be along in a while," the man said. "Highway Patrol." He patted the top of the car. "I'm in the truck just ahead of you, if you need anything."

"Thanks." Jimmy offered his hand. "Jim Stanowski. And this is my wife, Barbara."

"Reuben Wright." His beefy hand dwarfed Jimmy's. He nodded to Barb. "You'll be okay," he said, and then he was gone, swallowed up by the snow as he made his way farther down the line of cars.

Jimmy rolled up the window and buttoned his coat to the throat. "I guess we're in for a wait."

Barb hugged her arms across her chest and pressed her chin into the soft mink collar of the coat. It smelled of the Chanel No. 5 Jimmy gave her every Mother's Day. A comforting, familiar smell that seemed out of place in this remote, snowy world. "Go ahead and say it."

"Say what?" He leaned over the backseat.

"Do you know where my book is?"

"Say 'I told you so.' I know you would have rather stayed in Houston for the holiday." Every Christmas Eve, Jimmy and his golf foursome played eighteen holes, then exchanged joke gifts over drinks, then he stopped by the Honeybaked Ham store to pick up the Christmas dinner Barb had ordered. Sometimes they turned down the air conditioning and built a romantic fire in the fireplace. It had been cold enough to warrant the fire a few times, but they certainly never had so much snow they couldn't drive wherever they wanted.

"I didn't mind coming to see Maggie," Jimmy said. He straightened, paperback thriller in hand. "And it's not as if you can control the weather."

That was Jimmy — so calm it was practically inhuman. She was the emotional one in their marriage, but what was the use ranting about something when her words merely bounced off him with little effect?

He settled in to read his book and she stared at the falling snow. This was definitely not what she'd pictured when she'd proposed heading to Eureka for the holidays. The little mountain town where her best friend had relocated last year resembled a Victorian postcard. The holiday had offered the prospect of sleigh rides, shopping in cute little boutiques, evenings enjoyed mulled wine or cider by a roaring fire, and afternoons soaking in the hot springs, a gentle snow drifting around them.

No blizzards. No spending the night in the car on the side of the road, reduced to nibbling on energy bars and smoked almonds. She'd stashed a couple of bottles of wine in their luggage, but without glasses they'd have to swig from the bottles, like skid row bums.

She blinked hard. She would not cry. Crying was immature and useless and besides, it would ruin her makeup and make her eyes puffy and her nose stopped up.

She closed her eyes and inhaled deeply. *Think calming thoughts.*

At least she wasn't back in Houston trying to pry her son, Michael, off the couch, where he spent far too many waking hours focused on some violent video game. Michael had dropped out of college after two semesters and moved back into his old room. He worked various jobs — delivering pizza or selling shoes at the mall — but none of them lasted very long. When he wasn't playing video games, he tinkered in the garage or haunted the golf courses. Like father, like son in that respect.

Mainly, he drove Barb crazy. She liked things to have a certain order — some people might even call her a control freak, but it wasn't that she wanted to tell other people what to do, only that she wanted to have control over her own life. Grown sons were not supposed to live at home. They were supposed to be in school or on their own, self-supporting.

She probably should have felt more guilty about abandoning her only child at the holidays, but Michael had already planned to party with friends on Christmas Eve and he would spend the holiday itself with Jimmy's sister and her husband, who would lavish him with food and gifts and attention, so what more could he ask for?

With that comforting thought, she drifted off, lulled by the lingering warmth in the car and the steady drone of wind-blown snow. A tapping on the driver's side window woke her with a start. She let out a choked cry, heart hammering. She'd dreamed she was trapped in a snow globe, swimming through clouds of white glitter, trying to find her way out.

A young man in a dark leather jacket with a fur collar, a Colorado State Patrol shield over the breast pocket, peered in the window Jimmy had opened. "You folks doing all right?" he asked.

"A little chilly, but we're okay," Jimmy answered.

"We've got a place nearby for you to spend the night where you'll be more comfortable," the trooper said. "Grab a few overnight things and come with me."

The thought of a welcoming fire, a stiff drink and indoor plumbing lifted Barb's spirits. Whether their emergency shelter would offer the first two was debatable, but a woman could dream, couldn't she? She shoved open her car door and stepped into snow up past her knees. Her feet felt like ice in the thin leather boots, but she ignored that, and floundered her way around to the back of the car, where Jimmy had opened the trunk. He handed her her makeup bag and he took the suitcase. "I guess everything else will be all right here," he said.

"After I drop you off at the cabins, we can come back up here and get the rest of your stuff," the trooper offered.

"Cabins?" That sounded promising. She pictured oversized log furniture, a massive stone fireplace, maybe even a hot tub. Maybe this delay wouldn't be so bad.

"There are some vacation cabins by the lake. The owner has agreed to open them up for you all." He took Barb's elbow and guided her over a drift that had formed by the roadside. "I'm Officer Kates. What's your name?"

"Barb Stanowski. Do you all have snowstorms like this every winter?"

"Sometimes. Where are you from, Ms. Stanowski?"

"Please, call me Barb. We're from Houston. We're on our way to Eureka to spend Christmas with a friend." Maggie was Barb's best friend. When her husband dumped her and her late father left her property in Eureka, she'd decided to make the move permanent. Now she had a new job, a new love interest and a new spirit that had been missing before. Barb almost envied her. No matter how happy you were with your own life, there was something so tempting about the idea of starting over from scratch.

"Now you'll have a great story to tell all your friends back home about your Christmas in Colorado." Officer Kates stopped beside a snowmobile. "If you'll just climb on back here, I'll take you to your temporary home away from home."

Trying to look as if she did this sort of thing every day, Barb swung her leg over the snowmobile and straddled the leather seat. Jimmy slid in behind her and put his

435

arm around her. The trooper climbed on in front of them. "Ready?" He called over his shoulder. He revved the engine. "Hang on!"

With a roar, the snowmobile surged ahead. Barb grabbed hold of the trooper with both hands. If he had any objections to her holding on, he'd have to stop to make them, but the snowmobile surged forward, flying over drifts and bouncing through ditches. Some other time, the ride might have been fun. But the swirling snow made it impossible to tell anything about the landscape around them and the icy wind froze Barb's cheeks and ears. She buried her face against the cold leather of the trooper's coat.

The machine sputtered to a stop. "You can let go now, Mrs. Stanowski. We're here." The trooper gently pried her hands from around his waist.

She sat up straighter and studied the pair of gas pumps to her left. Not new gas pumps, but old metal boxy contraptions, the green and white Sinclair logo faded and flecked with rust. "A gas station?" she asked.

"There are some cabins." The trooper helped her off the snowmobile. "Technically, the place is closed for the winter, but you'll be more comfortable here than bedding down on the floor in some makeshift shelter."

Looking around, Barbara saw other snow-mobiles unloading other passengers. She recognized Reuben, the trucker who'd been in front of them. Next to him stood a family — mother, father and two small boys, everyone looking puffy and awkward in layers of parkas, scarves and extra clothing.

"Everyone, this is Mae Harper." An older trooper addressed them. He indicated a tall wisp of a woman in a man's long overcoat and green Wellington boots. A gray, black and white dog with upright ears and a plumed tail stood at her side, quietly surveying the visitors. "This is her fishing camp and she's agreed to open it up for you to stay."

Mrs. Harper scowled at them, clearly not happy about this intrusion. Barb wondered what kind of threat or bribe the troopers had made in order to persuade her to take in the refugees. "Don't expect nothing fancy," she said. The wind whipped a cap of straw-colored hair around her pale face. She looked anywhere between fifty and seventy, her skin leathery and lined, as if she'd spent a lot of time in the sun and wind. But her eyes were a brilliant, piercing blue; she regarded the travelers without sympathy. "These are summer cabins, not properly set up for winter use, but I suppose it's better than spending the night in your cars." She fumbled through a handful of keys and thrust one at Barb. "Number three, next to the last toward the far end of the row." Then she turned toward the family and Reuben and distributed the keys to cabins one and two.

"Come on. Let's get out of this wind." Jimmy took Barb's elbow and led her toward the end of the row of cabins. The structures had all been painted a dark green once, though much of the paint had flaked off, leaving bare, gray boards. Snow drifted on the windowsills and across the threshold. Jimmy fit the key in the lock and shoved open the door.

It was almost as cold inside the cabin as it had been outside. Jimmy flipped the light switch and a single bare bulb suspended from the ceiling cast a jaundiced glow over bare floors, a pitted brass bedstead with a sagging mattress, a wooden table carved with graffiti and three ladder backed chairs. A kitchen with a two-burner stove, half-sized refrigerator and rusty sink filled the corner of the space, and a door next to that led to what Barb supposed was the bathroom.

"It's horrible." She started to touch the table and drew back her hand. A thin layer of grime covered everything, and the room smelled of mouse.

Jimmy set down the suitcase and crossed to the thermostat by the bed. "It has heat — that's something."

Barb stared at him as he adjusted the thermostat. "Where is my husband and what have you done with him?" she asked.

He stepped back from the thermostat, rubbing his hands together. "What do you mean?"

"You hate the cold. You hate snow. You hate being inconvenienced. Yet you're acting like this is all a big adventure."

He shrugged. "Might as well make the best of the situation. It'll be fine."

"How can you say that? We're supposed to be spending Christmas with Maggie and Jameso in Eureka, a perfect postcard of a town. Instead, we're stuck in a hovel in the middle of nowhere."

"It'll be okay." He moved to her side and patted her shoulder. "This reminds me of our honeymoon."

Truly, the man had lost it. "We honeymooned in Paris." Her voice rose at the end of the sentence, tinged with hysteria.

He laughed. "True. But don't you remember how the hotel lost our reservation and we ended up staying at that *pension* at the end of the tube line? The room had two twin beds and we ended up squeezed together in one of them."

Barb had a sudden flash of memory of the thin woman in the black skirt and sweater who had shown them to their room and pretended not to understand Barb's halting French. There was a certain resemblance to Mae, in attitude, if not appearance. "Then I hope this works out like our honeymoon — the hotel found our reservation the next day and upgraded us to a suite."

"We'll be all right." He gave her a quick hug. "Come on. Where's your sense of adventure?"

Not waiting for her answer to the question, he headed toward the door. "Where are you going?" she asked.

"Back to the car to get the rest of the things we need."

CHAPTER TWO

As soon as Jimmy was out the door, Barb pulled out her phone and hit the speed dial for Maggie's number. If nothing else, her friend would offer sympathy, and maybe some advice for getting away from here as soon as possible. She worked at the newspaper in Eureka — maybe she had connections who could tell her when the highway would be open.

The phone was silent. Not even a dial tone. Barb stared at the message on the screen. No Service.

"Of course," she said out loud. "Why would I expect a place like this to have modern conveniences like phone service?"

A knock on the door made her jump. Expecting the grouchy landlord, Barb hurried to give the woman a piece of her mind about the filthy state of this place. Instead, she stared down into the soft brown eyes of the mother of the two little boys. "Hi. I'm

Elena Ramirez. We're in the cabin next door." She pointed at the next cabin over. "I came to see if you have an extra chair. We only have three and there's four of us."

"Uh, sure. Come in." Barb stepped out of the doorway and ushered the woman in.

Elena spotted the three chairs at the table. "Three must be what everyone gets," she said. "Could we use your extra? Otherwise, one of us will have to stand to eat."

"Help yourself." She snugged the coat more tightly around herself, though she could feel the first waves of warmth from the cabin's baseboard heaters. "Is your place as filthy as this one?"

"For sure." Elena picked up the chair. "But cleaning it will give us something to do. Better than sitting around twiddling our thumbs." She paused in the doorway and looked Barb up and down, no doubt taking in the pricey fur and designer boots. "I can send my boys over to help if you want. They're used to hard work."

Barb didn't have to be a mind reader to know what Elena was thinking. The helpless rich woman wouldn't want to risk breaking a nail scrubbing floors. "Oh. That won't be necessary. Thank you." She wasn't completely incompetent. It had been a few years since she'd had to clean her own house, but it wasn't as if plying soap and water was beneath her.

On her way out the door, Elena almost collided with Mae Harper. "Where are you going with that chair?" Mae demanded.

"Our cabin." Elena kept walking.

"You put it back before you leave," Mae called after her.

"Every cabin is supposed to have three chairs," she grumbled as she moved into Barb's cabin. The dog squeezed through the door behind her. Mae set a black plastic garbage bag on the table. "There's sheets, blankets, and towels in there," she said. "Nothing fancy, and don't expect maid service. You'll have to do for yourself."

"I can see you weren't expecting company," Barb said, deciding diplomacy might be more effective than demands.

"You're not company. The state is paying me to put you people up." She looked around the cabin, perhaps noting the grime for the first time. "I shut the place after Labor Day and the college girl who cleans for me goes back to school. I've got no cause to touch the place until May. I've got some buckets and rags and stuff you can use to clean up. Come up to the house and I'll give them to you."

"Thank you." What else could she say?

She couldn't very well ask this old woman to scrub down the cabin for her. "What's your dog's name?"

"This is Pearl. You don't have to worry about her. She's friendly."

As if to demonstrate, Pearl walked over and nudged Barb's hand, and looked up at her with one blue and one brown eye. Barb patted the soft fur between the dog's ears. "She's beautiful. What breed is she?"

"Australian Shepherd. They're herding dogs, but she seems content to herd me."

"Do you run this place all by yourself? Except for the college girl, that is."

"The fishermen who rent these cabins aren't much trouble," Mae said. "Most of them have been coming here for years, since my daddy opened the place when I was a little girl."

"So you inherited the family business."

"I guess that's what you could call it. My dad needed help and I didn't have anywhere else to go, so here I am still."

"It must be a pretty spot in the summer." Barbara had no idea if this was true; she merely wanted to keep the woman here, talking. She didn't want to be alone right now, when thoughts of all she was missing by being stranded here would crowd in on her.

"Some people think so. Mostly it's just the lake and the highway. Not that scenic in my book."

"It was snowing so hard I had no idea there was even a lake here," Barb said.

"The largest lake in Colorado."

"I don't know much about the state. This is only my second time to visit. We're on the way to Eureka, to spend Christmas with a friend who lives there."

"Never been there." Mae shook her head. "One of the old gold mining towns, isn't it?"

"That's right. My friend even owns a gold mine that she inherited from her father." The French Mistress hadn't yielded any gold, but just the idea of owning a gold mine made for good conversation.

Except that Mae wasn't interested in conversation. "Come get the cleaning supplies when you're ready," she said, and turned away.

Mae and Pearl left, and Barb stared in dismay at the bag of linens. The prospect of a night, perhaps even several days, in this dreary place was too depressing to contemplate.

The roar of a snowmobile announced Jimmy's return. Barb raced to the door and opened it to see him climbing off the back of the still-running machine. He carried the rest of their luggage — a large suitcase and a matching duffle. Barb ran to stand beside Officer Kates. She put a hand out to stop him from racing away. "How long do you think we'll have to stay here?" she asked, raising her voice to be heard over the idling engine.

"The road's completely blocked and it's still snowing. Could be a few days."

"A few days?" Christmas was a little over two days away. "Through Christmas?"

"Looks like it, ma'am." He touched his hat brim. "I'll check back with you in a day or two. Stay warm."

He sped off, a rooster tail of snow marking his path, until even that was gone. Barb felt colder than ever, like a child who realized that, no matter how good she was or how hard she wished, she wasn't getting the one thing she really wanted for Christmas.

"Come inside and get warm." Jimmy put his hand on her shoulder and she let him lead her into the cabin. He'd piled the luggage on the table and the unmade bed. "I brought everything," he said. "I figured if I left anything in the car, it would be the one thing we needed." He dug through the pile of boxes and bags and pulled out a gift-wrapped package. "This is for you. Might as well open it now."

She turned the box over and over in her hand. The paper was crooked — a sure sign Jimmy had wrapped it himself.

"Go on. Open it," he urged.

She tore the paper and lifted the lid on a pair of fur lined boots with ridged rubber soles. "The clerk said they were really warm," he said. "I thought you'd need them here in the snow."

"Thank you. They're beautiful." She sat and began to remove the thin-soled, high-heeled leather boots from her freezing feet. The fur lining of the new pair was soft and yes, warm. Not something she'd ever have needed in Houston, but perfect for here. She forced a smile. "Do you want your gift now?" She looked at the jumble of bags and boxes on the table. "I'm not sure where it is."

"That's okay. It can wait." He began opening and closing cupboard doors until he found a kettle, and filled it with water from the tap. "We've got those tea bags you were bringing Maggie. She won't mind if we take a couple."

"I tried to call her, but we don't have phone service. I hope she doesn't worry."

"She'll get the report the road's are closed. Hopefully, she'll figure out we're

447

somewhere safe."

Barb looked around the cabin. "I guess this is what I get for wanting a white Christmas." She swallowed a knot of tears and reminded herself once more that crying wouldn't solve anything.

"We can have Christmas here." Jimmy found the box of tea bags and opened it. "There are plenty of evergreens around. We can cut a tree, make decorations. It could be fun."

"I can't believe you're so ready to play rugged outdoorsman." After twenty-one years, he could still surprise her.

"Hey! I'm more than some office drone."

"At least you'll have a good story to tell when you go back to the office."

He dropped the tea bags into two mugs. "I'm not going back."

She laughed. "You'll just stay here in the woods and play Paul Bunyan?"

"I'm serious." Indeed, his expression was grim. Barb's stomach clenched. "I turned in my notice last week."

The words floated between them, refusing to penetrate her brain. "You did what?"

"I quit. I'm not going back to work there."

Jimmy had been Chief Financial Officer for Edmunds Oil for ten years. He'd held various other positions in the company for twelve years before that. He worked hard and put in long hours, but she'd never heard him complain. "When were you going to tell me?" she asked.

"I told you last month that I thought I could make a business out of that golf ball washer Michael and I invented."

She had a vague recollection of him talking about his latest project; as long as she'd known him, Jimmy had created things at a work bench in the garage. Michael had inherited the interest. "I didn't know you were serious."

"I was serious. Serious enough to resign."

She sank into a chair, suddenly too shaky to stand. "What are you going to do?"

"Michael and I are going into business together. Recycling golf balls. That washer we invented works great and he's already approached half a dozen courses in Houston about diving in their water hazards. We'll wash the balls, repackage them in egg cartons and resell them. It's green, it saves golfers money — the timing for this is perfect."

He grinned, as delighted as any kid. He looked ten years younger, while she felt at least that much older. She knew he and Michael had been spending a lot of time in the garage working on this latest creation, but she'd never dreamed it would come to this. "Are you serious? Do you really think you can make a living washing golf balls?"

"Absolutely. It's the perfect job, centered around two things I love — golf and my son."

"But . . . Michael drives you crazy." Michael was a dreamer, completely unmotivated, while Jimmy had always been so practical and dedicated. Jimmy said Michael was lazy. Irresponsible. He and his son clashed all the time over what Jimmy called foolish choices. Yes, they enjoyed tinkering with machinery together, but was that really enough to build a business on? "How are you going to work with him?"

"We've been working together on this for months. This is just what he needs to get his life together. It'll be great."

"So you're actually making money at this?"

"Not yet, but we will."

The sick feeling returned to her stomach. "What are we going to live on in the meantime?"

"I thought you could go out and get a job."

He laughed at what must have been a horrified expression. Barb had not held a paid job since she was eighteen, when she'd quit a part-time gig as a waitress to enroll at

Southern Methodist University in Dallas. She'd put in plenty of hours organizing and fund-raising for various charities, but she wasn't delusional enough to think anyone would pay her for that — not in this economy.

"I'm just kidding," he said. "I have money put aside. Everything will be fine."

She stared at him. How could he be so calm? "You didn't think maybe this was something you should have discussed with me before you made such a drastic change?"

"I tried to talk to you about it, but you clearly weren't interested. You're always telling me I work too hard. I thought you'd be pleased."

"I meant you should cut back on your hours, not quit altogether."

"Now I'll have more time at home."

He said this as if he thought it was a good thing. She suppressed a shudder. Of course she loved spending time with Jimmy, but she had her routines — she didn't want him around all the time.

"And this will be a lot less stress," he continued. "Much better for my health."

"You don't think getting a new business off the ground is stressful?" And what about financial stress? He'd just thrown away a six-figure paycheck for the promise of nothing.

"I've always taken care of you, haven't I? Everything will be fine."

"You should have asked me." A combination of terror, disbelief, and anger rocked her, so that she had a hard time breathing. And the tears that had been threatening all morning rose dangerously close to the surface. She pushed up out of the chair and headed for the door.

"Where are you going?" Jimmy called after her.

"Out." Away from this depressing cabin, and from him, and from the damning knowledge that he didn't see her as a partner in their marriage, but as someone who needed protecting — a helpless person who needed taking care of.

CHAPTER THREE

The wind had died down, but the snow still fell in a gentle white curtain, settling onto Barb's hair and the shoulders of the mink. If she stood still long enough, she'd come to resemble a frozen bear, or maybe a snow sculpture — Socialite On Ice.

The cabins were separated from each other by a small yard that contained a picnic table and a charcoal grill, both now cloaked in white. Barb picked her way along a path to the next cabin in the row of four. In front of the Cabin Number Two, two little boys pounded the dry snow into a misshapen snowman while Pearl romped between them, wagging her tail and barking.

"Hello!" The younger of the two boys grinned at Barb, revealing a missing front tooth. His brown eyes were the color of melted chocolate and his cheeks glowed red in the cold. His snow suit was a little big for him, and patched with silver duct tape at the knees.

"Hello." Barb stopped beside the boys, hands shoved deep in her coat pockets. "You two look like you're having fun."

"Mama said we should build a snowman so Santa Claus would know where to find us," the younger boy said. He hugged the dog. "Pearl is helping."

"Roberto is worried Santa won't know where we are if we have to stay here Christmas Eve." The older boy dumped a double handful of snow on the squat body of their creation and began patting it into place.

"Santa knows," Barb said. "He'll find you, come Christmas." She hoped that was true, that the boys' parents had presents with them in the family car.

"But how do you know he knows?" Roberto asked.

"If he knows when you've been sleeping and he knows when you're awake, then he knows where you're doing the sleeping and waking," she said. Geez, Santa sounded like some CIA spy.

"That's what I told him," the older brother said. He was taller than Roberto, with a thinner, more solemn face. Maybe eight or nine, Barb decided. No longer a believer, but trying to keep the dream alive for his little brother. She remembered Michael at

454

that age, fighting to hang on to Santa for a little longer, for his parents' sake as well as his own.

"Mama says we can have Christmas here just as well as at our Tito Ramon's," the older boy said.

"Papa said we can cut a tree and decorate it," Roberto said.

The door to the cabin opened and Elena looked out. She was a petite woman, at least four inches shorter than Barb, with eyes so brown they were almost black set in a heart-shaped face, and thick, dark hair that fell straight almost to her waist. She looked more like the boys' older sister than their mother. "The boys are telling me their plans for Christmas," Barb said. "They're pretty excited."

"This isn't what we planned for Christmas, but we'll make do," Elena said. "How you coming on your cabin?"

"I was on my way to get the cleaning supplies now."

"The woman who runs this place doesn't seem happy about having us here."

"I guess seven unexpected guests is a lot to take in at once." Barb didn't know why she felt the need to defend Mae; she had been unpleasant and there was no getting around that. "But yes, she is a bit of a grouch."

"She ought to be happy she's getting money in winter, when no one else is around." She looked toward the boys. "Come inside, niños, and help me make the beds."

Barb moved on, toward the main house. Pearl, abandoned by the boys, fell into step beside her. The house, which was painted the same faded green as the cabins, sprawled in a series of added-on rooms and porches. Assorted fishing memorabilia was tacked to the walls — a bait net, old fishing rods, even a pair of rubber waders with a hole in one heel.

She found a door marked "Office" and knocked. After a moment, Mae opened it. "I came for some cleaning supplies," Barb said.

"Come in and I'll see what I have left. You're the last to ask."

Barb wondered if this comment was a criticism of her slowness to launch into cleaning mode. Did Mae think she'd been waiting for someone to do the cleaning for her and had given up? She stepped into the house and waited for Pearl to follow before she shut the door behind her. She stopped in the small entryway to stamp snow from her boots and look around.

The large front room was paneled in dark wood, though little of the paneling showed behind a gallery of patchwork quilts. More quilts covered the sofa and two easy chairs, and draped over tables — their bright reds, blues, green and yellows lending vibrancy to the dated maple furniture and worn rugs. "Did you make all these quilts?" Barb asked. She fingered a coverlet composed of crossed pick axes against a background of muted browns.

Mae paused in her search through a closet and looked back at the quilts, as if she'd forgotten they were there. "I did. After my husband died and the kids moved out, the winters got pretty long. It was either quilt or drink."

Barb shuddered at the thought of being alone all winter in this isolated spot. "I guess I'd have had to take up drinking. I don't have a crafty gene in my body."

"This ammonia in water will clean just about anything. Just be careful of the fumes." Mae thrust out a blue plastic bucket that contained a wad of gray rags and half a bottle of yellow ammonia.

"Thanks," Barb said. "Do you really stay here alone all winter?"

"I have Pearl."

They both turned to look at the dog, who

457

had stretched out on a dog bed by a worn tweed recliner. "She's pretty good company. My son got her for me from a shelter in Denver a couple of years ago."

"Your son lives in Denver?"

"One of them does. They're always inviting me out to see them, but after a few days we all grate on each other's nerves too much. Better to stay put here."

And how many years had she "stayed put"? A lot, judging by all the quilts. "You said your father started the business?"

"Back in 1965. He bought the land before the lake was ever built. There wasn't enough water in it to float a boat when he opened the first cabins, but it didn't take too many years before the fishermen and boaters came flocking."

"And then you and your husband took over running it?"

"*I* took over running it. Moved back here when the boys were little." Her gaze focused on Barb's coat. "You might not think it to look at me now, but I had a mink like that once. When we lived in Chicago. My husband was in real estate. We had about as different a life from this as you could imagine."

"What happened?" Had her husband decided to chuck his job for the carefree life

458

of the self-employed?

Mae's eyes narrowed. "I don't see as how that should make any difference to you now."

Ouch. Barb backed up. "Well, thanks for the supplies. I'll return everything when I'm done."

"Wait a minute." Mae put up a hand, then disappeared into a back room. She returned in a few minutes with a bundle of clothing. "You're about my size, just a little shorter. You can roll up the pants legs." She thrust the bundle at Barb. "You don't want to ruin your clothes cleaning."

"Thanks. That's very thoughtful of you."

"I'll put it on the state's bill." She stepped back, as if afraid she'd done or said too much. "Go on. I've got plenty to do without wasting my time talking all day."

Dismissed, Barb stepped back out into the whiteness that felt even colder and bleaker. She wondered if Mae still had her mink coat somewhere. Did she ever put it on and remember a fancy house and exciting parties in Chicago? Or was it better to lock those kinds of memories away, to only look forward because looking back hurt too much?

Jimmy made himself scarce when Barb

showed up with the cleaning supplies, which was fine with her. She changed into the worn jeans and denim shirt Mae had lent her and attacked the cabin with the bucket full of sudsy ammonia. The stinging odor of the cleaner made her eyes water, and brought back the memory of Saturday housecleaning with her mother in a series of shabby rent houses in Beaumont, Texas. As the oldest of six children, Barb had been her mother's chief helper. All those Saturdays trying to clean houses that were marred by years of ingrained grime had strengthened Barb's determination to leave and never come back.

She'd never been particularly brainy, but she'd always been pretty — blonde and blue-eyed, with big breasts and a little waist. She'd been genetically blessed and she worked it for all she was worth, spending hours poring over magazines to learn how to dress and do her hair and makeup. In high school she was a cheerleader and a runner-up in the Miss Texas pageant. She'd gone to SMU to get her MRS degree and one of the first things she did after she and Jimmy were married was hire a maid who came every week.

Clearly, the woman's Christmas bonus wasn't large enough, Barb thought as she surveyed the cabin an hour later. She'd managed to banish the smell of mouse and the worst of the grime, but the place still reminded her too much of those dismal rent houses in Beaumont. She pushed the memories back into the shadows where they belonged, and changed into wool slacks and a sweater.

Jimmy came in, balancing a covered pot carefully in front of him. "What's that?" Barb asked.

"Dinner. Elena Ramirez made some stew and sent some over for us."

"Where did she find ingredients for stew?" Had her husband gone out and shot a deer in the blizzard? Or did she have the makings of the meal in their car?

"She found a bunch of canned goods in her cabin and figured with all the cleaning you were doing you wouldn't feel like cooking."

"She was cleaning, too. And she had two children to look after." Did she think Barb looked that helpless?

Jimmy set the pot on the table, and pulled bowls from the cupboards. "Let's eat before it gets cold."

When the aroma of the stew reached Barb, her stomach rumbled. Suddenly, she was starving. Bless Elena. "Do you really think it will take two more days for them to get the roads open?" she asked after her first few bites of stew.

"I guess that depends on how long it keeps snowing. Reuben told me he was once stranded in a hotel outside of Rifle for four days during a blizzard."

"When did you talk to Reuben?"

"He and I walked down to the lake. It's a pretty nice place — a boat ramp and a picnic area. If the weather clears I might try ice fishing. I'll bet Mae has some gear I can borrow."

"We're not here on vacation," she said. "We're here because we're stuck."

"Might as well enjoy ourselves."

He might enjoy himself ice fishing, but there was precious little here to distract her from thinking about the fun Christmas she was missing. "We should have stayed in Houston," she said. "We'd be at the Davidsons' party right now."

"Phil Davidson is a bore. He always corners me and wants to talk about his stock portfolio."

"But I like Sandy. And the food at their parties is always wonderful."

"Only because you gave her the name of your caterer."

"True. I hope she's thinking fondly of me now."

"I hope Michael hasn't decided to invite all his friends to the house to drink all my Scotch."

She laughed. "Do you really think he'd do that?"

"I would have at his age."

"I was married to you at his age. My parties were always perfectly proper. I was too busy learning to be the perfect wife for an up-and-coming executive to do anything wild."

"You've had your moments." He gave an exaggerated leer that made her laugh.

"One advantage of getting older is that it's supposed to make you braver about taking risks," she said. But was she really brave? She still cared what people thought of her; she wasn't really so different from that nineteen-year-old bride who'd been so determined to make a good impression, though maybe she hid the insecurity better behind expensive jewelry and a fur coat.

"Exactly right. Risks like starting my own business. Or heading to Colorado for Christmas in a snowstorm."

"Let's hope your business venture turns out better than this trip."

"We'll get to Eureka eventually." He

pushed away his empty bowl. "For now we're safe and warm and fed, and that's what counts."

"I hope we're not stuck here through Christmas," she said.

"You'll feel better in the morning," he said. "It's been a rough day."

The bed was narrower than the one they shared at home, the mattress hard and the sheets scratchy. Barb closed her eyes and tried to count her blessings, but instead her thoughts turned to the idea of risk. She put on a bold front, and she wasn't afraid to try new things, but she wasn't a daredevil, either. She would have thought at this point in her life she'd have been past the age where she had to take chances, but the opposite seemed to be true. All around her, the people she loved were risking everything, changing their lives completely. Not just Jimmy, quitting his job and launching this new business, but her best friend Maggie had moved to Colorado to live in a remote town where she hadn't known a soul and started over with a new job, a younger man, and a completely different life.

Barb didn't want a different life. She liked the life she had. But she also didn't want everyone moving on without her. The worst feeling in the world had to be that of being taken for granted.

She would have thought she couldn't sleep in the strange cabin, on the creaky bed, but she eventually surrendered to weariness and dozed. She woke a few hours later, cold, and curled into Jimmy, who put his arms around her and drew her close.

"Jimmy, are you awake?"

His only answer was a soft snore.

She shook him. "Wha?" he moaned.

"You should have made me listen to your plans to open a business," she said. "You should have made me see how important it was to you."

"Mmm." He pulled the covers closer around him.

"I'm not helpless," she said. "You don't have to protect me. We're supposed to be partners."

"Partners," he muttered.

She sighed and laid her head on his shoulder. He draped his arm around her. "Go to sleep," he said.

So she closed her eyes and to her surprise, drifted off almost immediately.

Chapter Four

After a breakfast of tea and a protein bar, Barb set out to return the cleaning supplies and clothing to Mae.

"It's stopped snowing!" Roberto ran up to her almost as soon as she stepped out of the cabin.

"That's great news," she said. The sky was still low and gray, but the air was clear and still, though stinging cold.

"Papa says we can get a tree today," the older boy said. "We're going to make paper chains and stuff to decorate it."

"That will be fun." And it would keep the boys occupied a while.

The door to their cabin opened and Elena emerged. She wore a man's checked flannel shirt over jeans, the shirt much too big for her, giving her the appearance of a child playing dress up. "Good morning," she said. She hugged her arms around herself and looked up at the sky. "It's stopped snowing."

"Maybe they'll open the roads soon."

"Maybe." She didn't look confident.

"Roberto said you were going to his uncle's for Christmas?"

"Not just for Christmas. We're moving there. My brother thinks Ernesto can get a job with his employer, at a machine shop."

"Is that the kind of work he did in New Mexico?"

Her eyes narrowed. She was silent so long Barb wondered if she'd asked the wrong question again. "Ernesto can do a lot of different things," Elena said finally. "He's a good mechanic and he knows about engines and fixing stuff. His main problem is he has a temper and that gets him in trouble at work. If he doesn't like something a boss is doing, he tells him." She shrugged. "He's lost a few jobs for speaking his mind. I'm hoping this will be a fresh start."

"We're making a fresh start in the new year, too," Barb said. "My husband's decided to go into business for himself, with our son."

"Maybe that's what Ernesto should do. Then, if the boss messed up, he'd only have himself to be angry with."

"Not so easy to do, though." Barb scuffed

467

the toe of her boot in the snow. "My husband says things will be fine, but change is scary."

"I hope this is a good change for us," Elena said. "Though we hadn't planned on this detour."

"Mama! Can Roberto and I dig a snow fort over by those trees?" The older boy, a snow shovel over one shoulder, gestured toward a cluster of trees just beyond the gas pumps.

"All right, but be sure to keep your mittens on. I don't want any frozen fingers."

"How old are they?" Barb asked as they watched the boys race for the trees.

"Carlo is eight and Roberto is five. My brother has boys near their age, so they're looking forward to seeing their cousins."

"I guess you'll have to make Christmas for them here."

"We were waiting to get presents until we got to Durango." Elena hugged her arms more tightly across her chest. "If they were older, we'd explain that they needed to wait, but Roberto still believes in Santa Claus. He'll expect something in his stocking, and Carlo pretends to believe, for Roberto's sake."

"Mae told me she had two sons. Maybe she has some things left from when they were little . . ." Barb's voice trailed away. The older woman might not be so willing to part with her belongings. "I wish I could think of something to give them." She doubted they'd appreciate any of her jewelry or clothes. Having money meant she didn't have to be creative. When she needed something, she went out and bought it. But money — and all those years getting by on her looks — weren't doing her any good now.

"They'll have plenty," Elena said. "Ernesto is carving little wooden animals and I'm knitting new hats and gloves. I started in the car on the trip over, so they won't be a surprise, but . . ." She shrugged. "It will be all right." She turned back toward her cabin.

"Thank you for the stew last night," Barb said. "That was very thoughtful of you."

The younger woman shrugged. "We've got a bunch of cans in the cabinet here. Someone must have liked that brand of stew a lot. If you want more, let me know. I have to go in now. It's cold."

"I'll talk to you later, then." Barb moved on, past where the boys were building some kind of fort, digging up snow and piling it into walls. She struggled against a sharp, fierce longing for Michael. Not as he was now — tall, lanky, uncommunicative young adult — but Michael as a cheerful, chubby toddler. They'd been inseparable then. She'd stayed home to look after him, and as he grew she'd been den mother and home-room mother and band boosters mom. She'd been a good parent, even if the last few years had been a struggle.

Maybe she should have pressed harder for him to come with them to Eureka. It would have been a time for them to bond as a family . . .

She shook her head. Michael would have hated being stuck with his parents for a week, with none of his friends. And she'd have been just as miserable. As much as she loved her son, she had to admit she didn't always like him these days. If only they could stay little longer.

Though the snow had stopped, the temperature was still freezing. She shivered, and hurried toward Mae's house. Pearl barked before Barb even had a chance to knock, and Mae called from the other side of the door. "Who is it?"

"Barb Stanowski. I brought back the things you loaned me."

She waited, and after a few seconds, Mae opened the door and reached for the bucket and clothes. Barb had a feeling the woman intended to snatch the items away and retreat behind the door once more; the idea annoyed her. Why shouldn't the woman want to talk to her? "Can I come in a minute and warm up?" she asked.

Mae hesitated. The old woman clearly wanted to be left alone, but when people pushed her away, Barb's natural tendency was to push back. Trying to win Mae over would at least help her pass the time waiting for the road to open.

Mae opened the door a little wider and motioned her in. "I guess the cabin's looking better now," she said.

"Yes. Thank you." Not that it would ever be a showplace.

Silence stretched between them. "Everything all right last night?" Mae asked after a long moment.

"I was a little cold," Barb said. "Do you have any more blankets?"

The lines on Mae's forehead deepened. "I'd have to dig around in the storage closets."

"I don't mind looking, if you show me where they are."

Mae sighed. "Maybe you could borrow some of my quilts. They'd brighten up the place, and keep you warmer at night."

"That would be wonderful." The lump in her throat surprised Barb as much as Mae's offer. These quilts probably meant a lot to the older woman.

"I used to try harder to decorate the cabins and make them look nice." Mae moved to the recliner in front of the wood-stove and motioned Barb to a worn chintz armchair opposite. "But the fishermen and hunters who stay here don't appreciate nice things. They want a cheap room they can drink and smoke and clean fish in, so I stopped bothering."

Had that been a hard concession for her to make — or an easy one, a relief even, that she didn't have to try so hard?

"You said one of your sons lives in Denver. Where is the other one?"

"Troy is an electrician in Denver and Gary manages a chain of restaurants in Green Bay."

"My son, Michael, is nineteen and he doesn't know what he wants to do with his life. He just quit school and moved back home."

"My boys were like me," Mae said. "They couldn't wait to leave. They loved it here when they were little. They ran wild, fishing and throwing rocks and exploring the woods. But when they got to be teenagers, we were so far from the things they wanted — movies and malls and other kids their age. Girls."

"You left," Barb said. "You told me you went to Chicago."

"Yes. But I got sucked back in. I couldn't escape."

She tried to imagine what it would have been like if she'd had to move back to Beaumont, to a life of cheap rental houses and bars filled with oil workers and waiting tables at Denny's, and shuddered. She'd been lucky to have Jimmy and her safe, easy life. "It seems so lonely here," she said.

"Sometimes it is. But I like my own company."

"Did you come back here to help your father?" She steeled herself for another outburst from Mae.

But the older woman's voice was mild. "Nosy, aren't you?"

Barb smiled. "Yes. But I like to hear people's stories. And I'm curious, since it seems you and I may have a little in common. How did you get from wearing a mink coat in Chicago to living alone out here in the middle of nowhere?"

"My husband was very successful." Mae leaned forward, her sapphire eyes pinning Barb in her chair. "A little too successful. He embezzled money from some of his clients. He went to jail for a few years and everything we had went to pay his victims. So I came back here."

"I . . . I'm sorry." Jimmy might have rashly quit his job, but at least he wasn't going to jail.

Mae shrugged. "We do what we have to do."

"I guess so." It was a lame answer, but the best she could come up with.

"At least the boys made something of themselves. Neither of them are married, but Gary has a steady girl I think he might marry one day. When he's ready."

"I sometimes think grandchildren would be nice, but I don't know if I'm ready for that just yet," Barb said. Being a grand-mother sounded too old for her — it didn't fit with her picture of herself as still young, though every year it became harder and harder, and more expensive to keep up the illusion of youth.

"Those two little boys in cabin two are cute as bugs," Mae said. "They remind me of Troy and Gary at that age."

"Their mother told me they don't have any presents for them for Christmas," Barb said. "Their father is carving little wooden animals and their mother is knitting caps and gloves. But I wondered if you had anything from your boys . . ."

Mae frowned. "There might be a busted bicycle or something in the sheds. You're free to look around. But there's nothing in the house."

"Maybe I will look around," Barb said. "My husband is pretty handy at making things."

"What does your husband do for a living?"

"He was an accountant. Well, that's how he started out. For the last ten years he's been the chief financial officer of an oil company in Houston." She sighed. "But apparently he quit that job last week and has decided he's going into business with our son, recycling golf balls." Saying the words out loud made his plan sound even more ridiculous.

"My husband got tired of his job, too. He was a high flyer, selling luxury properties inside the loop, pulling in mid six figures every year. But that wasn't enough. He wanted more, so he cooked up a scheme to siphon off money from his employer. Idiot got caught after only a few months."

"I can't even imagine how awful that was for you."

"I didn't mind leaving town. I couldn't face all the friends I'd made there. At least out here nobody cared if I'd once had a mink coat and a townhouse overlooking

Lake Michigan." She shrugged. "When you have kids, you do what you have to do."

"But to lose everything like that, including your husband."

Mae's laughter was a harsh bark. "Oh, I didn't lose him. When he got out of jail after a couple of years, he came here, too." Again the shrug. "I still loved him, though I didn't respect him anymore. And the boys needed him. By then my dad was gone and I needed the extra help. He was good with the customers, still charming and friendly."

"And he's gone now?"

"Died of a heart attack three years ago. That's when I took up quilting. I've got enough fabric here that I ordered off the Internet that I could open my own quilting store." She sat up straighter, hands on her knees. "I bet I've even got something I could sew into a couple of shirts for those boys. I've got patterns stashed somewhere from when Gary and Troy were little." She stood. "Let's go look."

Curious, Barb followed her toward the back of the house, into a room lined with plastic storage tubs, the kind people used to store Christmas decorations. Mae began pulling out tubs and popping off the lids, revealing stacks and stacks of cotton prints in every color and design imaginable.

"Here's what I'm looking for," she said, and yanked out a sheaf of fabric printed with horseshoes and six-guns and cowboy hats. "Little western shirts, with pearl snaps. I've got a contraption here for putting on the snaps." She handed the fabric to Barb and turned to another stack of tubs along the back wall. "My patterns are in here somewhere. Do you sew?"

"Not a stitch. I don't know how to do much of anything practical or useful." She laughed, making a joke of her purely ornamental existence. She was a good friend and wife and mother, but sometimes she wished the things she did really mattered. The last real contribution she'd made to the world was Michael and so far he hadn't exactly made a big splash.

"Here are the patterns." Mae held up a browning paper envelope that showed two sixties-era boys in cowboy hats with toy pistols, wearing colorful western shirts. "I don't suppose kids' fashions change that much with time."

"I'm sure the boys will love them." She was still the cheerleader, smiling big and never letting them see her sweat. "I guess I'll leave you to your work."

"Don't forget the quilts. I put a stack by the door for you. And you could take some to the boys' mother."

"Elena. She and her husband were on their way to her brother's in Durango."

"Take her a few of the quilts."

Barb found the stack of quilts on a chest by the door. The fabric was cool against her fingers and smelled of lavender. The real herb, she'd guess, not a purchased sachet. She managed to open the door and staggered out under the weight of the coverings, struggling to see over them.

"Let me take some of those." Reuben stepped up and relieved her of half her burden. The truck driver was an imposing man, over six-feet tall, broad shouldered and muscular, with close cropped hair, golden brown eyes and skin the color of fudge. He had the solemn demeanor of an undertaker, very grave and formal.

"Thank you," Barb said as she surrendered half her burden. "Mae is lending us these." She peeled off the top quilt — a maze of tiny, colored squares like a cloth mosaic in muted greens, blues and browns. "Take this one." Mae hadn't said anything about Reuben, but he probably needed a quilt for his bed, too.

"Thanks." He tucked the quilt under one arm, still balancing the stack of others in one hand.

Barb glanced at the three covers in her hand. Reuben had four more beside his own. "I'll take these and you can give those to Elena," she said.

"I told Ernesto I'd go with him to cut a tree for their cabin. He's sharpening the hatchet we found." They started walking toward cabin number two.

"That's good of you. Do you have family who'll be missing you over the holidays?" Barb asked, hoping she wasn't opening up any painful wounds. Maybe he'd just tell her to get lost.

"When I'm home, I have dinner with my mothers and sisters, but they know I'm working so they won't miss me."

"That must be hard, working on the holidays."

"Christmas is just another day to me. I'm Buddhist, so it's not my holiday."

"But you're helping with the Christmas tree."

"Just because I don't celebrate doesn't mean I'm against kids having fun."

"Sure. That makes sense." She cleared her throat. Why did she feel so awkward with this man? She prided herself on being able to talk to anyone about anything. "What's in the truck you're driving?"

"Groceries. It's a King's Grocery truck.

You didn't notice the big logo on the back end?"

"I wasn't paying attention. Speaking of groceries, what are we going to eat while we're here?" A couple of power bars, almonds and tea bags weren't going to take them very far.

"There's some canned goods in the cabins. Didn't you look?"

"No." Clearly, he thought she was the original dumb blonde.

"Mae said the fishermen and hunters are always leaving stuff behind, so she just lets it accumulate."

Barb wrinkled her nose. "So no telling how old the stuff is."

"Beggars can't be choosers."

"Right. Well, thanks for helping with the quilts. I'd better make sure my husband hasn't cut off his thumb or something."

Not that that was likely. Like everyone else around here, Jimmy was ridiculously competent. Only Miss Jefferson County, 1985 lacked any significant talent. She'd always suspected the only reason she hadn't been crowned Miss Texas that year was because the contest judges were less than impressed with her ability to do the splits and turn cartwheels while cheering. And even those dubious accomplishments had deserted her long ago.

CHAPTER FIVE

Back at their cabin, Barb found Jimmy sitting at the table with his book. "Go out for some fresh air?" he asked, not looking up.

She dumped the coverlets on the bed. "I visited with Mae and she lent us some of her quilts. I woke up in the middle of the night freezing."

"Really? I was comfortable."

She told herself he wasn't being contrary on purpose, but she had to resist the urge to whack him on the head. She didn't want his opinion; she wanted sympathy and commiseration. Instead, he remained so stolidly positive.

So enough with the pity party, she told herself. It wasn't as if they weren't all in the same situation, and considering, she and Jimmy had it pretty good. "I talked to Elena, too," she said. "She and Ernesto don't have presents for the boys. Well, not many, anyway."

Finally, he closed the book. "That's not good. They'll be expecting Santa Claus."

"Exactly. I told Mae about it and she's going to make shirts for the boys. I was hoping she had some toys left from her children, but she didn't. She said we could look in the shed — wherever that is — but she didn't think there was anything useful in there."

"I know where it is. I saw it this morning when Reuben and I were exploring. Let's take a look anyway." He stood. "Maybe I can make something."

"I was hoping you'd say that."

She waited while he put on his coat, hat and gloves, then she followed him around to the back of the row of cabins, where a wooden garden shed, painted the same faded green as their lodgings, stood half-buried in the snow. An open padlock hung from the hasp, and the door creaked in loud protest after Jimmy had kicked snow from around it and tugged it open.

She shrank back from the interior of the shed, half-expecting some scary form of wildlife to scuttle out of the jumble of discarded items heaped on the dirt floor. Paint cans, nuts and bolts and odd bits of metal filled shelves along two walls. A pair of old, narrow skis leaned against the door jamb, and the hulk of a rusting riding lawn-mower crouched in the corner. A thick layer of grease and dirt overlay everything.

"There's bound to be something useful in all this." Jimmy rubbed his hands together in anticipation, then waded into the mess and began teasing items from the tangle on the floor.

"It's just a bunch of junk," she said. She picked up a dented paint can. It was so old the label was gone.

"There might be some things I can use." He crouched and pulled a skateboard from the tangle of junk on the floor. The decking was warped and split.

"You'd have to be a miracle worker to fix that," Barb said.

He grabbed one of the skis by the door, then dragged out a broken push mower. "I can cut the ski to make a new deck, attach the wheels, add the handle from the mower, polish everything up and it'll be a scooter."

Handed the same assortment of junk, she'd have been just as likely to turn it into a really ugly paperweight. "Really?"

"Really. The boys will love it. Come on. Help me carry this stuff back to our place."

She helped him lug the various parts to their cabin, along with a tool box and some steel wool he found on one of the shelves.

"Is there anything I can do?" she asked as she watched him arrange everything on the table.

"Nope." He surveyed his haul, a mad scientist ready for another session in the lab. "This is going to be fun."

She picked up her book and tried to focus on the story, but she had a hard time sitting still. Back in Houston, she'd be decorating the house, getting ready for parties, delivering gifts, shopping, picking out clothes and tending to dozens of last-minute errands in preparation for the holidays. In Eureka she'd be helping Maggie with her holiday preparations and catching up with her friends in town, shopping and decorating and partying and generally celebrating.

Here in this cabin she was stuck, with nothing to do and no way to really celebrate.

The sound of raised voices just outside the cabin made her drop her book and sit up straighter. "Maybe they're opening the road," she said, and raced to the door.

But instead of a road crew, she found Ernesto and Reuben with a snow-covered evergreen between them. The two boys followed along behind the men, jumping and giggling and shouting with glee. Pearl brought up the rear of the procession, barking and wagging her tail. "We found a good one," Reuben called to her.

"It looks huge," she said. "Will it even fit in the cabin?"

"We might have to trim a little off the top."

"What are you going to do with it now?"

"We're going to decorate it."

Finally, here was something she could help with. She had years of experience, decorating for parties and fundraisers. "I'm going to help with the tree," she told Jimmy as she slipped into her coat.

"Sounds good."

A blast of cold wind shook her when she stepped out of the cabin door. She pulled the mink more tightly around her and leaned into the gale. She never paid much attention to the weather in Houston. Summers were oppressively hot, spring rains occasionally flooded side streets and made traffic worse, and every few years a hurricane threatened and everyone stocked up on bottled water and batteries. But weather was merely a background to her days, not something that dictated her activities or interfered with her plans. Here in this desolate place the snow and cold and wind seemed so much more threatening — more personal and real and uncontrollable.

Carlo answered her knock. "Did you see our tree?" he asked, and held the door wide.

"I saw your father and Mr. Wright carrying it," she said. The two men were wrestling the massive evergreen into a corner of the cabin, Ernesto on his knees, Reuben steadying the top of the tree. Roberto stood on the end of the bed, grinning from ear to ear.

"Carlo, shut the door. You're letting in the cold." Elena peered from behind the tree. "Oh, Mrs. Stanowski. I didn't realize it was you."

"Please, call me Barb. I thought I might help with the tree." She felt suddenly awkward, intruding on this family scene. "But you seem to have everything under control."

"Come in, come in." Elena waved her forward and Carlo shut the door behind her. The smell of fresh-cut cedar filled the room. Melting snow dripped from the branches of the tree. Elena grabbed a towel and began wiping up the moisture. "Excuse the mess."

"We put rocks in the bucket to keep the tree from tipping over." Roberto jumped off the bed to stand beside Barb, admiring the tree. It sat a little crookedly in a yellow mop bucket.

"I think it will be okay now." Reuben stepped back and surveyed the tree critically. "You might want to trim it back a little."

"It's perfect," Roberto announced. "Can we decorate it now?"

"First, we have to make the decorations." Elena moved to the table. "Mr. Wright, Mrs. Stanowski, would you like to stay and help?"

"Please, it's Barb. Mrs. Stanowski was my mother-in-law." Jimmy's mother had been a very patrician woman who had intimidated Barb until the day she'd died. She'd left Barb the mink because, as she'd explained in the note attached to the coat, she had never approved of the cloth coats her daughter-in-law had preferred. Barb gave the mink an extra pat as she took it off and laid it across the end of one of the beds. She could guarantee Jimmy's mother would never have pitched in to help decorate a tree cut from the woods, in a fishing cabin temporarily occupied by a Mexican-American family. She joined the others at the table. Elena had assembled scissors, a pile of old magazines, a bowl and flour-and-water paste, a box of matches, and an assortment of empty cans.

"Barb, if you will cut strips of paper from the magazines, the boys can make chains."

"I know how! I can do it." Carlo reached for the scissors.

Elena swatted his hand away. "You wait and show Roberto how to glue the strips into chains."

"What are you going to do with those cans?" Reuben asked.

"The soda cans I can cut into stars and hearts and other shapes," she said. "If you cut the ends off the tin cans, you can punch holes in them with a nail to make patterns."

"I can do that." He picked up a soup can and studied it. "Do we have a can opener?"

"Right here." She handed over the opener. Ernesto took a second can and the men went to work.

Barb cut strips of paper and distributed them to the boys, watching as Elena deftly carved the soda can into a fancy star. The red, white and silver of the can was perfect for an ornament, but Barb would never have thought of turning it into a decoration. "Where did you learn to do that?" she asked.

"When I was a little girl in Mexico there was a man in my village who turned soda cans into all kinds of things — toy airplanes and cars, those spinning pinwheel things. He sold them to tourists."

Ernesto took the box of matchsticks and began to glue the tiny sticks into little stars and diamonds and pentagrams. The simple, geometric shapes made of overlapping matchsticks looked surprisingly delicate and beautiful. "Those are wonderful," she said.

Ernesto smiled, but said nothing. Perhaps his English wasn't very good, or maybe he was just very shy.

As they completed the decorations, they hung them on the tree with dental floss. The boys giggled as they draped yards of colorful paper chains in the branches, allowing their mother to add a few to the top of the tree. But most of the ornaments ended up at kid height. Barb admired the odd assortment of matchstick shapes and soda-can cutouts and smiled. She had decorated some fabulous trees in her time, but never with things she'd made. This tree wouldn't have won any prizes compared to some of the beauties she'd put together, but she couldn't deny its charms.

"We should ask Mae to join us," Reuben said.

"Do you think she would?" Barb asked. "I got the impression she'd just as soon we weren't here."

"She has to be lonely, stuck here all winter by herself," Reuben said.

"Some people like their own company." Elena carefully bent a piece of the aluminum soda can into the halo of an angel.

"She likes the boys." Barb smiled at Carlo; the tip of his tongue stuck out as he concentrated on gluing the paper strips into perfect circles. "She says they remind her of her sons."

"Then we should definitely ask her to join us." Reuben looked at Barb.

"Why are you all looking at me?" she asked.

"She likes you," Elena said. "She didn't invite me in or lend me her quilts."

"All right. I'll ask her."

"Tell her to bring some popcorn," Elena said.

"For the tree or to eat?" Carlo asked.

"Both."

Mae took so long to answer the door Barb wondered if she'd been asleep. "Hold your horses!" came a muffled shout that rose above Pearl's barking as Barb knocked a second time. The door jerked open and Mae blinked at her from behind a pair of wire-rimmed glasses. "What is it?"

"The Ramirez family cut a tree for their cabin and we wondered if you'd like to help us decorate it."

"Why would I want to do that?"

Clearly, Mae enjoyed being contrary. But Barb could be stubborn, too. "Because it's Christmas and decorating a tree is fun," she said. "Of course, then you'd have to actually come out of this house and talk to the rest of us."

"You're not my company I have to entertain."

"Maybe it's the other way around. Maybe we'll entertain you."

Mae removed the glasses and polished them on the hem of her faded blue turtleneck sweater. "I'll do it for the boys — not for any of the rest of you."

"Fair enough. Do you have any popcorn?"

"I suppose you want butter and salt, too." Despite her stern expression, Barb thought she detected a hint of laughter in the older woman's eyes.

"Only on half of it. The other half is for the tree. We'll need needles and thread for stringing, too. I know you sew, so you should have those."

"Come on in, then. This is going to take a while."

Barb followed Mae into a red, white, and blue kitchen — red linoleum floor, white Formica counters, and blue wooden cabinets. Mae pulled a quart canning jar half full of popcorn from the cabinet and shoved it at Barb. "You get the popcorn started and I'll get the thread. There's a pan in the cabinet by the stove."

Barb found the pan — a large aluminum sauce pan with a lid with a cracked black plastic handle. Fat lot of good this does me, she thought as she studied the jar of kernels. She knew it was possible to make popcorn in a pan on the stove; she just didn't know how to go about doing so.

"I'm afraid the only popcorn I've ever made was in little packets in the micro-wave," she said when Mae returned.

"Must be a pain going through life so helpless." Mae took the pan from her and shooed her toward the table. "And take off that coat. You're making me hot."

Amused, Barb removed the coat. She'd rather deal with Mae's open scorn than anyone else's silent pity.

"I'll bet you've never strung popcorn for a tree before either," Mae said as she shook the pan of kernels over the glowing stove burner.

"Nope. But you can show me," Barb said.

"It works better when the popcorn's stale. The kernels don't break as easily. But this will have to do. Fetch me that biggest bowl out of that cabinet." She nodded toward a cupboard to Barb's left.

The bowl was a massive yellow plastic container big enough to bathe a baby in. Barb passed it over. "Now get the butter out of the refrigerator."

"You like ordering me around, don't you?" Barb asked as she retrieved the butter dish.

"Does it show that much?" She cut off half the stick of butter and slid it into a small saucepan. "Tell me you're not one of these women who won't eat butter because you're worried it'll clog your arteries or make you gain a pound or two."

"Calories don't count when you're stranded over Christmas," Barb said.

Mae laughed. "That's my girl." She stirred the butter as it melted, then tipped the pan over the bowl of popcorn and stirred everything with her hand. "A little salt and we're done. Then I'll make some to string."

The hot, buttered popcorn was better than caviar or cashews, Barb decided as she munched a handful of fresh kernels. When she'd married Jimmy, she'd served those two appetizers at her first party; they were the most expensive, exotic offerings she could think of in her then-limited experience. She'd never eaten caviar in her life at that point, and cashews were something that might show up in her stocking at Christmas in a flush year.

Popcorn she could have any time she wanted, but it had never tasted better, no doubt due to the real butter and generous application of salt. She scooped up another handful. She'd hit the gym when she got home — if she ever got home.

When a second, only slightly smaller bowl was full, the women washed their hands, donned their coats, and trekked to cabin number two, Mae's pockets stuffed with a packet of needles and two spools of white thread.

CHAPTER SIX

The boys greeted Mae and Barb — or rather, they hailed the bowls of popcorn — with shouts of delight. Elena cleared a space at the table and distributed paper towels from a roll by the sink, and everyone helped themselves.

"We should have popcorn more often," Carlo said when the bowl was almost empty.

"My boys used to eat a lot of popcorn," Mae said. "It was a cheap snack to help fill two bottomless pits."

"That's my stomach," Roberto said. He picked a last kernel from the bowl. "A bottomless pit." He eyed the second bowl of popcorn. "Are we going to eat that one, too?"

"This one is for the tree." Mae moved the bowl closer to her and took out the needles and thread. "I'll show you how to string it. It looks really pretty on the tree, but you have to be careful. The kernels break easily."

"Maybe the boys should stick to paper chains," Elena said. "They'll eat more popcorn than they string."

"Where's that husband of yours?" Mae asked Barb.

"He's working on a project. Helping Santa."

"It's been a long time since Santa visited here." Mae deftly slipped a kernel of popped corn onto her needle and slid it down to the knot at the end of the thread.

"You don't think he'll have any trouble finding us, do you?" Roberto's forehead wrinkled in a worried frown.

"He'll know kids are here," Mae said. "And this is the only place along this side of the lake where anyone's living this time of year. He'll be able to see the smoke from my wood stove a long time before he gets here."

"How do you think Santa comes down all those chimneys without getting burned?" Roberto asked.

"He wears a fireproof suit," Mae answered, without skipping a beat.

Carlo's eyes widened. "I never thought of that."

Barb bit her lip to keep from laughing out

loud. So much for thinking the old woman was a sourpuss.

"Does Pearl talk at Christmas?" Roberto asked.

"Does she talk?" Mae looked at the dog, who lay stretched in front of the door, asleep.

"I heard a story that said animals could talk at Christmas," Roberto said. "On Christmas Eve."

"I've never heard Pearl talk, but that doesn't mean she couldn't," Mae said. "They say Christmas is a time for miracles."

"I'd settle for the miracle of the highway opening again," Barb said.

"I thought miracles were things like healing the sick or big stuff like that," Carlo said.

Elena smoothed his hair back from his face. "There are a lot of different kinds of miracles, I think."

"I have a story about a Christmas miracle." Mae set aside the popcorn she'd been stringing. "It happened a long time ago, to two little boys about your ages."

"What happened?" Roberto asked.

Mae leaned back in her chair, her hands in her lap. "Once upon a time, there were two little boys, brothers. They lived by the shore of a big lake with their mother. They had a father, too, but he was far away. They missed him very much, but their mother had told them not to expect to see him again for a very long time."

"Was he a soldier in the war?" Carlo asked. "Our friend, Danny, his dad went to Iraq and Danny didn't see him for a whole year."

"That would be one reason for a father to go far away, wouldn't it?" Mae said. "In this story, it was getting close to Christmas. The lake was frozen and there was a lot of snow on the ground. The boys spent a lot of time wondering if Santa would be able to find them so far away from any town."

She smiled at the boys, but Barb had a feeling she was seeing another pair of children, from many years before.

"The boys decided to write a letter to Santa. So they put their heads together and wrote a letter. They thought that, instead of asking for a whole long list of things, they should ask for the one thing they wanted most. They thought maybe if they asked for only one thing, they would have a better chance of getting it."

"Smart boys," Barb said.

"They thought they were smart, anyway," Mae agreed. "They took a stamp from their mother's desk when she wasn't looking and they mailed the letter, addressed to Santa

Claus at the North Pole. And then they waited for Christmas to come."

"What did they ask for?" Roberto asked.

"That was a secret," Mae said. "Only Santa knew what the boys wished for. They waited and waited, and while they waited they were extra good. They helped their mother with all the chores, and they didn't fight with each other. They wanted Santa to see that they deserved the gift they wanted."

"Was it a new bicycle?" Roberto asked. "That's what I want Santa to bring me."

"It wasn't a bicycle." Mae picked up the popcorn string and moved her fingers along it, the way a woman might worry the beads of a rosary. "Christmas Eve came and the boys were so excited they couldn't sit still. They sat by the highway and waved to every car that passed, and made up stories about the people in the cars — where they were going, and where they'd come from. When their mother asked why they were sitting by the highway, they told her they were waiting for their Christmas wish.

"It was almost dark and getting colder. It started to snow, and the boys' mother told them they had to come inside. They begged her to let them stay out longer; they wanted to see their Christmas wish the moment it arrived. Their mother told them they were being silly, that boys who waited up for Santa Claus were passed by.

"So the boys reluctantly came in and ate dinner and got ready for bed. They were very quiet, and even sad, worried they'd been wrong, and that Santa wasn't going to give them their wish. But just before it was time for them to go to bed, they heard the sound of a big truck on the highway — a noise like the truck's air brakes make when it stops. They listened, and after a minute, the truck rumbled on. But a little bit after that, they heard someone calling their names.

"They raced to the door before their mother could stop them, and they ran out into the snow in just their slippers. And then, walking toward them through the darkness, they saw a man. He had on jeans and a thin jacket, and a knit wool cap — nothing like the clothes he'd worn when they'd seen him last. Then, he'd been dressed in a fancy suit. But the clothes didn't matter. They recognized him right away, and ran to him.

"Meanwhile, their mother had put on her coat and come out into the yard. She recognized the man, too, and she couldn't believe what she saw."

"Who was the man?" Carlo looked

puzzled.

"He was the boys' father," Mae said. "And he was their Christmas wish. They'd told Santa that what they really wanted was for their father to come back to them, and so he had."

Barb blinked back stinging tears as she imagined the reunion between father and sons. And how had Mae felt about the return of her embezzling husband? She'd said she still loved him, but what a bittersweet reunion that must have been. How much had she given up in the way of independence and trust to have her family whole again?

"That's a better gift than a bicycle, isn't it, niño?" Elena squeezed Carlo's hand.

The boy nodded. "I guess so."

"That was a beautiful story, Mae," Barb said. "Thank you for sharing it with us."

"It's good to remember things sometimes, at Christmas. And to think about how, even the things we don't wish for can turn out for good." She stood. "I think you all have the tree decorating in hand now. Pearl and I are going to go back to the house. I've got work to do. Maybe even a few presents to wrap."

"I'd better go, too." Barb stood also. "And see what Jimmy is up to."

"I still hope Santa brings me a bicycle," Carlo said as Barb followed Mae out the door.

She fell into step beside the landlady. "Were you as happy to see your husband as the children were?" she asked.

"What makes you think I was talking about my husband? It was just a story."

"You don't strike me as the type to make up stories."

"What do you know? I might surprise you."

Barb said nothing, but kept pace with Mae.

"I was glad I didn't have to be both mother and father to the boys," Mae said after a moment. "And I wanted my husband back, but what I really wanted was the way our life had been before, and that wasn't possible. So we reached a kind of truce. It wasn't perfect, but it had its moments."

They stopped at the door to Mae's house. "I know people wonder about me, living here all alone," Mae said. "But I've never minded my own company. And there are worse things than being all alone. And worse ways to live than in the present, playing the hand life has dealt you. Regrets will kill you as fast as any cancer. And that's my two cents worth of advice for the day. Good afternoon."

"Good afternoon, Mae."

Barb walked slowly back to her cabin, snow squeaking beneath her feet, wind rattling the chain on the empty flag pole by the gas pumps. She wasn't a person prone to regrets, except sometimes when she wished she'd done more with her life. If she lost everything, like Mae, would she have anything left to carry her through? She never wanted to find out the answer to that question, but it was worth examining. Especially at Christmas, when anything seemed possible, and the world felt poised for a miracle, whether that was bringing a man home to his family, or uncovering the thing Barb Stanowski was meant to contribute to the world.

Despite his job as a desk jockey, Jimmy was good with his hands. He liked creating things, like that ball washer he and Michael had spent hours fussing with in the garage. When Barb came back to the cabin later that afternoon, he was polishing rust off the handle of the new scooter. Though built from scraps, he'd managed to give the piece a hip, retro look. "The boys are going to love it." She smoothed the plastic streamers he'd fastened to the handlebars. "Where did you learn how to do this — make stuff?"

"I was always messing with things around the house when I was a kid. I wanted to be an engineer, but my dad convinced me to be an accountant instead, so I could take over that position at the company."

"You never told me you wanted to be an engineer." Twenty-one years of marriage and the man still had secrets. The idea dismayed her.

He shrugged. "I liked being an accountant okay, but inventing things is more satisfying than adding up columns of numbers." He stepped back to admire the scooter. "Tomorrow night I'll take it over to the cabin after they're asleep."

Despite the fact that their holiday plans had been derailed, he looked happier and more relaxed than she'd seen him in years. Maybe his job had caused more stress than she'd realized. "Do you really think you can support us by recycling golf balls?" she asked.

"I know I can." He glanced at her. "Whether it will always be in the style to which you're accustomed, that's another story."

She thought of the weekly appointments with her manicurist, and the quarterly visits to the plastic surgeon for Botox touch-ups, the closet full of designer clothing and shoes and the twice-weekly sessions with her personal trainer. She'd often joked that it cost a lot of money to look like a trophy wife past age forty, but she was only telling the truth.

"If you want me to cut back on expenses, I will," she said. "It's not as if I don't know how to cut corners." When she and Jimmy had met, she'd been Barbie Sue Brown from Beaumont, former night shift waitress at Denny's.

"I don't want you to cut corners." He patted her hand. "And I don't want you to worry about money. We'll be fine."

Spoken like a man who came from money. Jimmy's family had made a fortune first from cattle, then cotton and oil. Now they leased their many acres for gas wells and wind turbines and fields full of solar panels, taking advantage of the demand for clean energy. The truth was, Jimmy could probably afford to tinker with inventions and play golf as much as he wanted.

And just like everyone else in his family, he'd make loads of money doing it. Barb really didn't have to worry. She didn't have to do anything — a realization which bothered her more than she cared to admit.

"I'm not some child you have to take care

of," she said. "Marriage is supposed to be a partnership."

He laid aside his screw driver and looked at her. "You're still upset because I didn't tell you about quitting my job, aren't you?"

"Of course I'm upset. You can't decide all by yourself to do something that turns both our lives upside down."

"My intention wasn't to turn your life upside down at all. You shouldn't notice much difference, except now I'll be home more — and our son will be gainfully employed. Those two things ought to make you happy."

Clearly, he just didn't get it. "This isn't about whether or not there'll be changes. It's about your not thinking my opinion on the matter was important."

"Of course I care what you think, but when I took the job you said the decision was up to me. I thought leaving should be my decision, too."

"When you took the job we weren't even married yet." She pulled out the chair next to him and sat. "I don't like you shutting me out of your life," she said. "I married you to be a part of your life, not just an accessory or a dependent."

He put his arm around her shoulders. "You're not an accessory, and I like looking

507

after you. I still can't believe a geek like me ended up with a beauty queen like you."

"I was going for the quarterback, you know."

"I know." He grinned. "Good thing he was a jerk."

It was a familiar exchange; the routine of it made her feel a little better. Southern Methodist University freshman Barbie Sue Brown had set her sights on the college's star quarterback, who was already being recruited by the NFL. She'd dazzled and charmed him into asking her on a date, but he'd gotten wasted at the frat party they attended and his roommate — a geeky accounting major named Jimmy Stanowski — had ended up rescuing Barb from what was turning out to be the date from hell. He'd taken her back to her dorm and they'd ended up talking all night about life, dreams, and everything. She felt he was the first man — maybe the first person, even — who'd really listened to her, who saw her as more than a beautiful doll.

Did he still think that?

"Maybe I could help you and Michael with the business," she said.

"What would you like to do?"

"I don't know. What do you need?"

"I'm handling the financing, Michael's

doing the marketing and procurement, and we're both working on design and manufacturing. I think we're covered."

"Maybe instead of spending all that time at the gym and beauty parlor, I should have learned a useful skill."

"I love you just the way you are." He turned his attention back to the scooter.

"Everyone is doing something to make Christmas for those little boys and I can't think of anything."

"We'll make the scooter from both of us. You can wrap it. You're good at making things look nice."

"When the zombie apocalypse comes, I'm sure decorators and party hostesses will be in high demand."

"What?"

"Michael was telling me about a movie he saw. Zombies take over the world and only people with survival skills can make it. Everyone else is expendable."

"You're not expendable. I'm getting hungry. Why don't you see what you can find for supper?"

She could have told him he was being a chauvinist to assume she should be the one to cook dinner, but if she'd done that, he'd have gotten up and opened the cans himself. Jimmy wasn't a fighter — but then, he'd never had to be.

Dinner was canned soup that had expired three months before. "At least we can have wine," she said, setting the bottle and two jam jar glasses on the table.

"If you can find a corkscrew."

"If you can make a scooter out of an old skateboard and skis, surely you can fashion a corkscrew."

He shook his head. "Not before the soup gets cold."

So soup it was. As Barb chased alphabet noodles around the bowl, she longed for crusty bread, wine and cheese, and a very large bar of chocolate. The thought of the dinner she could have been eating in The Last Dollar in Eureka made her want to whimper.

After washing the dishes, she lounged in bed, trying to lose herself in the romance novel she'd brought along. The baseboard heaters ticked and rattled, wind howled around the corners of the cabin, and Jimmy muttered to himself as he turned pages in his own book — all noises that reminded her she wasn't in her familiar surroundings, or any place else she wanted to be.

She had dozed off when the sound of singing awoke her — singing and banging on pots and pans and loud laughter. "What in the world!" Jimmy was already out of his chair, headed for the door. Barb followed, and reached him just in time to greet the boys and their parents. Carlo, a red T-shirt draped over his head and hanging down the back, stared up at her solemnly. "We have come to ask if you have room for us at the inn," he said solemnly.

CHAPTER SEVEN

"Room at the inn . . ." Something about the solemn pronouncement clicked in Barb's head, and she took in their attempts at costumes — Elena with a shawl draped over her head and a pillow stuffed under her blouse, next to Carlo, as a pint-sized Joseph with his T-shirt headdress and a stick for a staff. Beside him, Roberto had a similar headdress and staff, while Ernesto and Reuben hovered in the background, each carrying a lit candle. Were they shepherds or wise men or possibly angels?

She held the door open wider to welcome them in, but Elena put up a hand to stop her. "They have no room at the inn for us either. We must move on."

Carlo and Roberto drooped, the picture of weariness, though Roberto's grin as he peeked up at Barb to gauge the effectiveness of his performance gave him away. Barb hid her smile. "Good luck in your journey," she said as the group turned away.

Reuben stopped in front of them. "Now you're supposed to put on your coats and join the procession. We're headed to Mae's house."

They hurried into their coats, and Reuben handed them each a candle, and lit it from his, and they fell into step behind the others, who had waited at the end of the walkway. The Rodriguez family began singing again, in Spanish, so Barb didn't understand a word, though the children's and adults voices blended in a beautiful melody that filled the still night and brought a tightness to her throat.

They moved slowly across the parking lot, toward the main house, where one window showed a faint light. How would Mae react to this new development? It wasn't that late, but possibly she was already dressed for bed. Maybe she'd had enough of them today, what with decorating the tree and all.

The air was so cold breathing it in was a shock to the system, yet invigorating. Barb huddled into her coat and tilted her head back to take in the night sky. She gasped, and stopped walking. "I've never seen so many stars in my life," she whispered, as if speaking out loud would break the spell. Against the blackness of the sky, millions of stars glowed, like glitter scattered by a child's hand.

"No light pollution here," Jimmy whispered in return.

Starlight bathed the snow-covered landscape in a wash of silver. The firs and pines clustered around the cabins looked like black feathers against the paleness of snow and sky. The snow crunched and squeaked beneath their feet, providing a counter-rhythm to the family's sweet voices.

The procession stopped in a huddle in front of Mae's door, and Ernesto knocked. Immediately, Pearl responded with loud barking. The older woman must have heard their approach, because she opened the door right away, and frowned out at them. "What is it now?" she asked.

"We are celebrating *Las Posadas,*" Elena said. "A reenactment of the holy family's journey to Jerusalem for the birth of Jesus. We go from house to house seeking shelter. You are the last house."

Roberto stepped forward, shoulders straight, standing tall. "We have come to ask if you have room for us at the inn," he said clearly.

Mae looked at Elena. "How am I supposed to answer that?"

"You are the last house, so your answer is yes."

"So you all just come over and invite yourself in," Mae said.

"Yes. It is tradition."

Barb held her breath, afraid Mae might tell the young woman exactly what she thought of her tradition. She certainly had the right to guard her privacy, to refuse to participate in a tradition that wasn't her own. She looked out at all of them, with their candles and their breath freezing in front of their faces, these pilgrims who had sought refuge at her inn. She'd given them shelter, but did she want to welcome them into her life?

She stepped back and opened the door wider. "Come in, but I wasn't expecting company."

They crowded into the welcome warmth of the room, which was lit only by the television that flickered in front of the recliner. The remains of Mae's dinner — a bowl of soup and a packet of crackers — sat on the table beside the chair. Roberto's eyes widened at the sight of the television, and he headed toward it like a moth to a flame, but his mother took him by the shoulder and steered him away.

"Thank you for inviting us in," Elena said.

"Are you familiar with *Las Posadas*?"

"Can't say as I am." She switched on a lamp and punched a button on the remote to shut off the television. "Don't just stand around like a bunch of milling cattle. Sit down. I'm guessing refreshments are traditional, too."

"Hot chocolate," Roberto said, and grinned.

"Niño, do not be rude," Elena scolded. "We didn't come to impose," she said. "We only wanted to share our tradition with you."

"Let me see what I can find in the kitchen, then you can tell me about it."

"I'll help." Barb shed her coat and followed Mae to the kitchen. "I'm sure you didn't plan on feeding all of us," she said as Mae opened cupboards and took down cups and boxes.

"There's cocoa in the pantry there, and sugar. Being so far from the grocery store, I tend to keep things on hand, though I can't say I have a lot of variety. No cookies or chips or things children are likely to enjoy."

"The cocoa will be good." Her own mouth watered at the thought of chocolate in any form.

"I have plenty of bread and butter and cinnamon. I'll make cinnamon toast."

Again the tightness rose in Barb's throat. "My mother used to make cinnamon toast," she said. "For a treat when we got home from school." Had she ever made that simple snack for Michael? Probably not — he had access to all manner of pre-packaged snacks and microwave meals.

Ten minutes later, Barb filled mugs with hot cocoa while Mae sprinkled cinnamon and sugar on slices of buttered toast. She cut the toast into triangles and arranged them on a platter. Barb carried the cups on a tray into the living room, where someone had arranged the candles in a saucer in the center of the coffee table. The boys and Reuben sat cross-legged on the floor, while the adults filled the chairs and sofa. Jimmy rose and gave Barb his seat; they had left Mae's recliner open for her.

"I smell cinnamon," Carlo said.

"Cinnamon toast." Mae offered him the plate and he shyly took one triangle. "Take two," Mae said. "They're small. And have a cup of cocoa."

She settled into her chair with cocoa of her own. "Now. Tell me about this *Posadas*," she said.

"*Las Posadas* is a procession that takes place for the nine nights before Christmas, ending on Christmas Eve," Elena said. "It is done in memory of the holy family's journey to Jerusalem, and their search for a place for Mary to give birth to Jesus. The procession goes from house to house in the neighborhood, singing and praying. At each door they ask for shelter, but are turned away. At the last house, they're welcomed in for more songs and praying and food and fellowship."

"And the last night — Christmas Eve — there's a party," Roberto said. "With a piñata and presents and everything."

"No party this year, niño," Elena said. "And we don't have nine nights to celebrate, but the boys were bored and I thought this was a good way to take their mind off Santa Claus and onto the real reason for the holiday, at least for a little while."

Mae nodded. "So sing me a song."

The boys looked to their mother, who nodded. "Sing for us, niños. You know the words."

"En nombre de cielo, os pido posada . . ." Carlos began, and Roberto joined in, the boys' clear, sweet voices filling the still night. Elena harmonized in a gentle alto, while Ernesto added a surprisingly clear tenor.

They sang several verses, and though Barb couldn't understand the words, the music reminded her of long-ago church programs, when she was a girl in Beaumont. One year she'd played an angel, dressed in an old nightgown of her mother's and a halo of Christmas tinsel.

"*Entren, santos peregrinos, a este humilde rincon . . .*" The song ended and they all applauded.

"The song tells the story of the pilgrims searching from house to house," Elena explained. "Until at last they are welcomed in."

"To the humble '*rincon,*' " Mae nodded. "I got that part. I studied Spanish a long time ago in school. I guess I remember more than I thought."

"And you do this every year before Christmas?" Reuben asked.

"We didn't do the nine nights this year, because we were moving," Elena said. "But my brother is having a posadas at his house on Christmas Eve."

"Will they still have the party without us?" Roberto asked, his voice tremulous.

"Perhaps they will have another party for us when we join them," his mother said, and gathered him close.

"What about you folks?" Mae turned to Barb. "What do you usually do at Christmas?"

"We usually have a big party," Barb said.

"Do you have a piñata?" Ricardo asked.

Barb smiled. "No. But maybe next year we will."

Jimmy patted her shoulder. "Barb is known for her parties," he said. "Everyone wrangles for an invitation."

She flushed. "I do enjoy pulling everything together." The planning began early in the fall, choosing a theme, discussing the menu with the caterer, compiling the guest list and gathering decorations.

"How big a party are we talking about?" Mae asked.

"I think the guest list last year was two hundred," Jimmy said.

"Two twenty," Barb said. She'd rented outdoor propane heaters and arranged them all through the backyard, and strung lights in the trees so that the party could extend through the house into the yard. Her theme had been Christmas in Tuscany, with decorations of red, blue, and gold to resemble a Tuscan Christmas market. Strolling musicians entertained the guests, and a buffet loaded with fruit, cheeses, olives, meats and traditional Tuscan candies and pastries was featured on the cover of an upscale Houston magazine this past November.

For weeks afterward, Barb had basked in praise for her Christmas bash. While she'd entertained a smaller group of friends this year before she and Jimmy left for Colorado, she had to admit she'd missed the bustle and busyness of preparing for a really big celebration. As Jimmy had said, her parties were what she was known for — her biggest accomplishment every year.

"I like this cinnamon toast," Carlo said. He nibbled the last crust on his plate.

"You may have another piece if your mother says it's okay," Mae said.

Elena nodded and Carlo helped himself to a triangle of toast. Mae turned to Reuben. "What about you, Mr. Truck driver? How do you celebrate Christmas?"

Reuben set aside his empty plate and cup. "I don't. I'm Buddhist."

Mae lifted one eyebrow. "You were raised a Buddhist?"

"No. I was raised Southern Baptist, in Georgia."

"Your converting to Buddhism must have surprised some of your family."

"I guess so. I volunteer to drive over the holidays so another driver can be home with his family."

"You don't mind?"

"Why should I mind? There's less traffic, and for a day, at least, most people are in a pretty good mood."

"Have you ever been stranded by a snow-storm before?" Jimmy asked.

"At the holidays? No. But other times. I spent two days in my truck on the side of the road in Nebraska during a blizzard once. A highway crew had to dig me out."

"You were stuck in your truck for two days?" Carlo's eyes widened. "What did you do?"

"Mostly I slept. I watched movies on my laptop. Read books. Ate the peanut butter and crackers I keep for emergencies. This is a lot better." He looked to Mae. "Have you taken in stranded travelers before?"

"No. The few times we've had storms shut down the roads the Highway Patrol takes them to a Red Cross Shelter in Gunnison or Lake City. I think this is Bobby Kates's plan to not have me spend Christmas alone."

"Officer Kates?" Barb didn't try to hide her surprise.

Mae nodded. "He was a friend of my younger son, Gary's. He thinks it's his responsibility to look after me, since the boys don't live close. I've told him I don't need looking after, but he doesn't listen."

"What would you do for Christmas, if we weren't here?" Carlo asked.

"I'd have a quiet day at home. If the

weather was nice, I might go for a walk around the lake with Pearl. If it wasn't, we'd stay inside and I'd start a new quilt."

It sounded like a lonely kind of day to Barb, but peaceful, too, she supposed. Mae might be one of those people who preferred solitude.

"Thank you for taking us in," Elena said. "This is much better than trying to stay warm in our car, or sleeping on the floor in some shelter." She stood. "And now it's time for little boys to go to bed."

The boys started to protest, but a stern look from their father silenced them. Elena and Ernesto helped the boys into their coats, hats and gloves, and collected the props from their procession. The others stood also and said their good nights.

"Let me help you with these dishes," Barb said, and began to collect cups and plates.

"I'll take care of it." Mae made shooing motions. "Go on now. It's getting late."

Barb didn't argue. It must be close to ten o'clock, and maybe Mae had tolerated them long enough.

After the sleepy warmth of the house, the cold outside brought Barb fully awake. "If it weren't for the fact that it's keeping us away from Maggie, I'd say the snow was gorgeous," she said.

Jimmy took her hand and tucked it into the pocket of his coat with his own. "If I have to be stranded in the middle of nowhere by a blizzard, I'm glad it's with you," he said.

"So you're not going to trade me in for the beer cart girl at the golf course?" She wasn't really worried, but a woman could never be too sure. After all, Maggie hadn't seen her husband's defection coming.

"Never." He stopped and turned toward her. Moonlight smoothed the lines from his face and made him appear years younger — as young as the man she'd married. "I'm sorry I didn't talk to you about the golf ball recycling business. I can see how it might seem like a rash decision, but I've put a lot of thought and preparation into it, and I think it will really work. I want to at least try." He sounded so eager — so happy.

But she couldn't let him off too easily. She kept her expression stern. "Yes, you absolutely should have consulted me first. I'm even more upset that you never told me you've had this burning desire to be a golf ball entrepreneur."

"It's not as if I've ever pretended I thought my job was anything more than a way to pay the bills," he said. "You know I really enjoy making things with my hands. And I like the idea of building something I can pass on to Michael. This is important to me."

"Then it's important to me, too." She laced her fingers more tightly in his. "But no more secrets like this."

"I promise."

She fell quiet. Clearing the air with Jimmy ought to be a huge weight off her shoulders, but the tension inside her hadn't loosened much. She still felt unsettled and anxious. She wanted to blame him — his decision to change his life had unmoored her from her comfortable, safe routine.

But how comfortable was that routine if the prospect of it felt so empty to her now?

"What's wrong?" Jimmy bumped her shoulder.

"Why do you think something's wrong?"

"You've gone all quiet. And you're puckering your mouth, the way you do when you're fretting about something."

She pressed her lips together. She puckered? How unattractive.

"Out with it," he said. "I told you my secret; now it's your turn."

She shrugged. "I guess I'm a little jealous. I'm happy that you're realizing your dream, but what about me? I don't have a dream to realize. For years I knew exactly where I stood. I was the executive's perfect wife — the society hostess and the perfect volunteer. I was Michael's mom. Now Michael doesn't need me."

"He'll always need you."

"Not as much. And while the parties are fun, it's not as if you need me to further your career. The volunteer work is for good causes, but Houston is full of women who could do the same thing."

"Not as well as you."

"I'm not so sure of that."

"How long have you felt this way?"

She shrugged. "A while. Maybe since I got back from visiting Maggie in Eureka this summer. When she left Houston she was so sad and depressed; she'd lost everything, almost. But in Eureka she was so happy and doing all these new things — writing for the newspaper, climbing mountains, learning to do stuff for herself that she'd never had to do before. And she was doing great. I'm not so sure in her shoes I'd have been so resilient. It made me wonder if there was anything I'm really good at."

"You're good at being you. Isn't that enough?"

She shook her head. "If it was, would I feel so unsettled right now?"

"I guess the question is, what do you really

want to do?"

"Something I enjoy. Something I'm good at. I'm just not sure what that is."

He put his arm around her and hugged her close. "You're thinking about it. That's a first step. You'll find the answer."

He said that because his whole focus in life had been finding answers. He made things balance and solved problems. Barb had little practice in those arenas.

"That was fun tonight, wasn't it?" he asked as they resumed walking toward their cabin.

"It was. Those boys are so sweet. I hate that they're missing the big party with the rest of their family."

"They'll probably have another one when they get to their uncle's house. In the meantime, they'll have a good Christmas here."

"The scooter will be a surprise. They'll love it. But a Christmas dinner of canned soup isn't much of a celebration."

"I guess we're lucky to have that."

She sighed. "At home I'd call the caterer and the decorator and we'd whip up a winter wonderland they'd never forget."

"They'll never forget this Christmas either. Children have a knack for accepting the moment and not worrying about comparisons. This won't be better or worse than any other Christmas — it will just be Christmas."

She smiled at him. "Are you saying I'm spoiled?"

"Don't I spoil you? I do my best."

"Oh you do, do you?"

"Maybe you should try harder."

"Come to bed and I'll do my best."

"Mmmm. That sounds like an invitation I can't refuse."

Chapter Eight

Barb woke the next morning with her conversation with Jimmy still on her mind. He'd asked what she really wanted to do — well, that was the problem, wasn't it? For the first time in her life, she had no clear goal, nothing she could apply her talents to or work toward. When she'd met Jimmy, her goal had been to land a well-off husband. Some people would say that was a mercenary ambition, but she'd gotten lucky and found love along with a higher standard of living.

Once they were married, she devoted herself to the challenge of being the perfect executive's wife, and in the process she hoped to win over Jimmy's chilly mother. She quickly became the hardest working volunteer and the best hostess in their circle, and she liked to think she'd eventually won Mrs. Stanowski's grudging respect — didn't the fur coat show that?

Michael's arrival focused her attention on doing her best for him. She'd been there for every class party, every home and away game, every school committee and fund drive. Letting go of that role when he'd gone off to college had been a kind of relief. Time to fulfill some dreams of her own.

Except she didn't have any unfulfilled dreams. Just the growing awareness that, despite all her years of busyness, she was still Barbie Sue Brown, trying to prove she could be somebody — that she mattered somehow.

She was forty-one years old and what did she know how to do? How to give a great party. How to decorate a room and wrap a gift and dress up. And at Christmas — the one time of year when she could really put these talents to good use — she was stuck somewhere where none of that mattered.

Then again, the thought came to her, maybe they mattered more than ever. She sat up in bed, and tugged the covers up to her shoulders to ward off the chill. If anybody needed a party and celebrating right now, it was a group of stranded travelers. Especially those little boys.

Excitement fizzed in her like champagne. She threw back the covers and reached for her clothes. She knew what she had to do

— not with the rest of her life, but for today — Christmas Eve. She could utilize the one talent she had to make this a good Christmas — maybe even a great Christmas — for everyone here.

By the time she'd dressed and started water heating for tea, Jimmy was awake. "You're up early," he said. "Have trouble sleeping?"

"It's Christmas Eve. I still get excited about the day, even at my age. Isn't that funny?"

"Not so funny." He sat up on the side of the bed and ran his hand over his jaw. "You're one of those people who can always find a reason to celebrate. It's one of the things I love about you."

She stopped in the act of pouring instant oatmeal into a bowl and looked over her shoulder at him. "Really? That's one of the nicest things anyone ever said to me."

"I only tell the truth." He stood and began to dress. "Want to come ice fishing with me this morning?"

She did her best to hide her glee that he was so conveniently going to be out of her hair for the day and wrinkled her nose in feigned disinterest. "I don't think so. What are you going to use for bait?"

"I was thinking about that can of Spam

we found in the back of the cabinet."

"I'm not sure how I feel about eating anything that's attracted to Spam."

"Don't think about the Spam. Think about a nice trout or salmon grilled with a little olive oil and fresh herbs."

"Except we don't have olive oil or fresh herbs."

"A guy can dream."

"Then go on, dreamer. I'll stay here."

"What will you do with yourself?"

"Oh, I'll find something." Let him imagine her whiling away the day reading her romance novel and napping. Instead, she'd be busy pulling together a big Christmas surprise for all of them.

She could hardly keep from shooing him away. As if sensing her impatience, he dawdled, lingering over his tea and oatmeal, then taking his time gathering the things he thought he'd need — the Spam and a knife and extra layers of clothes. Then it was off to the shed to unearth an ancient ice auger and fishing tackle. At last, he trudged off toward the lake, down a path countless other anglers had worn from the cabins down to the lake shore, discernable even in the snow.

As soon as Jimmy was out of sight Barb went in search of Reuben. She found him in his cabin — from the looks of his bleary eyes she might even have awakened him. "I need your help," she said.

He raked a hand through his unruly hair and regarded her warily. "Help with what?"

"We're going to hike up to your King's Grocery truck and get everything we need for a Christmas party." Why no one had thought of doing this earlier, she couldn't imagine, except that they'd all forgotten about the truck full of groceries in their worry over everything else.

Reuben shook his head. "Uh-uh. We can't do that."

"Why not? It's all just sitting up there while we're stuck here eating canned soup and Spam. I admit, it might be a bit of a hike, but I'm willing if you are."

"No ma'am. None of that stuff in the truck belongs to us."

"But it's for sale, right? I'll pay you for everything. We'll find some paper and a pen and you can write down everything. I'll write you a check today if you like."

"Nope." He started to close the door, but she thrust herself over the threshold.

"You can't tell me you want to spend Christmas eating two-year-old canned soup — or that you want those children to wake up Christmas morning with no stockings and no candy or fruit or any Christmas feast, when you have everything we need to have a real celebration right there in that truck."

He looked pained. "I'm sorry. I wish I could help you, but I can't. I can't take the risk."

"Risk? What risk? You can't think anyone at King's is going to begrudge you helping to make Christmas for a couple of kids."

The lines on his forehead deepened. He shook his head slowly. "King's is a big corporation. Corporations don't think like people."

"Oh, please! Corporations are run by people. People who will understand, I'm sure. Honestly, what could be so bad?"

"You can say that because you're a woman who's never had trouble in her life."

"Reuben, you aren't making sense here."

He looked from side to side, as if making sure they were alone. He leaned toward her. "I've got a record," he said softly.

She frowned. "A record?" Did he mean he kept a journal or a log book?

"I've been in prison, all right? I've got a criminal record." His expression was a mixture of defiance and fear.

Barb swallowed hard, and tried not to show her shock at this revelation. "Well, I never would have guessed."

"What? I don't look like your idea of an ex-con?"

That was exactly what she meant, but she wasn't about to admit it. "It doesn't matter," she said. "This wouldn't be stealing."

"It does matter. King's took a chance hiring me. If I take anything from that truck they'll call it stealing and I'll be out of a job — not just this one, but any kind of job."

Maybe what he said was true. The idea made her angry. "Just let them try to say you stole anything. I know a couple of very good lawyers, a handful of journalists, and two U. S. senators."

"And you'd make a fuss for me?"

"Of course I would. I'd raise so much hell rock stars would be holding concerts on your behalf."

This surprised a chuckle from him. "I believe you would."

"Please." She hesitated, then took his hand, the fingers thick and calloused, so different from Jimmy's. "I want to make a nice Christmas for all of us," she said. "You have everything in that truck we need."

He gently withdrew from her grasp. "I don't know about that, but I'll do what I can to help."

"Thank you! Thank you!" She had to

restrain herself from jumping up and down like a girl who'd just been granted her fondest wish.

"Just remember your thanks if they come to arrest me." He stepped back and took his coat from a hook by the door. "Is that the only coat you have?"

She looked down at the fur. "I'm sorry. Does it offend your Buddhist sensibilities? I don't believe in killing animals for fur either, but I inherited it. And it is warm."

"I'm not offended — I just think you're liable to get it dirty digging around inside the truck."

"I'll be careful. And I don't have another coat." She'd worn this one as often as possible since Mrs. Stanowski had passed it on to her, out of a sense of obligation, or maybe it was her way of saying *I'm good enough to wear your coat, so why didn't you think I was good enough for your son?*

"You're going to need something to carry all that stuff on," Moe said.

"What do you suggest?"

"There's a couple of sleds in the shed."

The pair of children's sleds were actually nailed to the wall on the back of the shed, the old-fashioned type with wooden platforms and metal runners. Mae's sons must have used them when they were little. Did she even remember they were here anymore? Reuben wrenched them from the wall and dropped them in the snow. "They're so rusty and beat up they'd be hard to ride on, but they'll be okay for hauling groceries."

"Come on. Let's get out of here before someone sees us and asks what we're up to."

"Last night Elena said something about her and Ernesto taking the boys down to the lake this morning," Reuben said as he led the way around the shed.

"That's where Jimmy is, too. He said he was going to catch fish for our dinner, but I'm hoping to bring back something a lot better."

"Then let's go." He motioned for her to go ahead of him, but she hung back.

"You'd better lead," she said. "I'm not exactly sure where the truck is parked, or even how far away."

"And yet you're certain you can carry a load of groceries back here?"

"It can't be that far," she said. "And I'm determined to do this. I won't give up."

"And I guess I have to not give up with you."

"Come on. You'll be a hero."

"Can't say I've ever been one of those." He set off through the snow, the empty sled bouncing along behind him.

Having made the trip to the cabins on the back of a snow-mobile in a snowstorm, Barb had no idea how far they were from the highway, but she reasoned Mae's business couldn't be too remote. Still, the going was tougher than she'd expected, the unpacked snow rising past her knees, drifts making it difficult to gauge distance or landmarks. She clamped her mouth shut, determined not to utter so much as a squeak of complaint. Any hesitation on her part might make Reuben give up.

At least he was breaking trail for her, for which she was grateful. "What were you in prison for?" she asked when they were out of sight of the cabins.

He glanced over his shoulder at her. "Not anything violent, if that's what you're worried about."

"I wasn't worried, just nosy."

He faced forward once more. "I got popped for burglary. And drugs. I had a problem, but I'm straight now."

"Is that why you turned Buddhist? Part of your rehab?" Wasn't finding religion part of recovery for some people?

"Not exactly." His breath came in puffs of white fog as they trudged up a small hill. "I'm not really Buddhist. I mean, I've done

538

some reading and it seems like an okay religion, as religions go. I mainly tell folks that to get them off my back about the holidays."

"What do you mean?"

He reached the top of the hill and waited for her. "You okay, or you want to rest a little?"

"I'm fine." She panted, trying to catch her breath. She wanted to ask how much farther they had to go, but bit back the words. "Do you have something against Christmas?" she asked instead. "Bad memories or something?"

He set out walking once more and she hurried after him. If she let him get too far ahead she could end up lost in this world of white drifts and evergreen trees that all looked alike. "The reason I work on Christmas isn't because I don't believe in celebrating," he said. "It's just that I don't have any family to celebrate with. They washed their hands of me when I went to prison."

She heard no trace of self-pity in his words, but she ached for him just the same. "Have you talked to them since you got out?" she asked.

His shoulders hunched. "I called my sister once. She hung up on me. I don't blame them. I stole from her and from my mother, too."

"They might like the man you are now a lot more than the addict you were."

"Maybe. But maybe they can't forgive all the bad things I did."

Was that true? She supposed it might be possible for Michael to do something so awful she couldn't forgive him, but she was glad she couldn't imagine what that might be. "Maybe they couldn't forgive you right away," she said. "But time might make that easier."

"Better to stay away."

No, not better, she thought. Not better for the mother and sisters who had to miss him more at this time of year than any other.

But maybe not. What did she know, considering the sheltered, spoiled life she led? Maybe forgiveness was easier when you had money and position and no real trouble in your life.

"You should try again. This year. I guarantee they think of you over the holidays, and they probably think of the good things more than the bad. Your calling might be the one gift they've really been wishing for, even if they can't say it."

He grunted, a noise of dismissal.

"You remember the story Mae told, about

the man who came home to his sons at Christmas?"

"I figured that was her old man. So what was he — a soldier?"

"No. He came home from prison. Apparently, he embezzled some money and got caught."

He turned, brown eyes searching her face. "No lie?"

"No lie. She lost everything she had. It all went to pay back the people he'd taken money from. She was angry and hurt — but when he showed up at Christmas, she realized her boys needed a father. And she realized she still loved him, in spite of everything."

"Hmmph. I wouldn't have guessed that one."

"Your mother and sister still love you, even if they don't like what you became. I think you owe it to them to try for a second chance."

"You sure like bossing people around, don't you?" But there was no heat in his words.

"I guess I do." She smiled.

He turned away from her and started walking again. "I'll think about it," he said after a moment.

Maybe it was none of her business, but

she was sure she was right about his family. Blood truly was thicker than water and if he had been her son — if Michael had been sent to prison for stealing and doing drugs — she would never have stopped loving him, even if she'd ended up so angry she couldn't stand to be in the same room with him. That was the way mothers — good mothers, anyway — were wired.

They topped another rise and he raised his arm to point to their left. "We're almost there."

The truck was a boxy wall rising out of a snowbank, smaller mounds of snow behind it for Barb and Jimmy's car and the Rodriguez's pickup, the bed piled high with what she realized must be all of their possessions. All around them was a flat expanse of snow, sculpted into stiff waves by the wind. "I can't even see the road," she said, dismayed. "We'll be here until next spring, waiting for it to melt."

"You won't have to wait for it to melt. Those big rotary plows the state uses will cut right through it. As soon as the danger of avalanches in the passes ahead is gone, the highway department will bring a crew through here and open the road in a manner of hours."

"That would be the nicest Christmas

present I could think of," she said.

They trudged the rest of the way to the truck and kicked through drifts to reach the back of the trailer. Then they had to scrape aside the snow with their hands to free the door. "Don't know why I didn't think to bring a shovel," Reuben grumbled.

"My hands are frozen." Barb surveyed her soaked gloves, then stepped back from the now-cleared door. "But it doesn't matter. Open up."

He took a key from his pocket and fit it into locks on the double doors at the back of the trailer, then shoved one door open. The smells of citrus fruit, cinnamon, coffee and garlic descended on them in a cloud. Barb's mouth watered and her stomach rumbled. "Boost me up," she said. "Time to go shopping."

"I'll get in first and help you up." Reuben hauled himself into the trailer, then shoved boxes aside to clear a space for them to stand. He leaned down and Barb grasped his hand. "Be careful," he cautioned. "Watch for sharp edges and slippery spots."

"I will," she promised, and he helped her up beside him.

"What exactly do you want?" he asked.

She surveyed the stacks of boxes and crates. "We need a ham — that'll be easier to cook than a turkey. Stuffing. Potatoes. Fruit. Pies would be good. Milk for the children, maybe?"

"Produce is up here. Meat's toward the back. Canned goods on the left."

They sorted through and moved aside boxes in search of the items on Barb's list. She tilted her head sideways to read the stenciled labels on boxes and cartons. When she found something she wanted, she pointed it out and Reuben pulled the box down and set it in front of her. "What next?" he asked.

"I can't take the whole carton. Open it."

He hesitated, then pulled out a pocket knife, folded open a blade and slit the carton along the side. She pulled out a couple of packages of gravy mix and set them aside. "Now, how about that box up there labeled Green Beans."

She plowed her way through oranges, eggnog and eggs. "This is better than a sale at Sack's," she said as she handed him a spiral-sliced ham wrapped in gold and red foil.

"Don't forget, we have to carry all this stuff back," he said. "Don't get carried away."

"It's Christmas. Of course I'm getting carried away."

But at last even she agreed she'd done all the damage she could. She had candy for the children, coffee and chocolate for the adults, and even some treats for Pearl. "Hand me that package of paper plates and I guess we're done."

He obliged, then hopped to the ground and turned to reach back for her. "I won't let them fire you, I promise," she said, while he still had hold of her.

"I guess if anyone can stop them, it'll be you. You don't take no for an answer."

"No, I don't."

She tried to help him arrange her "purchases" on the sleds, but finally gave up. Her efforts were more of an impediment than a help. While he stacked and tied and muttered under his breath, she walked along what must have been the shoulder of the road and looked back toward the fishing camp. The tracks she and Reuben had made on their way to the truck showed clearly in the smooth snow, the choppy, crooked rambling of some ungainly creature.

For the first time, she noticed the small, faded sign hanging from a tree beyond the highway ditch. "Fishing Cabins" the sign advertised, with a painting of a group of log cabins beside a large trout hanging from a hook. An arrow pointed ahead. "You'd have to know the place was there to even find it," she observed when Reuben dragged the sleds alongside her.

"I think Mae likes it that way."

"I don't see how she stands being along here all winter."

"Not everybody enjoys a crowd," he said. "Maybe she had enough of that before her husband stole that money. Being alone gives you time to think."

"Think too much and you'll go crazy," she said.

"She's not all alone. She has friends, like that Officer Kates. Not everyone is a social butterfly like you."

"I guess not. All right. Let's head back. I have a lot of work to do." She took hold of the rope attached to her sled and tugged. The overloaded sleigh scarcely moved.

"You're going to have to put some real muscle into it," Reuben said. "Fortunately, most of our route is downhill."

But first they had to get over the line of drifts beside the highway. Barb tugged and fought and swore. "Maybe we should leave it and I'll come back," Reuben said, without enthusiasm.

"No. I'm going to do this." She grabbed the rope with both hands, dug in her heels, and hauled back with all her might.

The sled moved — an inch, then another. Barb huffed and puffed, plowing her way through the drift, afraid to stop moving for an instant. On the other side of the drift the ground sloped down, and the sled picked up speed. Soon Barb was running to stay ahead.

Reuben laughed and loped after her, his sled in tow.

Their return pace was faster. By the time they drew in sight of the cabins, Barb was soaked with sweat beneath her fur coat, and she could no longer feel her fingers and toes, but a sense of triumph warmed her from the inside out. She stopped on the edge of the woods beside the cabins.

"What do we do now?" Reuben asked, halting beside her.

"I want this to be a surprise, so I need to make sure no one sees us."

"I'll take care of that." He dropped the rope for his sleigh and strode into the clearing. No one came out to greet him, or called to him from the other cabins. He looked back toward Barb and motioned that the coast was clear.

She hauled her sled toward the last cabin in line, the only unoccupied unit in this front grouping. Reuben retrieved his sled and followed. She stopped in front of the door to the cabin. "Can you open it?" she asked. "It's locked and I don't want to have to explain to Mae why I need the key."

"If I say no you're going to convince me to do it anyway, aren't you?"

She grinned. "You catch on fast."

He took hold of the doorknob, put his shoulder against the door and shoved. The lock popped and the door swung open. "Hurry, let's get all this inside before someone sees," she said.

He helped her unload the sleds, piling all the groceries on the two double beds in the cabin. "Thanks." She turned up the dial on the thermostat by the door and peeled off her wet gloves. "You can go now. I'll take it from here."

"Oh, no. I'm in now. I'll help you clean the place up."

"If I was a more gracious person I'd insist that you didn't have to go to all that trouble." She wrinkled her nose. "But I really would appreciate your help." Like the other cabins, this one had clearly been neglected since summer. Dust coated every surface, and the air was musty and stale.

"I know where Mae keeps the maid's cart. What are you going to do once the place is clean?"

"I'm going to decorate. Then I'm going to cook."

"You can cook?"

She made a face at him. "Not a lot, but heating a pre-cooked ham isn't hard, and even I can do stuffing from a box and gravy from a jar. It won't be gourmet, but it will be better than canned soup."

"And when are you going to tell the others?"

"Tonight, when the children do the posadas thing. This will be the last house. They'll come in and we'll have a party. A real Christmas party."

He shook his head. "You're really something, you know that?"

"I'll take that as a compliment."

"The first time I saw you, climbing out of that Lexus in your mink coat, I thought you'd be one of those women who look down their noses on everything and everybody who wasn't up to your standards."

"And I knew you thought that." She laughed at his embarrassed look. "Women in mink coats get judged just as harshly as ex-cons sometimes," she said. "And sometimes the judgments are justified."

"And sometimes they aren't." He nodded. "You're all right."

"So are you." She patted his shoulder.

"Come on. We'd better get to cleaning. We have a lot to do before dark."

CHAPTER NINE

If Barbie Sue Bowman had decided to wow the beauty contest judges with her decorating and party organizing talents all those years ago, she might have won that Miss Texas pageant after all, Barb thought as she put the finishing touches on the old cabin. The place was truly transformed. As soon as they'd finished the heavy cleaning, she'd banished Reuben, telling him to make sure Mae was part of the night's *Posadas* procession, and that everyone should make cabin four their final stop.

She tacked up red paper tablecloths to hide the drab walls, and pushed the beds to one side and covered them with blankets and pillows to serve as makeshift sofas. She draped the scarred table with another holiday-themed cloth and piled oranges and apples in baskets and filled bowls with candy. Every saucer and shallow bowl in the cabinets had been pressed into service to hold a candle, and the aromas of pine, cinnamon, and vanilla drove out the scents of staleness and disuse. Paper plates decorated with poinsettias and plastic cutlery tied with red ribbon awaited the feast.

And what a feast it would be — ham and potatoes, green beans and broccoli and fruit salad. No one would mind that almost everything came from a box or can, and for dessert she would assemble a trifle of cubes of pound cake, canned peaches, pineapple and cherries, and whipped cream from a can. Coffee for the adults and milk for the children rounded out a meal they'd all never forget.

Decorating complete, and everything prepped for the meal that evening, Barb stepped back to admire her work. She thought of Christmases when she was a girl, in those drab rent houses on the poorer side of town. Even then, she'd been the one to "do" Christmas — the one who cared what things looked like, who tried to hide the ugliness of life around her with paper and ribbons and potpourri. She'd never seen it as a talent, just something she had to do. But here, in this remote little outpost, this could be her contribution to the celebration. Other people could carve toys and assemble scooters and cut trees, but she could set the table and arrange the feast. She could add a little holiday magic they could all enjoy.

Smiling to herself, she switched off the light and shut the door behind her, then hurried to her own cabin. Jimmy sat at the table, little pieces of something arranged neatly before him. "How was the fishing?" she asked, and kissed his cheek before she shed her coat and sat across from him.

"Apparently the fish don't like Spam any more than we do." He offered a rueful smile. "Sorry. No fresh fish for dinner."

"That's all right." What would she have done with a fish, anyway, with a ham the size of a stock pot ready to go into the oven? "Did you have a good time?"

"It was cold and windy and, I don't know — desolate. Out there on the ice, nothing to see for miles but more ice and snow and trees — it's hard not to feel insignificant." He squinted at the item in his hand. "I guess I'm too much of a city guy to feel at home in the wilderness."

"That's a relief. I love visiting Eureka, but I'm not ready to turn rustic. What are you working on?"

"The fishing reel I was using wasn't casting smoothly, so I thought I'd see if I could improve the action."

"When you were a little boy, did you take all your toys apart and put them back together again?"

"I did." He fit two pieces of the reel together and picked up a screwdriver. "I got in trouble for replacing the burned out heating element in our coffee maker, because my mother wanted one of those fancy new espresso machines and my father wouldn't buy one until the coffee maker we had wore out."

"Your parents didn't understand you."

"Do you understand Michael?" He shook his head. "I already know the answer to that — parents never really understand their kids. My father would have been much happier if I'd devoted myself to sports and girls. I can't tell you how thrilled he was when I took up golf. And when I brought you home he gave me the biggest compliment I ever heard from him."

"What was that?"

Jimmy set aside the reel and smiled at her. "He said, 'Boy, either she's after your money or you're better in the bedroom than I gave you credit for.' "

"I hope you told him it was the latter." Too bad Ken Stanowski wasn't still alive. Barb was old enough now that she'd give him hell about such a declaration. Unlike his chilly wife, Ken had always been nice to Barb — nicer than he often was to his son, come to think of it. He'd died of a heart attack more than ten years ago — one more reason Barb was always worried about Jimmy working too hard or being under too much stress.

"I knew you enjoyed the money, too," he said. "But there were a lot of men at school with money, and most of them were better looking than me, so I figured you meant it when you said you loved me, and that's all that really mattered."

"I do love you," she said. "You were the only one of those men who always looked me in the eyes when we talked, and you really listened to what I had to say."

"I was looking at your body, too," he said. "But I was smart enough not to show it."

"You devil."

He picked up the reel. "My plotting paid off. I got the prettiest co-ed at SMU to marry me and she's actually stuck around all these years."

"I'm certainly not going to go to all the trouble of breaking in a new husband now. And I can't think of anyone else I'd rather be stuck in a snowstorm with."

"Let me know when you're ready for your canned soup."

"How about never?"

He fit another part into the reel. "When we get out of here I think I'm going to pull over at the first steakhouse I see and order the biggest slab of meat they can bring me."

"Mmmm. On that thought, let's wait until after the *Posadas* procession."

"Smart woman. Maybe Mae will have something better than soup for refreshments."

"Maybe. After all — it's Christmas Eve." She stood. "I think I'm going to take a shower. I feel like dressing up tonight."

He glanced at her. "What are you up to?"

"Why do you think I'm up to something? I just thought it would be fun to dress up for Christmas Eve."

"You look very . . . smug. Like someone with a secret."

"You're imagining things." But she smiled to herself as she turned away, pleased that he still paid attention after all these years. She'd been smart to choose him over the quarterback. And his mother had been wrong — not only was she worthy of Jimmy, she was exactly the woman he needed.

While Jimmy took his turn in the cabin's tiny shower, Barb slipped next door to put the ham in the oven. She was back in her place at the table, pretending to read her book, when he emerged from the bathroom, freshly shaved and dressed in a suit. He was better looking now than he'd been when they were kids — a fuller face and graying hair suited him somehow. Impulsively, she leaned in and gave him a deep kiss.

"Mmmm. What was that for?" he asked.

"No special reason. I just wanted to kiss you."

"I'm happy to oblige, any time."

They heard the children singing about five-thirty, and Jimmy opened the door at the first timid knock, to discover they were the first stop on the procession. Roberto had the role of Joseph tonight, and he'd added a new touch to the costume — a long stick, curved at the end like a shepherd's crook.

"We have traveled a long way and are very tired," Roberto said, brown eyes twinkling with excitement. "We have come to ask if you have room for us at the inn."

"We have no room at the inn," Jimmy said, with equal solemnity.

Roberto's shoulders sagged. "Then we must keep searching."

Barb and Jimmy accepted candles, lit them, and joined the procession as they headed toward Reuben's cabin, where the request and denial were repeated, then they moved toward Mae's house. "I forgot something back at our cabin," Barb whispered to Jimmy.

"What?"

"I promised Mae I'd bring her that book I was reading."

"You can get it later."

"No. I'm afraid I'll forget. I'll be right back." She caught Reuben's eye, and he nodded, just once. His job was to make sure the little procession continued on to Cabin Four.

Barb hurried back toward her cabin, but moved past it to the last cabin in line. Inside, she stripped off her coat, then began opening cans and boxes, dumping the contents into pots to heat. With luck, the discussion at Mae's would take a few extra minutes; Mae might even try to argue with Reuben, and they'd have to wait for her to put on her coat and hat.

She lit candles, kindling the last tiny flame as singing filled the night outside her door.

She took a deep breath, then went to answer the knock. "Hello," she greeted the procession. Adults and children alike stared back at her with expressions of anticipation. "What brings you all out on this cold and lonely night?"

Elena nudged Roberto. "Oh!" he cried, then composed his face into an expression of adult solemnity. "My wife and I have traveled a long way, and she's going to have a baby. We want to know if you have room for us at the inn."

"Come in." She opened the door wider. "Come in and make yourselves comfortable and feast. There is plenty of room."

They filed in, everyone talking at once, Pearl barking with excitement.

"Oh boy, it's a party!" Roberto cried as he raced past her into the room.

"It smells good in here." Carlo raised his nose in the air and sniffed. "Like good food."

"Where did you get all of this?" Elena asked.

"I bet I can guess," Mae said. "From a certain King's Grocers truck stuck on the highway."

"We kept track and I intend to pay for everything," Barb said.

"I never saw a woman get so excited about shopping for groceries," Reuben said.

"There's a ham, and lots of other good things," Barb said. "And coffee, and even wine, if someone will open the bottles."

Jimmy hurried to do the honors. "I can't believe you did all of this." Elena stared, as if she expected the bounty to disappear at any moment.

"Reuben helped," Barb said.

Reuben made a snorting sound. "Like I had a choice. The woman won't take no for an answer."

"This is my Christmas gift to all of you," Barb said.

Mae accepted a glass of wine from Jimmy. "I hardly recognize this place. You could be a professional party planner."

"I could," Barb agreed. "Except that Houston is overrun with those. Besides, planning other people's parties wouldn't be nearly as much fun as planning my own."

"You could be a decorator, then." Mae looked around them. "You've made this old cabin look like some fancy bed and breakfast."

"That's an idea." Barb smiled, but deep inside she felt a tingle, as if something wonderful had happened, though she couldn't imagine what that might be.

Elena helped her assemble the rest of the meal, and everyone served themselves and found seats at the table or on the beds. "Reuben, will you say grace for us?" Mae asked.

To Barb's surprise, the big man bowed his head. "We're thankful that we can be together tonight, enjoying this good meal," he said. "And we're grateful for this shelter from the storm. Amen."

They ate like starving people, or maybe simply people for whom a diet of canned soup had grown dull. Even Pearl enjoyed a special plate of some gourmet dog food Barb had grabbed at the last minute. "She'll turn up her nose at her kibble tonight," Mae said, but she didn't look particularly upset as she helped herself to a third slice of ham.

Appetite sated, Barb sat back in her chair and surveyed the room. She felt warm and filled and . . . happy. Happier than she had been in a while. Two days ago, she would have said celebrating in this place, so far from where she wanted to be, and with a bunch of strangers, was impossible. But here they all were, and she felt such a tenderness for the people around her, as if they were all family.

"Merry Christmas, everyone," she said.

"Merry Christmas," they echoed.

She and Elena enlisted the children to help clear the table, stuffing the plates and cutlery into big trash bags, then arranging the few leftovers in bowls and on platters to fill the cabin's tiny refrigerator. While they were busy doing this, Ernesto and Jimmy slipped out to play Santa Claus and arrange the boys' gifts under the tree in their cabin.

The boys' eyes were beginning to droop by the time Barb blew out the candles and followed everyone outside. Moonlight illuminated the snowy landscape like a spotlight. Jimmy made a show of examining the ground in front of the Rodriguez's cabin. "Are those sleigh tracks?" he asked, and pointed to twin lines in the snow.

Mae came to stand beside him. "I believe they are." She pointed ahead of the tracks. "And are those reindeer hooves?"

Barb blinked at a confusion of deer hoofprints clearly marked in the snow. The boys stared, open-mouthed, then Roberto broke into a grin. "Santa Claus!" He turned and raced his brother to the door of Cabin Two. The boys arrived at the same time, and hurried to pull open the door. The adults followed, arriving just in time to witness the discovery of the scooter. "I can't believe it!" Carlo said. "It's even cooler than a bike."

The boys took turns gliding across the floor on the scooter, before their mother directed their attention to the other gifts. While they exclaimed over the shirts Mae had made and the animals Ernesto had carved, Barb sidled over to Jimmy. "The scooter was a hit," she said.

"I think so." He grinned.

"If the golf ball recycling doesn't work out, you can sign on as one of Santa's helpers."

He shook his head. "Too tall." He put his arm around her. "And how about you? Tonight was amazing. I can't believe you pulled it off without anyone knowing."

"Except Reuben. I couldn't have done it without his help."

"You were the mastermind. You're very good at organizing people."

"You mean I'm bossy. Reuben said the same thing."

"No, I mean you're good at coming up with an idea and making it happen."

"Party planning and decorating aren't going to save me when the zombie apocalypse rolls around." But her tone was teasing. What did she care about that now?

"I think you're wrong," Jimmy said. "When things are at their bleakest, that's when we need pleasant surroundings and a good meal the most."

"You may have a point."

Roberto ran up to her. He was wearing his new cowboy shirt and clutching a carved dog to his chest. "Thank you for the party, Mrs. Stanowski," he said.

"You're welcome. Merry Christmas."

"Merry Christmas." He threw his arms

around her, hugging her knees. She knelt and gathered him close, blinking back a film of tears. The boy pulled back. "Did Santa bring you a present?" he asked.

"I think he just did." She patted him and stood. Roberto ran to catch a ride on the scooter, which Carlo was piloting around the room again.

"Are you ready to call it a night?" Jimmy asked.

"Yes. I'm tired." And she was suddenly exhausted. Today had been a lot of work. "Let's get some rest. After all, tomorrow's Christmas."

"Do you have big plans?" he asked.

"Yes. I'm going to walk up the highway until I get a phone signal and call Maggie. And Michael. I want to wish my little boy a Merry Christmas, even if he isn't so little anymore."

"That sounds like a plan, then."

CHAPTER TEN

Christmas morning, Barb awoke to the sound of children's voices. For a moment, caught in the world between sleeping and waking, she thought she was hearing Michael and a friend, playing in the backyard of the house in Houston. She was ten years younger, and it was time to get up and see to breakfast for the children.

But then she opened her eyes and stared up at the water-marked ceiling of the cabin and remembered where she was, and why, and she felt a bit of a let down. Where had the years gone?

"Sounds like the boys are having fun with their new toys." Jimmy rolled over and pulled her close. "Merry Christmas."

"Merry Christmas." She nestled close.

"Do we have any coffee left?" he asked.

"Yes. In a bag on the counter."

"I never thought I'd be so grateful for coffee," he said, and slid out of bed, leaving her cold and grumpy.

But she felt better once she was dressed and sipping the coffee, with generous amounts of sugar and cream. She presented Jimmy with his presents — a contraption to monogram golf balls, and a very nice leather jacket, which he put on immediately. "I got the monogram thingie for your personal golf balls," she said. "But I suppose you could use it to mark the ones you recycle with the company name or something."

"That's a terrific idea." He kissed her. "Thank you."

"What is the company name?" she asked.

"What else? We're calling it Stanowski and Son. The logo is two esses joined by an ampersand. S&S."

"Of course." The obvious pride in his voice made her smile.

He went to the bed and pulled a box from beneath it. "I already gave you the boots, but there's this, too."

The box was too large to be jewelry, too small for books or clothes. Perfume, she guessed. Jimmy tended to buy things he was certain she would like, without being too adventurous. She carefully peeled back the paper and lifted the lid. There, in a nest of tissue, lay a silver bell with a carved wooden handle. She lifted it from the box and it sounded a clear chime.

"Do you like it?" he asked anxiously.

"It's beautiful." She smoothed her thumb over the pattern of birds, leaves and flowers carved into the handle. "But why a bell?"

He shrugged. "I guess I wanted to get you something beautiful and maybe not very practical. Something besides another bottle of perfume or earrings."

So much for thinking he was predictable. Clearly, he was anything but these days. She rang the bell again. The clear chime reverberated through the room and a shiver of anticipation raced up her spine. Maybe this was a sign — a good omen for the future. "I know just what I'm going to do with it," she said.

"What's that?"

She kissed his cheek. "I can't tell you yet. But I will, soon." She replaced the bell in its package. "Let's go outside and see what everyone else is up to."

The sun on the snow shone so bright that even wearing sunglasses, Barb had to squint. Carlo wobbled past her on the scooter. "Merry Christmas!" he called.

"Merry Christmas," she replied. Roberto raced after his brother, Pearl in his wake, the flag of her tail waving.

"Merry Christmas," Elena called. They

joined her and Ernesto in front of Cabin Two. "The scooter is a big hit," she said to Jimmy. "Thank you again."

"I had a blast putting it together."

"And thank you for the party last night," Elena said to Barb. "That was a wonderful surprise."

"You're welcome, but I did it as much for myself as for anyone else. It was the one thing I could contribute."

"I'll admit I was pretty glad of a cup of coffee this morning," Reuben said.

"Have your bosses call me if there's any trouble," Barb said. "Or you call me yourself."

"I'm hoping you're right and since it's Christmas, they won't raise a fuss."

"You're in a more positive mood this morning," Barb said.

He shrugged. "It's hard not to feel good on a day like today."

Barb had to agree. The sun shone brightly in the bluest sky she'd ever seen, not a cloud in sight, and snow sparkled in the trees and draped everything in a blanket of white, as if the world was a wedding cake, and they were figures in a tableau atop it.

The door to the house opened and Mae emerged, carrying a stack of folded quilts. Pearl rushed to her. "Go on now," Mae fussed at the dog. "If I slip and break something the two of us would be in a pickle." She made her way across the yard to where the rest of them stood.

"Merry Christmas," Jimmy said.

"I've got something for you all," she said. She handed Barb the quilt on top of the stack, then distributed the others to Elena and Reuben. "These are to keep in your vehicles, to use if you ever get stranded by weather again."

Barb unfolded her gift. It was smaller than a bed quilt, but bigger than a baby blanket, with a patchwork of blockish hearts framed by a border of postage-stamp sized squares. "Mae, it's beautiful! Thank you."

Mae looked away, toward where the boys and the dog played. "Just something practical to remember me by."

"As if any of us could ever forget this Christmas," Barb said. "Or you. Thank you for everything."

Mae waved away her words, then froze, hand in the air. "Do you hear that?"

"Hear what?" Reuben asked.

But Barb heard it — the sound of an engine, and of metal scraping on snow. "It's a snowplow!" she said, and pointed up the little road that connected the fishing cabins to the highway. The bright orange hulk of a plow hove into view, like a second sun cresting the horizon. With a screech of the heavy blade against pavement, it pushed a wall of snow to one side and chugged toward them. Behind the snowplow came a Highway Patrol SUV.

When the plow reached the end of the drive, it made a sweeping turn. The group standing in front of the cabins cheered and waved, even the boys and the dog adding their voices. The driver smiled and saluted, then headed back the way he'd come, widening the driveway with his second pass.

The SUV stopped and Officer Kates climbed out. "I've brought you all a Christmas present," he said. "The road's open."

Another cheer went up. "We can still have Christmas dinner with Maggie," Barb said, hugging Jimmy.

"And we can make it to Tito Ramon's," Elena said.

"Where are you headed?" Officer Kates asked Reuben.

The truck driver shoved his hands in the pockets of his leather bomber jacket. "I thought about something Barb told me. I think I'm going to finish my run to Montrose and give my mom and sister a call, wish them a Merry Christmas."

Barb resisted the urge to run over and hug

him; it would just embarrass them all, but she smiled and nodded at him, and he offered a shy smile in return.

"What about you, Mae?" the officer asked. "Will you be all right when everyone leaves?"

"Pearl's going to miss those boys." She nodded to where the children and the dog had resumed their play. "But it will be good to have my peace and quiet back." But she smiled when she said it.

"Are you sure you don't need help with anything?" Kates asked.

"What I need help with is eating all the food left over from our party last night," she said. "There's a huge ham, and a Christmas cake I baked when I couldn't sleep last night." She gave the officer a stern look, though her eyes sparkled with laughter. "You come and eat dinner with me. And bring the plow drivers and anybody else who's on duty near here. They're entitled to a lunch break, aren't they?"

He grinned. "All right, Mae. You asked for it. We'll come help you eat your leftovers."

"You do that." Mae turned to her guests. "As for the rest of you, you'd better go on and pack up. You'll want to be on the road, soon."

Barb hugged her. "Thank you for everything, Mae. I don't know what we'd have done without you."

"You'd have probably ended up in some hotel with cable." She patted Barb awkwardly. "This was a Christmas I'll never forget, that's for sure. Safe travels to you. And stop by anytime you're in the neighborhood."

Giving in to another impulse, Barb slipped out of the mink coat. "I want you to have this," she said, and draped the coat around Mae's narrow shoulders.

"No! I can't take your coat!"

"I'll wear Jimmy's jacket until I get to Eureka, then I'll borrow one from my friend, Maggie, or I'll buy a new one." She stroked the mink. She'd worn it all these years because Jimmy's mother had expected her to, but she wanted Mae to have it, to replace the one she'd had to give up, along with everything else when her husband went to jail. "I want you to have this. As a Christmas present."

Mae pulled the mink tighter around her neck. "Won't I be in style down at the grocery store?" She squeezed Barb's hand. "Thank you. I'll cherish it."

Afraid if she stayed with Mae any longer she'd burst into sentimental tears, Barb turned away and hurried to their cabin.

Jimmy followed and they silently began to pack, collecting all the belongings they'd scattered across the cabin in their short stay there.

"I'll have to buy Maggie some more tea," Barb said as she stuffed her makeup bag into the already full suitcase.

"And I'll have to buy you a new coat." He put his arm around her. "Why did you give yours to Mae?"

"You don't mind, do you? I know it was your mother's and everything . . ."

"It's been yours for years. I don't care what you do with it, I'm just curious."

"I wanted her to have something luxurious and special. And I didn't need the coat anymore. When I first inherited it, I felt like somebody every time I wore it, someone who was somehow worthy of everything I had. But I don't need to feel that way anymore."

He kissed her, the sweet, tender kiss only a couple who have been together a long time can share, a kiss that fills a silence filled with unspoken, but well understood, sentiments.

"What's that music?" Jimmy raised his head and looked toward the window at the front of the cabin.

"Music?" Barb listened, and heard the faint, tinny notes of a pop song. "I think that's my phone!"

She dove for her purse, which sat on the end of the unmade bed, and dug out the phone. "It's Maggie!" she cried, and punched the icon to answer the call. "Maggie!" she cried. "It's so good to hear from you. Merry Christmas."

"Merry Christmas to you." Maggie's voice was so full of happiness and life and love. Barb felt close to tears all over again. "I heard the road was closed. Did you get stranded?"

"We've been staying at some fishing cabins near a lake — us and a couple with children and a truck driver who was caught out with us. It's been an incredible time. I'll tell you all about it when we see you."

"I'm resisting the urge to open your presents and claim them all for myself," Maggie said. "The Highway Department website says the roads are open now, so will you be here soon?"

"As soon as we can get our car loaded and dug out of the drifts."

"Wonderful. I've got a lot to tell you, too. We've had a pretty incredible Christmas ourselves, thanks in part to the weather."

"We'll talk ourselves hoarse when we see each other," Barb said. "And I want to talk to a real estate agent while I'm there, too."

"Why? Are you planning on moving to Eureka?"

"Not exactly. But I need a big house. One with lots of bedrooms."

"Stop being so mysterious. What are you planning?"

Jimmy gave her a curious look, silently echoing Maggie's question.

"There aren't that many places to stay in the area, right?" Barb said.

"There's the hotel, and some tourist cabins . . ."

"Well, I've decided what I want to do when I grow up."

"What's that?"

Jimmy moved closer, expression still questioning.

Barb couldn't contain her grin. Excitement rose in her, just as it had when she was a girl and opened a particularly wonderful present. "I'm going to open a bed and breakfast. In Eureka. I won't have to be there full time — I can find someone to run it for me and spend part of the year there and the rest in Houston."

"That's a great idea," Maggie said. "But what made you decide this?"

"It's a long story, but let's just say that I've been thinking about what I'd really like to do, and this is the perfect job for me, the one that utilizes all my talents."

"I can't wait to hear all about it. Now hang up the phone and finish packing. I can't wait to see you."

"All right. See you soon."

She disconnected the call and looked at Jimmy. "What do you think about my new plan?" she asked.

He pulled her close in a bear hug. "I think you'd be great at anything you tried, but especially this."

"I'll put your bell on the front desk," she said. "Guests can ring it when they need help. And I'm thinking of asking Mae to make quilts for all the bedrooms."

"It will be beautiful."

"I hope so." She stepped back and returned to the suitcase. "Your mother would have been horrified by the idea," she said. "Some of our friends in Houston will be shocked, too. They'll think I'm doing this because we need the money."

"I hope the new business makes money — that's kind of the point. But you don't care what other people think, do you?"

"I'm trying not to." She zipped the case shut and set it on the floor. "It's a little scary, launching something like this when you've never done it before."

"Now you know how I feel, starting the

golf ball business."

"If you'd never decided to start your own business, I wouldn't be thinking of doing the same," she said. "And to think when you first told me, I was so upset about things changing. Now I'm looking forward to change."

"Should I buy you a new mink coat to celebrate?"

"No. I want to buy my own coat. And I'll figure things out for myself with this business, too. Scary as that prospect is, it's exciting, too." She looked around the almost empty cabin. "Are you ready to go?"

"I'm ready." He picked up the suitcases and headed for the door. She gathered up her purse, the box with the bell, and a totebag filled with books and other miscellaneous items. Time to get started with the rest of her life, and show the world — and herself — that Barb Stanowski was more than a pretty face.

Dear Readers,

I hope you've enjoyed reading Barb's story. You can read more about Eureka, Colorado and Maggie's story in *The View From Here,* Book One in my Eureka series. And be sure to watch for Book Two in the series, *The Mountain Between Us,* on sale this month!

Cindy